Praise for John Gilstrap

Hostage Zero

"Jonathan Grave, my favorite freelance peacemaker, problem-solver, and tough-guy hero, is back—and in particularly fine form. *Hostage Zero* is classic Gilstrap: the people are utterly real, the action's foot to the floor, and the writing's fluid as a well-oiled machine gun. A tour de force!"
—**Jeffery Deaver**

No Mercy

"*No Mercy* grabs hold of you on page one and doesn't let go. Gilstrap's new series is terrific. It will leave you breathless. I can't wait to see what Jonathan Grave is up to next."
—**Harlan Coben**

"The release of a new John Gilstrap novel is always worth celebrating, because he's one of the finest thriller writers on the planet. *No Mercy* showcases his work at its finest—taut, action-packed, and impossible to put down!"
—**Tess Gerritsen**

"...at hero, a pulse-pounding story—and the launch of a really exciting series."
—**Joseph Finder**

"...ntertaining, fast-paced tale of violence and revenge."
—*...ekly*

"No other writer is better able to combine in a single novel both rocket-paced suspense and heartfelt looks at family and the human spirit. And what a pleasure to meet Jonathan Grave, a hero for our time . . . and for all time."
—**Jeffery Deaver**

"*No Mercy* is entertaining, fun, and hard to put down. You will want to read it in a single sitting as Gilstrap engages readers in the novel's absorbing plot."
—*Reviewing the Evidence*

Scott Free

"Gilstrap hits the accelerator and never lets up."
—**Harlan Coben**

Even Steven

"Action-packed."
—*Publishers Weekly*

"Gilstrap has an uncanny ability to bring the reader into the mind of his characters."
—*The Denver Post*

At All Costs

"Riveting . . . combines a great plot and realistic, likable characters with look-over-your-shoulder tension. A page turner."
—*The Kansas City Star*

Also by John Gilstrap

FICTION

No Mercy

Scott Free

Even Steven

At All Costs

Nathan's Run

NONFICTION

Six Minutes to Freedom (with Kurt Muse)

COLLABORATIONS

Watchlist: A Serial Thriller

HOSTAGE ZERO

JOHN GILSTRAP

PINNACLE BOOKS
Kensington Publishing Corp.
kensingtonbooks.com

PINNACLE BOOKS are published by

Kensington Publishing Corp.
119 West 40th Street
New York, NY 10018

All Kensington titles, imprints, and distributed lines are available at special quantity discounts for bulk purchases for sales promotions, premiums, fund-raising, educational, or institutional use. Special book excerpts or customized printings can also be created to fit specific needs. For details, write or phone the office of the Kensington special sales manager: Kensington Publishing Corp., 119 West 40th Street, New York, NY 10018, attn: Special Sales Department; phone 1-800-221-2647.

PINNACLE BOOKS and the Pinnacle logo are Reg. U.S. Pat. & TM Off.

ISBN-13: 978-0-7860-2088-1
ISBN-10: 0-7860-2088-1

First printing: July 2010

10 9 8 7 6 5 4 3 2 1

Printed in the United States of America

CHAPTER ONE

Harvey Rodriguez waited till daybreak before he ventured out to look at the body. He wanted to make sure that the men with the guns were long gone before he turned himself into a target, so he'd spent most of the night lying still in his tent among the trees, trying his best to remain invisible.

If he'd had a brain in his head, he'd have used the cover of darkness to scoot out of here, but every time he'd flexed his legs to move, he'd talked himself out of it. He'd used the time to plot his strategy.

On the one hand, he'd been living out here long enough to be running pretty low on everything, and even if the killer had stripped the dead man's pockets clean, the corpse was likely to have something of value, if only a pair of socks that actually covered his whole foot. Or maybe a watch. Harvey's ten-year-old Timex had crapped out a month ago.

On the other hand, when you've got no home and you make your living—such as it is—off the sometimes unwilling largesse of others, the last thing you need is to get yourself wrapped up in a murder case. It wasn't as if he had people who could vouch for his alibi, you know? He could almost hear the interrogation in his head:

2 *John Gilstrap*

Where were you last night?

I was at home.

And where's that?

Wherever I make it. Last night, it was in the woods out by Kinsale.

Right where a murder happened?

Yes, sir. That's a hell of a coincidence, ain't it? I was just lying there in my tent, and I heard somebody in the woods. I started to peek out, and then I heard a gunshot, and I ducked the hell back in.

Who would believe that? But running away would make it sound even worse. Harvey didn't know many people, but nobody's completely invisible. Sooner or later, somebody would find the body, and the homeless drifter would be the first suspect. Especially if the drifter was wearing the dead guy's socks and watch.

Okay, stealing from the body was a bad idea. He wouldn't do that.

If he were a better citizen, he'd have called for help, but in all fairness, he thought he deserved a break there. He'd chosen this spot as his camp precisely because it was in the middle of nowhere, which meant that "calling for help" had to be taken literally—as in, cupping his hands to his mouth and yelling, "Help!" Hardly compatible with his plan to remain invisible.

Bottom line, he was screwed no matter how it turned out, but after all this time, he was by God going to take a peek at the body. He owed himself that much. Hell, the dead guy owed him that much after costing him a whole night's sleep.

Finally, it was time. Taking care to keep quiet, Harvey crawled out of his last-legs Coleman camping tent and scanned the scenery. It had been a cool night compared to some of the sweltering nightmares of the past couple of weeks, but even now, he could feel the sun doing its duty to deliver a blistering day. It's the way it was in this part of the world. At least winter was long behind and long ahead.

Winter was the hardest part of being Harvey Rodriguez.

People asked why he didn't spend his summers walking to someplace where they didn't have winters, but the truth was that he was now a Virginian through and through. In this part of the Commonwealth—along the Northern Neck on the Potomac River—winters were pretty mild. It rarely snowed, and nighttime ice almost always melted by midday. It was the rare day when he couldn't pull something edible out of the river and rarer still when he couldn't snare a squirrel or possum.

As he stretched to his full five feet eight inches, Harvey eyed his peeling Adidas but decided to leave them where they were. The rubber sole on the left shoe was about to give way to a hole, and he wanted it to last for at least one more rainy day. His eyes scanned the horizon as he adjusted the pull cord on the swim trunks he wore as shorts, hoping in vain to make them tighter. One thing about the hot weather: it was hard to keep weight on.

Making no sudden movements, Harvey turned a full 360 degrees, watching and listening for signs of danger. Satisfied that it was safe to move, he plucked his prized FBI T-shirt off the branch where he'd left it to air out overnight, and slipped it on.

Harvey walked carefully through the tall grass and scrubby bushes toward the water—toward the spot where he presumed the body to be. He watched his feet. Poking a bare toe into somebody's guts would be a disgusting way to start the day.

Something caught his eye, off at his eleven o'clock. He stopped in midstep and squinted. Had something moved? He didn't think so. It was one of those intuitive things that hit him from time to time, and he knew to wait it out until his brain could unscramble it. All around him, nothing stirred but the breeze, gently waving the top of the tall seed-tipped grasses in an undulating ripple that made land look like water.

So what was it?

A phrase popped into his head: background anomaly.

When someone's lying in wait—or lying dead—they think they're concealed by the tall grass that surrounds them, and they'd be right if it weren't for the background anomaly. When everything is waving in the breeze, the anomaly is the patch of vegetation that stands still. In this case, it was far more obvious than that. Harvey saw a very definite hole in the rolling surface of the grass—exactly the kind of hole that a body would leave after it had been dumped.

As he closed the distance, he thought briefly about the footprints and other damning evidence he was leaving behind, but if it came to that, at least he could show that the path of footprints led directly to his tent. Plus, if footprints were an issue, there should be at least one other pair that would implicate the real killer.

He was still ten feet away when he caught the first glimpse of blue fabric through the moving blades of grass.

It was definitely a body.

He slowed as he approached the last couple of yards. "Hello?" he said. "Hey, are you okay?"

The dead guy didn't move. If he had, Harvey may well have shit all over himself.

Nearly on top of it now, he could just make out the whole form. He gasped and clamped his hands over his mouth. Horror washed over him out of nowhere, gripping his insides and twisting them.

Without any thought or warning, Harvey Rodriguez did something he hadn't done in too many years for him to remember. He started to cry.

CHAPTER TWO

July in Virginia.

Though the sun had set, the weather still hung like wet wool as the two men climbed out of their rented Chevrolet Caprice and closed the doors. They wore the standard uniforms of the FBI agents they pretended to be—white shirts and rep ties under unimaginative pinstriped suits. Blue for the smaller of the two, and gray for his massive companion.

The big man—Brian Van de Meulebroeke by birth, but Boxers to his friends—pulled at his collar like a boy in church. "I swear to god, Panama was cooler," he grumbled.

Jonathan Grave smiled. "At least we've got autumn on the other end of it," he said. Back in the day when discomfort was part of their patriotic sacrifice to God and country, the two men had logged dozens of months in fetid tropics, but today's Brooks Brothers uniforms made Virginia way less comfortable. The latex facial prostheses didn't help.

Their destination lay half a block away, remarkable for its ordinariness. Low rise, and constructed of red brick trimmed in white stone, the Basin Jail looked like the result of a student architectural lesson gone bad. It might have been mistaken for a small elementary school or even a recreation center.

"That's the stupidest looking jail I've ever seen," Boxers said, nailing Jonathan's thoughts.

"Here's to thin walls and lax security," Jonathan quipped.

Despite their FBI cover, they parked in the pay lot, just like everybody else. Boxers seemed annoyed as Jonathan waited for him to fish through his pockets for three quarters to feed the meter. "The hell am I paying for?" Boxers grumped. "You're the bajillionaire."

Jonathan said nothing. As the man who signed Boxers' paychecks, his heart did not bleed for the big guy. He also knew that he'd see these six bits on Boxers' expense report.

"Any questions on the plan?" Jonathan asked as they closed to within fifty yards of the target.

"Not a one," Boxers replied. His role was anything but complicated. He was to walk around the facility to identify the strengths and weaknesses of its physical security, and to plot the most effective escape route. Lethal force was not an option in this first phase, but if the therapeutic application of high explosives proved to be necessary, that would be Boxers' responsibility as well.

"Are you with us, Mother Hen?" Jonathan asked, seemingly to the air.

The voice in their earbuds responded with crystal clarity. "Always." The voice belonged to Venice Alexander (Ven-EE-chay, and don't screw it up), the woman who kept Jonathan's life afloat administratively, and whose special gift was to make the electrons of cyberspace dance to music of her choosing. She had left countless IT and security managers around the world wondering how their "unbreakable" databases had in fact been broken.

Venice continued, "I've got the entire camera grid on my screens, and I've been recording for nearly an hour. As soon as you step through the front door, I'll be able to wave hello."

Approaching the main entrance, Boxers held back to remain outside the viewing perimeter of the exterior cameras. "Good luck, Boss," he said. "And nice nose." He split off and began his stroll around the perimeter.

Jonathan gave a wry smile. His disguise was a good one, filling his cheeks and expanding his nose to the point where facial recognition software would be stymied; but it wasn't the kind of thing he normally used. As close as they were to their own backyard, this mission required him to take extraordinary precautions. He'd even donned contact lenses to turn his normally blue eyes brown.

He pulled open the right-hand panel of the double glass doors and stepped into a public reception area that had the feel of a seventies-era ski lodge. Rough-finished beige bricks dominated the walls, arranged edgewise in horizontal courses that rose from the brown tiled floor to the acoustic tiled ceiling.

The admissions officer—it was the only title Jonathan could think of for the guy—sat at the long end of the rectangular room, and as his guest entered, his expression showed annoyance. "Visiting hours are over," the officer announced.

"Of course they are," Jonathan said. As he reached into his pocket for his occasionally legitimate Bureau credentials, he got the sense that the desk officer had been expecting him. "Agent Harris, FBI."

"Just what I need," the officer said.

"Care to guess who I'm here to see?"

The officer twitched a shoulder. "Only federal rap we got is Jimmy Henry. Kidnapping and attempted murder."

"That's the one," Jonathan said. He was close enough now to see his tag: DIANE. He hoped it was his last name, not his first.

The officer followed his gaze. "If you're gonna make a crack, get it over with now," he said. "That way, I don't have to get out of my chair."

"My name's Leon," Jonathan lied. "With a name like that, you don't make fun of others."

Male bonding. A beautiful thing.

"Go to the door," Diane said, pointing with his forehead to a heavy steel security door. "I'll buzz you in."

Jonathan walked the path he already recognized from

Venice's research. Just two hours ago, he'd been watching this very space from their offices in Fisherman's Cove. The first door led to a security air lock dominated by a chest-high counter. In a different context, it would have looked like a bar.

"Can't help but think you're wasting your time," Diane said as he entered the air lock from a door on the other side of the counter. He reached underneath and produced a long rectangular box. "I need your firearm and any other weapons. Jimmy Henry lawyered up first thing. Ben Johnson's representing him. You know him?"

"Never heard of him," Jonathan said. He drew a fifteen-shot 9-millimeter Glock from its holster on his belt, dropped out the magazine, and locked open the slide before placing the weapon and its ammo in the box. He noted the wall-mounted cameras near the ceiling, but saw no metal detectors.

"Well, Ben's good at what he does. After he told that kid to keep his mouth shut, that's exactly what he's been doin'."

"Hmm," Jonathan said. "Can I speak with him now?"

"You sure you want to? Nothin' he says can be used in court after he's lawyered up."

"Then I'll just have to be careful what I ask, won't I?" Jonathan mimicked the condescending tone he'd heard from dozens of federal agents over the years.

Diane raised a section of the deck and opened a door underneath to let Jonathan pass through. On the far side, he faced another heavy steel door. Diane plucked a phone from the wall and dialed an extension: 4272, Jonathan noted, though he didn't know how the number could possibly help him.

"Hey Chase, this is Bill. I'm letting an FBI agent in. He wants to talk to the Henry kid." A pause. "What, you think I don't have a clock up here? I didn't call him; he just showed up. Yeah, well, aren't they all?"

He hung up the phone and then pushed and held a button under the counter. The lock buzzed, and Jonathan pulled the door open to reveal the fluorescent hell of the cell block. As he stepped across the threshold, he could feel the years of institutionalized fear and misery exuding from the reinforced concrete walls. Whether they were built by the Commonwealth of Virginia or by Saddam Hussein, pervasive misery was the common denominator of all prisons.

Another guard stood just a few feet away. His name tag read BATTLES. "You're up late," he said. "I thought you Fibbies only worked the day shift."

Jonathan shunned the small talk. "I need to speak to Jimmy Henry," he said. "Do you have an interrogation room?" It was a question to which he already knew the answer.

Battles's demeanor darkened with the seriousness of the visitor's tone. He pointed to a secured lockdown about a quarter of the way down the center aisle of the cell block.

"I'd appreciate you bringing him to me," Jonathan said, and he started down the hall.

Battles trotted to catch up. "What's the urgency?" he asked. "You guys usually call ahead."

Jonathan ignored his question and walked to the door. "I want the recording devices turned off in the room while he's with me."

Battles pulled short. "That's not how we do things."

"Tonight's different. Now how about we get done what needs to be done?"

Battles didn't like this. It showed on his face. But he nonetheless unlocked the door and let Jonathan enter. "Sit here, and I'll bring him to you."

As Jonathan stepped inside, the door closed behind him, and the guard locked it. As if reading his mind—as she often did—Venice spoke in his ear: "Don't worry about them recording you. I have their soundtrack control on my screen. Even if they leave everything on, I'll be able to zero out all sound once Henry arrives."

Knowing that she could see him, he acknowledged her with a subtle nod. Jonathan helped himself to the one bolted-down metal chair that was not equipped with a ring to secure prisoners' shackles.

Battles made Jonathan cool his heels for ten minutes or more. Jonathan noted the video camera high in the corner, and despite his makeup did his best to avoid looking at it.

The lock turned, and Battles escorted Jimmy Henry into the room. The nineteen-year-old prisoner stood around six feet and appeared beneath the orange jumpsuit to possess the build of someone who worked hard during the day. His dark brown hair was a sleep-twisted mess, and his eyes seemed sunken into his skull. Clearly pissed at being rousted from his bed, he knew better than to voice his objection.

"Sit down," Battles said, pointing to the available chair.

Jimmy gave a sullen nod and shuffled his slippered, shackled feet over to the chair and sat. With arms pinioned to the waist belt of his shackle rig, he settled himself carefully. When you can't catch yourself in a fall, you become supremely aware of how fragile your nose and teeth are. Once the kid was settled in, Battles attached the chain to the chair.

"I don't think that's necessary," Jonathan said.

Battles glared, but continued with what he was doing. When all was secure, he said, "Pound on the door when you're ready to send him back." He locked the door behind him as he left.

Jonathan leaned back and crossed his arms and legs. "So, you're Jimmy Henry," he said.

"I already said I ain't talkin' to nobody," Jimmy said. "This ain't legal, bringing me out at this hour. It's sleep deprivation."

"The sound is down," Venice said in his ear. "They did it on their own."

"So, you know your rights, do you?" Jonathan asked, amused.

"Damn straight I do."

"Uh-huh. What do you know about why you're here?"

Jimmy glared. Silence meant silence.

"Good for you," Jonathan said. "So you've really been quiet the whole time? You haven't admitted to anything?" As he spoke, his voice showed an edge of approval.

Something changed behind Jimmy's eyes as he cocked his head. His belligerence had dimmed.

"I'll come clean with you," Jonathan said. He unfolded himself and leaned forward until his forearms rested on the cold table. "But first I want you to understand that the quickest way to die is to piss me off. And the quickest way to piss me off is to repeat a word of what I'm going to tell you. Do you understand?"

Now Jimmy seemed amused. Jonathan was easily three inches shorter than the man he'd just threatened, and frankly didn't look all that intimidating. But what he didn't possess in physicality, he projected through the intensity of his glare. As Jimmy absorbed it, the smile went away. "Yeah, okay, I got you."

"Be sure, Jimmy. There's no room for error."

"What the hell kind of FBI agent are you?"

Jonathan reassumed his comfortable posture. "Well, that's the thing," he said. "I'm not an FBI agent. I'm the friend you never knew you had. My job is to bust you out of here."

Jimmy shot a paranoid glance over his shoulder toward the door. "What do you mean?" He'd dropped his voice to a whisper.

"I work for people who don't want the details of what you did this morning to leak out. That leaves two choices: They can hire someone to kill you, or they can hire me to get you out. If I were you, I'd pick me."

"But *why*?"

"Because you were the only one stupid enough to get caught. You get credit for youthful stupidity, which is why you're still alive, but the offer to get you out expires in about three seconds. So, are you willing to cooperate or not?"

Another quick look over his shoulder. "How are you going to do it?"

"My concern, not yours. Just be ready to go at two a.m. And keep your mouth shut. I get paid for trying, not succeeding. If you betray me—"

Suddenly animated, Jimmy shook his head. "No. God no, I wouldn't do that."

Jonathan took his time. He wanted to instill even more fear. "Okay, then. I'll be coming back to visit around two. I need you to be in bed and as asleep as you can pretend to be. When you get up, dress just as you are now. Don't try anything on your own. When the time comes, all you'll have to do is what I tell you." He stood. "I'll see you in a little while."

As Jonathan strolled to the door, Jimmy shifted quickly in his chair. "Wait. How do I know you're telling the truth? How do I know I'll be safe coming with you?"

"You don't," Jonathan deadpanned. "But consider the alternative. You're a kidnapper, kid. If that guy you shot dies, that means a needle in your arm."

"I didn't shoot anybody. That was the crazy dude."

Jonathan stopped him with a raised hand. "Save it. I don't care. Not now, anyway. Keep on keeping your mouth shut, and everything will be fine." He pounded on the door for Battles.

CHAPTER THREE

The body was a little boy wearing torn pajamas, and Harvey hadn't been prepared for that. The kid lay on his back with his eyes closed, a loop of duct tape around his mouth. His legs lay slightly askew, but his hands lay on his stomach, as if placed there by a mortician. Harvey was no expert in these things, but he placed the age at somewhere around thirteen or fourteen years old. Maybe a little younger. It was always hard to tell with kids this age.

The sudden rush of emotion had come from nowhere. Harvey found it embarrassing at first, and then he found it just human. He'd seen his share of death over the years, and after a while you sort of get used to it. But not with kids. If you can get used to that, then there's no point living anymore. Slip to that level, and society has no use for you.

Harvey just stood there for a long time—probably three, four, five minutes—figuring out what he was supposed to do. It was one thing to leave some bum like himself out in the weeds to get eaten by buzzards and carried off a piece at a time by foxes and dogs, but you couldn't—

The boy's chest moved. It wasn't anything dramatic, but there definitely was movement.

As Harvey leaned closer, he saw that he'd been wrong. The kid wasn't dead. His face had too much color. Stooping to his haunches, he grasped one of the boy's hands. It was warm. With his own heart racing, Harvey dropped to his hands and knees at the level of the boy's shoulders and felt his neck. With the tips of two fingers, he located the larynx, and then slipped his fingertips into the groove between the cricoid cartilage and the anterior border of the sternocleido-mastoid muscle. He expected to find a weak thready pulse, but found a strong one, instead.

This wasn't right at all. He lifted one of the boy's hands from his belly and let it drop. It fell like a rock. The kid was out cold. A peek under his eyelids reveal pinpoint pupils. That meant drugs.

Harvey raised up straight, still on his knees. He again craned his neck, looking to see if help might have wandered by. Seeing none actually brought relief. This next step had to be done, but it would be a bitch to explain if anyone wandered by.

He had to make the kid naked.

There'd been a gunshot, for God's sake. He didn't see any holes or any blood on the pajamas, but that didn't mean there weren't any on the boy. Harvey's hands trembled as he undid the four buttons of the pajama top and peeled it away. The chest and belly looked normal, though he noted light bruising high on his chest, inferior to the clavicles. The kid looked on the thin side, but there appeared to be no nutritional issues.

The speed with which Harvey's skills returned amazed him. He used his fingers, left hand under the right as if making a forward dive into a swimming pool, to palpate the boy's belly. It felt loose and malleable, so there was no significant internal bleeding. Liver and spleen were both normal size.

There comes a point where a lack of a diagnosis is as concerning as a troubling one, and Harvey found himself rapidly approaching that line.

Scooting to the child's hips, Harvey slipped his fingers into the pajamas' elastic waistband and slid the fabric down to his shins. Again, no sign of trauma, but he'd definitely entered puberty, and he definitely was not a practicing Jew. Feeling progressively more optimistic that he'd find no bullet wound, Harvey leveraged the kid's thigh and ribs to roll him to his side, till he rested against Harvey's kneeling thighs. He shoved the pajama top up to his shoulders to expose the entire posterior surface and issued a sigh when he saw that there were no signs of penetrating trauma. He returned the boy to a supine position and pulled his clothing back into place.

What else was there? Harvey wondered. He fought to recall his Marine Corps training.

Of course! His arms. With bullet trauma off the table, the arms made the most sense. Sure enough, as soon as he wrestled the boy's left arm free from the sleeve of his pajamas, he saw an antecubital bruise. The injection point for whatever had knocked this kid out appeared as a bull's-eye in the middle of a purple halo at the crease of his elbow joint.

Sixteen hours later, the boy still had not awakened. He'd stirred a few times, and in the last couple of hours he'd made some mumbling sounds—all good signs—but he remained unconscious.

Harvey recalled the list of drugs that could have such lasting effect and realized how lucky the kid was to still be alive. Risks remained for liver damage or renal failure, but with each additional sign of recovery, the risks diminished.

As time passed, the *how* of the kid's situation mattered less, but the importance of the *why* continued to glow as brightly as ever. Anyone who was angry enough to inject an overdose of narcotics into a kid's system and then leave him for dead in the middle of nowhere was likely to be a person who'd be mightily pissed to learn that he'd failed. It was exactly the sort of person that Harvey wanted nothing to do with.

If Harvey'd had a brain in his head, he would have run away from this kid like a bunny rabbit on fire, putting as much space as possible between the two of them before finding a way to call for help. Woulda, coulda, shoulda. Fact was, he *didn't* have a brain in his head. He'd decided instead to play floor nurse, monitoring the boy's respirations and pulse, and making sure that if they faltered, he would be there to jump-start them.

And if the bad guys came back, well, that would just be the perfect ending to the perfect day, wouldn't it?

He was *so* screwed.

The boy lay in Harvey's tent now, in Harvey's sleeping bag and under his mosquito netting. Now that night had returned, recovery was all up to the boy and God.

Harvey's money—as if he had any—said that the kid would be fine after he slept it off. And then what?

Well, that was the question, wasn't it?

Harvey could see the headline now: HOMELESS MAN FINDS PARTIALLY CLOTHED BOY. Jesus.

Forget all those worries from last night about being associated with a dead guy. Being found with a live boy was the stuff of national headlines. These days, the mere appearance of impropriety made you a pedophile. Been there, done that. Thanks, but no.

So, just what the hell was he supposed to do? Going to the police was a ticket to prison. Not even the kid himself could testify that he hadn't done anything awful, so the cops would automatically assume that he had. Once they get that thought in their head, facts stop mattering.

After the first hour or two, when the kid still hadn't stirred, and his pupils were still pinpoints, Harvey had come *this close* to leaving him to get help, but what would have happened if the kid's vitals had crashed in the meantime? He'd have brought the police to the body of a boy who'd died in Harvey's tent.

Thanks again, but absolutely not.

Welcome to the land of crappy choices, starring Harvey Rodriguez.

Harvey sat way forward on his nylon sling camping chair, tending to the Coleman one-burner stove and the pot of re-heated coffee from lunchtime. To stay near the boy, he'd opted to dig into his emergency supply of canned tuna for both lunch and dinner, and he was hoping that the astringent twice-cooked java would take the dead fish taste out of his mouth.

The boy coughed.

Harvey spun his head. Coughing is a voluntary action that implies a higher level of consciousness. It meant that the boy was coming out of his coma.

Harvey left his coffee on the stove but turned the burner down as he pulled himself out of his chair and crawled back into the tent. He used a cigarette lighter he'd found in a trash can a month ago to light the single mantle of his propane lantern. Pulling the mosquito netting out of the way, he leaned in close to the boy's face and held the lantern off to the side, trying to tame the dark shadows thrown by the kid's facial features. He saw that the boy had ejected a bit of spit-tle onto his cheek, and he wiped it away with his thumb.

The boy twitched at his touch.

"Hey, kid. Are you awake?"

Nothing.

Harvey gently grabbed the boy's shoulder and shook it. "Hey, pal, come on and open your eyes."

They fluttered.

"That's it. Go ahead and open them. You're safe. You're okay."

The boy coughed again, and as he did, he raised his head a little with the effort. He was close to wakefulness.

Harvey rubbed the shoulder more vigorously. "You're almost there. Come on. Open your eyes. Let me know that you're okay. Talk to me. I don't even know your name."

Wrinkles appeared in the boy's forehead, and when his mouth twisted into a wince, Harvey moved the light away from his eyes.

"You've had a long hard day, my friend," Harvey said. "Open your eyes now and join the world."

The lids parted, though it took a few seconds for awareness to arrive. The boy raised both hands to his face and rubbed his eyes with the heels of his palms. For a few seconds, he looked like any other child waking from a long sleep, but then full awareness arrived. His hands shot back down to his sides, and the boy recoiled in terror, trying to roll away, but unable to flee from the tangle of the sleeping bag.

Harvey reached out to comfort him, but the boy yelled out at his touch. "Leave me alone!"

Harvey pulled back as if he'd touched a hot stove.

"Help!" the boy yelled.

Harvey felt a jet of panic. "Hush! Shit, kid, be quiet."

"Help me! Don't hurt me! Let go of me!"

It was the nightmare. Harvey shot a glance out the tent opening, half expecting a police officer to be standing right there. "I'm not touching you, kid," he said at a harsh whisper. "Jesus, I saved your life. Cut me a break."

The kid kicked at his covers, and the more he struggled, the more tangled he became. "Please don't hurt me anymore."

"Listen to me!" Harvey barked, loudly this time, hoping to startle the boy into sanity. "I'm not the one who hurt you. I *saved* you." He raised the lantern parallel to his own face. "Look at me," he went on. "I am *not* the one who hurt you."

At first, it was as if the boy hadn't heard him; he continued to wrestle with the sleeping bag as fear and frustration turned his efforts violent. Then, he stopped. It was as if Harvey's words had traveled the slow route and had only just now arrived. He pivoted his head and scowled as he studied the man's features.

"You're safe here," Harvey said, his voice soft again.

The kid darted his glance from one corner of the tent to another. "Where are they?"

"Gone," Harvey said. "About twenty hours ago."

This was a lot to process even when you were clear-headed. Given his drugged-up stepping-off point, the boy was having a particularly difficult time of it.

"You're safe now," Harvey repeated.

It was what the kid wanted to hear, but he wasn't ready to trust the words. "Where am I?"

"As close to nowhere as a human being can get," Harvey said. When the scowl deepened, he added, "You're in the woods. In Virginia. Near the Potomac River, and the people who hurt you probably think that you're dead."

Cobwebs remained. "*Am* I dead?"

Harvey smiled. "Alive and well. And lucky to be that." He extended his hand. "Harvey Rodriguez," he said. "Nice to meet you."

The boy looked at the hand, but retreated some more. "Where did they go?"

Harvey kept his hand outstretched. "They're gone."

The boy shook his head. "That's *what* they are," he said. "Not *where* they went."

Harvey chuckled and abandoned the handshake. "Fair enough. I don't have an answer for you." He recounted the events that led them to the present. "As surprised as you seem to be alive, that's half as surprised as I was to find you that way," he concluded. He allowed it to sink in, and then he extended his hand once more. "Let's try this again. I'm Harvey Rodriguez."

The boy accepted the hand. "I'm Jeremy Schuler." This time, the friendly touch seemed to relax him.

"I'm pleased to meet you, Jeremy Schuler. Are you hungry?"

Jeremy shook his head. "Could I have some water?"

As Harvey poured water from a converted plastic milk jug into a metal coffee cup, he fought the urge to pummel the kid with questions. After all he'd been through, he needed time to orient himself to the present before Harvey dragged him back to the past. He handed the cup to Jeremy. "Sip, don't gulp," he warned. "Your stomach might not be as awake as the rest of you."

The boy sipped and swallowed. "Thank you," he said.

"You're welcome." He watched Jeremy drink until it became awkward when the boy became aware of being watched. "Tell you what," he said with a single, gentle clap of his hands. "I'm going to leave the lantern here with you, and I'm going to go out there and cook some dinner. If you change your mind about eating, there'll be plenty for you."

While there was no critical medical need for the kid to eat right this minute, sooner or later he'd need sustenance, and sooner was better than later.

Harvey grabbed a flashlight from the piece of two-by-four that served as his nightstand, crawled back into the night and over to the surplus footlocker that served as his pantry. He spun the combination lock, lifted the hasp, and opened the lid.

Seeing as how Jeremy was his first company in five years, it only made sense to appeal to his young taste buds. He pulled out a packet of macaroni and cheese, courtesy of the United States Army. Last winter, on one of the truly cold days, Harvey had agreed to spend a night in a shelter. He hated the principle and he hated the crowds, but he was impressed with the generosity of the pastor of St. Katherine's Church, who handed out cases of Army MREs—Meals Ready to Eat—to anybody who wanted one. They weren't likely to put any restaurants out of business, but they tasted pretty decent, and on the days when you wanted to splurge a little, they came in handy.

Tonight, he decided to bypass the typical procedure of cooking the meal in its FRH (flameless rotational heater), and actually cook it on the stove. Somehow, food tasted better when a real flame was involved in the preparation process. He'd just gotten the water to boil when Jeremy appeared in the tent opening.

"Can I still have dinner?" he asked.

Harvey smiled and pointed to the camp chair. "Make yourself comfortable," he said.

CHAPTER FOUR

Venice Alexander had tried to nap on the sofa in her office, but it was impossible. Whenever she closed her eyes, the images of blood-spattered walls and the puddled gore on the linoleum flooded the darkness. She could still see the shock and sadness on the faces of the children. It was unspeakable that such violence could visit them literally at their doorstep. They'd already suffered so much in their young lives.

She tried to will the thoughts away. They were counterproductive. Right now, everything was about the mission. She labored not to fixate on the right or the wrong of things anymore, hoping that she could one day find that emotional place where Digger lived at times like these, but she just wasn't wired that way.

She could pretend—she could push herself when the time came to don her game face and be one of the boys—but when quiet returned, she always remembered that there really was good, and there really was evil, and that in the end, good always prevailed, even if at a daunting price.

Her years at Security Solutions working with Digger Grave had taught her that when the stakes were as high as

Digger ratcheted them, outcome often trumped means. When the prize was important enough, any law was expendable if it stood in the way of justice. They were in the business of reuniting families, after all, and for Digger and Boxers, shattering rules was a part of the game that energized them. Venice could intellectualize immorality as necessity, but she'd never be able to fully embrace it.

That's part of the reason why Jonathan called her the soul of the team.

With sleep out of the question, she'd spent the last half hour rechecking her connections to the Basin, Virginia, jail. Unlike Jonathan, whose ground-level view saw only one-third of the building, she was responsible for controlling the whole thing. The jail's graveyard shift, which started at ten and would run until six o'clock the next morning, consisted of six deputies who divided their time between the front desk and the three cell blocks, all of which were connected by a series of steel security doors.

Looking at the plan view she'd pulled up on her center screen, she once again noted the important landmarks. The adult portion of the detention facility resembled a wide, asymmetrical V, with the men's cell block taking up the longer left leg, and the women's portion the shorter right leg. The two legs joined at the administrative section of the facility, where the admissions desk and the main security air lock were located.

The hallways through the cell blocks were further controlled by intermediate security doors which, in the event of a prisoner uprising, could isolate the event to one-third of either wing. Guards who were not patrolling the hallways worked at a warren of desks in the heavily secured apex of the two wings.

Watching her screens, she could see every corner of the jail, including the insides of the cells if she were so inclined—which she was not. There was nothing remotely engaging in watching men and women in their alone times, especially at night.

When the balloon went up on this operation, she was

going to have a lot to do in a very short period of time, with no room for error. She'd programmed all the appropriate commands and committed them not only to memory but to a list that lay beside her keyboard, and in these final moments, she waved her fingers over the keys, practicing the strokes the way a piano player will silently practice a concerto before stepping onto the stage.

Finally assured that she'd done everything she could, she pulled up Spider Solitaire in a separate window on her computer and stacked up four wins.

At 01:45, she donned her headset with its boom microphone and waited for the boss to check in. Knowing Jonathan and Boxers, they'd probably spent the last three hours at a restaurant somewhere having a nice meal before another day at the office.

Her earpiece crackled, "Mother Hen, this is Scorpion. Are you there?"

Relief. Then the flutter of anxiety. "I'm here," she responded. "What about Big Guy?"

"I'm on the Net," Boxers replied.

"What are your screens showing?" Jonathan asked.

"Just a boring night at the jailhouse," Venice said.

"Any questions on the plan?"

Venice resisted the urge to answer quickly. "I've run every scenario I can think of, and I think we're ready," she said. Never mind that every plan goes to the dogs five seconds after it shifts from theory to reality.

The movie screen in her mind played the images of blood-spattered walls again. "Hey guys?" she said. "Get this son of a bitch, okay?"

Jonathan and Boxers exchanged glances in the darkened van. "Did Venice just cuss?" Boxers gasped. It was the equivalent of a Muslim taking a drink. It just didn't happen.

"Yes, I did," said the voice in their ears. "And I'm sorry, but I just . . ." Her voice trailed off.

"I know exactly what you mean," Jonathan said. "Let's do it, then."

The dome light had been disabled, so when Jonathan opened the passenger door and let himself out, the world around them remained dark. He addressed Boxers' silhouette. "Be patient, Big Guy," he said. "Trust twenty-first-century solutions."

"I always do," Boxers replied. "But I'll never stop trusting nineteenth-century backups." Boxers felt a deep love for blowing things up.

If everything went according to plan, Venice would be the key player in this op, controlling all the moving parts from her computer terminal sixty-plus miles away. Jonathan didn't understand the technical details, but he'd witnessed Venice's skills enough times in the past to trust that she could perform every task she had promised.

Boxers' point was a valid one, though: If things went to shit, a great big boom would be their only escape.

Jonathan followed his footsteps from before, even duplicating his gait. As he approached the front desk, it occurred to him that this was all feeling very easy.

In his line of work, that was never a good thing.

Granville George caught action out of the corner of his eye—movement on the one video monitor that rarely showed anything but a still life at this hour, and he knew right away that it was the FBI agent from earlier in the evening. Granville had read Bill Diane's entry in the logbook after shift change, and he'd heard a personal account from Battles in the locker room when they were changing out. What was it about these federal guys that made them be such pricks all the time? He figured there had to be special courses on ego inflation at the FBI Academy.

No Fibbie would ever believe it, but Granville wouldn't trade places with a fed for anything, doubled salary included. He liked living on the water in a community where the spectrum of crime was more or less the same as you'd get in a big city, but at a fraction of the scale. His current penance of jail duty—the mandatory six-month sentence for wrecking a police cruiser in a high-speed chase—would be fulfilled in another fifteen days, and then he'd be back on the streets, doing what he loved.

He glared as the man in the suit crossed the waiting room to the reception window.

"I'm Agent Harris, FBI," he said, producing the obligatory credentials case. "I need to speak with Jimmy Henry."

Granville took the black leather folder from him and examined it—not because he had to, but because he could. The weight of it told him that the man was legit. Fake IDs were rarely made of the same quality of metal as the real thing. "A little late, isn't it?" he grumped, returning the creds to their owner.

"The law never sleeps," the agent said.

Granville rolled his eyes. "Yeah, well our inmates do, and rousting them at two in the morning is a good way to start a riot."

"That's what locks are for," the agent said with a smirk. "I really need to talk with him."

"About what?"

"About things that are confidential. Now can you please wake him?"

Granville sighed to signal what a pain in the ass it was to do this, and then he stood from his chair and pointed toward the door to his left, his visitor's right. "Wait for me over there." Technically, it was within his power to make the agent cool his heels until 6:30 wake-up, but he couldn't see any good coming from returning shittiness with shittiness. He'd already pissed off his bosses enough to get jail duty for half a year; it made no sense to piss them off more.

Venice waited for the guard to leave his desk and then counted to five before she went to work. With everything cued up ahead of time, it was just a matter of a few keystrokes. The video monitors at the front desk went black for an instant, and when they returned to life, they showed Jonathan dressed just as he was right now, being let in through the security air lock, just as he was right now. Except the pictures were all about six hours old.

She'd rerouted everything she'd recorded earlier to their respective monitors. All but the camera facing the lobby and the front desk, which would continue to project a live feed. It wasn't a foolproof plan, but given the short time they'd had to put it together, she thought it was pretty darn good.

Jonathan followed the second deputy—a blond string bean of a man whose tag read R. SHENTON—to the interview room and walked with a determined gait to the waiting table.

"I'll be back with the Henry boy in a minute," Shenton said before leaving. Jonathan noted that unlike his evening-shift colleague, he did not lock the door behind him.

"He's walking toward Jimmy Henry's cell," Venice said in his ear. When Jonathan didn't reply, she added, "The guards are all watching camera loops. The audio in the interview room is down."

He nodded. "Thank you," he said, and then added, "I don't need to know what's going right, only what's going wrong." He hated radio chatter.

Unlike his last visit when he was performing for the camera, Jonathan didn't bother to sit. He paced the strip of tile between the door and the table. When it came time to react, he was going to have to move quickly.

A glance at his watch confirmed that it had only been two minutes, but it felt like fifteen. He understood that Shenton needed time to shackle Henry up and shuffle him down the hall, but knowledge did nothing to move the hands on the clock faster.

"They're in the hallway, coming at you," Venice said. "Give it ten seconds."

Jonathan turned toward the door as it opened and stepped aside to greet his guest. Jimmy Henry wore the shackle rig as before, with his hands cuffed to his waist and his ankles hobbled by a three-foot chain. The defiant swagger from earlier had been replaced with a pale, meek aura of fear.

"Put him in the chair," Jonathan instructed. He gestured with an outstretched arm the way a maître d' would show a guest to his table. It was a presumptuous thing to do in the deputy's own house, but nowhere near as rude as what was coming next.

He let the prisoner pass, and then, just as Shenton came into range, Jonathan launched an open-handed punch, nailing the deputy with the heel of his hand at the spot where his lower jaw hinged with his upper jaw. It was the sweet spot that every boxer aims for, and Shenton was out cold before Jonathan had even finished the punch. Jonathan caught him under the arms as he spiraled toward the floor.

"Holy shit!" Jimmy shouted, jumping back and then tumbling over his designated chair. "Holy fucking shit!"

"Shut up," Jonathan hissed. He dragged the deputy to the bolted-down table and gently laid him on the floor in front of it. Moving smoothly, as if in one continuous motion, he produced a pair of handcuffs with a flourish and attached Shenton to the table leg.

"Did you kill him?" Jimmy said as he tried to find his feet again. "Jesus, he dropped like you killed him."

"I didn't kill anybody," Jonathan said. He just hoped he hadn't broken Shenton's jaw. He stooped to go through his pockets.

"So what do we do now?" Jimmy asked. He darted to the door and leaned out, looking both ways down the hall.

"Get inside and close the door," Jonathan commanded. He found a ring of keys in the deputy's front pocket and shuffled through them. He saw a standard Schlage key, probably for his house, plus a Honda key and another for a Ford. None looked like it was made for a high-security lock. He did find a handcuff key, though, and that was enough of a reason to slip the ring into his suit-coat pocket.

"There!" Jimmy said, pointing. "You just had it. That was the key to these fucking things." He raised his hands as best he could and rattled his chains.

Finished with the unconscious guard, Jonathan stood and thrust a forefinger at Jimmy Henry. "Listen to me," he said. "This is my op, not yours. I don't need suggestions, and I don't need advice. My job is to get you out. Yours is to do exactly what you're told. Tell me this isn't too complicated for you."

Jimmy reared back, clearly insulted. "Dude, there's no reason to be hostile."

Jonathan stepped forward until their noses were nearly touching. "I'm breaking you out of prison, shithead. There are armed guards everywhere, and I want very much to wake up alive tomorrow morning. There is every goddamn reason to be hostile."

The prisoner jingled as he took a step backward. "Really, dude—"

Jonathan silenced him with a raised finger. "Remain silent, do exactly what you're told, and don't do anything I don't tell you to do. Remember that, and we'll be just fine." He waited for the nod that confirmed that his words had penetrated. "Good. Now when we get into that hallway, we're going to head left, and we're going to keep going till we're outside. Then we're going to catch a ride out of here."

The prisoner cocked his head. "Just like that?"

"Just like that."

His earbud popped. "Scorpion," Venice said, "we have a problem."

CHAPTER FIVE

For not being hungry, Jeremy Schuler faked it well. The way he wolfed down the mac and cheese, he was lucky he didn't lose a finger. Ditto the baked beans and the orange pound cake. Skinny thing that he was, he scarfed more calories in a single sitting than Harvey consumed in an entire day. Clearly, he was a kid who didn't go wanting very often. In Harvey's experience, people who understood scarcity ate with more appreciation.

"That was really good," Jeremy said as he licked the last of the cake from his fingers.

"Glad you liked it."

"Is there more?"

"Not tonight." As he spoke the denial, Harvey was half prepared for an argument, and surprised when it didn't come. The kid merely nodded, and put his plate on his lap.

Harvey picked up the plate and poured some boiling water onto it from the pot on the burner. With the water balanced in the center, he used a ratty dish towel to clean it off. Through it all, Jeremy said nothing. But he stared a lot, and that was annoying.

"You got something on your mind, son, it's best to get it out," Harvey said.

The observation seemed to startle the boy. "I want to go home," he said.

"I imagine you do," Harvey said. "Where *is* home?"

"I go to a school in Fisherman's Cove. I live there. It's called Resurrection House."

Harvey had heard of the place. It was affiliated with St. Katherine's parish, the very one that had given him tonight's dinner. Except he'd always thought it was an orphanage. "Well, let's take that on in the morning. It's a long walk, and I don't have a car. It's even longer in the dark."

"But what if they come back for me?"

Now that was the panic-inducing question, wasn't it? "I wouldn't worry about that," Harvey said. "They've had all day to come back for you. If they were coming, they would have come then." Maybe if he said it definitively enough, Harvey would believe it himself. The simple truth of the matter was that Jeremy wasn't yet ready to make that kind of trek.

Jeremy thought for a while before asking, "Don't you want to know what happened?"

"Of course I do. But only if you want to tell me."

"I got . . . *kidnapped*," he said. He stumbled on the last word, and in the uneven glare of the lantern, Harvey could see Jeremy's eyes glistening.

"A bunch of men crashed into my room." Jeremy struggled to keep his tone even. "They tied up Anthony, and then they . . ." His voice trailed off, but then he settled himself with a deep breath. "And then they killed Mr. Stewart."

A knot formed in Harvey's belly. "Who's Anthony?" he asked.

Jeremy covered his eyes. "My roommate," he squeaked.

Harvey's head swam. This was worse than he'd thought. "A bunch of men came into *your* room and took you away?"

Jeremy let his hands fall away, and nodded as he pulled his legs up into the chair Indian style.

"And who is Mr. Stewart?"

Jeremy answered to his lap. "The janitor. He was my friend."

"Why would someone do that?"

"They took other kids, too," Jeremy said. "At least one."

"Are you sure?"

As he sat there in the camp chair, Jeremy seemed to shrink, as if growing younger and smaller. His shoulders slumped, and his head drooped. For a few seconds, Harvey thought maybe the boy had fallen back to sleep.

But then he looked up again. He drew a huge breath, and he told his story.

CHAPTER SIX

Granville George looked up from his daily log reports and leaned back in the medieval torture device that posed as his chair. He swore that the sheriff had specially ordered this uncomfortable piece of crap just to make his six-month sentence as miserable as possible. As if the mind-numbing work weren't painful enough.

As he arched his back and stretched, he caught a glimpse of himself on the security monitor. Without paying attention, he scanned the other monitors as well. In the women's wing he saw Terry Milan strolling her patrol, just as she was supposed to, while in the men's wing, the hallway remained empty—not unexpected, given the fact that Rob Shenton would be babysitting Agent Harris for the time being. Meanwhile, three other guards attended to their various admin duties in the center security section.

But that didn't really add up, did it? Granville shifted his gaze to the interview room, and sure enough, there was the Henry kid sitting at the interview table across from his Fibbie visitor. So where was Rob? He must have been standing in the corner where there was no camera cover.

Only, that didn't make sense either. Chase Battles had

told him during shift change that the asshole from the FBI was very specific about wanting to talk to his prisoner alone.

In fact, there was Chase Battles on the screen right now, leaving the interview room and beginning his patrol.

Not Rob Shenton. Chase Battles. From evening shift.

"Oh, shit!" Granville spat. "Oh, fucking shit!" He snatched the phone from its cradle and mashed the emergency alert button with his palm.

Venice knew something was wrong from the way the desk attendant launched upright. She shot a look to the feed monitor, and right away saw what had happened. He recognized the guard.

As he reached for the phone, she was a step ahead of him, and she typed in the code to shut the phone system down. It was one of the emergency precautions she'd planned for.

"Scorpion, we have a problem," she said into her boom mike. As she uttered the words, she saw the desk attendant reach for something on his console, and an instant later, her monitor speakers erupted with an earsplitting squeal.

"What the hell is that?" Jonathan barked.

She ignored him, because she hadn't a clue what to tell him.

"The fuck?" Jimmy Henry said, though his voice was lost in the squeal of the alarm.

He'd articulated Jonathan's thoughts exactly.

The radio on Shenton's belt crackled to life. "Emergency. Emergency in A-Wing."

Jonathan planted his hand in the center of Jimmy's chest. "We're still on plan," he said, feigning calm. "We're just on a tighter schedule. Stay close to me." He reached for the door and pulled.

It was locked.

* * *

"Mother Hen?" Jonathan asked over the radio. Venice recognized the concealed rage. "The door is locked."

None of this had been built into their contingencies. "The panic button must have locked everything down," Venice said.

"Then how about you *un*lock something?"

Venice refused to reward his snarky attitude with an answer. She wasn't going to reward him with an unlocked door anytime soon, either. The panic button had done something to wipe out all of her prepared codes. All of the door annunciators were showing red, meaning they were locked, but when she glanced up at her screen, she saw the front desk guy typing furiously, and then the annunciator for the front Receiving Area blink to green. The guard was selectively undoing the lockdown protocol to allow guards to respond.

Now it was a race to see who was the better keyboard operator.

Granville tried to push his mind away from figuring out who had overridden the cell-opening protocols in the computer. Neither the who nor the why mattered right now, and they sure as hell didn't affect the immediate future. Right now, all that mattered was that someone was trying to escape on his watch.

And that, sports fans, was not going to happen.

Back when they'd designed the system, they'd put in a fail-safe mechanism that would lock down all the cells simultaneously in the event of a prisoner disturbance. That done, it would be a simple thing, according to the manual, to mouse-click individual doors to reopen them as necessary. Only that wasn't working tonight. Whoever had been fucking with the computer system must have screwed up the presets, leaving him with no choice but to enter key codes individually.

There was a manual for this somewhere on the shelf behind his desk, but he only had time to wing it from memory. In the boredom of desk duty, he'd actually read all that shit—probably the only deputy in the department who could say that and not blush. He'd never thought he'd need it, but as a lifelong geek, he'd sort of enjoyed it. Now all he had to do was remember it.

Each door required a lengthy series of keystrokes, beginning with the individual door identifier, followed by command codes. His fingers flew as he tried to enter the number for the air lock between the central security area and A-Wing, the men's cell block, but when he hit ENTER and saw the RECEIVING AREA icon go green, he realized that he'd fat-fingered the door identifier and opened the wrong one. He spat a curse under his breath.

He settled himself. At least it was one door open. He started on the next.

And then the RECEIVING icon went red again.

Jesus, he was fighting an active enemy live! Someone was undoing every command.

Venice typed in the code to lock all the doors simultaneously. It would undo the progress that the guard was making and also buy time for her to find her cheat sheet with the doorway codes on it.

From the way the guard cursed when the lock turned green, she knew he'd made a mistake, and that now he'd be working on a more useful door. If he got his guards loose before she got her boss loose, this was going to get very ugly.

She found the crib notes on the far right-hand side of her desk and snatched them up. But she'd fallen too far behind in the race. The guard had such a head start that she'd never win without cheating. She once again entered the code to lock all the doors, but she waited to push the ENTER key until she saw the icon for the main administrative office shift to green.

The instant it did, she made it turn red again.

The guard slammed his fist. "Who the hell are you?"

CHAPTER SEVEN

Jeremy Schuler squinted against the light, bright enough to backlight the tiny blood vessels through his closed eyelids. He tried to roll away, but the light followed. "Quit it," he tried to say, but his vocal cords were still sleeping, so it came out as a meaningless groan.

A thick hand clenched itself over his mouth. "Make a sound and I'll cut out your eyes," a hoarse voice growled from very close to his face. The man smelled of garlic and cigarette smoke. "Do you understand me?"

The pressure from the hand cut off all air, making it impossible for him to answer. He must have nodded, because the pressure eased.

"What's your name?" the man hissed.

"Jeremy," he wheezed. He coughed to clear the block in his throat and tried it again. "Jeremy Schuler." There was a sound of tearing fabric to his right, and a quick glimpse revealed three men clustered by his roommate Anthony's bed. The other boy was bucking and trying to yell, but it sounded like his mouth was full. After the sound of a hard smack, the kicking and the noise stopped.

"Look at me," the voice said.

Jeremy squinted back into the light.

"Don't you look at them. Keep your eyes front. How old are you?"

Jeremy felt himself trembling, his whole body vibrating with an involuntary tremor that wouldn't stop. "Th-thirteen," he stammered.

"Well, Jeremy Schuler, if you want to see thirteen and a half, you do everything we say, understand?"

Jeremy nodded.

"Say it."

"I'll do everything you say."

"You're a smart boy."

The ripping sound from Anthony's side of the room stopped, and the men left that bed to surround Jeremy's. *"We're set,"* one of them said.

The flashlight shifted from Jeremy's eyes to Anthony's bed. It looked like they'd mummified him with strips of duct tape. The light returned, once again gouging Jeremy's retinas. *"Stand up,"* his attacker said, stripping off the sheet and blanket. *"Get out of bed."*

It was only a couple layers of fabric, but somehow that cover felt like protection. Now he was so terribly exposed. He drew himself up into a ball.

The hesitation pissed off the attacker, who grabbed Jeremy's arm and pulled him off the bed and dumped him in a heap on the floor. *"I said get up."*

Jeremy found his feet and rose to his full height, adjusting his pajamas as he stood. At Resurrection House, everyone wore the same light blue pajamas with dark blue piping—like something out of a Leave It to Beaver *rerun.*

"Don't cross me, kid," the attacker said. *"Killing you wouldn't bother me a bit."*

Jeremy nodded. And trembled harder. His head still felt fuzzy from sleep, giving him hope that maybe this was just a very real, very bad nightmare that would set a new standard for nightmares everywhere.

"Do you know Evan Guinn?" Garlic Breath asked.

Jeremy nodded again. "Yes." Then as a self-preserving after-thought: "Sir."

"Do you know where his room is?"

"What did he do?" A lightbulb popped behind his eyes when a slap he never saw connected with his cheek. He smelled blood inside his head. A moment later, it was trickling down his lip onto his chin. "Yes," he said. "I know where his room is."

His upper arm disappeared into Garlic Breath's fist as he was nearly lifted off the floor. "Take us there," the man said. He stuck out a finger so close that the boy couldn't focus on it. "And don't make a sound."

Jeremy sniffed and nodded emphatically. The sniff brought a mouthful of blood.

Evan Guinn lived with Zaiem Ahmed, six or seven doors down the hall to the right, on the opposite side from Jeremy and Anthony's room. Both of them were losers. Between the two of them, they had no friends other than each other. Too damn smart, and too ready to let everybody else know it.

Jeremy led the way into the hall. It was shocking how quietly they moved as a group. No one's shoes even squeaked on the gleaming tiles, though Jeremy was keenly aware of his own blood trail. He could hear Mr. Stewart grumbling already as he had to wipe it up in the morning.

One of the men darted ahead and used a key to open Evan's door—just a crack at first, and then wide enough for two men to slip into the darkness on the other side. Jeremy briefly heard a bed skid along the floor, and then the sounds of a struggle. Before he could figure out the details, Garlic Breath lifted him by his biceps and pulled him away from the door.

When they got to the fire door at the end of the hall, they stopped abruptly. "What's through this door?" Garlic Breath asked, pointing toward the far end.

Jeremy answered quickly. He was learning. "The girls' wing. But it's alarmed."

What was he doing? Why did he warn them? If they set off

*the alarm, maybe these guys would run. But the reaction to
warn was instinctive—visceral.*

"Does it lead outside?"

Jeremy shook his head. "I don't know. I've never been
there."

A man boomed from behind them, "What's going on
here?"

Without looking, Jeremy recognized the deep rumble of
Mr. Stewart's voice. They turned together and there he was, a
blue-black mountain of a man. The face that normally radi-
ated with cheer—especially when he saw Jeremy—was
twisted into a frightening scowl that warned of danger to
anyone within reach. Jeremy was surprised to see that Mr.
Stewart wore the same dorky blue pajamas as the boys did.

One of the men who had wrapped Anthony in duct tape
produced a pistol from someplace. "Mind your own business," he warned.

If the gun frightened Mr. Stewart, his face didn't show it.
If anything, his eyes set even harder. "None of you belong
here," he growled.

"Yet here we are," Garlic Breath said. Then, in the same
tone you'd expect from someone asking to pass the salt, he
added, "Shoot him."

Jeremy yelled, "No!" but it was too late. The pistol
boomed—it was impossibly loud in the confines of the hallway—and Mr. Stewart dropped to the floor. He landed in a
heap and didn't move.

Jeremy shrieked, "Mr. Stewart!" and a hand clapped his
mouth closed. Garlic Breath lifted him by his head until his
bare feet could no longer find the floor.

From behind them, down the hall, someone yelled, "What
the fuck?" and one of the men who'd disappeared into the
dorm room darted back out into the hall with a gun in his
hand.

"Gotta get going," Garlic Breath said.

Jeremy couldn't believe the lack of emotion. They'd just

*killed the nicest man at Resurrection House. He dug his fin-
gernails into Garlic Breath's hands and kicked his feet
wildly. He wasn't leaving Mr. Stewart. Not like this.*

*His attacker's grip only tightened. "Get the other one
out," he commanded, and the other man disappeared again
into the room.*

*"Let me go!" Jeremy yelled, but it was as if he were in-
visible.*

*Another door opened, and a boy yelled. Jeremy recog-
nized the face but couldn't remember his name. Jeremy
yelled, "Help!" but the boy disappeared back into his room
and slammed the door.*

"To the stairs!" Garlic Breath called.

It hurt too much to fight. Jeremy let himself be taken.

Another door and another scream.

A man's voice yelled, "Mitch! Look out!"

*And then Jeremy got hit by a train. That's what it felt like,
anyway. Without warning he was airborne, and then fireworks exploded behind his eyes as he was driven into the unyielding concrete block wall.*

*Things went fuzzy after that, but there were definitely
more screams. As his head cleared, it took a second or two to
realize what he was seeing. Mr. Stewart was fighting his kidnapper! He and Garlic Breath rolled on the floor, cursing
and struggling for advantage as blood smeared and spattered everywhere.*

*"Help!" Jeremy cried, and while more doors opened,
none of the children filling the jambs did anything.*

*In seconds, the man from down the hall joined the fight
and pulled Mr. Stewart away from Garlic Breath by his pajama top. When it ripped and the buttons pulled away, the
custodian launched himself at the attacker again. But he'd
lost his element of surprise. The second man grabbed him by
the arms this time, and Mr. Stewart could barely move as
they stood him up. His chest and belly were slick with blood,
but he kept up his struggle as best he could.*

"Run, Jeremy," he said. *"Children, get to your rooms and lock—"*

Garlic Breath punched him hard in the ribs, in the spot where the blood seemed to be flowing from.

Mr. Stewart's face twisted into something beyond pain, but he didn't yell. Instead, he locked eyes with Jeremy and said again, "Run." At least he tried to say it. No sound came out.

But Jeremy couldn't move. Not to save his friend, not to save himself. He didn't even know he was crying as he covered his mouth and watched them hit Mr. Stewart again. And again. One more time and they let him slide to the floor.

"I said it was time to go," Garlic Breath said to his accomplice. Then he walked to Jeremy, stooped and grasped his arm, almost gently this time. "You, too, Jeremy," he said.

Jeremy stood. The last thing he saw before they placed the foul-smelling rag over his face was the faces of all those kids staring at him, letting him be taken. Letting Mr. Stewart die.

Darkness.

"That's all I remember," Jeremy concluded. His voice had been growing softer as he droned on with the story, until now it was barely audible, speaking to his crossed ankles on the camp chair. He rocked his head up, and in the dark illumination of the lantern, Harvey was surprised to see that the boy's eyes were dry. "Why would they do that?" he asked.

"I don't know," Harvey said, but his words were merely place-takers in the night. His mind raced in step with his hammering heart as he tried to come up with some plausible explanation. It was worse than a mere kidnapping. These men—whoever they were—dragged Jeremy all the way out here to kill him. And then they didn't. Why take him in the first place if they just wanted him dead? They killed Mr. Stewart, after all; why not just fire a second shot into the boy? Worse, why fire a fake shot to pretend they'd killed him?

Harvey felt the panic attack blooming like a mushroom cloud. It was a big one, he could tell, forming like an off-shore tidal wave and rising higher and higher until it would finally break over him and crush him. He hadn't had one like this in years.

He had nowhere to run. He had possession of a child he didn't know, who was supposed to be dead, and undoubtedly had people bearing down to correct their mistake. If they got the kid, they'd get Harvey, too, and then what?

No, sir. He'd chosen this ridiculous lifestyle specifically to keep things like this from happening. He'd been responsible for too many people, thank you very much. He'd fought other people's wars. He wasn't going to do that again.

He had to get rid of this kid. He should have just let him die. He should have let the boy become a body, and then just packed up his shit and gotten out of here. What was he worried about protecting, anyway? A footlocker full of MREs and a few utensils?

The air seemed suddenly too thick to breathe. Harvey clamped his arms across his chest and squeezed, trying to bring the rush of panic under control. Sometimes this worked, sometimes it didn't. When it didn't, things got ugly.

He closed his eyes and tried to summon the image of the serene lake where the long-ago shrink had taught him to seek refuge when the attacks came. If he could get to the lake before the wave broke, the whole incident could pass. If it didn't, then he guessed he'd see another blackout. He'd go wherever his mind would take him, and when it was over, he'd have to assess the damage he'd done.

Come on, he begged himself. *Let me win.* To lose was to wipe four successful years completely off the books. *Please, God, don't let that happen.*

He saw it. On the movie screen behind his eyes, he saw the mirror-smooth surface of the water reflecting the flawless blue sky and the green pines. He saw himself as a little boy sitting on the edge of the dock casting for bass, his bare feet swinging, his toes cutting *V*-shaped wakes in the still water.

The image was born of hypnosis, and when it arrived, it always felt real. He could feel the warmth of the sun on his neck, feel the chill of the water on his toes. Those sensations were every bit as real as the slowing heart rate and the regulated breathing. He'd broken the wave before it could break him. He'd won, and he was proud for it.

"Are you okay?"

It was Jeremy. He'd climbed off his chair and taken a position on his haunches in front of Harvey. The touch of the kid's hand on his shoulder brought him back from the lake.

"Are you okay?" Jeremy asked again.

Harvey inhaled deeply through his nose and blew it out as a silent whistle. It steadied him. The panic was gone.

"You and I have some serious thinking to do, young man," he said.

CHAPTER EIGHT

"I'm setting up a breaching charge," said Boxers' voice in Jonathan's ear.

The framed explosives that the big guy had brought along would make easy work of the security doors, but not without leaving an unholy mess. Jonathan wanted to say no, but things were looking grim. "Fine," he said. "But don't blow anything until I give the command." They were here to free one prisoner, not a whole jail.

"What the hell is going on?" Jimmy Henry demanded. He looked terrified, fully ready to join the other side. "And who do you keep talking to?"

Jonathan ignored him. "Mother Hen, speak to me," he said.

"It's bad," Venice said. He could hear the computer keys clacking in the background. "They figured out what we're doing, and they're trying to stop us. So far, they're as locked in as you are, but that won't last long. Once you're out, you're going to have to move fast."

As if I were planning to dawdle, he didn't say.

The lock buzzed, and Jonathan pushed Jimmy Henry ahead of him through the open door into the hallway. He pushed him to the left, toward the fire door, but as he glanced behind him, he saw a living mural of faces pressed against the reinforced glass of the central security station. He knew none of them, but there was no mistaking their desire to kill him.

Jonathan tried to move his precious cargo faster, but the shackles limited the kid to baby steps. They were five feet from the fire door when the security station door slammed open down the hall behind him and released a tidal wave of five pissed-off guards.

"You!" one of them shouted. "Stop!"

"They're coming!" Jimmy shouted.

"I see that," Jonathan growled. "Mother?"

"I've got it," she said, and the fire-door lock buzzed.

"Don't be stupid!" a guard yelled.

Jonathan threw open the door and hurled Jimmy Henry through the opening with enough force to send him sprawling on the linoleum. He slipped through, and pressed himself against the door till he heard the lock slide home, a heartbeat before the wave of guards slammed into it from the other side.

"Too close," Jonathan said. But in the instant he dedicated to making eye contact with them, he noticed with great relief that none of them were armed with guns. He wasn't surprised, given all the things that could go wrong by having a firearm in the presence of hardened criminals, but he was definitely relieved.

Now they were one-third of the way to freedom, trapped in a box in the middle of the cell block. All around them, inmates who'd been awakened by the commotion pressed against the rectangular windows in their cell doors, screaming profanity or words of encouragement. Just as Deputy George had predicted, the residents of the Basin Jail did not appreciate being awakened out of a sound sleep.

That's why you have locks on the doors.

His own smartass comment returned to his mind without warning. "Holy shit," he said. "Hey Mother, I have an idea."

"Not now," she snapped. Again, he heard the furious tapping of computer keys in the background.

"Unlock the doors," he said. "All of them. Cell doors, too. It'll give the guards more to do."

He correctly interpreted the silence he got in return as her appalled response.

"They won't all rush out together, but we only need one or two. Once the guards have someone else to occupy them, we'll get a break." Ahead of him, Jimmy Henry had already waddled to the next fire door.

"But I can't—"

"Do it, goddammit." He missed the days when people didn't question his orders.

Granville sensed that he was winning. Whoever was on the other side of his computer system knew it, too. Why else did they keep locking all the doors simultaneously instead of opening the doors for their coconspirators? He'd just finished the last digit to open Fire Door C in the middle of A-Wing, and as he hit ENTER . . .

The annunciator for every friggin' door in the jail went green.

The locks all buzzed at once just as Jonathan arrived at the second fire door. It opened easily, as did the one containing the guards, and for a moment Jonathan thought he'd miscalculated. As the plug of guards raced down the hall toward him, the inmates all remained behind their closed door.

"Y'all are free, goddammit!" he yelled.

The lead guard—a man only slightly smaller than Boxers, and mad as hell—was only ten feet away from Jonathan when the first cell door flew open and a mostly naked behemoth with long hair and complete sleeves of biker tats charged into the hallway.

If the guard saw him, he made no indication. He wanted

Jonathan and Jimmy Henry. From the flame in his eyes, it was a safe bet that he wanted them dead, in fact. Jonathan squared away and braced himself for the fight that was on its way. If killing were an option, it would have been easy, but that was off the table, which meant that it would have to be about pain tolerance.

The guard had committed himself to a high-velocity take-down that would have torn Jonathan in half, but you could tell by his eyes that he wanted to take him out at the chest. At the last instant, Jonathan ducked at the waist and charged forward two steps to body block the big man and send him sprawling to the floor.

It was all the time Jonathan needed to dart through the fire door and swing it shut behind him. "Lock it!" he yelled. "Lock it, lock it!"

He heard the bolt slip closed, and then it buzzed again.

"What the hell are you doing?" he snapped at Venice.

"It's not me," she said. "They were anticipating. Hold it closed."

Jonathan threw his shoulder into the door and braced his legs against the slick linoleum. On the other side, he heard the riot blossoming, but that didn't stop somebody from launching an enormous blow against the door. It parted a couple of inches from the jamb, but it wasn't enough to launch the door open all the way. If there was one more like that, or the guy on the other side got some help, this exercise was over.

A shadow approached from behind, and before Jonathan could react, two black hands planted themselves on either side of Jonathan's hands, and he felt heavy breath on his neck. "Gotta press harder," a voice said. "Otherwise, they'll get through."

Jonathan craned his head to get a look, and saw the owner of the voice and the hands: a young man—another weight-lifter, judging from his heavily muscled arms—and he was all business.

"He came from one of the cells," Venice said, answering his question before he could ask it. "Okay, got it."

The bolt slid home again. They had a little more time.

Boxers said, "Charges are in place, boss."

"Stand by," Jonathan said. "I'm still not ready to shoot."

"Shoot who?" his new companion said. "Who the fuck you talkin' to?"

"Never mind," Jonathan said.

"The fucking door's locked!" Jimmy yelled from the far end of the hall. He was one door away from freedom, and he could feel the pull. What he didn't know was that if Boxers shot the door with him standing there, no one would ever find his pieces.

The inmate said, "The fuck you doin' here?"

"We're breakin' out!" Jimmy called, and his words raised a hell of a ruckus behind the cell doors. They wanted out, too.

"That true?" the inmate asked Jonathan.

Jonathan nodded. "Afraid so, yes." He started moving toward the final door.

The inmate followed. "Antoine Johnson," he said, offering his hand.

Jonathan stifled an ironic chuckle and shook the hand as he continued to walk down the hall. "Nice to meet you."

"I'm coming with you," Antoine said.

"No, you're not." Jonathan answered without eye contact.

Antoine grabbed him by the biceps and jerked him to a halt. "I don't think you heard me."

This time, Jonathan's eyes burned through the man's brain. "Take your hands off of me," he growled. "I appreciate your help, so I don't want to hurt you."

Antoine seemed to surprise himself as he let go and took a small step back. "C'mon, man. I don't belong here. I'm innocent."

"I'm sure you are," Jonathan said. "But I'm only here for him." He indicated Jimmy with a toss of his head.

The lock on the final door buzzed, and Jimmy reached for

it. "Freeze," Jonathan commanded. "Don't move until I tell you." He looked back to Antoine. "Do not follow us," he said.

"How you gonna stop me?" He seemed to grow an inch as he tried to look menacing.

Jonathan took a step closer and lowered his voice nearly to a whisper. "If I see you on the other side of that door, I'll kill you. You helped over there, and I appreciate it. Don't make me kill you, Antoine."

The inmate took a step back. "Then what am I supposed to do?"

Jonathan shrugged. "Wait for your cell door to open again and go back home."

"Scorpion, we gotta go," Boxers said.

"I'm on it," Jonathan replied. He held out his hand to Antoine. "Thank you," he said. "And good luck to you."

Antoine looked at the hand as if it were something poisonous.

"Trust me," Jonathan said. "Within the next twelve hours, you're going to get a big laugh out of this."

"Digger!" Venice barked in his earbud.

Antoine cocked his head. "A laugh, huh?"

Jonathan smiled. "I promise."

The inmate accepted his hand, and they shook. "You one crazy motherfucker."

Jonathan ended the conversation with a quick flick of a nod, and then he disappeared out the door into the night. The lock slid home immediately.

Two steps into the fresh air, Jonathan and Boxers together grabbed Jimmy Henry by his arms, bent him low, and more carried than pushed him to the van that Boxers had staged on the far curb. It was exactly the same maneuver that the Secret Service would use if a protectee was under fire.

The back doors were open and waiting. When they closed

to within a few yards, Boxers broke off to slide behind the steering wheel while Jonathan half tossed, half slid their precious cargo onto the steel deck of the stripped-down van. He hadn't even stopped tumbling before the van was rolling. As they turned the first corner, Jonathan leaned out to close the back door.

"That was awesome, dude!" Jimmy laughed. "I mean, really fuckin' awesome. I thought for sure we were—"

"Shut up," Jonathan barked.

Jimmy was only a silhouette in the dark, but Jonathan saw him rear back. "Christ, dude, you don't—"

Jonathan grabbed the ankle of Jimmy's orange jumpsuit and pulled, sliding the kid flat onto his back. Before the inmate could react, Jonathan fired a savage punch to his testicles, and the response was instant. The kid retched and curled himself into a tight ball. He was still struggling to regain his breath when Jonathan started wrapping Jimmy's eyes with duct tape.

"Dude, what the fuck—?"

Jonathan clamped his hand over the kid's mouth hard enough to loosen a tooth and pressed his head into the floor of the van. "Shut up, punk," he hissed. "Just shut up until I tell you to talk. And I swear to God, if you call me 'dude' one more time, I'm going to take a hammer to your nose."

Jimmy was crying now, in agony from the blow to his groin, and clearly terrified. "I'll do anything," he whined. "Honest to God, I'm on your side, okay?"

"Don't be so sure, kid," Boxers called from the front.

"W-what are you going to do?"

Jonathan punched him in the balls again, harder this time. "What part of 'shut up' confuses you?" he growled.

The kid retched more, and when he vomited, Jonathan felt comfortable that he'd finally made his point. Jimmy wouldn't risk another punch, so Jonathan wouldn't have to fire another one. As sensitive as testicles are to pain, they're actually fairly indestructible. Pound a guy in his nuts and you not only get his attention but you gain a huge psychological advantage. The younger the target, the more profound the advantage. It's as if God had interrogators in mind when he designed the human body.

As for the vomiting, it was an unfortunate but predictable side effect—and the reason why Jonathan hadn't taped his prisoner's mouth. He didn't need the kid choking to death before he gave them what they wanted.

They drove eight miles into the flat vastness of Virginia's Northern Neck, past thousands of acres of farmland that was devoid of all but the occasional shade tree, the entire tableau dyed blue-black in the late-night darkness. Without the GPS preset on their navigation device, Jonathan doubted that Boxers would have seen the narrow driveway that marked their first turn.

They drove confidently in the darkened vehicle thanks to the night-vision goggles that Boxers and Jonathan had come to see as an extension to normal vision. As the van bounced along the rutted path, so did Jimmy on the metal floor. But beyond the occasional instinctive reaction to pain and fear, he kept his mouth shut.

Ahead, at the end of the long driveway, an open gate in a clapboard fence marked the way to a massive barn. The door had been propped open just as they'd arranged. The owner of this spread was a man named Horne, an old acquaintance of Jonathan's, who knew better than to ask detailed questions but had made the appropriate assumptions about the nature of Jonathan's business and didn't mind cooperating one bit.

They drove into the barn and stopped. Jonathan waited quietly as he heard Boxers get out of the van, close the barn door, and then return to the van to open the double back doors.

"Listen to me, Jimmy," Jonathan said. His tone was soft, almost soothing. "We're going to move you now, and I want you to cooperate. Do you understand?"

Jimmy's breathing rate doubled as panic set in. Blinded

by the tape over his eyes and aching from his beating, the kid was terrified. That was the whole point.

Jonathan jerked his chin at Boxers, and the big man grabbed the cuffs of the kid's pants and dragged him along the flatbed to the edge above the back bumper. When he let Jimmy's legs drop, the kid naturally sat up, and Boxers dipped to get his shoulder low enough to lift him into a fireman's carry. Another panic response made the kid squirm, but he caught himself right away and settled down.

"You're doing good," Jonathan encouraged. "The next part's going to seem worse than it is, so don't panic. Once my friend puts you down, just stand still. This will all make sense in a minute."

In the dim light cast by a half dozen bare lightbulbs suspended from the twenty-foot ceiling, Boxers carried his charge to one of the twelve-by-twelve-inch hardwood columns that held the roof up. He rotated the kid off his shoulder into a standing position, and then held him tightly against the post by a massive hand pressed to the center of his chest.

"This is the scary part," Jonathan soothed. "Just relax, and nothing will hurt."

"Please don't hurt me," Jimmy begged. He couldn't help himself.

Mr. Horne had driven an enormous nail into the center of the post, per Jonathan's instructions, exactly six and a half feet off the floor. On it, he'd placed a thick leather dog's collar, with a leash hanging from the built-in loop. Without saying a word, Boxers took the collar from the hook and looped it around the prisoner's neck.

"We're not going to choke you," Jonathan said, getting ahead of the natural panic. "We're not even going to cinch it tight. We just need you not to get away."

The kid's breathing rate doubled.

Boxers did just as Jonathan had promised, securing the collar with two fingers' clearance around the skin of Jimmy's neck. Then he secured the leash to the spike with enough slack to keep Jimmy from choking, but not so much that he might forget that he was helpless. They let him stand there for the better part of a minute, no one saying anything as Boxers returned to the van to retrieve his tools for the next stage.

Jonathan felt his own heart hammering as the big man leaned into the open doors and removed a heavy rubber truncheon. About the size and shape of a baseball bat, the weapon had enough flex that it wouldn't break a bone, but enough heft that it would hurt like hell.

Boxers rolled his shoulders to loosen them up as he returned to his spot at the kid's left and set his feet in a batter's stance. He glanced to Jonathan for the final go-ahead, and when he saw his boss nod, he let loose with a homerun swing. The truncheon's sweet spot connected squarely on Jimmy's hip bone with a sound that reverberated through the barn like a muffled pistol shot.

Jimmy howled. It was a guttural, choking scream that was equal parts fear and agony. Blinded by the tape over his eyes, he couldn't know what had caused the pain, and with his arms shackled and his neck secured, he couldn't protect himself. "Please!" he shouted. "What do you want from me?"

Jonathan let ten seconds pass before he answered. He abhorred these kinds of interrogation techniques, but two children were missing, and he had neither the time nor the luxury to be subtle. By establishing a baseline for pain, he hoped that the one swat with the truncheon would suffice.

As he watched this nineteen-year-old sob for mercy, Jonathan felt sympathy for him. "Jimmy, I need you to listen to me," Jonathan said softly. He made his voice sound gentle.

"Please don't hit me again."

"Don't make me, and I won't," Jonathan said. "But you need to know that what you felt right then is only the opening act. We can keep that going all night long. You wouldn't like that, would you?"

Jimmy shook his head frantically. "I'll do whatever you ask."

"I hope so," Jonathan said. "But I'll be honest with you. My friend hopes just the opposite. He would like nothing better than to beat you till you'd spend the rest of your life in a wheelchair." It was a classic good-cop, bad-cop banter, but in this case, it was a statement of fact.

"I swear to God, I'll do whatever you ask."

"All right, then. Let's start with last night. When I know everything that you know, I'll be out of your life."

"All I did was drive," Jimmy whined. "I never went inside. I had nothing to do with the shooting. I swear to God."

"But you knew you were there to kidnap children," Jonathan said.

Jimmy said nothing.

Jonathan figured he was looking for the right answer. "Lying to me will be a mistake," he said. "Do we need to hit you again?"

"Yes," Jimmy said. "I mean no! You don't have to hit me again. Yes, I knew that we were going to be snatching kids."

"For what reason?"

"They never told me."

"Didn't you ask?"

Jimmy shook his head. "I didn't want to know. I didn't need to know."

"You must have heard names," Jonathan prompted. "You must have heard who they were coming to get."

"I knew there'd be two," Jimmy said. He spoke emphatically, clearly anxious to prove that he was being truthful. "But I only heard one name. It was Evan something. An Irish name."

"Guinn," Jonathan said.

"That's it. But then they came out and I heard they'd shot somebody. I was like, what the fuck?"

"So Evan Guinn is the only name you heard," Jonathan recapped.

"I swear to God." Despite the slack in his leash, he stood on tiptoes and kept his jaw extended.

"Why him and not the other one?" Jonathan asked.

Jimmy's breathing quickened again. It was his tell for not having the answer he thought they wanted to hear. "I don't know. I swear to God. I only know about Evan Guinn because I overheard the name."

"Why did they take him?"

"They didn't say."

"You mean you didn't ask."

Jimmy hesitated. "Yeah, that, too. Look, all I know is that this guy paid me six hundred bucks to drive a car, okay?"

"You knew it was for kidnapping children," Jonathan pressed, "but you never thought to ask why?"

Jimmy dared to bring his heels to the ground and lean against the column. "I figured it was obvious," he said with a barely perceptible shrug. "I mean that place is an orphanage for criminals' kids, right? I figure somebody pissed off somebody else, and they wanted to snatch their kid because of it."

Before Jonathan could intervene, Boxers swung his rubber truncheon with everything he had into the heavy timber pillar, shaking the barn with an enormous *boom*. "And that seems all right to you?" he growled.

"Hey, I'm just telling you what happened!" Jimmy yelled, once again on his toes.

Jonathan held out a hand to settle Boxers and fired a glare that told him to back off. The vigilante that lived in Jonathan's soul wanted to beat the kid to death, too. But they were professionals, and they had a job to do. There was no room for that kind of outburst.

"Everybody just calm down," Jonathan soothed. "Take a deep breath, both of you. And I mean that literally." He gave himself a few seconds to follow his own advice. "Jimmy, it's hard for us to understand how someone can agree to kidnap a pair of children and not ask why."

"If they wanted me to know why, they'd have told me why," Jimmy said. "Plus, like I said, I figured I already knew. It's about criminals doing what they do best."

"Who hired you?" Jonathan asked.

"A guy named Sjogren. Jerry, I think. Or maybe George, I'm not sure. A *J* sound. But I've done a couple of things for him before."

"Kidnappings?" Jonathan asked.

Jimmy shook his head vehemently. "No, nothing like that. One bank thing that didn't turn out to be much, and a convenience store thing. Nothing where anybody got hurt."

"But they could have," Boxers suggested.

"They *didn't.*"

Jonathan shot another disapproving glare. Boxers knew better than this. For an interrogation to work, there had to be one contact, one focus. Boxers knew this as well as anyone, but he was pissed.

"What happened to that guy who was shot?" Jimmy asked.

"Why do you care?" Jonathan asked.

Jimmy blew a puff of air through his nose and shook his head. "I was the fucking *driver*, okay? I didn't plan any of this shit. I'm not some fucking animal who snatches kids, but I also know that I'm fucked by the law because I was part of it. Doesn't mean I want some guy to die." His voice dropped in volume. "I was earning a living. I didn't think it would go like this."

Jonathan kept to the point. "This Sjogren guy. Is it S-H-O-G-R-E-N?"

"I don't know how he spells it. It's not like we wrote letters back and forth."

Jonathan conceded the point. "Was he with you at the school?"

Despite the fear and the discomfort, Jimmy was able to cough out a laugh. "Sjogren? Hell no. He never gets his hands dirty."

"He's just the middleman," Jonathan helped.

"Exactly. People need help and they contact him."

"Who were his customers?"

"The first jobs I did with him were about a thug named Sammy Bell. I don't know if you know that name."

Jonathan shot a knowing look at Boxers. Sammy Bell used to be an enforcer for the Slater crime family, whose interests often clashed with those of Jonathan's father. When Old Man Slater kicked the bucket a dozen years or so ago, Sammy had stepped in to take over.

"This was Sammy Bell's operation?" Jonathan asked.

"No, no, no, no. I didn't say that. I said that's how I first met Sjogren. I don't know if Sammy Bell is involved."

"Where can I find this Sjogren guy?" he asked.

The breathing tell kicked in again. "I don't know," Jimmy said. "I've never tried to find him. I don't have to. He finds me when the time comes."

"Is Sjogren his real name?"

"It's all I've ever called him."

"And what about the others?" Jonathan asked, moving on. "What did you call them?"

Frustration took root. "Jesus, you make it sound like we're drinking buddies. I didn't call them anything. Hell, I didn't even want to talk to them."

"Why's that?"

"Scary, scary dudes. Like they were pissed at the world. They growled and snapped at each other like they were married or something."

"How many of them were there?"

Jimmy hesitated long enough to verify the number in his head before answering. "Four," he said. "Five, including me. Only, they all seemed to know each other, and they weren't happy about me tagging along."

The wording made Jonathan cock his head. He noticed Boxers doing the same. "What does that mean, 'tagging along'?"

"Like when you have to take you little sister with you on a date."

"I know what the phrase means," Jonathan said. "It was an odd choice of words for you."

"But that's what it was like. I think something happened to their original driver. That's why I was brought in."

"Something happened like what?"

Jimmy's frustration peaked and he shouted, "I don't fucking know!"

The outburst brought another explosive but harmless blow from Boxers' truncheon onto the heavy pillar.

"Go ahead!" Jimmy yelled. "Go ahead and hit me again, you stupid shits. But before you can beat information out of me, you've got to beat it into me first. I just don't know this stuff you're asking me."

"Everybody settle down!" Jonathan commanded.

"Who are you people?" Jimmy asked.

Jonathan was shocked that it took him so long to ask. "Trust me when I tell you that you don't want to know," he said. "Are you telling me that you never heard any names from these guys you were with? They must have called each other something."

Jimmy steeled himself with an enormous breath. "A guy named Ponder seemed to be the guy in charge. He was the one who was pissed when shit started to fall apart."

"How did your time with these people end? When did you last see your friends?" Boxers asked.

Jimmy drew another deep breath. "I dropped them off at a storage place in Kinsale," Jimmy said. "It had some stupid name that used the letter U instead of the word 'you.' They off-loaded the kids and never looked back."

"Why the storage place?"

"I guess they had stuff stored there," Jimmy said. He quickly added, "I'm not being a smart-ass. They honest to Christ didn't tell me about their plans."

"What did you see?"

"As little as possible. I'm telling you, these are really scary dudes. You know how when you get mugged you don't want to look the dude with the gun in the eye so he won't have to kill you to keep you from testifying? It was like that with these guys."

Jonathan had never felt that way himself, but he'd inflicted the feeling on others a time or two. "What *did* you see, then, when you were trying not to see anything?"

This time, Jimmy hesitated a long time—probably twenty seconds. That kind of internal debate usually portended something big.

"First promise you won't kill me," Jimmy said.

Jonathan shot a look to Boxers. This was an interrogation, not a negotiation. The rules prohibited any deals with the target. To maintain the command position, the book said you had to make your target feel utterly helpless.

Jonathan decided to trust his gut instead. "I'm not an assassin," he said. "I wouldn't shed a tear if you got hit by a truck, but as long as you continue to cooperate, I'm not going to kill you."

Another pause. Another gut-check for Jimmy. "They had a helicopter in there," he confessed. "It wasn't very big, and the propellers or whatever the hell you call them were, like, folded back, but I could see the front of it."

Jonathan's stomach fell. "So they moved the children by helicopter."

"I think so." Jimmy's tone turned whiny. "I saw that, and I knew I was in deep, deep shit. A chopper, for Christ's sake. Who does that? Who's got the money for that? I just boogied the hell out of there as fast as I could."

Jonathan's brain was stuck on the image of the chopper. Jimmy had asked all the right questions. Who the hell *did* have those kinds of resources? "Where did you boogie to?" he asked.

Jimmy managed a laugh. "To jail," he said. "I was supposed to ditch the van at a McDonald's parking lot in Montross, where there was supposed to be a Mustang waiting for me. Only, I got pulled over on the way." He sighed. "I guess I got a little heavy-footed."

Jonathan didn't share with him the fact that his van had been spotted by a witness. If it hadn't been for that one insomniac, Jimmy probably would have skated with nothing more than a speeding ticket.

He found himself out of questions. He looked to Boxers and got a shrug. The big guy was out of questions, too.

CHAPTER NINE

Granville George struggled to contain his amusement as he watched the teams from the FBI and the Virginia State Police try to make sense out of all that had happened. Whoever planned this mess had every right to feel proud of himself—even though Granville himself was probably looking at an extended tour of duty behind the desk.

Sheriff Charles Willow had hauled his shriveled ass out of bed to be a part of the investigation, and from the looks of him, with his sleep-twisted hair and his white beard stubble, the usually media-savvy sheriff had forgotten to glance at a mirror on his way out of the house.

Presently, the sheriff seemed most concerned about remaining relevant among the state troopers and FBI agents, all of whom had taken the position that as keeper of the jail system, Sheriff Willow was more a target of the investigation than a participant in it. Still, since he literally had all the keys, there was no keeping him out of the reception area as the very attractive Sergeant Lindsey Wilson of the Virginia State Police ran Granville through his story for the third time.

"But there's no such person as Special Agent Leon Harris

with the FBI," she said, responding to the information he'd just recited.

"I'm not hard of hearing," Granville said. "And I'm not especially dim-witted. Right around the time that he was coldcocking my colleague I think I began to consider the possibility that he was an imposter. How many times must I say it?"

Sheriff Willow rose to his opportunity to make noise. "I'd watch my tone if I were you, Deputy," he said.

Granville ignored him.

So did Sergeant Wilson. "When you explain how you let an imposter into a secured area, I can stop asking."

"He was an imposter with legitimate FBI credentials," Granville explained. Again.

"Not possible." This from Special Agent William Meyer, FBI, whose role in this was not clear to Granville, beyond the fact that Jimmy Henry was being held on federal charges. "They had to be counterfeit."

"Then they were good ones."

"Perhaps to the untrained eye," Meyer said. Wilson nodded in agreement. It seemed that the federal government and the Commonwealth of Virginia had jointly decided that there was a certain dimness between Granville's ears.

Granville gestured to them both. "You two met before?"

"Actually, no," said Sergeant Wilson. And judging from her tone, this was a good thing.

"Then how do you know he's really with the FBI?"

Meyer puffed up like an indignant fish.

"His credentials, right?" Granville answered for her. "I mean you didn't do a quick background check or take any fingerprints? It was the attitude, the badge, and the gun, right? Same with me."

Sergeant Wilson smiled as she got the point. Special Agent Meyer did not. "Let's move on," she said.

"No, let's not move on," Granville said. He struggled to keep his tone even, but the more he spoke, the more difficult that became. "Let's stay right where we are until we all embrace the fact that I am not an idiot. In fact, let's all agree that I am not only *a* victim, but in many ways the *primary* victim of what went down here."

Sheriff Willow took a step forward.

"Save it, Sheriff. I understand that this is embarrassing to the department. Christ, of all the people in the room right now, I understand that better than anyone."

"You're getting defensive," Meyer said with a roll of his eyes and a wave of his hand.

Granville shot to his feet, toppling his chair with his knees. "Defensive, my ass. Shall we talk about what really happened here tonight?"

"What we've been trying to do since we got here," Sergeant Wilson said.

"Bullshit. Y'all have been trying to dig a bunker for yourselves with a door that's too small to let me in." As he felt the color rising in his cheeks, he knew that his dreams of getting away from the desk were done, but he didn't give a shit anymore. "What *actually* happened here is a very carefully planned and brilliantly executed prison break."

"That better not be admiration I hear in your tone, Deputy," Willow said.

Granville glared. "Jesus Christ, Sheriff, open your eyes. 'Admiration' might not be exactly the right word, but I gotta tell you it's close. It was a flawless plan." He turned on Agent Meyer. "And why would you doubt that a team that was able to hijack our entire security system—and, in the process, erase every goddamn trace that they were ever here, *despite* the eyewitnesses—could figure out a way to forge a hunk of metal into a precious FBI badge, and some papers into convincing creds?"

He paused. It was a real question, but Agent Meyer's only answer was to make his ears turn red.

Granville shifted his attention to his boss. "You know, Sheriff, as you struggle to find the right kind of message to send out to the voting public, you might want to mention the fact that thanks to me and all the other competent deputies *you* hired, we came *this close* to stopping them, and we limited what could have been a mass breakout to only one."

Sheriff Willow prepared to be angry, but then the words got through, and he backed off.

Granville lowered his voice as he closed the deal. "What I saw happen tonight was nothing short of heroic. One deputy was overpowered and severely beaten, and then the rest of the team risked their lives to keep everything from going to hell."

He turned to Meyer. "I'm guessing that your guy has some damned important friends, and they didn't want him spending time with you. The kind of help he got doesn't come cheap."

"But he's nobody," Sergeant Wilson said. "Jimmy Henry is a small-time crook, in and out of the system two or three times, but no known ties to anyone important. No known ties to anyone at all."

Just like that, Granville saw that he'd earned his way inside the circle. She was speaking to him, not at him. "He was accused of shooting up that school yesterday, right?" he asked. He knew the answer, so he kept going. "Maybe it was just a vigilante thing. People broke him out to string him up."

"For God's sake, Deputy George," Sheriff Willow growled.

Again, Granville decided not to engage the boss, deciding to cut a break for the guy who was watching his career implode.

"Was there anything in this Leon guy's words or actions that make you think that might be the case?" asked Sergeant Wilson.

Granville shrugged. "No. But then again, there was nothing in his words or actions that made me think he wasn't an FBI agent."

"Seems awfully Zane Grey to me," Meyer said, alluding to the famed writer of pulp Westerns.

"You know what goes on at the school, right?" Granville

pressed. "Every single student there is the child of an incarcerated parent. If ever there was a group that could open up a can of Zane Grey vigilantism, that would be the one."

"It's worth looking into," Wilson said, jotting a note to herself. "We start with the parents of the two who were kidnapped—"

A state trooper who looked too old not to have any stripes on his sleeve interrupted Wilson by clearing his throat. He held a cell phone in his fingers, ready for it to be taken. "Excuse me, Sergeant, but this is a park ranger. He first asked for Sheriff Willow, but when I told him you were running the investigation, he said he wanted to talk with both of you."

"A park ranger?" Wilson said. She looked to Willow. "Any objection to putting it on speaker?"

The sheriff shrugged.

She pressed the button on the phone. "This is Sergeant Wilson with the Virginia State Police," she said. "I'm here with Sheriff Willow. How can we help you?"

The background noise through the speakers made it clear that the ranger was outdoors. "Yeah, hi," said a young voice. "This is Paul Johnson with the National Park Service. I'm at the George Washington Birthplace Memorial here on Popes Creek?"

Everyone in the room shrugged together. "Okay," Wilson said.

"Well, I think I've got something here that belongs to you." A smile appeared in his voice. "Some*one*, actually. He says his name is Jimmy Henry. Does that mean anything to you?"

The morning crew at the Washington Birthplace Memorial had been shocked to find the shackled man chained to the base of the obelisk that marked the entry to the park. According to the incident reports they'd filled out for the National Park Service, the young man had been sleeping soundly on the ground. Once the workers saw the chains and the orange jumpsuit, they were able to link what they were seeing with the reports they'd heard on the radio, and they'd called higher-ups without actually approaching the fugitive.

Granville George was waiting at the jail when Jimmy Henry arrived. The overtime hadn't been approved, but he didn't care. If he had to eat a couple of official hours on his own nickel, that would be fine, just so long as he saw justice done.

They'd sent a car from Middlesex County to Westmoreland County to make the pickup, and when Jimmy was escorted in, Granville made a point of being right there in his face to let him know that actions had consequences in this part of the world, and that Jimmy had chosen poorly.

The rules in a case like this were clear. Jimmy Henry was processed just as if he were a first-arriving prisoner. His personal effects—none—were catalogued, and then he was escorted to the processing bay, where he was stripped naked and cavity searched. It was a part of the process that Granville didn't particularly enjoy, but he'd long ago lost his guy-shy instincts. It doesn't take but one incident where someone literally pulls a weapon out of his ass to make you respect the importance of a cavity search.

He'd accordingly been prepared for the humiliation; but he hadn't been prepared for the bruises. Jimmy Henry's left leg was bruised beyond purple. It bore a deep black stripe from what must have been a brutal attack. When they called in the jail physician—actually a local doctor who moonlighted for folding money—they also found bruising around the kid's throat, in addition to the more typical stress wounds inflicted by the unyielding shackles.

"Who did this to you?" the doctor asked.

"I don't have to tell you anything," Jimmy answered.

"Seems to me it serves your best interests to talk about the people who tortured you," Agent Meyer said. Sergeant Wilson was in the room, too, but remained silent. If Granville wasn't mistaken, she was embarrassed by the prisoner's nakedness.

"Who said anything about torture?" Jimmy asked. "These bruises are from falling down."

"Must have been a hell of a fall," Granville said.

But the prisoner had shut down. "I know my rights," he said. "I don't have to tell you anything without a lawyer."

"Who broke you out of here?" Sheriff Willow asked.

Sergeant Wilson put a hand on his shoulder. "He asked for a lawyer," she said. "We're done with questions."

With that, it was over.

Granville stayed with Jimmy as he dressed himself in fresh orange coveralls, and then escorted him back to the cell where his evening had begun only a few hours before. As they walked together down the central hallway, Granville called out to the other inmates, "Take a look, gentlemen. You can try to run, but you'll never get away." Faces appeared at the windows in cell doors. "Jimmy Henry is back with us after only five hours on the run. He raised all that ruckus, and what did it buy for everyone? Forty-eight hours in lockdown. When y'all start going stir-crazy in there, I don't want you getting pissed at me and the other guards. I want you to remember that Jimmy is the one to blame."

Jimmy shot him a panicked look, and Granville shook it off. This was the kind of announcement that could get an inmate beaten to shit, but Jimmy should have thought of that before.

"You're a kidnapper," Granville said to his charge as they arrived at his cell door. "And you're the guy who cost every inmate a lot of privileges. I'd be careful if I were you." Jimmy's eye grew large as the truth sank in. "If I were you, I might think about cooperating a little."

Something happened behind the kid's eyes, but it was gone as quickly as it arrived. Fear, maybe? Perhaps just a grim acceptance of what lay ahead. "Well, I tell you what, Deputy George. If I was you, I'd have killed myself a long time ago. Now, why don't you just quit worrying about me?"

Granville opened the cell and let Jimmy inside.

As he pushed the door closed, he glanced to his left and saw another prisoner, Antoine Johnson, grinning widely as he strained to see what was happening.

"What are you looking at?" Granville barked.

Antoine gave a little giggle. "I'm just happy to learn that I'm smarter than I thought I was," he said.

Evan Guinn knew that he was moving.

He couldn't see or hear anything, and his head hurt like it had been pounded with a hammer, but he knew he wasn't lying still anymore. He had the sense of floating. Maybe the sense of spinning. It wasn't a good feeling like the ones you get when you dream about flying on Harry Potter's broom. This was a sick-making feeling, not unlike the morning after the night when Powell Andersen had treated a bunch of the RezHouse crew to the moonshine that had been sneaked into the dorm via his Uncle Ed. Evan had always thought that Father Dom had suspected something that day, but he'd never called the question.

Even as he was floating, though, he had the sense that he was somehow anchored down. He couldn't feel any ropes or chains, but as he tried to move, his arms and legs felt as if they weighted a hundred pounds apiece.

He needed to run. But why?

Men in the dark. Men with tape and heavy hands. The foul-smelling rag over his face.

He'd been kidnapped. *Kidnapped.* Was that possible?

Who would want to kidnap him?

The more he thought about it, the more his head boomed. He wanted to move, to run; but he was paralyzed.

Except his eyelids. If he really struggled against the weight that burdened every part of him, he could get them to open. First his left eye, all by itself, and then his right. It was hard to focus, but when he forced himself, he could make the scenery come together.

He lay on his back, staring up at a low ceiling that had knobs and things he'd not seen before. They cast shadows that cut straight across at a sharp right angle, and from that he knew that the light was coming in at him from the side, instead of from above, as he would have expected. He turned this head to the right—carefully, to keep the hammers inside from beating against each other—and he saw an oval window that looked out on the sky. It was a little thing, nowhere big enough to climb through.

He was on an airplane. He'd never been on one before, but he'd seen enough of them in movies. The fact of being airborne made him feel fear for the first time since awakening. There's kidnapped, he thought, and then there's *kidnapped*. If they flew you to where you were going, you'd be gone forever, right?

Moving his head to the left, he confirmed his suspicion. This was definitely an airplane.

"He's waking up," a voice said, and Evan feared he'd done something wrong. If he could have made his vocal cords work, he would have apologized.

"Not for long," said another voice.

The shadows shifted, and a man appeared in his field of vision. "You must have a hell of a liver, kid," the man said. He bore the faint scent of garlic.

Unable to do anything—to talk or scream or even roll over—Evan watched as the man lifted a plastic tube and stuck a needle in it.

He had the fleeting thought that the other end of the tube must be stuck in his arm someplace, but then his thoughts and his mind went blank.

CHAPTER TEN

A stick cracked.

While it could have been caused by anything, Harvey knew that someone was coming to kill him.

He'd dozed in the camp chair, leaving the sleeping bag and the air mattress for Jeremy. He hadn't intended to sleep deeply. He hadn't intended to sleep at all. Hell, he hadn't intended a single moment of what had happened during the last twenty-four hours.

It didn't matter, because he was wide awake now, and so was the new day, the sun hanging low and golden in the east. Without moving his body, he opened his eyes and scanned as far to the sides as his eyes could shift. The morning revealed nothing.

Another crack. Rustling.

From the darkness of the tent, Jeremy whispered, "Harvey?"

The words were barely audible, but they registered on Harvey's ears as a shout. "Shh," he hissed. "I hear it."

The boy's face appeared in the triangular opening of the tent. "Who is it?"

"Maybe it's just a deer," he hoped aloud.

"But I heard a car," Jeremy said.

Harvey's stomach fell. He hadn't really believed that it was a deer, anyway.

Jeremy crawled out farther. "It's them, isn't it?"

Keep it together, Harvey told himself. Losing it now wouldn't help a soul.

"Harvey?"

"Shh!" This time, the hiss was emphatic. More than anything else, they needed silence. Silence and invisibility. A trip back in time to undo his decision to get involved in this crap would be good, too.

"I'm scared, Harvey."

What part of "Shh" did the kid find confusing?

Jeremy kept coming. He crawled all the way into the open, and then over to Harvey, where he crouched next to the camp chair. He clutched Harvey's arm.

He expects me to protect him, Harvey thought. What a stupid move that was. Harvey Rodriguez had room for exactly one important person in his life, and that was Harvey Rodriguez himself. If Jeremy—a stranger—thought for an instant that he would risk even momentary discomfort for some larger, nobler cause, then he was woefully mistaken.

The sounds of movement grew steadily clearer. Within a minute, he could hear voices. A few seconds later, he could hear what the voices were saying.

". . . no goddamn sense."

"When was the last time this job made sense to anybody?"

"So I gotta pay for it? This shit just ain't right."

Both voices were male, and both sounded neither young nor old—a conclusion confirmed just a few seconds later when Harvey got his first glimpse of them. Thirty yards away, they both wore jeans and T-shirts, and as they waded toward the tall grass, they headed directly toward the spot where Harvey had discovered the unconscious boy.

Jeremy's hand tightened on Harvey's arm. "It really is them, isn't it?" he squeaked.

"Don't move," Harvey said. With the sun rising over the tent, into the eyes of the visitors, there was a chance that they could remain unseen if they just didn't move. These guys weren't moving with any sense of danger, which meant that they were likely to accept their surroundings as is. It's human nature to accept a first impression as normal—making it possible to literally hide in plain sight. But thousands of years of evolution still had not erased the instinctive alarm triggered by movement.

Both men had a wiry athletic look about them, a clear source of pride for the one closest to Harvey. His T-shirt was at least two sizes too small, straining the fabric at his biceps and pecs. He was also the one who carried the folded gray body bag under his arm. It bothered Harvey that he could recognize it for what it was.

"Lie down," Harvey whispered. "Very, very slowly." As he spoke, he wrested his arm free from the boy's grasp and pressed down on his shoulder. Jeremy did not resist. He lay flat on his belly, his arms tucked under his chest.

With the kid stable on the ground, Harvey edged his own butt to the front of the camp chair and pressed his shoulder blades against the sling backing. The effect was to lie flat, his front to the sky, though his eyes never moved from the visitors. Warnings against movement notwithstanding, a smaller target was always better than a larger one.

"So where is he?" asked Body Beautiful.

"I know what you know," the other one said. He was as powerful looking through his shoulders as the other one, but wore his T-shirt looser. And his hair was longer—over his ears but not over the top. "He's here somewhere."

"Sayin' it don't make it so. Jerry said to go to the end of the parking lot and then straight till you're almost in the water. That's what he said, and that's where we are. Show me a dead kid."

His butt on the ground now, Harvey could still see the tops of the visitors' heads above the swaying grass.

"Then he's got to be here somewhere."

"Maybe somebody moved him," Muscles said.

"No way. Somebody found him, this place would be lousy with cops. It'd be all over the news. They're already ape shit over the shit at the school. Can you imagine the shit if one of the kids was found dead?"

Muscles nodded. "Have it your way. How'd a dead kid get up and walk away?"

A long silence followed as they continued their search. As the sun rose higher, the details of these men's appearance grew clearer, and Harvey had the terrifying thought that they were cops. They looked like cops. It was the military bearing, the focus on the task at hand. His already-pounding heart picked up more speed. Cops trying to kill a kid, with him stuck in the middle. He was so screwed.

"Hey, Billy," Long Hair said. "Look at this over here." By Harvey's calculation, he was standing at the exact spot where he'd found Jeremy. "Look at this grass. It's all matted."

Harvey tried to recall what he'd left behind, but he pulled up a blank. He'd been concentrating too hard on the kid.

Billy joined his partner. "And what fine matted grass it is. Where's the body?"

"Christ, I don't know. Maybe animals dragged it off."

"And where's the blood?"

For the first time, Harvey considered bolting off into the woods and taking his chances. The kid was the one they wanted. If he ran . . .

. . . they'd still hunt him down and kill him. Who was he kidding?

"I'm beginning to think maybe he was never killed," Long Hair said.

A long pause. "You can't just stop there."

"Think about it. Explains a lot."

Billy was genuinely lost. "You're saying he was wounded and wandered off."

"Maybe. Or maybe . . ." He shifted his gaze directly toward Harvey's campsite. "What the fuck is that?"

In unison, they drew firearms from underneath their T-shirts and pointed them at Harvey.

"You there!" Long Hair shouted. "Don't you fucking move."

"Ah, shit," Billy whined. "Who the hell is he?"

Singular, Harvey thought. *I'm the only one they see.*

"Stand up!" Long Hair said. "And be really fucking careful if you don't want to die."

Harvey's head raced faster than his heart. Dying was nowhere on his list of things to do today.

"Harvey . . ." Jeremy whined.

He ignored the boy. As he stood, he pressed down on Jeremy's head for leverage, as if it were a rock. It was important that the kid stay out of sight. If they saw him, they'd shoot him. And if they shot the kid, what incentive did they have to let Harvey go on breathing? Jeremy needed to disappear, and since that wasn't possible, he needed to keep out of sight.

"Hello," Harvey said, as brightly as he could. He recognized the pistols in the man's hands as 9-millimeter Berettas, standard military issue. Police departments hadn't gone to that particular weapon in most cases, certainly not here in Westmoreland County.

"What are you doing there listening to us?" Billy asked.

Harvey pegged him as the hothead of the two, the one to be talked down first. "It's hard not to listen to a conversation in an open place," he said. "It's quiet out here." As he spoke he took a couple of steps forward, hoping that if they couldn't see the boy, they wouldn't make the connection. He also moved to his left to break their sight line away from the kid in case he moved in the background.

"Why are you hiding there?" Billy asked.

Harvey forced a chuckle that he hoped sounded more genuine that it felt. "Y'all heard what you were sayin', right?" he quipped. "Wouldn't you think about stayin' outta sight if that's what you heard?"

Billy raised his arm perpendicular to his body and drew a bead on Harvey's chest. Harvey recognized the look. It was over for him.

But the other man grabbed Billy's wrist and spoiled his aim. "No," he said. "Not yet."

"We've got to."

"Not *yet*," his partner repeated.

"Sean—"

"I said *no*."

So the other guy's name was Sean. It was always nice to know the names of the people who were going to kill you. Harvey's heart continued to pound, but he was surprised how clear his head felt. "Yeah, Billy, he said no," Harvey said.

"Christ, now he knows our names," Billy spat.

Harvey had thought that a little levity might defuse things. He'd been wrong.

Sean let go of his partner's wrist and allowed him to reacquire his target. "This would be a good time for you to do some explaining," he said.

Harvey had been moving left the entire time, never closing an inch, but continuing to draw their aim away from the campsite. He stopped now. "I'm not a threat to you," he said. "It's like you said earlier. If I'd wanted to bring the police into my life, this place would be alive with them. Do you see any cops?"

Billy and Sean exchanged confused glances.

Harvey used the brief silence to design a lie that would buy him some time. "I was here night before last," he said. "I saw them drag that boy out here and shoot him. Then I heard the chopper. Scared me to death." He let the news settle on them. "If I was going to call somebody, that would have been the time, don't you think?"

He could almost hear Sean's brain trying to process it. He knew what the inevitable question would be, so he moved ahead with the scary-big lie. "Fact is, you're about three hours too late."

It registered on the visitors like a slap. As they recoiled with another shared look, Harvey noted movement behind them and off to the right. It was two men, one huge, the other average. He didn't allow himself to look directly at them because they appeared to be armed, and through his peripheral vision, Harvey would swear that their aim was trained on the men who would kill him.

"Two guys came and took the body away," Harvey went on, thankful that the new additions to the cast gave him more inspiration. "One was really big, and the other one just normal."

"He's lying," Billy said. "You can see it in his face."

Sean regarded him for a moment, then nodded. "I think you're right." Then to Harvey, "You'd suck as a poker player."

Harvey couldn't help himself. He shot a look directly at the new arrivals, a silent plea for help.

It came instantly. "Drop your weapons!" one of them yelled. The rest of it unraveled in mere seconds, but Harvey was too busy dropping for cover to see a thing.

Boxers drove the Batmobile while Jonathan rode shotgun. Boxers had christened the heavily armored and electronically enhanced Hummer H2 with its nickname due to the impressive technology it carried, and it stuck. Jonathan had finally shed his Leon Harris makeup and changed out of the suit that might have linked him to the breakout. He'd left them and their rental van at the farm with every confidence that everything would be properly disposed of, sanitized, or returned. During their ride back from the George Washington Memorial, he and Boxers had been generous in praising each other for the brilliance of their plan to return Jimmy Henry to jail.

The U-Lockit franchise in Kinsale had been the next logical stop in their quest to pick up the trail. Given the early hour, he didn't know what he might find, but experience

taught that delaying the inevitable rarely paid dividends in
the long run. Besides, it had already been twenty-eight hours
since the assault on the school.

"You know," Boxers said as they closed within a mile of
the place, "you're gonna get your ass in a crack keeping the
FBI out of this."

"Let them collect their own evidence," Jonathan said.
"They don't appreciate our methods."

"Don't you think this one's a little close to home for piss-
ing contests?"

Jonathan shot the big guy a curious glance. Boxers didn't
often push back like this. "They couldn't use what we gave
them even if we gave it to them," he explained. "Fruit from
the poisonous tree and all that." Jonathan considered it one
of the great weaknesses of the United States's system of ju-
risprudence that even in egregious cases like this one, the
process used to obtain evidence was given equal weight to
the evidence itself.

"Besides," he continued, "I'll tip our hand to Doug when
we get back to the Cove." Doug Kramer was the chief of police in Fisherman's Cove, and a childhood friend of
Jonathan's. Whether by accident or intrepid investigation,
Doug had connected enough dots over the years to know the
basic outlines of the illicit side of Jonathan's firm, Security
Solutions, and he'd made it very clear that badge notwithstanding, he saw no reason to interfere.

A moment later, Boxers pointed ahead through the windshield. "What have we here?"

An unremarkable black Chrysler sedan sat parked in
front of the U-Lockit office, which was dark and appeared
empty. The storage units themselves ran in parallel blocks
behind it.

Jonathan checked his watch. Five forty-five. "Go in quietly," he said, instantly on alert. Never a believer in coinci-
dences, he concluded that this car had to belong to a bad
guy.

Boxers coasted to a halt just inside the driveway and turned off the ignition. "How do you want to handle it?"

Jonathan said, "Let's keep it light. Weapons holstered but ready." He opened the door and slid to the ground.

Boxers joined him at the front bumper. "Who are you expecting them to be?"

It was a good question. As Jonathan thought through Jimmy Henry's story, it could be anyone from a bad guy returning to the scene of the crime to a cop investigating a lead. "I just want to be ready for the worst," he said.

As they approached the Chrysler, Jonathan noticed that the engine was still ticking as it cooled under the hood.

"Sounds like they just got here," Boxers said, speaking his boss's thoughts.

Jonathan cocked his head, listening. Something wasn't right about this. "Who just parks in a storage lot at this hour? If you're retrieving something from storage, you park in front of your unit. Whoever drove this car isn't here for what's in the units. They want something else."

"Like what?"

That was the million-dollar question. Jonathan beckoned with his chin for Boxers to follow as he walked toward the woods at the edge of the lot. As the approached the grassy patch at the edge of the woods, he pointed to the ground. "Look here," he said.

Clearly, people had recently walked this way. They drew their weapons and started into the woods.

Jonathan heard voices. On a still, humid morning like this, sounds traveled easily. He could clearly make out the hum of men's voices in the distance, but a career of firearms, helicopter insertions, and explosives had made it impossible for his abused ears to decipher individual words.

Three minutes later, they were on top of what looked to be a mugging in process. Two clean-cut guys in T-shirts had drawn down on a gangly Latino hippie who appeared to have established a campsite near the edge of the water. From the look of the place, Jonathan guessed that the guy had been living there for a long time. The body language of all three men telegraphed an urgency that told Jonathan he'd arrived in the proverbial nick of time.

Moving with a choreographed unison that came from years of cooperation, Jonathan and Boxers spread out slightly to create a more difficult target, and they both brought their weapons to bear. As they approached to within twenty yards, Jonathan made brief eye contact with the bearded victim, and noted with interest how cool the guy remained as he continued to pivot in a wide circle away from the campsite. To Jonathan, that meant that there was something worth hiding in the camp.

At this range, their words were clear. The hippie was talking a mile a minute—something about these guys being three hours late.

Jonathan felt Boxers' gaze on him and returned it with a nod. The time had come to intervene.

"Drop your weapons!" he yelled.

The hippie, who seemed to have been expecting the confrontation, reacted instantly, dropping to the ground to leave an unobstructed sight picture.

The men in the T-shirts whirled, with guns at the ready and murder in their eyes. There was no time for negotiation.

Jonathan and Boxers fired simultaneously, and the men died on their feet—triple-tapped with two shots to the heart and one to the forehead in the time that it took for the first spent shell casing to hit the ground.

Even with the targets neutralized, neither man broke his aim. Jonathan yelled, "If I didn't just shoot you, you'd better by God stand up and show me your hands."

Nobody moved. Boxers shrugged.

"Last chance!" Jonathan yelled. "If I have to come and find you, you will not be happy."

As he spoke, he kept his aim trained on the spot where the hippie had disappeared. It surprised him when the man slowly rose above the grass thirty feet to the right. He and Boxers pivoted their aim in unison.

The guy looked older than he had before. Scrawnier and dirtier, too. He rose straight up, as if on an elevator, his large hands extended more out than up, his fingers splayed wide. He looked scared to death.

"Very well done," Jonathan coached. "Very smart."

He sensed movement near the campsite at the exact instant when Boxers said, "Left."

Since Jonathan held the left flank, the target belonged to him. He pivoted as Boxers held fast.

Jesus, it was a child. The look of terror in the boy's face didn't touch the feeling of horror in Jonathan's stomach as he broke his aim and redirected the muzzle of the .45 to the ground. The weapon was still at the ready if he needed it, but even an unheard-of accidental trigger pull couldn't do any harm.

"Don't let that one move an inch closer," Jonathan said, pointing to the hippie. He moved in closer to the boy, and within two steps, he recognized him. "Jeremy?" It seemed too good to be true.

The boy's mask of fear morphed into a mask of confusion. Then, finally, recognition. "Mr. Jonathan," he said.

Jonathan holstered his weapon, still cocked as always, and rushed to the boy. He stopped, though, when Jeremy recoiled. "Are you all right?" Jonathan asked. He shot a contemptuous glare at the hippie, whose hands remained high. Jonathan dared another couple of steps, stopping just a foot or two outside the kid's personal space. "We've been worried sick about you," he said. He resisted the urge to ask about the other missing child, Evan Guinn. Maybe he didn't want to know. Maybe he just wanted to savor this victory before finding out awful news.

Still, Jeremy didn't move. He just cocked his head a little, as if trying to fit together the pieces of too complex a puzzle.

Jonathan had memorized the dossiers on the missing children, so he knew Jeremy Schuler to be thirteen years old—a seventh grader just three years away from having a driver's license—but at this moment he could have been ten, or even eight. Six. Pick a number. As his features melted, he transformed from young man to little boy.

He launched himself at Jonathan, wrapping his arms around his chest in a crushing bear hug, and he dissolved into deep racking sobs. Jonathan wasn't ready for it. The rawness of the emotion made him self-conscious. He patted Jeremy's back, and then he cupped the crown of his head and pulled him in closer.

In Jonathan's job, nothing good ever came from crossing the line that separated the heart from the head. His world was about life-and-death decisions made quickly, in the vacuum of professional detachment. That meant shunning hugs from relieved victims and constructing emotional walls to separate him from the people he helped.

As Jeremy Schuler trembled and sobbed, his hot tears soaking into the fabric of his shirt, Jonathan felt his defenses crumbling. A few yards away, Boxers searched the hippie for weapons.

This was a victory, Jonathan told himself. With one still missing, it was only one half of total victory, but it was a moment to be celebrated nonetheless. In the midst of a thousand unanswered questions, Jonathan Grave knew one fact beyond even the slimmest sliver of doubt: Whoever had hurt this child—whoever might still be hurting Evan Guinn—was going to pay an extraordinary price.

CHAPTER ELEVEN

Brandy Giddings sat comfortably in the upholstered antique chair in the hallway, pretending not to notice the stares from the stern-faced Secret Service agents who stood in their assigned corners of the anteroom. She marveled at the way they could simultaneously project lethality and professional indifference. She wondered if The Look—easily recognizable by anyone with eyes—was specifically taught in the academy.

Did they even have an academy? she wondered. Surely they learned their craft somewhere, but she'd never heard mention of such a place. FBI Academy, yes—everybody knew that was in Quantico, Virginia, the place where Clarice Starling (Jodie Foster's character in *The Silence of the Lambs*) received her orders—but a Secret Service Academy? Never heard of one.

Even a year and a half after her dream job had grown to become her oh-my-God-I-can't-believe-it job—a year and a half after American voters had voted an exciting newcomer into the White House—she still had to pinch herself from time to time.

She'd been all over the world, meeting the prime minister

of England and the Pope in Rome, the premier of China, and the president of Russia, but through it all, nothing brought the same sense of awe and raw power as sitting right here in the West Wing of the White House. The very lack of pretense—the low ceilings and time-worn moldings—only added to the majesty of the place.

Brandy's title was special assistant to the secretary of defense, but she knew what people thought. She listened to talk radio and knew that Denise Carpenter—"The Bitch of Washington, DC"—had christened her Defcon Bimbo. Those were just ugly words from the conservative queen of an ugly town. Harry Truman had said it best: If you want a friend in Washington, get a dog.

Brandy Giddings didn't care what people thought. Her boss, Secretary Jacques Leger, would be the first secretary of defense to stress peace over war, embrace inclusion over exclusion. And Brandy was part of it all. It was just too much to believe.

At twenty-eight, Brandy was blessed with the looks of someone ten years younger, and the body to go with them; but what would have been a blessing in Hollywood was a curse here in its East Coast sister city. Washington was the city of Birkenstocks and minimal makeup. "Look like a dyke or die," as one of her fellow Georgetown grads had told her.

To hell with them. Looking hot had worked very well for Brandy, first landing her a spot on then-Senator Leger's staff, and then propelling her into the E-Ring of the Pentagon, where the office accommodations put those of the White House to shame. While nothing trumped the greatness of the Oval, her boss's digs were known throughout the world as the most opulent in the federal government.

Brandy's was a job that led to Great Things. She commanded the attention of four-star generals and forty-year career bureaucrats, and it drove them all mad. As Secretary Leger's right-hand lady for matters not directly related to national defense, she rarely waited more than ten minutes for her calls to be returned. With official cover from her boss, she traveled the world in tricked-out executive military jets that would make corporate titans blush.

Talk-show blabbers and late-night hosts could say whatever they wanted. None of their words could undo the reality of where she was and where they were not. When the history books were written, Brandy Giddings's fingerprints would be there, if only through the victories of the man she served.

Note the lowercase *S* in "served." There was no romance between Secretary Leger and her. Had he offered the opportunity it undoubtedly would have been different, especially during his senate years, but as it was, their mutual loyalty was built entirely of trust and hard work. As time progressed, she'd learned to accept that as best.

Today, as she waited in the narrow hallway outside of the Oval for the cabinet meeting to adjourn, Brandy scrolled absently through the e-mails in her BlackBerry, developing her strategy for breaking the bad news to the secretary. Their efforts to control the outcome of one very important matter had taken a bad turn, and it fell to her to keep the boss in the loop without propelling him over the edge. The roots of this particular matter reached back to the earliest days of his career.

When her electronic leash revealed that the news had not yet improved, she thrust it back into her purse and checked her watch again. Six-thirty. It hadn't yet been eight hours since her previous seventeen-hour day had ended. For a job that delivered so many perks, the hours sucked.

The president had always prided himself in being an early riser, but in the three months since the *New York Times* had played up that element in the profile they'd done on him, he'd become maniacal about it. Of course, when you have the ultimate home office and you're an early riser by nature, why not call 6:00 a.m. meetings? It's not as if anyone's going to say no.

Brandy sighed and recrossed her legs, this time daring to return the agent's glance. If she didn't want men to notice her body, she'd have long ago surrendered to her French fries jones. If she didn't want them to drool on her boobs, she'd quit wearing push-up bras. It was becoming obvious that a recognizable love life would be the price paid for her patriotic zeal, so why not encourage a few stares from the Secret Service? There were far worse bed partners in this life than a hard-bodied man who lived for the opportunity to sacrifice his life for others.

Besides, you know what they say: *Big hands, big feet, big . . . gun.*

The door to the cabinet room opened, and her fantasy lover snapped back to attention. Brandy stood. As the lesser ranks of Washington royalty filed past—the secretaries of agriculture and interior departed the meeting first—Brandy might just as well have been invisible, and their studied indifference amused her. In the two-plus centuries of the republic, no one who held their positions had left so much as a dent on history. Ditto Transportation, Commerce, and, God help us, Health and Human Services. For them to have any self-respect at all, she figured, they felt compelled to pretend she wasn't there. She almost felt sorry for them. How difficult it must be to be at the pinnacle of your career and know that you'll be banished to obscurity.

"Cheer up," Secretary Leger said as he powered into the anteroom. "Don't think of it as early; think of it as a running start on the day."

"I try, sir," she said, forcing a smile. She hurried to catch up with the stride that never slowed.

He gave her a sideward glance. "Did you just call me sir? Sounds foreboding."

As they approached the door that led to Executive Drive and the waiting limos, Brandy slipped into her proper place three feet behind the secretary, just in case any reporters had infiltrated this deep. A second rule of power in Washington was to never risk hogging the frame of a picture that was being shot of your boss.

While all cabinet secretaries got a car and a driver as part of their package of perks, only the secretary of state and

SecDef got their own security details. Granted, SecDef's was a small one—a driver and a shotgun rider, plus a single follow car—but it was enough to add to the mystique of the position. The shotgun rider was the man in charge, a thirty-something Army major in civilian clothes, and as Secretary Leger approached the right rear door of the town car, the major opened it for him and then closed it as soon as his butt hit the seat. On the opposite side, Brandy was left to fend for herself. A few weeks ago, during a conversation that Brandy had mistakenly thought was flirtatious, the major—his name was Binder—had made it clear that his duty to protect the secretary in no way extended to her. In fact, he'd emphasized his point by explaining that staffers like her were considered by bodyguards to be de facto human shields whose presence made it more difficult for an assassin to take a clear shot.

Once they were moving, Leger settled into his corner of the seat and crossed his legs. "Let me have the bad news," he said.

Brandy's jaw dropped.

Leger laughed. "Don't fake surprise," he said. "I can read you better than my wife. You've been guarding bad news since before the meeting."

Brandy had a better poker face than people gave her credit for, but she could be transparent as glass when she wanted to. Bad news was always easier to deliver when it was asked for. "Our special operation hit a snag," she said.

Leger's ears turned red at the news, and his right eye squinted just a little. Apparently, it was not the bad news he'd been expecting.

"It turns out that the team didn't completely follow the protocol. We just recently found out that one of the targets was killed on U.S. soil."

Now Leger's jaw twitched. "You mean the janitor? He died?"

Brandy shook her head. "No, I mean one of the *targets*."

He closed his eyes and massaged his forehead with three fingers. "Which one?"

"Bravo," she said. Notwithstanding the fact that the limo was sealed and checked daily for listening devices, neither of them felt comfortable speaking of these matters in plain English. It'd be different if they were planning an invasion, but as it was, this sort of business needed to be guarded with the utmost secrecy.

"Why am I just hearing about this now?" He asked the question through clenched teeth.

"I was hoping to be able to report on solid damage control."

He looked at her like she was crazy. "Damage control? He's dead, for God's sake."

This was the part she'd been dreading most. Her strategy all along was to just blurt it out and let the storm happen, so she said, "We've got people going out to pick up the body."

Something happened behind his eyes. For an instant, she thought Secretary Leger might hit her. "*Pick up the body?* Pick it up from where?"

Brandy chose her words carefully. "Because of the shooting, the team panicked a little. They knew that the police would go crazy, so they were in a hurry to get out. The pilot of the chopper told them that he couldn't handle all the weight, so they took Bravo to the woods and shot him."

Leger's eyes grew huge, an expression of genuine horror. "Jesus."

Brandy went on, "I didn't find out about it until Viper called at three this morning. He swears there was no alternative. He told me where they'd stashed the body, and I've sent a team out to recover it."

Leger scowled. "Viper called at three *this* morning? Twenty-four hours after the event?"

"Yes, sir. Apparently there was a communication breakdown."

Secretary Leger stared at her, as if he wasn't sure he understood the words. Then he shifted his gaze to the front of the limo, to the panel with the Defense Department shield that separated them from the security team. His face drooped.

Brandy said, "Sir, I assure you that this is under control. We knew going in that there were risks, but overall—"

"Brandy." He turned his head and looked at her with an expression that defined exhaustion.

"Sir?"

"Shut up for a while, okay?"

CHAPTER TWELVE

"I didn't do nothin' to the kid," the hippie insisted. Jonathan detected a slight Spanish accent. "I saved his life." The guy kept putting his hands up as they walked toward the Batmobile, and Jonathan kept telling him to put them down. They were beyond the cover of the trees, back out in the open, and few images could draw attention quite like a scruffy man in full surrender.

Jonathan thought it was important to move Jeremy away from the bodies as soon as possible. Poor kid already had enough to deal with; he didn't need to see spattered brain tissue. Boxers was still back there, though, rifling through the men's pockets and gathering intel.

Jeremy might as well have been welded to Jonathan's side. More behavior that seemed too young for the boy exhibiting it. Jonathan needed to get him to Father Dom's head-shrinking couch as soon as possible.

"Tell him, Jeremy," Harvey said. "Don't let me hang out to dry like this. Tell him I saved your life."

Jeremy wasn't talking to anyone about anything. He kept his focus straight ahead.

Harvey went on, "Look, Mister, I swear to God—"

"I believe you," Jonathan said, cutting him off. They were still thirty feet from the Hummer, but Jonathan stopped the parade.

Harvey's face showed only distrust.

"Swear to God," Jonathan said. "I saw how you were protecting the boy. I saw you pulling their aim away from the campsite, and I know you didn't take him. So relax, okay?"

Fear gone. Cue the anger. "Relax!" Harvey erupted. "How the hell am I supposed to relax when there are two dead guys in the camp that everybody knows is mine? And, all respect, how the hell am I supposed to relax when I'm talkin' to the guy who killed 'em?"

Jonathan shot a nervous glance down to Jeremy. He didn't like this kind of talk in front of a child. Then he realized how far out of the bottle that particular genie was. "Any idea who they were?" Jonathan asked, softening his tone in the hope that Harvey would follow suit.

"I know they were killers!" Harvey said. "They were there to get his body"—he thrust a finger around Jonathan to Jeremy, who continued to reside in his own world—"only he wasn't dead because I saved his life. They'd drugged him—I could tell from the pinpoint pupils—and they were supposed to have shot him, only they missed." The details spilled out in a rush of words and arm flaps. He covered all of the details of his medical ministrations. "I swear on a stack of Bibles that I didn't do nothin' but good for that boy. I sure as hell didn't touch him inappropriately or nothin' like that."

That struck Jonathan as an odd detail to emphasize. Why deny an accusation that had not been made? "Where did you get your medical training?" he asked. It was a legitimate question, but he intentionally timed it to pull the hippie away from his anger.

"Who says I have medical training?"

"You said you knew Jeremy was drugged because of the 'pinpoint pupils.' Not only is that specialized knowledge, but the phrase 'pinpoint pupils' is sort of . . . esoteric."

Harvey didn't flinch a bit from the five-dollar word. "I was in the military a while back," he said. "I was a medic. A good one. Saw action in both the Bushes' wars."

"Which branch of the service?" Jonathan started leading them toward the Hummer again.

"Marines." Harvey glared for a few seconds, then shook his head. "No need to talk about bad times," he said. "And who the hell are you, anyway?"

Something about the delivery—the sheer incredulity—of the question made Jonathan laugh. "Well, now, that's complicated," he said.

"You with the government or somethin'?"

"No." He didn't bother to add, *not today, anyway*. "Let's just say I'm a friend."

"Whose friend?"

They arrived at the Batmobile. "Jeremy's certainly," Jonathan said. "And yours, if you'll play along."

"Play along with what?"

"Just answer the questions as they come. You're not the only one who saved a life today, you know?" In case the hippie's memory had failed, Jonathan tossed a glance back toward the woods and the bodies they concealed. He noticed that Boxers was just emerging and heading their way.

"You look like government," Harvey said.

"Actually, I'm told I look like an aging Boy Scout."

Finally, a smile from the guy. "Yeah, that, too. But I think those guys you shot were government, too. It was the way they held themselves. The way their hair was cut."

And the car they drove, Jonathan thought.

"At least give me a name," Harvey said. "Somethin' to call you."

He hesitated. His was a world of pseudonyms and fake credentials; he didn't like being this far out on a limb under his own name in his own backyard—almost literally. Jeremy knew who he was, though, and soon Harvey would know where he came from, so it didn't make a lot of sense to keep unnecessary secrets. "My name's Jonathan," he said as Boxers approached within hearing distance. "My friends call me Digger."

Harvey considered that for a while. "Well, Jonathan," he said, his eyes squinting to slits, "what the hell is going on here?"

Jonathan unlocked the Hummer and opened the front and back doors on the passenger side. "You stole my line, Harvey. I wanted to be first on the record with that very same question." He looked beyond the hippie to Boxers. "Did you get it all?"

The big guy nodded. That meant he'd recovered the spent brass from the shootings, and he'd stripped the bodies of identification.

"Good," Jonathan said. He leaned into the truck, across the massive front seat, and into the center console, from which he removed a black box about the size of a pack of cigarettes. Turning to face Harvey he said, "I need to see your hand."

Harvey shoved them into his pockets. "What for?"

Jonathan opened the box and displayed a flat surface that might have been an iPod but wasn't. "I want a fingerprint from you. Just want to make sure you're not scarier than you seem to be."

"Fuck you."

Boxers loomed over the man. "Watch your mouth, friend," he growled. "The kid doesn't need that kind of language."

When Boxers wanted to look intimidating, even the toughest of men cowered. Harvey Rodriguez was nowhere near the toughest of men. He withdrew his hand and held it out flat. It was trembling.

"Thank you," Jonathan said. He took the hippie's forefinger and pressed it against the tiny screen, and then repeated the process for his thumb. After verifying that the images were clear, he pressed SEND. Within minutes, Venice would begin the process of matching the prints to people.

"That wasn't so hard, was it?" he said. "Now I want you to climb into the backseat here, while Jeremy rides up front with Boxers."

The big guy shot a furious glare at the sound of his real name. Jonathan ignored it.

"Why?" Harvey asked.

"Because I asked you to?"

"Where am I going?"

"Where Boxers takes you." He paused for a smile. "Harvey, you're safe, okay? You're no longer in any danger."

"What about my stuff?"

"It'll keep," Jonathan assured.

"Everything I own is out there."

Jonathan cocked his head and let the words hang, hoping that Harvey would hear the nonsense of his own words. "You think those two guys are the last ones?" he asked. "When they don't show up to wherever they're supposed to be, don't you think there'll be more? I don't think you want to be around when they arrive."

Understanding bloomed in Harvey's eyes. "People are gonna think I did that," he said. "Whether it's those guys' friends or just some hiker, somebody's gonna walk by and see those corpses, and they're gonna think I'm the one who offed them."

"No, they won't," Jonathan said.

"Of course they will."

Jonathan placed a reassuring hand on Harvey's shoulder, and as he reached, the hippie flinched. "Trust me, Harvey," he said. "I know how to take care of these things."

Lightbulb moment. Harvey got it.

"Now, please get into the vehicle. And please behave yourself when you're in there."

He hesitated, but finally climbed inside.

"The front seat's for you," he said cheerily to Jeremy.

The boy's hand clamped tighter.

"Jeremy," Jonathan said. The boy kept staring straight.

"He okay?" Boxers asked.

"Not now he's not," Jonathan said. "Jeremy, please look at me."

The boy's face pitched up.

"It's okay for you not to be okay right now. You've been through a lot, but you're safe now. My big friend here, Mr. Boxers, is going to take you back to Fisherman's Cove. He's going to take you to see Father Dom. You like Father Dom, right?"

Jeremy's nod was barely perceptible.

"Nothing can happen to you now, understand? It's been a terrible couple of days, but you're completely safe now. I need you to get into the truck."

"Are you coming, too?" Jeremy asked. His voice was a raspy whisper.

Jonathan was glad to hear him finally speak. "I'll be along in an hour or so. Maybe two. I have some things I need to take care of."

"What kind of things?"

Jonathan exchanged glances with Boxers. "Stuff that doesn't involve you. Now, be a good kid and hop into the truck. Boxers will drive carefully for you."

It took another two minutes of negotiation, but when it was done, Jeremy was strapped into the front passenger seat, and Jonathan closed both doors.

"You sure you don't want me to take care of this for you?" Boxers said when they were shut off from prying ears. "We can trade places."

Jonathan would rather walk through fire than deal with Jeremy's anger and sorrow for much longer. "No, I'm good," he said. "Just take them right to the mansion. Call Dom ahead of time and see if he can be there waiting."

"And your scraggly friend?"

"Find a room for him. Make him comfortable while we sort him out."

Boxers handed over the keys he'd pulled from one of the dead men's pockets. "Let me know if you have any trouble," he said, and then he walked around to the driver's side.

Jonathan stripped to his boxer shorts to load the bodies into the Chrysler's trunk. He felt more than a little ridiculous, but if someone wandered up in the next ten minutes or so, embarrassment would be the least of his problems.

Among the biggest surprises of this day that was filled with surprises was the fact that the gunmen—he'd sent their prints off to Venice as well—had already lined the interior of the trunk with plastic. How could you not smile at the irony of that?

Then the despicability of what they were planning came back to him, and the ironic smile dissolved to anger. These assholes' mission had been to stash the body of a dead child in here. One of the House's children, which made him one of Jonathan's children. How dare they? Hell had two new residents tonight, and he suspected that even Satan held child killers in contempt.

He'd moved the Chrysler as close to the bodies as he could without running over them so that once he had the corpses hoisted onto his shoulders it would be as short a walk as possible. Both of the dead guys had been in good shape. The muscle tissue made them a little heavy for their size, but the lack of flab made them less slippery and therefore easier to flop into the trunk bed. He took perverse pleasure in the way the heads collided when he deposited the second body.

With arms and legs all tucked in, Jonathan shut the lid and looked himself over. Blood streaked his hands, chest and arms. It caked his fingernails. He could only imagine what his face looked like. It wouldn't do. He wandered to the hippie's tent, rummaged through his stuff, and found the bar of soap he knew had to be there somewhere. With the Ivory in one hand and his pistol in the other, partially concealed by a purloined towel that he'd draped over his forearm, he trudged through the tall grass all the way down to the river.

He kept the bath to only a few minutes. Part of him continued to worry about being caught in such a compromising condition, but all of him worried about God only knew how many microbes were invading his body from the waters of the Potomac.

Clean, dry, and redressed, he climbed behind the wheel of the Chrysler and dropped it into gear. When he'd put a couple of miles between himself and the crime scene, he slid his cell phone out of his pocket and pressed the button for the voice command. "Call Niles Decker," he said.

The man he was looking for answered on the third ring. Jonathan told him what he wanted.

Decker sighed. "I'll meet you at the office," he said. "Drive straight to the back."

"See you in thirty," Jonathan said, and he closed the phone.

It only took him twenty-five.

The Decker family had been in the undertaking business for generations, building one of the most recognizable brands in the Northern Neck. Their sprawling edifice on the outskirts of Montross was an architectural icon. Tall, fat pillars in front suggested the north portico of the White House. Inside, the viewing rooms rivaled the world's most opulent mansions with fabric wall coverings and ornate chandeliers. For members of a community of working-class farmers and fishermen, this was the one chance they had to live in the style of their dreams. It's a shame they had to live it when they were dead.

Jonathan and Niles Decker had been classmates from first grade through high school. While they were never close, they were linked by the industry their fathers shared. Officially, Simon Gravenow—Jonathan's father—made his fortune in the scrap recycling business. In fact, Jonathan still owned that business, and it still made more than enough money to support a very wealthy family. Jonathan had ceded direct control to Leonard King years ago, limiting his involvement to the occasional board of directors meeting, but he enjoyed the tie to real industry.

In his spare time, Simon Gravenow was a thief and a murderer, a key player in what the press had glibly labeled the Dixie Mafia. He bought and sold politicians at will as he kept the drug trade thriving. Those who got in his way were removed with extreme prejudice. Now Simon was a guest of Uncle Sam in one of his finest maximum-security prisons, where he was scheduled to spend the rest of his life.

Jonathan had made it a point to stay out of his father's affairs—to know as little about that part of the family business as possible. That had always disappointed his father, and when Jonathan turned eighteen and legally changed his name from Gravenow to Grave, communications between them had pretty much shut down.

But some details had leaked through, and some had worked to Jonathan's benefit. One was the connection with the Deckers.

Decker Funeral Home sat at the crest of a hill. Recognizing that the distasteful part of the dead-body business was conducted in the basement, they'd excavated the site to allow for a below-grade loading dock that allowed hearses—or in this case a Chrysler sedan—to pull through overhead garage doors and disgorge their cargo just steps away from the parlors where their guts and blood would be replaced with preservative chemicals.

Jonathan turned the vehicle around in the driveway and backed into the garage where Niles Decker was waiting for him. Even through high school, the guy had been a clotheshorse. Now that his business required a certain for-

mality, he was never seen without an expensive suit. Today it
was navy blue, with a crisp white shirt and a wildly pat-
terned tie. Short and stocky, he didn't fit the Ichabod Crane
archetype of an undertaker, but his bloodline had evolved itself out of a sense of humor.

"Hello, Niles," Jonathan said as he climbed out of his vehicle. The roll-up door was already on its way down.

"Good morning, Jon." The Digger nickname was a product of Jonathan's Army years, but even though most of the
people he knew had taken it on, Niles's sense of propriety
would never allow it. He stood aside as Jonathan opened the
trunk and displayed his cargo. "The plastic lining is a nice
touch," he said. "Good of you to be prepared."

Jonathan didn't bother to explain that the preparations
were not his. It wasn't the undertaker's business, and he undoubtedly wouldn't care.

"Dare I ask what these gentlemen did to deserve their
fate?"

"They tried to shoot me," Jonathan said.

"When will people learn?" Niles unbuttoned his suit coat
and placed it on a hanger that dangled from a hook next to a
closet near the door to the inside. From the closet itself he
withdrew two rubberized long-sleeved aprons. He offered one
to Jonathan. "Would you mind helping with the transfer?"

Jonathan took the apron and pulled the collar over his
head. "Not at all." He slipped his arms into the sleeves.

Niles next pulled open a cabinet that sat next to the
closet, revealing a stack of disaster pouches—the civilized
term for body bags. He removed two, then took a minute to
spread them open just so on the concrete floor. Finally, the
cabinet produced two pairs of rubber gloves, the kind you'd
use to wash dishes in very hot water.

"Do we have names?" Niles asked as they hefted the one
whose mangled head sprouted blond hair.

"Not yet," Jonathan said. "I didn't realize that would be
important to you."

Niles shot him a disapproving look. "Some of us are disturbed by the things we occasionally must do."

Jonathan held the body's head and shoulders, and as they closed to within inches of the floor, he let go, allowing the corpse to fall. "So long as you're disturbed, Niles. That's important. Just not disturbed enough to stop doing it."

Niles found the zipper tab near the corpse's feet, and he pulled it closed. "If I could, I would."

Jonathan let it go and turned his attention to the second body. Again, he had the heavy half. Niles no more had the balls to stop disposing of bodies than Jonathan had an inclination to deal with the undertaker's other illicit customers.

The mechanism of disposal could not have been simpler or more reliable. When dead people are on display in a funeral home, that thin mattress they lie on is suspended by nylon webbing, not unlike the webbing used in folding lawn furniture. By adjusting the height of the webbing, the mortician can position skinny corpses and fat corpses at just the right height relative to the edges of the casket. The dirty little secret that Niles Decker's father had discovered and passed along to his son was that the void created by the webbing was the perfect place to stash an additional body. Inside a sealed body bag, there'd be no stink, and with all the bedding in place, the hitchhiking corpse would be invisible. As for the extra weight, everybody just wrote that off to a heavy casket.

Thanks to the Deckers, more than a few graves in Westmoreland County were double occupied.

"How long before these two are in the ground?" Jonathan asked.

"By tonight," Niles said. "We have two events this afternoon, and I'll see to it that they're a part of it."

"I appreciate that," Jonathan said. He waited as Niles disappeared back into the building and returned with first one gurney and then another. He helped lift the bodies onto the carts. "You need more help than that?" he asked.

"I can take it from here," Niles said.

Jonathan could see that the emotional burden of being a mob cleanup man was beginning to crush him. "Hey, Niles?"

The man turned.

"These are the guys who shot up Resurrection House yesterday." It was close enough to the truth not to be a lie. If they weren't the ones who did the shooting, then they were close associates. "Don't shed any tears for them."

CHAPTER THIRTEEN

The food court in Pentagon City Mall was like every other food court in every city in the world. The same pizza, the same Chinese food, the same burgers. One thing that set it apart, Brandy thought, was its location on the bottom floor. Weren't most such places on the top floor of major malls? It made sense here, though, because the Pentagon City Metro Station was only a couple hundred footsteps away. Located between the stops for the Pentagon and Crystal City, it was the perfect spot for meeting like this.

For 10:30 on a weekday morning, Brandy thought the food court was unusually busy—not that she had any current frame of reference. SecDef had his own personal chef, and as special assistant, those perks extended to Brandy as well, free of charge. When five-star food was available for free, why would she ever dine outside the E-Ring if she didn't have to?

In order not to draw attention as she waited, Brandy sipped a Starbucks latte and nibbled on a cinnamon scone that tasted like sugared sawdust. Every bite needed to be chased with a sip of coffee to keep it from turning to concrete in her mouth. As a security hedge, she'd chosen a seat in the middle of the sea of identical white tables, figuring it would be far harder to sneak up on her. You don't make your living tying up these kinds of loose ends without developing a healthy paranoia.

The personal meetings were a necessary evil. Every phone call into and out of the Pentagon was a matter of public record—if not the what, then certainly the who. It had been that way for as long as there'd been phones, she supposed, but previous administrations had never learned the lesson that was first etched in marble during Nixon years: Every electronic trail will trace directly back to the thing that you want most to keep secret. She could have handed over her cell phone number, she supposed, but she didn't relish the likes of Jerry Sjogren knowing more about her life than he already did.

That left face-to-face meetings like this one. If nothing else, the shopping mall felt like familiar ground.

She spotted Sjogren when he was still on the escalator heading down, but she didn't make eye contact. She dared just a brief glance, during which she noted that he was likewise avoiding any sign of recognition. This was the way the game always was played, though she didn't understand why. Since they were going to be sitting together anyway, she thought it might make more sense to smile and wave like they were lovers.

Actually, no one would believe that. Jerry was easily fifty years old, and he was built like a bear. Thick gray hair covered his head, his ears, and his upper lip, and when he spoke he sounded like someone doing a disrespectful parody of a New England accent, complete with the nasal "ah" sound where there should have been an "are." Although he was quick to laugh and grandfatherly in his demeanor, there was no doubting after two minutes of conversation that Jerry Sjogren was capable of all the things he was hired to do.

Brandy waited till his shadow loomed before she looked up from her scone. "You don't look like a man bringing good news," she said.

Sjogren helped himself to the opposite seat and leaned his forearms on the table heavily enough to make it shift. "There's rarely 'good' news in this line of work," he said. "If you know what I mean." This was his grandfatherly side, patronizing at its roots. He somehow pulled it off without insulting her. "But in this case, it's worse than it otherwise might be." .

Brandy felt a chill. "So we in fact lost him?"

Sjogren cocked his head and chuckled. "Well, that would have been bad enough, wouldn't it? But it's even worse. We didn't just lose the kid. We lost the men sent to find him."

She felt herself going pale and tightened her stomach muscles to keep blood flowing to her head. "You lost them? What does that mean?"

He leaned back, releasing his psychic hold. "Exactly what it sounds like. They're gone. Misplaced. Disappeared. Poof. Sent them out, never heard from them, and then when I sent another crew to follow up, they got nothing but some bloodstains in the grass."

"The boy's bloodstains?" she asked hopefully.

He shrugged. "Red bloodstains. That's the best I can do for right now."

"Well, what happened?"

Sjogren laughed. "I guess I should have defined 'poof' a little better. I got no clue. They're gone, the car's gone. Everything. Gone."

"How can that be?" As soon as the words left her mouth she knew that they were stupid. It made no sense just to keep repeating the same question with different words. "There has to be something."

He conceded that much with a shrug. "There's a campsite nearby that appears to be somebody's house, but nobody's home. I got people wandering around asking questions to see who owns it. That might be a lead."

"'Might' is not a word my boss is going to like."

"You'd rather I lie?"

Actually, yes, she didn't say. That way when it all went to

hell she could blame it on their contractors. "Do you think
they're . . . dead?" She nearly whispered the last word.

"They're two tough dudes," Sjogren said, cocking his
head again. "I have a hard time believing that some homeless guy got the drop on them."

"So why—"

"But it's even harder for me to believe that they're still
alive but didn't report in. They just wouldn't do that. So,
yeah, I think they're probably not with us anymore."

Brandy noted the utter aloofness in his tone. He might
have been speaking about a couple of lost screwdrivers. "Do
the police know?"

This time, Sjogren's laugh was loud enough to draw attention. He let the moment pass, then leaned back and
crossed his legs. "And just exactly what would I tell the police?" he asked. "Especially when I get to the part about why
they were down there?"

She'd asked another stupid question. Thing was, she
couldn't think of any smart ones. Nothing was going as it
was supposed to. "So what do you want to do next?" she
asked.

"I was going to ask you the same thing."

"I'm not the one who fumbled the ball," Brandy said. She
was pleased that her tone sounded strong despite the panic
that coursed through her body.

Sjogren's features hardened. "I guess that depends on
when you start counting, doesn't it? Between you, me, and
your boss, which one is tearing up the countryside to make
an old problem go away?"

Brandy tried to return the glare in kind. "Of the three of
us, you are the one being paid to make it go away. The rest of
it isn't in play."

Sjogren's eyes narrowed, and for the first time, Brandy realized that her paranoia was justified. This man was not accustomed to being told off by anyone. For it to come from a
woman half his age had to hurt.

She held her ground, and his expression softened. "I've given this a lot of thought," he said at last, his tone as even and easy as before. "You heard about that jailbreak nonsense down in Buttscratch, Virginia, where the op went down?"

"The news said it involved someone suspected in the event."

"We must have heard the same report. They said he had help from somebody masquerading as an FBI agent. Pretty slick."

"If you say so," Brandy said. From where she sat, slick was not the operative adjective. Disastrous came a lot closer.

"Well, have you heard the latest?" Sjogren went on. "Despite all the high-class help, they recaptured the guy who broke out."

Brandy in fact hadn't heard. She weighed it and didn't know what to do with it. "Is that good news or bad?"

"Personally, I wish they'd shot the son of a bitch. What bothers me is the fact that they found him all trussed up and packaged for Christmas. Whoever broke him out never intended to keep him out."

Brandy knew she should understand where he was going, but the pieces weren't there yet. Rather than admit it, she waited for him to connect more dots.

"They broke him out to squeeze him for information," Sjogren said. "He's back in custody because he gave them something worthwhile. Otherwise they'd have killed him. As I understand it, he's got some pretty good bruises."

"Who was pressing him?"

Sjogren sighed noisily. "I. Don't. Know." He spoke as if to a slow child.

"What could he have given? You said he didn't know anything."

"Everybody knows something. In this case, he knows, for example, where the drop-off point was."

"Where?"

"Do you really want to know?"

Good catch, she thought. "No."

He smiled. "It's the same spot where the kid was shot. Same spot where my guys disappeared."

It dawned on her in a rush. "Somebody attacked them," she said.

He acknowledged the possibility with his eyebrows. "That's what I'm thinking. Jimmy Henry gave them just enough to figure out a big one."

Brandy closed her eyes. "So, where do we stand?"

Sjogren made a show of crossing his arms and his legs. "Maybe we can find the guy that owns the camping gear," he said. "If we do, I guess there's a glimmer that we might be able to press him for information. Tit for tat. Quid pro quo."

"Is it wise to bring another stranger into the loop like that?" Brandy asked. "I mean, just by asking the questions, you're going to make him wonder . . ." She cut herself off in response to his overplayed look of patience. "Oh, of course," she said, looking down. Answering questions would be the poor man's last earthly act. "But you still have to find the body. Someone still has to take care of him. I still don't understand what went wrong there."

Sjogren grew uncomfortable. "Well, now, that's interesting, too. We're not looking for the kid's body anymore. We're looking for the kid. We think he's alive."

Brandy's jaw dropped. "Oh, my God."

"I pressed our friend Mitch Ponder on it pretty hard, and it turns out that Jenkins couldn't bring himself to shoot a child. Instead, he carried the kid out into the woods and pumped him with an overdose of sedative. He thought it would take care of him. He fired a shot in the air for the benefit of the others, and they left."

"This is what qualifies for 'professional' in your firm?" Brandy asked. She wanted to regain control of the conversation.

Sjogren drew his forefinger from the crook of his folded arm as if drawing a weapon from a shoulder holster, and he pointed it at her. "You'd best be careful throwing that word around, missy," he said. His cheeks and forehead glowed red. "Until you've done some of the wet work you order, you ought to keep your judgments to yourself. I'll make good what needs to be made good, but you need to remember that you and your boss are two different people. He crosses me, I might take it. You cross me, and I might just give you an inside look at the kind of work I do."

Brandy broke eye contact.

Sjogren said, "I'm going to sniff around to find this tent-dweller. The fact that he moved out without packing tells me he knows something. My not-insubstantial gut tells me that if I find him, I'll find the boy."

"And when you do, will you . . ." She let her voice trail off, confident that he would catch her meaning.

"You can pull me off of this thing anytime you want," Sjogren said. "But unless you do, I've got a job to finish. You want me to stop looking and just let the kid go?"

Brandy closed her eyes and inhaled. How could it possibly have come to this? "No," she said, her lids still closed. "I want you to finish it." The words seemed to come from someone else. Seven years ago, when she was graduating from Georgetown with her degree in political science, the thought of ordering the murder of a child would have been inconceivable. Now she'd just done it for the second time in less than a week.

CHAPTER FOURTEEN

Jonathan entered the mansion at ten-thirty, feeling human again after a very long, very hot shower. The two hours of sleep didn't hurt, either. Officially, the massive colonial-style behemoth held the administrative offices for Resurrection House and housed Venice and her family. Unofficially, to the rest of the town, it would always be the Gravenow mansion, Jonathan's childhood home. He'd happily deeded it away at his first chance for the whopping sum of one dollar.

Its towering, wainscoted memories were worthy enough of forgetting that Jonathan rarely entered the place anymore. When he did, it was only for a very good reason.

He barely slowed as he strode the ornately inlaid foyer and crossed under the massive staircase to open the narrow door that led to the basement. Jonathan tried not to remember the days when the basement suites housed teams of servants. Back then, they all worked for Mama Alexander, who, with her daughter Venice, had qualified for better-ventilated quarters on the mansion's third floor.

Jonathan thought it curious that the basement suites looked bigger than he remembered, and far less like a dungeon. The hallways were wide to accommodate the various food carts and cleaning apparatus that used to be shuttled from one service elevator to the next, and the sleeping quarters on either side were reminiscent of his dormitory days at William and Mary, twelve feet square with ten foot ceilings. Now these spaces were largely empty, except for a few that were stacked with junk that someone had deemed worth saving.

"Ven?" he called.

"Down here!"

He looked behind him to see Venice step into the hallway and beckon with one hand. In her other, she held a manila file folder. She looked five years older than she did two days ago. Her chocolate-colored skin had a slack, sallow look to it that spoke of too many tears shed over too short a time.

"Is Jeremy in there?" Jonathan asked as he closed the distance, nodding to the room Venice had just left.

She shook her head. "No, he's in the rectory with Dom."

"Is he okay?"

"Physically, he seems okay," Venice said. "Dom had Doctor Hamilton come in to take a look at him."

Jonathan felt a flare of anger. "I thought I told you—"

"Dom impressed on him the need for secrecy," Venice said, heading off the exact objection that Jonathan was about to launch. "He'd been drugged, Dig. We had to have him looked at."

She was right, of course, but at this juncture, the best way to keep Jeremy alive was to let everybody think he was still missing. Whoever had lost track of him the first time wanted him back badly enough to dispatch a team of killers. That kind of desire doesn't go away just because it gets difficult to do.

"Just make sure that the word is limited to as few people as possible."

"Does that include Doug Kramer or not?"

"Not just yet," Jonathan said. "Let's keep him out of the loop until we don't have a choice. He's busy enough handling this firestorm. How's Mr. Stewart?"

Venice winced and shrugged with one shoulder. "They think he'll come out of it okay, but they're worried about his liver and spleen. Apparently the bullet did damage to both, and then when they punched him . . ." She stopped as her voice broke.

Jonathan didn't need to hear the rest. The important part was that he'd survive. On a day when few things were going well, he'd take it. "And what about our new friends?"

"Of the two you shot, one is invisible. I can't find any record at all. He's like you—he never officially existed."

Jonathan's stomach tensed. In this day and age, *everybody* had a fingerprint on file somewhere—all except those whose fingerprints had been deliberately erased. To do that on every file was not easy. "What about the other one?"

"Sean O'Brian," Venice said. "We only know that because he was fingerprinted as a child offender twenty years ago. That's the *only* print on file, even though his juvie record shows that the judge pushed him to join the Marine Corps, which he did. That's clearly documented in his criminal file."

"Let me guess: the Marine Corps has no record."

Venice nodded. "Databases never heard of him."

Jonathan folded his arms and leaned against the wall. "So they were government agents," he thought aloud. "Or civilian contractors working for them. That fits with what Jimmy Henry told us, too." He briefly recapped the prisoner's version of his role in the kidnapping.

"Why would the government be involved in an assault on a school?" Venice asked.

"Clearly, they wanted those boys."

"But they're only *children*. What could they have done to deserve this?"

Jonathan suspected that they hadn't *done* anything—at least not knowingly. There are only so many reasons to kidnap someone. When governments get involved, the list boils down to three: to extort information; to ensure silence; or to leverage cooperation. He chose not to mention any of the options to Venice.

Instead, he said, "I need any and all information you can find on the shooters and on the children. Those boys have something in common—a shared secret—and we need to know what it is." He paused for a breath and a change in topic. "What about the hippie?"

Venice pointed toward the closest room. "He's in there," she said. "He's not talking, though. His name is Harvey Rodriguez. Born in Venezuela, moved to the States when he was fifteen. He's a child molester."

Jonathan recoiled.

Venice handed him the file. "It's all right here. In fact, there's a lot in there. You should give it a read before you talk to him."

He took the folder, but held Venice's gaze for a couple of seconds before he opened it. Was there anyone left on the planet who just wanted to let kids grow up normally?

"Don't tell Boxers about this," Jonathan said, hoisting the file. "He'll kill him."

"And that would be bad because . . . ?" She headed for the stairs.

It took Jonathan only a few minutes to absorb the basics of Harvey Rodriguez's file. When he was done, he opened the door and entered.

Despite the availability of a chair and a desk, Harvey stood in the corner, his back to the wall and his arms folded across his chest. An empty plastic water bottle lay on its side on the desk next to a full one. "You have no right to hold me here," he said in a rush as soon as Jonathan crossed the threshold. It was as if he'd been rehearsing the line and needed to say it quickly before he lost his nerve. "You're not a cop. You can't make me stay."

Jonathan cocked his head, then shrugged. "Leave," he said, stepping aside and clearing the way.

Harvey's eyes narrowed. "You're serious?"

"As a heart attack. As far as I'm concerned, we're protecting you, not imprisoning you. You want to leave, leave. The easier a target you are on the street, the less I have to worry about you bringing trouble here."

Harvey hesitated.

"Seriously," Jonathan said. "Go."

The hippie's eyes darted, as if looking for the scam. Then they grew wide as the reality dawned on him. "People are going to try to kill me if I leave," he said.

Jonathan helped himself to a folding metal chair on the front side of the desk. "It certainly seemed to be on the agenda a while ago," he said.

"Where's the boy?"

"Someplace that's none of your concern. Why don't you take a seat?"

"He's the one they were after," Harvey said. "They left him for dead. Did you know that?"

"And you saved him. You did a good thing. And now I'm saving you." He paused for effect. "Unless you want to leave."

Harvey thought on that for the better part of a minute. "You know I can't do that."

"I do."

"What am I supposed to do?"

Jonathan took his time answering. This was a negotiation of sorts, and as in all negotiations, the elements needed to be put in terms of the other party's best interests. "I'd like to think you'd accept this hospitality for what it is."

"You put me in the basement."

"Only because it's out of sight," Jonathan explained. "Things are happening here that don't yet make much sense to me. But I know this: If people are willing to kill a child, they're willing to kill anyone."

Harvey's face turned wistful as his eyes focused on a point that didn't exist in the real world. "I don't like people," he said. "Never had much use for them. Then this happens right in front of me, and I'm stuck holding the bag." His eyes rolled up to bore through Jonathan. "Does that make any damn sense to you?"

Jonathan liked this guy. He couldn't articulate why, but he liked him. "There's a lot in this world that doesn't make sense to me, Harvey." He let a beat pass. "Like how a man like you—a Marine Corps medic—ends up molesting children."

Harvey's jaw set at Jonathan's accusation, but his eyes just remained tired. "You've done your homework," he said.

Jonathan nodded. "I have. And I have to tell you that knowing this makes me wish you'd died out there with the others."

Harvey's eyes went red. He said nothing.

"Is it true?" Jonathan pressed.

"It's true that I'm a registered sex offender, yes."

Jonathan scowled. "Is there a 'but'?"

Harvey smiled without humor. "Not one that you'd be interested to hear."

"Why do you say that?"

"Because nobody's interested in hearing it. I'm a kid toucher on the record, and that's all that matters."

"That's a lot," Jonathan said.

Harvey glared through Jonathan's brain. "You tell me what your mood dictates," Harvey said. "Do you want to draw conclusions, or do you want to hear the truth?"

"The truth always works for me."

Harvey sat in the chair on the opposite side of the desk from Jonathan. He took his time assembling his thoughts, then launched into the story. "I had . . . *difficulty* in 2004 after the first battle for Fallujah. I don't know if you know anything about military operations, but that was pretty intense. They called it 'urban warfare' and I guess it was, but to me 'urban' means city. Fallujah was like a thousand years old. I was with Company K, three-five, and we caught nothing but shit for days on end."

Jonathan recognized "three-five" as Third Battalion of the Fifth Marine Regiment.

"Those Hadji fuckers were everyplace. We took a lot of casualties. I was up to my elbows in brains and intestines for days on end. I'd get one Marine packed up for transport and then another one would get hit. It was fucking awful."

It was also the most intense urban combat that United States armed forces had ever encountered, Jonathan didn't add, although he had studied it. He'd been separated from the Army for more than a few years by the time Operation Iraqi Freedom was launched, but he'd stayed in touch with many of his buddies who were still on active duty. The American press denied people at home the story of the stunning victory, choosing instead to concentrate on U.S. casualties and collateral damage, but the strategy and tactics developed during that weeklong battle would be studied in military textbooks for generations to come.

Harvey continued, "Anyway, if you've never been there, it's hard to describe how something just breaks inside of you. I just wasn't the Marine I thought I was. One day I was a damn good medic—and I mean *damn* good, even thinking of a way to use G.I. benefits to get to medical school—and then I just couldn't do it anymore."

He stripped the cap off his water bottle and took a long pull. "They called it PTSD, post-traumatic stress disorder. That's a great name when you're using it on someone else. When it's you, it just feels like 'crazy.' They sent me to Bethesda for a while, but then they drummed me out. I was fine with that, but what was I going to do for a living? I didn't want nothin' to do with the blood-and-guts business anymore, so I thought I'd try to help kids. You know, the future of the world?"

His bitter sarcasm triggered a humorless chuckle. "I took a job at a community health club in Braddock County, up near Brookfield."

Jonathan recognized it as a neighboring county in Northern Virginia.

"I taught swimming, did some lifeguarding. Even taught first-aid courses. It was exactly the kind of gig I needed. Kids are basically, nice, right? They live in a world where the only violence is the stuff you see on TV. They're refreshing to be around."

Jonathan jumped ahead. "So, refreshing, in fact that you—"

A white-hot glare cut him in half. "You gonna listen, or are you gonna talk?" Harvey spat. "See, this is why it's not worth explaining the facts to people. You see the label, and then everything just falls into place for you."

"I'm sorry," Jonathan said. And he meant it.

Harvey's eyes held him for a while longer, testing. "All right. Well, the fact is that kids are shit, too. I had one, Amanda Goldsbury, a loudmouth punk maybe thirteen years old whose parents dropped her off every day in the summer at seven in the morning, and then picked her up at eight at night. Our job was to babysit her ass for the six-buck-a-day admission charge. She wasn't the only one like that, but she was the one who was easiest to hate. She thought she was queen shit. She terrorized the other children, and she had no compunction about telling an adult to go fuck himself. You know the type?"

Jonathan smiled and chose not to say that he established a whole school for kids like that. They didn't stay that way for long after arriving at Resurrection House, but most students arrived either as bullies or as victims of them.

"So one day, this girl gets in my face, and I told her what I thought of her antics. I mean I *really* told her. Embarrassed the shit out her in front of her buddies and victims." He inhaled deeply through his nose, closed his eyes, and shook his head. "Next day, five cops show up at the center and arrest me for second-degree sexual assault on a minor. She went home that night after I pissed her off, and she told her parents that I had fondled her in the locker room.

"The prosecutor, a first-degree prick named J. Daniel Petrelli, decided to make an example out of me. He got the press involved, somebody leaked my history of 'mental instability'"—he used finger quotes—"and I was cooked. Everybody knows kids wouldn't lie about such a thing, even though they lie through their asses about every other damn thing, and suddenly I'm looking at serious prison time. I don't know if it's true, but I've heard that child molesters are beaten to shit in prison by the other inmates. I wanted none of that.

"So I took the plea agreement that my public defender told me was a sweet deal. I pleaded guilty in return for no jail time, but I agreed to seek psychiatric counseling and to stay away from children forever. I also landed on the registered sex offender list."

His eyes turned red as tears balanced on his lids. "And that, my new friend, is a life sentence in and of itself. There are no jobs to be had, and because you're not allowed to be within two thousand feet of a school or a church or a playground, there's no place to live, either. Not unless you got land in the country, which is really difficult when you don't have an income."

Harvey spread his arms wide, as if to say, *Ta-da!* "So here I am, hero of our nation, brought to nothing by single lie told by a single child who no doubt will one day be president of the United States."

For a long while, Jonathan just stared, allowing the story to soak in. It was the oldest cliché that everyone accused of disgusting crimes was innocent in his own mind. Over the years, Jonathan had lost track of the number of terrorists and kidnappers who had stared him straight in the eye and sworn that they were the innocent victims of happenstance. The wrong place at the wrong time. Merely exercising their right to practice their own religion. Simply trying to help the victims. These excuses and many more abounded even as their victims' blood congealed on their clothing.

Jonathan was anything but an easy mark for a sob story; yet he believed Harvey Rodriguez. Perhaps it was the absence of histrionics, the simple, bare-bones telling of the story. No, he realized, it was none of those things. It was the absolute absence of self-loathing that convinced him.

"Your life sucks, Harvey," Jonathan said. He didn't mean it to be cruel; he was merely stating a fact.

"Thank you," Harvey said. "Made even suckier by recent events." He laughed as he scratched his beard aggressively with both hands. "I am open to any suggestions you might have on how to un-suck it."

"I think I just might have one," Jonathan said. "How'd you like a job here?"

"What, at a school? Maybe you weren't listening to the part where—"

"The law?" Jonathan laughed. "Tell me one thing that's happened since we met that complies with the law."

"Easy for you. I'm the one looking at the jail time. I can't be around kids. Hell, I don't even *want* to be around kids anymore. I've had enough of that shit."

All things considered, Jonathan didn't blame him. "Well you can't just hang around here. Not without a job. Even if I said it was okay, there's no way Mama Alexander would let it happen."

"Mama who?"

Jonathan let that go. Mama defied explanation to anyone who hadn't met her. "We have an opening for a custodian here," Jonathan said. "It's yours if you want it."

Harvey scowled. "What, slopping toilets and cleaning up puke on the floors?"

"And earning a salary for your efforts. It's better than living in the woods and getting shot to death."

"Again, easy for you to say."

"I'm just trying to help."

Something changed behind Harvey's eyes.

"What's wrong?" Jonathan asked.

"What's your angle?"

"I don't have one."

"Bullshit. Everybody's got an angle—even the ones who don't think they do. You expect me to believe that you suddenly give a shit about me? Hell, look at me. Even I don't give much of a shit about me."

Jonathan scooted his chair back and crossed his legs. As he reopened the manila file folder that Venice had given him, he said, "I have a soft spot for veterans."

Harvey laughed bitterly. "I swear to God, if you say 'thank you for your service to our country' I'm going to barf all over your floor."

Jonathan read from the file. "Purple Heart, Navy Distinguished Service Medal and Navy Cross." He looked up. "That's some pretty high cotton." Among Marine Corps awards for gallantry, the Navy Cross was trumped only by the Congressional Medal of Honor.

"Don't mean nothin'," Harvey said with a dismissive wave. "Not anymore."

"They mean a lot around here," Jonathan countered. His own medals for gallantry remained classified top secret and were displayed only in Unit headquarters at Fort Bragg. "I'm alive because of medics like you."

Harvey looked at his hands. "I'm not a medic anymore. I'm not a Marine anymore. I'm the creepy loner who lives in a tent, and that's just fine by me." He raised his eyes. "What are you doing wandering through the woods shooting people? And what did you do with the bodies?"

Harvey Rodriguez posed a special kind of problem. The clandestine side of Security Solutions required extreme secrecy that had all been blown to hell by the events of this morning. It was bad enough that one of the children of Resurrection House had seen him kill; now he had to deal with direct knowledge held by a nominally unstable homeless drifter.

He considered every word as he spoke. "What do you know about the school next door?"

"That every one of the kids in there can probably do algebra better than me."

Me, too, Jonathan didn't say. "It's a residential school for children of incarcerated parents. Last night, the boy you helped, Jeremy Schuler, was kidnapped from that school."

"So you're a cop," Harvey said.

"No, I'm a good Samaritan."

"Who shoots people and disposes of their bodies. That's a lot of attitude for a good Samaritan."

Jonathan chuckled in spite of himself. He was liking Harvey more and more. "Can we just leave it at that for now?" he asked. "You really don't have the need to know." He hoped that if he invoked military-speak for "back off" Harvey would get the hint.

"The police don't even know about you, do they?" Harvey guessed. So much for taking hints. "And you're not just hiding me from the killers. You're hiding me from the cops, too." His eyes narrowed as they became crystal clear. "You've got some interesting secrets, don't you, Mr. Graves?"

Jonathan cocked his head and smirked. "It's Grave," he said. "No *s*. And I believe I'll neither confirm nor deny."

"Sounds like a 'yes' to me." Harvey was like a different man. For the first time, he seemed fully engaged, his fear evaporated. "Don't worry, though," he added. "Your secret's safe with me. I got no one to tell it to, anyway. It's interesting, though."

Jonathan believed him, though he still had no idea why. He'd come to trust his sense about people over the years—a valuable confidence when working backcountry with local tribal leaders and inner-city miscreants to accomplish tasks that would get them all killed if word leaked out.

"It's important to me that you stay close for a while, Harvey. And I think it's important to you to be useful."

"Ah, so you're a psychiatrist, too."

"A legend in my own mind," Jonathan said with a smile. "Think about it, okay?"

A knock at the door let him off the hook.

It was Mama Alexander, Venice's mother, and the hand holder in chief for every child in Resurrection House. In her late sixties, with the stamina of a forty-year-old, Mama bore a striking resemblance to the actress Esther Rolle from the seventies sitcom *Good Times*. After Jonathan's mother had died when he was still a little boy, Mama had stepped in as surrogate. In Fisherman's Cove and the surrounding communities, the name Mama meant Mama Alexander.

"You wanted to see me, Jonny?" she asked. Of the 6.8 billion people who walked the earth, she was the only one who got away with calling him that.

Both men stood. "Mama Alexander, I'd like to introduce you to Harvey Rodriguez. He was instrumental in saving Jeremy's life yesterday, and I want you to consider him to be a very special guest."

Mama's face lit up like a full moon. "I'm very pleased to meet you," she said, reaching out to embrace his offered hand with both of hers. "The Lord smiles on any man who offers what little he has to the betterment of others."

Harvey smiled uncomfortably and shot a look to Jonathan.

"Mama is one of the Lord's messengers," Jonathan explained with a wink.

She gave him a playful smack on the shoulder. "You make fun, Jonny, but you know I'm right."

"How is Jeremy doing?" Jonathan asked. He sensed Harvey's heightened interest.

"He's frightened," Mama said. "And he wants to return to his friends."

"Well, we've talked about that," Jonathan said. "We need to keep his rescue a secret. At least for the time being. It's for his own safety."

"I'm not arguing with you," Mama said. "I'm just answering your question."

"And I appreciate it. Now I need you to take Mr. Rodriguez upstairs, and give him one of the guest rooms on the third floor."

He could see the concern in her eyes, but knew that she would cut off a finger before insulting a guest.

"Hopefully, he'll be with us for quite a while," he continued. "Of course, that decision is his."

CHAPTER FIFTEEN

This time, consciousness returned with a harsh shake.

"Wake up, kid," a voice said. Kid sounded like *keed*. "Nap time is over. Time to open eyes."

Evan Guinn had been vaguely aware for some time, he thought. He knew it was impossibly hot and that he wanted to roll over into a cooler spot, but his body wouldn't cooperate. His limbs still weighed a hundred pounds apiece. So he'd just drift off again.

A harder shake this time, accompanied by a smack to the back of his head. "No more sleep. You wake now. Work to do."

Work? Did he just say work? What kind—

Hands landed heavily on his shoulders. They grasped his arms and dragged him. For an instant, Evan was suspended in the air, and then he hit the hard ground.

"Hey!" he yelled, arms and legs scrabbling for traction. "Leave me—"

The surroundings didn't make sense to him yet, but the reality of being lifted by his hair brought a certain focus. His attacker was a squat, beefy man not a lot taller than Evan's five feet, four inches, but outweighing him by at least a hundred pounds. Without thinking, Evan threw a punch at the man. It was a girlie, roundhouse swing with no power behind it that wiffed.

The counterpunch, however—more an open-handed slap, really, or it would have broken something—landed full-force in Evan's belly, a resounding *whack* that startled more than hurt. He tried to double over, but the grip on his hair tightened.

"Don't be stupid," the man growled. *Stoopeed.* "You make me hurt you, I hurt you. You do as I say, I be nice. *Entiende?*"

Evan coughed twice and took a deep breath. "Yes," he said. "Okay." He thought he recognized the language as Spanish.

"Good," the man said. "I let go then."

It felt like having his scalp reattached. Evan used his fingers as a comb to straighten his hair. It was wet and greasy. "Who are you?" he asked. He heard the accusatory tone in his voice and braced for another smack. It didn't come.

Instead, the man handed him a thick stack of clothes and said something he didn't understand. Something about "ropas."

Evan scowled. "What?"

The man repeated himself, shoving the clothes into his chest. "Put on," he said.

"Why?"

This time when he shoved the clothes, a finger poked him in the same spot where the slap had landed. Evan couldn't tell if he did it on purpose or not, but either way, it served as a reminder. He took them the way a linebacker takes a pass from a quarterback, a hand above and below the stack. They felt heavy.

The man held up his beefy hand, fingers splayed wide. "*Cinco minutos,*" he said.

You didn't have to speak Spanish to get "five minutes" out of that.

The man turned and left, closing a flimsy door behind him, and leaving Evan alone. Suddenly, five minutes seemed like way too much time. The room—if that's really what you could call it—was tiny, maybe eight feet square. The walls and floor seemed to be made of the same wide wooden planks, but the walls didn't actually go all the way to the floor, leaving a gap of six inches or so. The room didn't have a ceiling, really, just an elevated cap that looked like it was made of grass. The walls didn't meet there, either.

Behind him, his bed turned out to be a wooden door nailed to sawhorses. That platform was the only object in the room, except for a bucket that had been shoved into the corner on the wall opposite the door.

Evan placed the pile of clothes on the plank and sorted through them. This couldn't be right. "Hey!" he called. "Hey mister! *Señor!*"

He waited a few seconds, and when no one answered, he tried again. With still no answer, he padded barefoot to the door and pulled it open. "Hey!"

Jesus, he was in the jungle! Five feet away, two men wearing camouflaged green uniforms jumped at the sound of the door opening and whirled, leveling rifles at his chest.

Evan yelled, wrapped his arms protectively around his head, and dropped to his knees.

Someone shouted, and heavy footsteps ran up to him. Again, he was lifted by his hair, and this time he was shoved back inside. He landed on his back and skidded.

"Don't shoot me!" Evan cried.

"You crazy boy!" It was the same man as before. "*Loco!* Crazy to escape."

Evan brought himself to his feet, again adjusting his hair. "I wasn't escaping!" he yelled.

"You escaping!"

"No!"

"Then why run outside?"

"I needed to talk to you!" Evan said. The fear remained, but anger swelled as well. "Look at those clothes!" He pointed at the pile on the plank bed. "They're for winter!"

Indeed, the man had handed him blue jeans, a turtleneck, and a heavy wool sweater.

"Yes. You wear."

"It's a thousand degrees."

"You wear," the man repeated. He held up three fingers. "*Tres minutos*." He turned to the door, then turned back and said something.

"What?"

He mimicked knocking on the door. "No get shot." He turned to leave.

"Wait."

His jailer turned again, annoyance blooming on his face.

"I have to go to the bathroom."

The guard scowled. They weren't communicating.

Evan went knock-kneed and bounced, the universal pantomime for needing to go. "Pee," he said. "I need to go to the bathroom."

The guard's scowl turned to a grudging smile. He pointed to the bucket in the corner

Evan's jaw gaped. "You're shitting me."

"*Sí*," he said, pointing again. "Sheet." He closed the door as he exited, then shouted, "*Dos minutos!*"

The offices for Security Solutions occupied the third floor of the same one-hundred-year-old converted firehouse whose first two floors served as Jonathan's residence. He resisted the pull of home as he walked to the public entrance and smiled at the security camera. There'd been some major renovations to this entryway in recent months, following some unpleasantness involving invaders who had let themselves in by hacking the security code. Now, every employee had to offer up a thumbprint and an encrypted card key to gain access, while security cameras verified each visitor's identity before anyone could be buzzed in.

As the owner of the company, just the smile worked for Jonathan. The door hummed, and he pushed it open.

A rabbit warren of cubicles greeted him. In this front part of the office—everyone called it "the pit," but he had no idea why—Security Solutions' team of twenty investigators and their support staff took care of the public, legitimate side of their business, whose clients included some of the most recognized corporate names in the world.

Jonathan's team was waiting for him in the War Room—the teak conference room in the Cave, Security Solutions' executive suite, where the clandestine side of the business was run. Precious few in the company knew exactly what went on in the Cave, and that was fine. Even those who guessed knew to keep their mouths shut.

Boxers and Venice were seated around the table, as was the newest addition to the inner sanctum, Gail Bonneville. They each nursed a steaming cup of coffee. "Good morning, everyone," Jonathan said.

Return greetings were more mumbled than spoken. The mood in the room was funereal, with all three of the others averting their gaze to anything but the three-foot-by-four-foot image of a sullen boy that glowed from the projection screen at the far end.

Jonathan had made it clear to Venice that until this case cleared, the image of Evan Guinn would be inescapable. It spoke volumes, Jonathan thought, that the only recent clear photo they had of the kid after four years in their care was this one, taken seven months ago at the school Christmas party. Resurrection House was supposed to be a home, for God's sake. The fact that this boy's life was so sparsely documented pissed him off.

The face staring back from the screen emanated a plain vanilla expression from a plain vanilla place. The smile was as bright as it's supposed to be when someone's taking a picture, but it was all teeth and mouth. The eyes showed institutional emptiness—the show-nothing-so-no-one-can-hurt-you expression of every young inmate of every prison: equal parts fear and resolution. The boy's most striking feature was the long, wavy mane of white-blond hair.

With his own supply of caffeine in hand, Jonathan helped himself to the seat at the head of the table and rested his palms flat on the polished surface. "Look at me," he said.

Their eyes rose to meet his.

"How's Dom?" he asked Venice. If Mama Alexander was the soul of the House, then Father Dom D'Angelo was the heart. He and Jonathan had been friends since college.

Venice sighed. "He's doing as best he can. Handling the children's concerns is difficult, but the newspeople are being pretty brutal."

"Fuckin' reporters are gonna crucify everybody who has anything to do with the House," Boxers said.

"They're going to do what they're going to do," Jonathan said. He rubbed a hand through his hair and scratched the back of his head. Those who knew him well recognized it as a gesture of frustration. "We're staying out of it. Ven, after this meeting, I want you to get Matt Baker and Anne Hawkins involved. Let's let Dom concentrate on helping the kids to get whole."

Venice made a note without uttering her usual condemnation of Jonathan's preferred public relations and legal experts. Maybe even she recognized the need for the best of the best, despite the combined price tag of nearly two grand an hour.

"Who's spoken with Mr. Stewart?"

Venice and Gail both raised their hands.

"He's as sweet as ever," Gail said. "He's more worried about the kids than he is about himself."

"But he doesn't know about the kidnappings, right?" Jonathan hoped.

"I wish," Gail said. "A reporter called his room."

"Fuckin' reporters," Boxers repeated. "Why didn't somebody intercept the call?"

"They are now," Venice soothed. "Thanks to that call." She looked at Jonathan. "Dig, it would really help for him to know that Jeremy's okay."

Jonathan shook his head. "I know it would, but we can't

afford the chance of a leak. Not yet. But Mr. Stewart is still on track to recover?"

"He's still critical but stable," Venice said. "But offline, the doctor told me that he's past the point of major worries."

"Thank God for that," Jonathan said. He took a long sip from his coffee mug, and then caught the entire team up on what the last few hours had revealed. As he did, he rose from his chair and parted two paneled doors to reveal a white-board, on which he listed the salient points.

"So here's where we are," he concluded. "The driver, Jimmy Henry, was hired through some guy named Sjogren, who apparently has ties to the old Slater crime family through its new leader, Sammy Bell. That establishes a possible organized crime connection." He jotted that point on the board.

"Isn't that the same group that your father had all the trouble with?" Boxers asked.

"The very one," Jonathan said. "But it doesn't end there. There's a government connection, too." He deferred to Venice to relay her discovery about the gunmen's backgrounds.

"There's not a hard government connection," Venice concluded, "but it sure smells like one to me."

Gail Bonneville raised her hand. "I hate to be the slow one," she said, "but you're all talking like this makes some kind of sense. Government operatives attacking and trying to kill children. What am I missing?" Gail had cut her law enforcement teeth in the FBI, rising quickly through the ranks and ultimately snagging a leadership role on the Bureau's Hostage Rescue Team out of the Chicago field office. A tumultuous end to that career had led to a gig as a county sheriff in Indiana, which itself ended as collateral damage to one of Jonathan's earlier missions. Trim and athletic, Gail was to Jonathan's eye movie-star beautiful. Her dark brown eyes matched her dark brown hair, and she carried an air of intelligence that seriously stirred his juices.

"Nothing ever makes sense at this stage of an op," Boxers

said. He had a dismissive way about him that frequently put others on edge.

Venice ignored the big man and looked at Gail. "It's not completely outlandish when you think about it. Every child in the House has criminal parents. Some of those parents have run afoul of federal law enforcement. Many of them have run afoul of people whom federal law enforcers are looking to prosecute."

"Okay, then," Gail said, having clearly connected those two dots on her own. "So, pick one. You've got organized crime snatching the boys as retribution. Maybe. Let's stipulate to that for the sake of argument. But why the feds?"

Jonathan watched his new protégé with mixed feelings of admiration and desire. Gail's strongest professional asset was her ability to process information and reach a well-considered conclusion in just a few seconds.

She continued, "I have a hard time believing that agents of the government of the United States are going to apply such resources to the kidnapping and murder of children. It just doesn't make sense."

"The government connection to Sean O'Brian is clear," Jonathan said. "And frankly, the fact that there's no information on the other shooter is also damned convincing evidence of Uncle Sam's handiwork."

Gail wasn't buying. "Tell me organized crime, and I'm with you. Tell me government, and it just makes no sense."

Jonathan loved the way her ears reddened when she became passionate about a topic. "Maybe the mob happened to hire the same shooters Uncle Sam uses from time to time. Wouldn't that explain the link?"

Bingo. At least it was plausible.

Jonathan shifted his gaze. "Ven," he said. "Catch us up on what you found about the parents involved."

Venice pulled a file folder from her stack of meeting-prep materials and opened it. "Let's talk about Frank Schuler first," she said, spreading the papers out in front of her. She held up a mug shot labeled with the man's name. "This is

Jeremy's father. He's on death row here in Virginia for murdering his wife, Jeremy's mother."

Boxers made a noise like air escaping from a canister.

"She was cheating on him with a guy named Aaron Hastings. Schuler shot her. He maintained his innocence all the way through the trial, but the jury didn't buy it. Unless a miracle happens, he gets the needle in nine days."

She slid the Schuler papers back into their folder and opened another. She displayed another mug shot. No one would doubt the relationship between Evan and his father. They had the same light hair and blue eyes, the same angular features. "This is Arthur Guinn," Venice said, "and here is your connection to the mob. He was an enforcer."

"Hit man," Gail said.

Venice tossed off a shrug. "If you'd prefer. He killed people for money and got caught." She looked at her notes again. "He murdered an aide to then-Congressman Mark Levy from New York. Guinn said he was bent out of shape because of the congressman's politics, but according to the record, the feds always suspected a connection to the Slater mob."

Jonathan noted her satisfied smile as she delivered that last line. "Where do he and Schuler intersect?"

The smile went away. "They don't," Venice said. "At least not so far as I can tell. I don't see where they've ever occupied the same state, let alone town."

"There's got to be a link," Boxers said.

"No kidding?" Venice returned. "Golly, I wish I'd thought of that."

Boxers reared back in his seat. "What the hell did I do?"

"You implied that Venice didn't know how to do her job," Gail said.

"I did not! All I said—"

Jonathan held out both hands, like a cop stopping traffic in both directions. "Nobody start," he said. "Gail, I want you to interview both of these fathers. With their kids missing, maybe they'll be willing to open up a little. Work with Doug Kramer if you get push-back from the prison guys."

Gail jotted something in the speckled composition notebook that was as attached to her as her arm. "You bet."

"That'll get a little frustrating when you go to talk to
Arthur Guinn," Venice said. "I called the Illinois Department
of Corrections to see what I could find out, and I learned that
Mr. Arthur Guinn is no longer in the system."

Jonathan stopped in mid-stride and turned. "What does
that mean?"

"You tell me."

Jonathan looked to Boxers and Gail, and saw no indication of a theory. "What did they say?"

Venice consulted her notes. "They said that there's no immediate disposition of the case against him, but that he is no
longer part of the Illinois system. When I asked him if that
was double-talk for him being moved to someone else's system, I got 'I can neither confirm nor deny.'"

Jonathan saw where Venice was leading him. "You're
thinking witness protection," he said.

She smirked.

"The feds want him to testify," Gail said. "They must be
going after Sammy Bell, and to get him to talk, they made
him a deal."

Jonathan liked it. He pointed to Venice and said, "I know
Dom is swamped right now, but I need him to contact—"

Venice beamed. "I already talked to him," she said.
"You're meeting Wolverine at one."

CHAPTER SIXTEEN

Evan Guinn followed every direction to the letter. They'd led him from the tiny hut, flanked by the two guards who had nearly shot him, to a spot about twenty yards away that looked like it had been turned into a movie set. They'd cut a swath out of the dense green foliage to expose a large rock, which had been painted with stripes of white. The ground all around the rock had been painted white, too, and sprinkled with what appeared to be that fake plastic snow stuff that you put around Christmas decorations.

Through words and gestures, they directed him to stand in front of the rock. They handed him a copy of *The Washington Post* and told him to hold it just so under his chin, and pantomimed for him to smile. The squat man from the shack did all of the communicating while taking direction from a darker skinned man dressed in black slacks and a long white shirt who held a cell phone camera at arm's length, composing his shot, Evan assumed. Clearly, they wanted to make the picture look like he was somewhere cold, but he was sweating like a pig and barefoot. Who was going to believe it?

He'd seen this trick with the newspaper before in movies

about kidnapping victims. They used the headline on the paper as proof that the victim was still alive so that they would pay the ransom. He felt a sudden flash of fear. Who was going to pay ransom for him? Mom was dead, Dad was in jail, and there wasn't anyone else. Nobody had anything of value to trade for him. There wasn't a reason in the world to keep him alive.

But apparently there was. They'd gone to a lot of trouble to get him here to wherever the hell he was. And where was that, exactly? Mexico? South America?

Jesus, how long had he been asleep? South America and Mexico were both a long way from Virginia. Geography was one of his worst subjects, but he knew that much.

What were they going to do with him? Another jolt of fear. He'd been alone in the company of sweaty men before, with the last foster family before moving to RezHouse. He knew what they were capable of, and the fact that he saw no women around made his stomach churn. Evan had meant what he'd said to Father Dom during one of his counseling sessions: He'd never allow himself to be used that way again. The last time, he was little and didn't have the strength to break their bear hugs.

He was nearly fourteen now, though, and he knew a thing or two that he hadn't before. He knew what was worth killing for, and what was worth dying for. More to the point, he knew what wasn't worth living after.

The whole picture-taking process took less than ten minutes.

Apparently satisfied with the results, Shack Man beckoned Evan away from the rock and handed him a pair of well-worn short pants of an indefinable color. Somewhere between gray and black. Evan wondered if they'd once been white.

"You . . . wear," Shack Man said, and he pointed to the shack. Then he prattled about something while he made a sweeping motion in the air up and down the length of the boy's body.

"Huh?"

Shack Man pinched the shoulder of his sweater and tugged lightly. "*Esto . . .* sweetshirt?"

Evan processed it. "Sweater?" he guessed.

Shack Man nodded and pointed to Evan's jeans. He searched for a word. "Give back."

Evan didn't hesitate for a moment to shed the sweater and turtleneck. He pulled them over his head, and handed them over, leaving him bare-chested. He got that he was supposed to return the pants, too, and for that he walked back to the shack. He noted for what it was worth that the guards didn't follow him this time.

Inside, he changed into the shorts and lay back down on the plank door, after folding the blue jeans and using them for a pillow. He draped his forearm over his eyes and took a deep breath. *I will not cry*, he told himself. It doesn't accomplish anything, and it shows weakness.

Worse, the weakness hands power over to the people who want to hurt you.

Who *were* these people? And what were they planning to do with him?

What were they planning to do *to* him?

His stomach fluttered, and he closed his eyes tighter. *You have to learn to cope with the reality of what is*, he heard Father Dom telling him. *When bad things happen to us—especially as children—we want there to be a reason. We search so hard for meaning in yesterday that we can lose sight of today. Today is all that matters. Today and tomorrow. Yesterday is past and needs to be shoved aside until the Lord makes it our business to understand.*

Lying in this sweaty stinkhole, he felt homesickness sliding in. He felt sadness knocking at the door. They were the same sensations that threatened to suffocate him in the first months after the social workers finally listened. He had been nine years old then. It was hard not to allow the darkness in; but maybe it was supposed to be hard.

"What's happening to me?" He spoke just loudly enough for him to hear his own voice.

When God wants you to know, He'll tell you.

Evan brought his arm down quickly and whipped his head to the side, expecting to see Father Dom standing there. His voice had been that clear in his head.

When He wants me to know, He'll tell me.

A sense of utter clarity washed over him, flooding away the darkness.

He didn't have time for a pity party. Evan needed to grow a pair and embrace the reality of today. That meant he had to wrap his arms and his mind around the fact that he'd been taken from a place he liked and shoved into a place that smelled like mold and was hot as hell. He had no friends, so that meant he was on his own.

How do you run away if you don't know where you are to begin with? You've got to start from someplace, and Evan didn't even have a compass point to shoot for—as if he had a compass in the first place, or would know how to use it if he did.

His first decision, then, was easy: He'd wait things out for a while. So far, he saw no reason to tempt people to kill him. If the time came to risk death, Evan figured he would know it, and he would make the big decisions then. For the time being he'd just hold tight and—

His door slammed open, revealing Shack Man silhouetted against the harsh light of the day. "Come," he said, beckoning with his whole hand. "Time to go."

"Go where?" Evan asked.

"*Appurate,*" the man said. Evan knew "hurry" when he heard it. He left the jeans where they lay, folded on the plank, and he walked cautiously to the door. As he approached, he saw that a beat-up four-wheel-drive vehicle was waiting for him.

CHAPTER SEVENTEEN

The Sussex 1 State Prison on Musselwhite Road in Waverly, Virginia, sprawled like a concrete cancer in the former tobacco fields south of Richmond. First opened in 1998, the place featured the overly sterile look of the modern supermax prisons that are so popular these days.

This was home for the worst of the worst, and they were treated accordingly, closed into their soundproofed concrete cells for twenty-three hours a day, the twenty-fourth hour dedicated to indoor recreation. In its own way, the stifling nature of the new cell design had to be even more oppressive than the barred cages of days gone by.

After a lifetime in law enforcement—first as an FBI agent and later as sheriff of a small community in Indiana—Gail Bonneville still could not abide the oppressive tightness of the air inside a prison. The filtered body odor seemed harder to breathe than air on the outside. She wondered if it was possible to lock the doors so tightly that the oxygen levels actually dropped. Add to the general misery of the place the meter-pegging humidity of the otherwise stifling July day, and you begin to realize just how little the penal system in the United States has evolved from the torture chambers of medieval Europe. Where, she wondered, were the protesters who forced the closing of Guantanamo when places like this—new construction, no less—continued to thrive?

At least the noise levels that were so common of older prisons were kept in check here.

The deal that Gail had made with Marie Brady, Frank Schuler's attorney, had left no room for variation: She would allow her client to appear in the same room with Gail, but all questions would be addressed to the attorney. She would then make the decision as to whether or not he could answer. At this stage, with Schuler's execution date less than two weeks away, they could afford for nothing to go wrong. In a perfect world, Schuler would speak to no one even distantly related to law enforcement. This exception was being made only because his son had been kidnapped.

Per Jonathan's instructions, Gail had mentioned nothing about the boy having been recovered safely.

In deference to the hopelessness of Frank Schuler's situation, she'd dressed plainly and unprovocatively. That meant gray slacks with a black blouse, chosen in part to help conceal any filth she picked up from the furniture.

Marie Brady had arrived first and was waiting in the reception area for Gail when she arrived. Neither tall nor short, the lawyer was likewise dressed plainly, but less formally than Gail had come to expect from attorneys. Her black slacks and top were clearly off-the-rack, and her shoes hadn't seen polish in a long, long time. They were the clothes of the working poor, and it occurred to Gail that such was the lot of a lawyer who specialized in saving the condemned from their court-ordered fates.

The women greeted each other cordially, and then Marie walked Gail through the process of gaining entry into the death row interview room. Throughout the process, Gail noted with interest the respect shown to the attorney by all of the correctional officers. It bordered on deference, in fact.

As they ran through the perfunctory checklist of dos and don'ts, she got the feeling that they wanted to apologize for the inconvenience.

"You seem comfortable here," Gail said as they cleared the security air locks and followed their escort down the brightly lit concrete hallway.

"Comfortable is not the word," Brady said. "Not when you factor in the mission. But I am certainly a regular. Secretly, I think they all want me to prevail in the cases I represent."

"Murderers?" Gail's voice demonstrated more shock than she wanted it to.

"Human beings," Brady corrected. "Over the years, the corrections staff develops relationships with these men. It's hard to watch them walk off to their deaths for crimes that were committed so long ago." As they approached yet another door, the attorney added, almost to herself, "If politicians were half as human as the worst of these guys, we'd be done with sanctioned murder."

Under the circumstances, those were the politics that Gail had expected.

"Sometime soon," Brady continued as they walked, "probably in the next three or four days, they'll transfer Frank to the death house at Greensville. That's about thirty-five miles from here. I've even seen a few tears among these COs when inmates depart for the final trip. This is an emotional business."

For reasons that no doubt made sense to someone, the Commonwealth of Virginia had decided to separate death row from the execution chamber. In fact, the death house was located in a medium-security prison. You had to love bureaucrats.

After another door, Gail and Brady arrived at the tiny glass-walled interview room. To Gail's utter shock, the furniture was spotless—shiny, even, carrying forward that oppressive, astringent sterility.

"You know I've got to have the recorder on, right, Marie?"

the guard asked, his first words since they started their long walk.

"I do," Brady replied with a smile. To Gail, she explained, "Normally, my talks with Frank are privileged. But since you're not an attorney, and you'll be hearing what he says, the state gets to listen in, too."

Gail found this alarming, though she could not say why.

"That explains the importance of all questions being directed at me," Brady went on. "If anything you ask even knocks on the door of something Frank shouldn't be saying, I'll cut you both off. I'll ask you not to question that decision until after we are out of the prison."

Gail agreed. The lawyer was impressive, she thought. It wasn't everybody who could rattle off instructions like that and not seem patronizing or haughty.

Within a minute or two, a door opened on the opposite side of the room from where they'd entered, and a different guard escorted Frank Schuler into the room in a full shackle rig. He looked twenty years older than his eight-year-old induction photo. Thin to the point of appearing frail, he sported a pate of sparse gray hair. He moved with the institutional shuffle of a lifer. He needed no instruction as he turned to make his wrists more accessible to the correctional officer's key.

With his hands free, and clearly resigned to his ankles remaining restrained, he shuffled to the table and accepted Brady's warm embrace. "They said something about Jeremy," he said in a rush. "Do you know something? Tell me it's good news."

"Frank, this is Gail Bonneville, a private investigator from Fisherman's Cove."

Recognition came instantly. "That's the town where the school is," he said.

Gail offered her hand, and he eagerly shook it. "It is the same town, but I'm afraid I have no news for you," she said. The lie tasted especially foul under these circumstances.

The prisoner's face fell. "Then why are you here?"

Gail indicated the chairs. "Let's sit."

"Let's stand," Schuler countered. "Why are you here?" Desperate fear emanated from him like a hot flash.

"I've been hired by the school to do an independent investigation."

"How could something like this happen?" Schuler said, his institutional pallor reddening along his jawline. "They're children, for God's sake! Why isn't there security?"

Gail again swallowed the temptation to set his mind at ease. "I'm working *for* Resurrection House, Mr. Schuler. I don't work *at* Resurrection House. I'm trying to get a handle on who might have taken your son, and why they would have done it."

"How about finding *where* they took him?"

Gail paused before answering, a tactic used in interviews to take some of the wind out of angry people's sails. "It's all part of the same packet, sir. We're hoping that the who and the why will lead us to the where. I know you're upset—"

"You *think*?"

"—but ranting about what is past does nothing to advance the future." Gail tuned her voice to being the ultimate in reasonableness.

The redness deepened in Schuler's face, but something changed behind his eyes. He shot a look to his lawyer.

"She's the real deal," Marie said. "I think you should talk to her."

A moment passed in which no one moved.

"Let's sit," Brady said, pulling a chair out for herself. With that, it was done. She'd let him vent a little, let Gail respond, and now it was time to get on with the business at hand.

Frank Schuler turned awkwardly to lower his butt into his chair. "I'm sorry for that outburst," he said. "But I don't know if you can imagine what it's like to be where I am and hear that your child has been taken."

"I'm sure that the worst I could imagine wouldn't even come close to the reality," Gail said.

Schuler relaxed a little. "Why a private dick and not a cop?"

"The police haven't already talked to you?" Gail didn't try to mask her surprise.

Brady answered for her client. "Remember the rules, Ms. Bonneville."

"Please call me Gail."

"And I'm Marie. This is Frank. Formality seems a little silly under the circumstances. But to answer your question, I'm sure that the police will get around to us sooner or later. I don't think they consider us to be a priority at the moment. In fact, I'm a little surprised that you do."

Gail chose not to offer a theory of her own, or to address the open question. She opened her speckled notebook and dug right in. "Do the names Evan Guinn or Arthur Guinn mean anything to your client?"

Marie nodded her approval to Frank. Clearly, this hands-off interview style was a common occurrence for them.

"Who are they?"

Gail started to answer, but stopped herself. "Can I answer him?" she asked Marie.

The attorney smiled. "Your questions and his answers are the only concern," she said. "Not the other way around. Trust me, you'll get used to it after a while."

It sure felt weird now, Gail thought. "Evan is the other boy who was taken from the school," she explained. "Arthur is his father. Do you know who they are?"

Frank Schuler looked off the side and scowled. When his gaze returned, the regret was obvious. "Nothing," he said. "I mean, the name might be familiar, but how would I know? I've met a lot of people over the years. Are those the only names you've got?"

Gail invoked the name of the only shooter they'd been able to identify. "What about Sean O'Brian?"

Another moment of intense reflection, begun even before the nod from Marie. "Another common name. Who is he?"

Gail found herself on the precipice of the proverbial slippery slope. They had no legitimate trail to these identities. By answering the question, she'd be showing a card in her hand. To be evasive, though, would shove Frank into anger or insolent silence; neither of which would advance their case a bit. She decided to take a chance.

"We think he might have a connection to Sammy Bell. Does that—"

Marie's hand shot up. "Stop. Move to your next question."

"The mobster?" Frank asked.

"Frank, no."

Gail moved quickly. "Yes, the mobster."

Marie's raised hand became a pointed finger. "Gail, you promised me."

"He asked me," Gail said, her palms upturned in a gesture of innocence.

"Do you think that Sammy Bell had something to do with this?" Frank pressed.

Marie slammed her hand on the metal table. "Damn it, Frank, stop it."

He turned angry. "Stop what, Marie? This is my son we're talking about. My only child. What would you have me stop doing?"

"I would have you stop talking!" she snapped. "Sammy Bell is a known mobster. Anything you say—"

"What?" Frank interrupted. "What could I possibly say that would turn my situation into anything shittier than it already is?"

"We still have an appeal left," Marie said. "Anything and everything you say—"

"Fuck the appeal, Marie."

The attorney looked like she'd been slapped.

"They're not going to grant me a stay. In nine days, they're going to tie me to a bench, put needles in both my arms, and they're going to kill me. If I can die knowing that I've done everything I can to help Jeremy, then that's a hell of a lot better than dying without knowing where he's been taken." Frank turned to Gail. "Ask your questions."

"Goddammit, Frank—"

"Do I have to *fire* you, Marie?" he shouted. "I don't want to, but I will, if that's what it takes. The decision's yours, but make it now."

Gail realized that she hadn't taken a breath in a while. For her part, Marie Brady looked injured, on the verge of tears. "It's only over if we give up," she said, but the words trembled.

Frank Shuler's eyes burned hot. "You were talking about Sammy Bell," he prompted Gail.

She swallowed hard. "Um, well . . . Marie?"

"He's the client," she said with an angry flick of her hand. Even though it looked petulant, Gail recognized it as resignation.

She returned her gaze to Frank Schuler. "Yes, we think that Sean O'Brian was an affiliate of Sammy Bell, the mobster."

"Is he dead now?"

Marie threw up her hands. "Jesus."

"Is who dead?" Gail asked. This conversation was beginning to feel like a windstorm.

"This Sean guy. You referred to him in the past tense."

Oh, shit, Gail thought. "I meant that as in he used to work for Sammy Bell." She hoped her poker face held.

"What did he do for him?" Frank asked.

Gail took a deep breath and sighed. "Look, Mr. Schuler—"

"Frank."

"Okay, Frank. I know you're anxious to learn as much as you can, but I need to ask you to let me ask the questions."

"You have something to hide?"

Jesus, Gail thought, *this guy is sharp as a tack.*

"We all have *something* to hide, don't we?" she countered. As she asked the question, she offered a coy smile.

He acknowledged her with a little nod. "Yes, I suppose

we do." He regrouped. "I do know who Sammy Bell is—and for the benefit of the transcriber, I'll note that you, too, Mr. Transcriber, have also probably heard of him—but Sean O'Brian still means nothing to me."

Off to her left, Gail noticed that Marie had relaxed a little. She looked like a dental patient whose procedure hadn't hurt as much as she'd feared.

Frank continued, "But if you believe in six degrees of separation, I'm only two away from Sammy Bell."

Marie sat tall in her seat. "Holy shit, Frank." Relaxation gone; welcome, raw horror.

"Actually, maybe I'm three degrees separated. I guess it depends on how you count."

Marie said, "As your attorney, I am advising you in the strongest possible terms to shut the fuck up."

Frank laughed—a deep, throaty laugh that showed he was genuinely amused. "Marie, I love you. And I agree that 'shut the fuck up' ranks right up there with the strongest possible terms."

Gail found herself laughing along with him.

When the moment passed, Frank continued, "My wife, Marilyn, used to work for one of Sammy's mouthpieces. One of his attorneys."

Gail clicked her pen open. "What was his name?"

Frank's face folded into the now-familiar faraway scowl. "Navarro," he said, snapping his fingers as the name returned to him. "Bruce Navarro."

Gail made her note. "Do you know what his legal specialty was?"

"Keeping crooks out of jail, I would guess."

Obvious enough, Gail supposed. "I was hoping for something more . . ."

Frank waved off her words. "I know what you were looking for. I was just being an asshole. He did contract law, whatever that means."

"It means five hundred bucks an hour," Marie grumped.

Gail continued, "And what did your wife"—she consulted her notes—"Marilyn do for him?"

He shrugged. "Clerical stuff. Secretarial stuff. Nothing terribly important. I just thought it was interesting that Bell's name came up."

Something churned in Gail's distant memory, something from the notes she'd read from the research file. Something about Bruce Navarro. More specifically about Navarro & Associates.

"Aaron Hastings," Gail said.

Marie groaned, "Oh, please shut up."

"Marilyn's lover," Frank said. "He's also the man who I think killed Marilyn and framed me for it."

Gail had read that such had been Schuler's claim all along, but there'd always been problems with his argument. "But you don't know why," she reminded.

"The whole world doesn't know why, because the police decided from the very beginning that I was their man. They never bothered to investigate anyone else."

Gail looked to Marie for confirmation and got a nod. "From Day One, Frank was the only suspect in their crosshairs," she said. "Remember how the system works: The Commonwealth doesn't have to *be* right; they only have to convince a jury that they're right."

To someone outside the system, the statement might have seemed overly cynical, but Gail understood that Marie was stating fact. The entire industry of private investigation—such as it was—was built around the all too frequent occurrences of prosecutorial misconduct. At the end of the day, lawyers on both sides were merely human; and humans were hardwired to reject failure. Gail had known a dozen or more prosecutors in her time—at both the local and federal levels—who would consider a win at the expense of justice to be a perfectly fair deal. Even the venerated FBI had recently been caught fabricating evidence for the purpose of convicting those who were presumed guilty.

Gail didn't want to let him go that easily. "You have a theory, though? For why Aaron would have killed Marilyn?"

He gave a tentative glance to Marie, then took a deep breath. "Theory is too strong a word," he said. "I have questions, though, and I think that by stitching them together with answers, you'd have her real killer."

"I'm listening."

"Did you know that Bruce Navarro disappeared around the same time that Marilyn was murdered?"

"What do you mean, disappeared?"

"I mean just that. He was around one day, fat and happy with a flourishing practice, and then he was gone. Nobody ever heard from him again, as far as I know."

"You think he was killed?"

"I don't know one way or the other," Frank confessed. "But there's a guy in here who swears that there's a contract on Navarro's head that would pay a fortune. You don't put that out for someone who's already dead."

"Anyone can say anything," Gail observed.

"True enough. But this is a guy who would know."

"Who?"

Frank shook his head. "Not your concern."

"But if I could talk to him—"

"No. Being in this place on these terms, I don't have much, but I won't turn into a rat in my last days on the planet. You'll have to take it from me that if you talked to him, he'd tell you what I just said. I got no reason to lie. Not to you, anyway."

Gail searched his face.

"You're not seeing it, are you?" Frank pressed. "I can see it in your eyes." He leaned in closer to the table and rested his forearms on it. "Navarro, Hastings, and my wife all worked together for a law firm with mob connections. Now, they're all missing or dead. You say you're a private investigator, Gail. How big a stick do you need to be hit with?"

Gail turned to Marie. "How did the police just write that off?"

She shrugged. "They had the guilty party they were after."

"Have you ever tried to trace it all to ground?"

Marie's expression said, *Give me a break.* "Of course we have. But the time for suppositions and alternative scenarios passed the moment a jury found Frank to be guilty. It takes a twelve-to-nothing vote to make that happen. In Virginia, once the jury has spoken, it takes truly incontrovertible evidence to turn things around. DNA is working for wrongly accused rape convicts, but even that can be hard to get introduced into the system. Too many political careers get harmed when a prosecutor is found to have made a mistake. Some would rather see an innocent man die than look in his eyes and apologize for countless years lost to wrongful incarceration."

The cynical words stung. Gail had been a part of that system for long enough to know that the threads of truth within the bitterness were thick and strong.

"I think it might be even worse than you think it is, Frank," Gail said.

His face darkened as he connected the dots for the first time. "Oh, my God."

Gail said it out loud for both of them: "They're all missing or dead, but you're in prison scheduled to die, and now Jeremy is—" She stopped herself. *They'd left him for dead,* she didn't say.

Frank's eyes filled with tears. "Oh, Christ, they're going to kill him, aren't they?"

"No," Gail said. Her tone was too emphatic for the ruse she was trying to sell. "I won't let that happen," she added.

Marie's eyes narrowed. "You know something," she said.

Gail felt her heart rate double. She'd never been a good liar; she wore her thoughts on her forehead. She stared straight into Frank Schuler's eyes. "I think you need to have faith that Jeremy will be fine."

Frank scowled. He started to say something, but when Marie rested her hand on his arm, he swallowed the words.

"Do you have any more questions for us?" Marie asked.

Gail knew that she'd blown the secret, but she couldn't help but feel relieved. No one should be allowed to think that his child is in danger when it simply is not true. "No more questions," she said. She stood.

The others stood with her.

"Thank you," Frank said. "For whatever you've done. Whatever you're going to do."

Gail scooped her notes into her arm and shook Frank's hand. "I think there's an injustice under way here."

"Welcome to our very small club," he said.

CHAPTER EIGHTEEN

Jonathan arrived ten minutes early.

The Maple Inn on Maple Avenue in the heart of Vienna, Virginia, had been a meeting place for spies and miscreants for decades. Known locally for its chipped floors and do-it-yourself coffee station, the Inn poured more beer than restaurants three times its size, and hauled cash in by the bucketful, one chili dog at a time. Actually, it was two chili dogs at a time, because no one had the willpower to stop after one.

Situated six and a half miles south of CIA Headquarters, the Maple Inn provided neutral ground, where known sworn enemies could occasionally sit down and discuss matters that would forever remain off the record, even as they changed the course of history. Jonathan had first come to know the place back during his days with the Unit, when his own duties occasionally required him to eavesdrop on conversations that weren't as off the record as the participants might have thought.

He loved the food and the cheerful atmosphere, and appreciated the unofficial role it played in shaping policy and strategy. Dozens of such hangouts existed throughout the world, but this was the closest one to Fisherman's Cove, and it was therefore a common place for him to break bread with his contacts.

As he approached across the packed parking lot, he noted the unmarked black government vehicle backed into a spot close to Maple Avenue, and knew that Wolverine had beaten him here. The beefy guy sitting behind the wheel with the pigtail wire in his ear looked none too pleased to be excluded. Jonathan thought about offering him a friendly little wave, but in the end opted for discretion. Venice would have been proud.

Jonathan pulled the door and entered, unleashing the wall of noise that was typical at lunchtime, which at the Inn ran from noon to midnight. Even though he knew where he'd find Wolverine, he made a cursory scan of the inhabitants to reassure himself that it was safe to proceed. His concerns had little to do with violence—given the clientele, if you pulled a gun in this place, you'd be torn in half by the crossfire. What he really worried about were nosy observers with cameras.

It would advance no one's agenda for Jonathan and Wolverine to be spotted together. They never spoke on the record, which was why Dom D'Angelo always made the arrangements for them to make contact.

Confident that his anonymity would be maintained, he navigated through the first line of booths, and then around to the far side of the bar, where he saw Wolverine nestled into the farthest, darkest corner on the left. Whether by happenstance or design, the acoustics of the corner made it ideal for clandestine conversation. You didn't have to shout to be heard, yet the ambient noise of the room made casual eavesdropping virtually impossible.

When she saw him, she smiled. And what a smile it was. Wolverine was a holdover code name from years ago, when Uncle Sam had been a client. While they'd occasionally found themselves on opposite sides of certain tactical deci-

sions, Jonathan had always liked her. Now that she was *the*
Irene Rivers, director of the Federal Bureau of Investigation,
he admired her even more. Not only was she the first female
to hold the seat, she was the only director in history to actually step out for occasional field work.

He leaned in for the cheek-peck that would sell their
cover, and as always, he sensed that she kind of liked it. "Hi,
Irene," he said as he sat in the seat that placed his back to the
room. He much preferred to be oriented the other way, but if
anyone could cover his back—literally—Irene would be as
good a choice as any.

"Hi, Digger. Long time, no see."

He smirked, "Well, with you being a rock star and all, I
figured you didn't have time for us little guys anymore." The
last time they'd worked together—if that's what you could
really call it—Jonathan's discovery of a cache of chemical
weapons had brought a lot of great press to the Bureau in
general, and to Irene in particular.

"Alas, fame is such a fleeting thing. Things are changing
since the new sheriff came to town." He knew she was referring to the new president. "The way we used to do things
doesn't fly anymore."

"You mean that part where we used to fight to win?"

Irene gave a wry smile and shook her head. "We still win,"
she said. "It's just that the strategy has changed. We pretend
that our enemies like us now, so that takes all of the pressure
off." She sighed and took a long sip of water. "Speaking of
pretending, that was a clever bit of work this morning. George
Washington's birthplace, for God's sake." The chuckle became a laugh.

"I have no idea what you're talking about," Jonathan said,
but he made no effort to bluff with his eyes. Given what
these two had on each other, neither had any cause to play
that game.

"Did you get any good information from him?" Irene
asked.

A waitress approached from the area of the kitchen, but when she saw Jonathan shake his head, she turned on her heel to become scarce.

Jonathan leaned on his elbows and beckoned with his fingers for Irene to lean closer. "We've had a lot of interesting times, Wolfie. Please don't start gaming me now."

She recoiled, offended. "What do—"

"They came into the school I built," Jonathan said. He felt his temper fraying. "They shot the place up, critically wounded one of the most decent men on earth, and they took two boys in the middle of the night. Don't. Play. Games with me."

Irene's veneer of disgruntlement faltered just long enough that even she knew that her bluff had been called.

"You know who did this," Jonathan said.

Irene glared at the table as she considered her options. "No," she said. "We think we know who planned it. And we definitely know why."

"Are you squeezing Arthur Guinn?" Jonathan asked, cutting straight to the heart of it all.

This time, her face showed genuine surprise. "Wow," she said. "You're good."

Part of him worried that she would lose respect in him if he 'fessed up to how ridiculously easy it had been to figure out. "Is it Sammy Bell?"

Irene's eyes darted around the room, no doubt searching for eavesdroppers. "Honestly, Digger, no one's supposed to know any of this."

"And Evan Guinn and Jeremy Schuler are supposed to be in English class now. Funny how things don't always turn out the way you want." He was careful to imply that Jeremy was still missing. "Sammy Bell?"

Irene sighed. "We *think* it's him. Obviously, if we had evidence to that effect, we'd have him in custody. But yes, we've reached a deal with Arthur Guinn that would get him a new identity if he came clean with his activities for the old

Slater operation. On the second day of questioning, the kidnapping happened. We've already received a picture of Evan in custody holding today's *Washington Post*."

"I want a copy," Jonathan said.

"I've got the best photo analysts in the world—"

"I want a copy," Jonathan repeated, this time more forcefully.

She took a second. "Fine."

"And I want to speak with Arthur Guinn."

"Not possible." She raised a finger as he inhaled to argue. "Don't bother. That is one thousand percent off the table."

Jonathan had expected that to be the case. When people went into witness protection, the secrecy had to be absolute, or else what would be the sense? "I want transcripts, then."

Irene shook her head. "No." Her eyes were hard as obsidian. Another nonnegotiable point. "But that doesn't mean I don't want your help."

"On the record or off?"

Her expression said, "Don't be an idiot."

"What do you want me to do?"

She swept the room again with her eyes. When she spoke, her voice was barely a whisper. "I want you to get Evan Guinn back."

Jonathan laughed. "Oh, well, if *that's* all . . ." Then he saw she was serious. "Irene, you've got the full power and authority of the United States government at your disposal. Why don't *you* get him back?"

"Because we're not allowed to go there anymore."

"Where's *there*?"

"Your old stomping grounds, I believe. Colombia. They won't allow us on their soil anymore, and the president won't approve a covert op. The secretary of defense won't even recommend it. Hell, he won't even approve the intel."

Jonathan cocked his head. "So, what do you want me to do?"

She shrugged. "What you always do. Ignore the law and do what needs doing." When her levity didn't earn a smile, she said, "Look, Digger, I'll say it again. The rules have all changed now. The rules are real rules. I can't ask my people to break them. Not like this. It would mean jail."

Jonathan laughed. "Well, thanks a lot."

"This is what you *do*. This is your gift. I'm only asking you to do what you'd do anyway if I told you you couldn't."

Jonathan rubbed his forehead to make the confusion go away. "How is your sanctioning me doing it different than you actually doing it?"

She looked away, and then he got it. "Jesus, Irene. I have to pay for it, too? At least half this op belongs to you, doesn't it?"

She waved that idea away. "No, I can find funds from somewhere. The administration is too new to know where all the hiding places are. That way we can go to jail together if it comes apart. Does that sound better to you?"

Jonathan chuckled. "Actually, it does. Both parts—the money and the company in jail." He shifted gears. "Colombia's a big place for a small country. Do you know *where* he is?"

"I have a contact there. He's generally pretty reliable, and he tells me that a guy named Mitchell Ponder is the kidnapper, and he's got the boy with him."

"Who's Mitchell Ponder?"

"A bad egg. He used to do some wet work for the good guys back in the day, and then he went after the bigger money. We've never been able to catch him, but he's suspected in a number of shootings from years ago. Now we think he runs Sammy Bell's cocaine operations in Colombia with a wink and a nod from appropriately grafted politicians. But again, in official Washington, this is none of our business."

Jonathan was confused. "Why would they take the boy there? I mean of all the places in the world, why there?"

Irene shrugged. "I think it makes sense. It's out of the country, in a corner of the world that is safe from America's prying eyes. And it's a place they have to be anyway. Why not?"

Jonathan felt the weight of the challenge bearing down on him. "So out of hundreds of little factories dotted all over the mountainscape, how are we going to find one boy in one place?"

"Now, there we got a break. Because the Colombian government is a willing partner in the drug trade these days, we hear that Ponder has been able to consolidate his operations into just a few good-sized factories."

"You mean slave farms," Jonathan corrected.

Irene showed her palms. "Truer than false. By all accounts, Ponder is a butcher when villagers don't cooperate. I don't know if it's true or not, but my contact tells me that Ponder's MO is to gain cooperation by killing the men and teenage boys of a village, and then putting the younger boys to work in the fields and the factory."

"And the girls?" Jonathan asked. The instant he heard his own question, he knew the nauseating answer.

"They become the playground for the men. It's a disgusting business."

Jonathan inhaled. "Tell me what you know about someone named Bruce Navarro."

Irene's eyes grew large again. "Jesus, I've got entire field offices that are slower on the draw than you," she said. "He was a lawyer for Sammy Bell. He's one of my dream witnesses, but he pulled a Jimmy Hoffa and disappeared on us. Why?"

Jonathan smirked as he recalled his debriefing from Gail. "Did you know that he was Marilyn Schuler's boss?"

Irene scowled. "Who's Marilyn—" Then she got it. "Holy shit. No, I didn't."

Jonathan filled her in on the details of Gail's jailhouse interview. "I think if we can find him, we can get some nifty answers."

Irene got a faraway look. "He's got a sister in New Jersey," she said. "We've always suspected that she knows where he is—at least if he's still alive—but she won't say a word to us."

Jonathan raised his eyebrows. "To you. I wonder if she'll speak to me."

"I doubt it. But from what I know of Gail Bonneville . . ." She let him finish her thought for her.

Jonathan liked that idea. "We'll give it a shot." He snorted a laugh. "What an honor it is to be the boss. She gets New Jersey, and I get the armpit of the world." He shook his head at the irony. "Tell me about your Colombian contact."

Irene hedged, "I can give you a name, but you need to understand that he's an independent contractor."

"Is he any good?"

"He's done good work for me," Irene said. "Problem is, his loyalties are not predictable. He likes chasing the highest bidder."

"What's his name?"

"José Calderón. He lives in Panama City now, but he—"

Jonathan's face brightened. "Jammin' Josie? Guerrilla fighter, used to work out of Cartagena?"

"You know him."

Jonathan chuckled at the memory. "Sure, I know him. He led us to Pablo back when I was with the Unit. Twitchy little guy, but he knew his business. I thought he was PNG in Colombia now." He knew that Irene would understand the acronym for persona non grata.

"Did I not mention that he runs to the highest bidder?"

"Has he worked for you guys recently?"

Irene shook her head. "Not for us. Not for years. He did some work with the DEA toward the end of the last administration, and I heard he was trolling for work with the Agency in Nicaragua, but all of that has dried up. This getting-along business is putting a lot of contractors out of business."

"How do we know the other side hasn't picked up where we left off?"

"We don't. In fact we don't know a lot anymore."

Jonathan always did admire blunt honesty. He'd also had a lot of good fortune with Jammin' Josie. The man knew everybody, was trusted by people who counted, and was able to raise a small army, complete with weapons, on relatively short notice.

"And you know where you can find him?" Jonathan asked.

Irene gave a coy smile as she reached into the pocket of her suit jacket and handed him a card, complete with name and number. "He's waiting for you to call," she said.

CHAPTER NINETEEN

The jungle had grown progressively thicker during the four-hour ride from Evan's first prison compound. Mile after mile, the foliage pressed ever closer to their SUV as the road disappeared to little more than a trail. All the jungle had to do was take a deep breath, and the road would disappear completely.

Evan rode in the backseat next to a white man who seemed nearly as out of place as Evan did. He didn't say anything, but he kept casting glances to the boy and then returning his eyes to the front as soon as Evan caught him looking. *Stare away*, Evan thought. *No harm in that.* But if he even thought about touching him, he'd wish he hadn't.

As Evan had told Father Dom in the past, there wasn't much good to come out of a shitty childhood, but you learned how to take care of yourself. If those assholes back at the school had attacked when he was awake instead of sound asleep, he wouldn't be here right now.

He might not be alive, but he sure as hell wouldn't be here—wherever *here* was. And the people who took him would be blind and walking funny.

"I am Mitch," his seatmate said, extending a friendly hand. "And you are Evan, no?" The English was fine, but he had a different kind of accent. Sort of a cross between Mel Gibson (when he was being Aussie) and Michael Caine being Alfred the butler.

Evan looked at the hand, but didn't move to shake it.

"So, you are fourteen?" Mitch pressed.

"Don't talk to me, you fuckin' perv," Evan spat. He turned away to look out the window. He'd seen guys like this before. If you let them believe for even a second that you were an easy mark, they'd think they could do whatever they wanted.

The hand remained outstretched, unmoving. "Believe it or not, Evan, I am your friend."

Evan tried ignoring him, but when the words wouldn't dissolve into the air, he turned back around to face the man. "My friend, huh? Well, Friend Mitch, how 'bout you take me home?"

Mitch rolled his hand closed and replaced it on his lap. "I know that is what you would like me to do," he said, "but for the moment that is not possible."

The SUV hit a huge rut, jarring all of them, and making Evan feel good about putting his seat belt on. He kind of hoped that the bump might have knocked the others out, but was disappointed that they'd been wearing their seat belts, too.

"If you wanted it, it would be possible," Evan said.

"Actually, no," Mitch corrected. "I'm sure it's difficult for you to understand, but even I could not make that happen."

"*Even I could not make that happen*," Evan parroted, mocking the accent. "It really sucks to be a victim, doesn't it? Just you and me, sharing a jail cell."

Mitch looked amused as he folded his arms and legs and nestled himself into the corner near the door. "Has anyone put you in a jail cell?" he asked.

The sudden change in demeanor made the boy uncom-

fortable. He couldn't put his finger on it, but Mitch was pro-
.jecting a new air of menace.

"It's a real question, Evan. Have you seen the inside of a
cell here?"

"I've seen my share," Evan grumbled.

"I mean since you've been a guest with us. Have you seen
a cell?"

"Yeah. That shitty little room where I woke up."

Mitch raised a forefinger and wagged it slowly, duplicating the movement of his head. "That was a hut," he said.
"Every bit as nice as all the other huts in the camp. Only, unlike the others who live there, you had accommodations to
yourself. You were being treated not as a prisoner, but as a
guest."

"Bullshit."

"Such foul language from such a little boy."

"I'm not as little as you think I am," Evan said.

The smile returned. "Indeed. Have you been bound and
gagged? On this trip, I mean."

"Worse. I've been drugged."

Mitch acknowledged the point with a twitch of his head.
"But since you've awakened. No ropes? No handcuffs?"

"Doesn't mean I'm not a prisoner," Evan said. He genuinely didn't like this man.

Mitch held his gaze for a few seconds, then turned to the
men in the front seat. "Tito," he said, drawing the driver's
eyes to the rearview mirror. He said something in Spanish.

The driver looked surprised, and Mitch repeated himself.

The driver spoke to the guy in the shotgun seat, and then
brought the vehicle to a stop, right in the middle of the trail.

Mitch gave another command, and the electric lock on
Evan's door popped up. "Okay, go," Mitch said.

Evan looked at the door, and then at Mitch, unsure what
to do.

"Go ahead," Mitch said, making a shooing motion toward
the door. "You say you're a prisoner, and I say you are free to
go. So go."

It had to be a scam, Evan thought. He'd open the door, and they'd shoot him. Or maybe they'd just drag him back inside and punish him for having failed some half-assed loyalty test.

"Go on," Mitch said again, shooing more energetically this time. "Get out. Be free."

Evan shifted his eyes back and forth again. What was he supposed to do? If he stepped out, then what? He was in a goddamn jungle, for God's sake, nowhere near the top of the food chain anymore. He didn't move.

"It's no longer your choice," Mitch said. His tone had turned harsh. "Get out of my fucking car."

Evan felt the panic building. If he stepped out of the car now, and if they drove off, he'd be dead in days—sooner if the snakes and cougars and whatever the hell other creatures out here had anything to say about it.

Mitch unclasped his seat belt and leaned across Evan's chest to pull the latch on the door and push it open. "If you make me physically throw you out, it will hurt you. Badly." He popped the latch on the boy's seat belt and pushed him toward the open door.

Evan shot his arms out to the side, bracing himself against the doorjamb with one hand while the fingers of the other tried to find something to grab onto in the leather seat. But his fingernails weren't long enough. "No!" he yelled.

Mitch pushed harder. "I said get out of my car!"

The man turned in his seat and used the sole of his shoe to push him. Evan tried to hold on, but he could feel his butt slipping. One cheek cleared the seat, and he kicked out with his foot, snagging the map pocket behind the shotgun seat with his toes.

But it wasn't enough. After three more inches, it was all about gravity. He felt himself slipping toward the ground. His right elbow and hip rebounded off the filthy chrome running board, and then he was surrounded by weeds. It was like drowning in green. For a moment, there was no up or down; leaves were everywhere.

He heard the door slam and felt the percussive thump that went with it. They gunned the engine. Not knowing where the tires were, Evan dropped to his side and curled up, trying to make himself the smallest possible target so that he would not get hit by the heavy vehicle. In his mind, he imagined his legs being slowly crushed under the tires. For the first time since he awakened in that shack, he felt real fear. Paralyzing fear.

"Don't leave me!" he yelled, still curled in a fetal ball. His feet found the ground, and he stood. He could barely see the top of the truck above the high foliage. "Please don't leave me!" He shrieked it this time. To his own ear, his voice sounded high and squeaky, like a girl's.

He had to find the road. Without that, he knew he'd be lost forever. And once he found it, he could run after the truck and convince them not to leave him behind.

The road—the path, really—couldn't be but a few yards away, but as he took his first step toward where he thought it was, a vine or some damn thing snagged his ankle and made him fall. Everything here was wet. The whole world smelled of mildew and rot.

Of dead things.

Of dead boys.

"Don't leave me!" he shrieked.

A second attempt to run made him fall again, so he decided to crawl. Sticks scraped the bare flesh of his back and belly as God only knew what stabbed at his hands and knees. Effectively blind in the foliage, he pressed forward. They were driving away, for God's sake. He *had* to press forward. If he stopped—if he even slowed—they'd be too far away, and he'd never be able to catch up.

His head broke into the clearing first. Actually, it wasn't a clearing as much as it was the absence of jungle. Leafy shit stopped brushing his face and shoulders, and all at once it felt as if there was more air to breathe.

It was the roadway. It had to be. It had wheel ruts. What else could it be?

But there was no truck.

"Hey!" he yelled. In return, he got only the sounds of a million insects and other creatures that he wanted nothing to do with. He had no intention of being something's dinner tonight.

He turned to his right, the direction where the truck had driven off and started walking—a slow, dejected gait at first, burdened with the knowledge that he'd been left to die. A horrible daytime nightmare image of his body being ripped apart by vultures invaded his mind. He saw the stringy cords of his flesh and his intestines being pulled free of his carcass—just the way he'd seen buzzards and crows consume roadkill at home—and he picked up his pace.

Maybe there was still a chance that he could catch the SUV. Maybe they hit a rut in the road or they had to cross a stream so they'd have to slow way down. That would give him time to catch up.

But he had to move faster. He started to jog, and then to run. Rocks and sticks dug at his bare feet, but he didn't feel any pain. There wasn't room for pain today.

He picked up his pace even more, pumping his arms the way that Mr. Jackson, the PE teacher at the RezHouse and taught him. Evan had always been a good runner—a good athlete in general—and Mr. Jackson had taken a special interest in him. He said that he might be good enough to get a scholarship one day, but that when you get to that level of competition, all the little things mattered. Like pumping your arms just-so to get a little more out of every stride.

God, it was hot! As Evan rounded the first turn in the road, he felt the soaked, greasy tendrils of his hair bouncing against the back of his neck, and he swiped them away from his eyes. A hill loomed ahead, not steep but long.

Don't stop, he told himself. Stopping was too easy. That meant that dying was too easy. If he was going to die, it was going to be from exhaustion or dehydration. It wasn't going to be for his nutritional value. He lowered his head and forced himself on. He watched his feet instead of the terrain because the terrain was too depressing.

How could people live in this heat?

After eighty-five steps, it became easier. He hadn't even realized that he'd been counting. When he looked up, he saw that he'd crested the hill.

And there was the SUV, a hundred feet away. He could hear the engine idling above the noise of the insects.

Mitch stood at the back bumper. He wore all khaki, long pants with a short-sleeved shirt open at the neck. He'd assumed an expectant posture, leaning against the spare tire, his arms folded and his feet slightly extended and crossed.

Evan stopped at the sight of the man. He froze in his tracks, his chest heaving, his eyes stinging from sweat. He swiped at them with the palms of his hands, but that only made them sting more. Gasping for air, and his heart pounding, his body wanted to collapse onto the ground, but his brain wouldn't let him—wouldn't give Mitch the satisfaction.

Seeing the smirk on the man's face, Evan understood right away that he'd been played. Just like with most grownups, this was all about power. *You need me, kid* was the message. *Without me, you've got nothing.*

"Yeah, well you need me, too," Evan mumbled aloud. He was done running. He kept his stride as casual as his trembling legs would allow as he closed the distance to the truck.

"Took you long enough," Mitch said with a mocking smile.

Evan said nothing as he headed for his door. As he passed within range, Mitch reached out for him, but Evan twisted out of the way. "Don't touch me," he said.

He was vaguely aware that both the driver and the shotgun guy were also out of the car, watching with amusement.

Mitch seemed startled by Evan's speed. He folded his arms again. "You don't learn so good, do you, kid?"

Evan said nothing.

"Now, you need to ask permission to get back into my truck."

Evan didn't fully understand the look in the guy's eyes. The way he kept shooting quick glances to the other men, he almost looked embarrassed.

Evan started for the door again, and again Mitch tried to grab his arm.

"Don't *fucking* touch me!" Evan shrieked. The fierceness of his tone startled the henchmen.

"Don't *fucking* tell me what to do!" Mitch shouted back. "Now, either you ask permission to get back into that vehicle—either you show some respect—or I swear to God I'll leave you out here to die."

Evan had never felt his heart hammer so hard. In the past, on the few occasions when he'd found himself in this kind of blustering power play, the worst that would come from the ensuing fight might be a busted nose or a loosened tooth. Here, the penalty for being wrong was the biggest one there was.

But the rules don't change with the size of the bully. You can't ever afford to show weakness. What was it that Father Dom always said? *Victory can be claimed, but surrender has to be offered.* To Evan, it was a fancy way of saying, *Die trying.*

"*You* kidnapped *me*, remember?" Evan shouted. "You can't let me die."

This time, as he walked toward the car door, he noticed that the henchmen seemed amused, even as Mitch clearly could think of nothing to say.

Evan planted himself back in his seat, closed the door, and fastened his seat belt.

* * *

Apparently, in the world of killers and spies, it was never allowable to meet in the same place twice, at least not within too short a time. Thus, the food court at Pentagon City was out, and Founders Park in Old Town Alexandria was in.

If Jerry Sjogren had had his way, they would have met in an underground parking garage à la *All the President's Men*, but Brandy Giddings had aborted that idea before it could even take a breath. If she was going to be killed by some whack job, she wanted the murder to be witnessed by as many people as possible.

She'd followed Sjogren's orders to the tee. Metro from the Pentagon to the Braddock Road Station, and then two taxis just in case: the first one to Reagan National Airport and then a second to the Torpedo Factory—a trendy artists' colony located in a building on the Potomac River that had in fact manufactured torpedoes through the end of World War II. From there, it was an easy stroll to the park.

Brandy had promised herself that Sjogren would be the one made to wait this time; yet even though she arrived ten minutes late, the man was nowhere to be seen. She considered the possibility that her tardiness had pissed him off and he'd left, but then she remembered that this was his meeting, not hers.

She randomly chose an empty bench and waited to be found.

She never heard him approaching from behind.

"We playing power games now, Missy?" Sjogren boomed from a few feet away on her blind side.

"Jesus!"

Sjogren walked around to her side of the bench and sat next to her. "Being late never gives you the upper hand," he scolded. "Just so you know. I've been here for forty-five minutes. I can tell you everything about everyone we can see, and I watched you arrive. You looked right at me, you know."

She'd had no idea.

"They call it tradecraft, and if you're going to play these spooky kinds of games, you'd do well to learn some of it."

She looked away, stung by the rebuke. It was a little like disappointing your grandfather. Your burly homicidal grandfather.

"Besides, it's rude to keep people waiting," he said.

"I'll keep it all in mind for the future," Brandy said, struggling to recover face. "I thought you were supposed to be hunting for a homeless guy."

"In due time. But first I thought you should know that things have gone even further to hell since last time we spoke."

The familiar fist returned to Brandy's stomach. She didn't realize that it was possible to sink farther than dead bottom.

"A private investigator visited Frank Schuler today," Sjogren went on. "They've connected the dots to Sammy Bell's organization, and they know that Bruce Navarro is involved." He recounted the details of the conversation he'd heard in the digital audio file he'd received from a contact in the Virginia Department of Corrections.

Indeed, the bottom was only the beginning. "This is unbelievable," Brandy said. "We go through all of this, only to be taken down by some Lincoln Rhyme wannabe?"

Sjogren clearly understood the reference to the star of Jeffery Deaver's novels. "I don't believe I used the phrase, 'taken down,'" he said. "I'm just reporting facts as I know them."

He reached into his shirt pocket and produced a folded piece of paper. "I have a research project for you," he said, handing it to Brandy. "Give me everything you can dig up on this guy."

Brandy read the name. "Who is Jonathan Grave? Is this the investigator who visited Schuler?"

Sjogren shook his head. "No. That was a lady named Gail Bonneville, an up-and-comer in the Indiana Democratic Party until a shoot-out caused her to resign as sheriff in a little town called Samson. She left that gig to join on with that guy Grave."

Brandy tried to give back the piece of paper. "Find out for yourself," she said. "You seem to be doing just fine on your own."

Sjogren let the note hover between them. "Not this guy," he said. "I can tell you that he grew up as Jonathan Grave-now in Fisherman's Cove, and I can tell you that he runs a company called Security Solutions, which in turn employs Ms. Bonneville."

He paused, and when Brandy tried to repeat her sugges-tion, he raised his hand for silence.

"I know that he joined the Army," he continued, "some-time after changing his name from Gravenow to Grave. His father is Simon Gravenow, a mobster now pulling a life stretch in federal prison."

Another pause. "Sounds like you're doing just fine," Brandy said. "I don't want to have anything to do with this. Our office cannot be linked in any way to—"

"Yours is the only office that can do it," Sjogren inter-rupted. "After he entered the Army, he disappeared. I've got him through basic training and Ranger school, but then he's gone. Nothing. Then I find out that he doesn't even have a set of fingerprints on file. Call me crazy, but that sounds like a guy who learned special enough skills in the military that Uncle Sam made him invisible."

Brandy chose to say nothing.

"That means, Missy, that your office is the *only* one that can do the research I need done."

Brandy understood the implications—that this Grave guy was some kind of a spook—but she didn't understand the ur-gency. "I can't do this sort of data mining on my own," she said. "I'll have to involve others. It seems to me that the risks posed by expanding the universe of knowledgeable parties outstrips the benefit of gaining a couple more data points."

Sjogren's face morphed to a patronizing sneer. "Please

tell me you're faking right now. Tell me that you're not really that dense."

Brandy felt heat in her cheeks.

"We're talking about a man with ties to the mob who also has commando training. On the day when two of my best men disappear, an associate of G.I. Joe goes right to the heart of everything in a Virginia prison. Given all of that, you only see data points? Again, please tell me you're faking."

Now I wish I was, she thought.

CHAPTER TWENTY

It was hard for Harvey Rodriguez not to feel at least a little like a prisoner. With his beard shaved and his hair cut—courtesy of a hot black chick named Venice, who turned out to know her way around a pair of clippers—all it took was a hot shower and a change of clothes to make Harvey feel and look like a new man. Officially, he was free to come and go as he pleased, but it's hard to wander around in the open when people you don't know are looking to kill you.

Still, he needed fresh air. Blame it on the hundred bucks Jonathan gave him. With no bills to pay and a guaranteed roof over his head—in a *mansion*, no less—cash in his pocket meant beer in his belly. The way he saw it, dying with a couple of Coronas on board had to be better than dying parched.

Jimmy's Tavern sat on the water, three blocks downhill from the mansion. At 8:30 in the evening, the parking lot was three-quarters full, a surefire sign of the kind of place where Harvey could enjoy killing some brain cells.

His expectations dimmed, however, as he closed within a few dozen yards of the place and noticed that the pull hardware on the doors was fashioned in the form of fish—a yin and a yang, one sniffing the other's ass as they swam counter-clockwise.

He grabbed the fish belly on the right and pulled, hoping to be greeted by the aroma of booze and stale cigars, but instead was assaulted by the stench of chicken fingers and French fries. He missed real bars. This family-fare shit was for the birds.

If you ignored the left-hand side of the building, where a forest of empty tables awaited the dinner crowd, the smaller right-hand side featured a bar fashioned from pine planking and old seafaring barrels of grog. He knew the barrels were supposed to be grog, because the word was stenciled on every other one. The alternating barrels bore the mark of the ass-sniffing fish from the front door along with the word JIMMY'S stenciled in the open circle.

You never judge a bar by its bar, though; you judge it by the number and diversity of bottles stacked against the back mirror, and by the forest of beer taps. Measuring by that yardstick, this place was just fine.

The kid behind the bar didn't look old enough to be serving liquor. "Welcome to Jimmy's," the kid said, sliding a cardboard coaster at him. More of the damn fish. "What can I get you?"

The tap handles advertised an embarrassment of riches. With a hundred unearned bucks in his pocket, he ignored the cheap domestics that he'd normally order and went for a Harp Lager. Three or four of those and he'd be feeling a lot like a leprechaun.

The kid placed a heady pint onto the coaster and extended his hand. "I'm Chris," he said.

"Harvey." They shook hands.

"No kiddin'?" Chris said with a chuckle. "You missed a friend of yours by about ten minutes."

Harvey recoiled, instantly pissed at himself for giving up his name so easily.

"A big guy," Chris expounded. "Gray hair, mustache.

Boston accent." He mocked the word as *Bahston*. "He didn't leave a name, but he asked me to keep an eye out for you. Ring any bells?"

Absolutely. Big guy he'd never heard of. Sounds just like a guy sent to avenge two friends he didn't kill. "Not a clue," Harvey said. He took a pull on his beer, but now it tasted like piss. Maybe that was one of the thirty-four flavors of fear. "Did he say *why* he was looking for me?"

"Something about being an old Army buddy."

A wiry guy two seats down wearing denim on denim and sporting a close-cropped goatee piped in, "Said you were a war hero." The unspoken rule of neighborhood bars everywhere: Any conversation with the bartender is open for group participation.

"That's right," Chris confirmed, his face brightening with recognition. "He said that he found some medals that belonged to you. I don't know, in a basement or something. Said he wanted to get them back to you."

New flavor: acid. The next mouthful almost made him gag. He kept his Navy Cross and Distinguished Service Medal in their original cases, hidden in a hole he'd dug under his tent. He fought the urge to bolt from his barstool and tear for the door.

"Now that I see you, though, that might be bullshit," said Denim. "He must be twenty years older than you. I have a hard time seeing you two serving in the same unit. You might want to be careful."

Harvey eyed the denim guy carefully, then shrugged it off. He wanted this conversation to end.

"I think we all need to be careful," Chris said, absently wiping the bar top even though it didn't need it. "That stuff at Resurrection House the other day. I don't like stuff like that happening around here. If little kids aren't safe, then nobody's safe, know what I mean?" He shook his head sadly, and then seemed to realize he was bringing the mood down, so he became a little too cheerful. "So, where are y'all from?"

Harvey's gut jumped again. He'd assumed that Denim was a regular.

"I'm from everywhere," Denim said. "I'm willing to hang my hat wherever I can find work."

"Oh yeah?" Chris said, clearly intrigued by the prospect. "What kind of work do you do?"

Denim shrugged. "None, right now. I'm sort of looking around."

Was Harvey imagining things, or was this guy glaring at him as he spoke? One of the problems with being a diagnosed paranoid is that you never know when the paranoia is justified.

"For what?" Chris pressed. "What's your specialty?"

"I was in the weapons business for a long time," Denim said. "But this new outbreak of peace is killing me."

Chris laughed, but Harvey's hand started to shake. Weapons business. New in town. Happened to be here right at this moment. Coincidence or strategy?

"And you, Harvey?" Chris asked. "Where do you come from? What do you do?"

He knew the kid was just trying to be friendly, but Harvey wanted to shove a wad of napkins in his mouth. He should have prepared an answer for this. "I used to work for a charter fishing company," he lied. "I got laid off, though."

Chris looked concerned. "Which one? I didn't know charters were laying off."

"In Georgia," Harvey clarified. He had no idea why he'd just said that. He'd never even *been* to Georgia. "Out of Savannah." *Please, God, let Savannah be on the coast.*

"Well, that's a great line to be in around here if you're any good at it," Chris said. "Where are you staying?"

Jesus Christ, did he not have an off switch? "With friends."

The kid's smile brightened even more. "Anybody I know?"

Harvey opened his mouth to say something, but no words

formed. His library of lies had just checked out its last edition. He found himself staring.

"Give the guy a break," Denim said. "He just found out
that a stranger is looking for him, and you keep leaning on
him for information. Would you want to be answering your
questions if you were him?"

A lightbulb went on over Chris's head. Almost literally.
"Oh, jeeze, I'm sorry. I didn't mean to push too hard. I was
just—"

Harvey waved him off. "Don't worry about it," he said.

"Sure looked spooked, though," Denim said. He toasted
him with what looked to be a pint of Coca-Cola.

Harvey forced a smile, and tried to devise an exit strategy.
Denim worried him. Assuming he was a bad guy, Harvey
would be foolish to leave a public place. The guy would only
have to follow him, wait for the right moment, and then do
whatever he came to do. On the other hand, waiting would
guarantee a meeting with the big Bostonian.

Even if Harvey did leave, where would he go? He wasn't
the most selfless guy in the world, but there's no way he
could lead killers back to the mansion.

When you've got no good options, all you can do is hope
to choose the least shitty one. In this case, it meant finishing
his Harp and getting out of here. He waited a couple of minutes after he drained the pint to ask for the check. While
Chris rang the order, Denim defused everything by dismissing himself from his stool and heading to the men's room.

"I hope our friend isn't stepping out on his bill," Harvey
quipped as he slipped a twenty into the little plastic folder
embossed with yet another set of ass-kissing fish.

Chris smiled and shook his head. "Nah, he looks honest
to me." As he cashed out the change he added, "Sure you
don't want to stick around for your friend?"

Harvey spun himself off the stool. "Chris, I gotta tell you.
I don't know anybody who fits the description you gave, and

I've never won any medals. If he comes back, feel free to forget you ever saw me." He eyed the cash in Chris's hand. "Keep the change."

The kid's eyes saucered at the three hundred percent tip. "Forget I saw who?"

CHAPTER TWENTY-ONE

Jonathan settled into his chair at the head of the conference table in the War Room and gave the floor to Venice. Behind her, at the far end of the room, Evan Guinn's face continued to watch them from the projection screen. It disappeared only when she began to speak, replaced by the face of a man in his mid-forties, shot at an oblique angle, clearly through a telephoto lens.

"This is Mitchell Ponder," she began. "Of the few pictures of him that are available in any of the databases we can access, this is both the most recent and the most identifiable."

Identifiable was a relative term, Jonathan thought. Sure, the guy had features—he had a nose and a mouth and a set of eyes just like everyone else, but nothing about him truly stood out as unusual, which meant that even the best facial recognition software would be only marginally useful.

Venice clicked the remote control in her hand, and the image on the screen changed to a much younger version of the same plain vanilla face, but this time accompanied by a complete set of fingerprints. "This is his Army induction photo from twenty years ago," she explained. "His service record is unremarkable. In and out in six years with an honorable discharge as an E-5."

Jonathan recognized E-5 as the Army's rate of sergeant. To achieve a third chevron in six years was admirable, but nothing special.

"The big break," Venice went on, "is the set of prints. Since we know who we're looking for, and we know where to look for him, I was able to trace him down." She clicked again, and brought up a picture that could have been snapped at any immigration counter at any airport in the world. Obviously shot by a security camera, the photo showed the same man as the other pictures—Mitch Ponder. "Because the Colombians are still pissed at us for our hundred years of meddling, they require fingerprints of any American, Brit, or Frenchman coming in and out of the country." The time stamp on the photo showed he'd been in country for just over eighteen hours. "He's traveling under the name Robert Zambrano. I don't know if there's significance to the alias."

"Who else arrived on the same flight?" Jonathan asked.

"Too many to help us," Venice said. "He came in on a commercial flight from Houston with about a hundred of his closest friends."

"Houston?" Boxers asked. "Not Dulles, which would have been much closer." He looked to Jonathan. "I guess they took their collapsible chopper to a private airport somewhere and then took a private jet to Houston? Why not just fly him to Colombia?"

Venice explained, "The Colombian government pays very close attention to incoming civil aviation traffic. And the U.S. government pays even closer attention to outbound civil aviation traffic."

"But why Houston?" Jonathan wondered aloud. "Of all the outbound connections, why there? Were there any children who look like our boy?"

Venice shook her head. "I've done an initial run-through of faces and didn't see anything that even came close."

"So where could he be?" Boxers asked.

"Assuming he was on the plane, there's only one other place I can think of," Venice said. "In with the luggage."

Gail sat forward. "Wouldn't he suffocate?"

"I thought the same thing," Venice said. "But the research says no. I'd never really thought about this before, but they have to keep cargo holds pressurized now because of people transporting pets and such. With the pressure, there's plenty of oxygen to survive and temperature controls to keep you from freezing to death. I verified this on the Internet. But the key . . ." She paused for dramatic effect, hoping the Jonathan would complete her thought for her.

"Ven, please. You know I hate this game."

"The key is to properly sedate the passenger you pack."

Now he saw it. "Jeremy Schuler was sedated, too."

Venice licked her finger and affixed a gold star to the air. "Bingo." She pressed her remote and revealed a sea of luggage being managed by uniformed airline personnel. "It turns out that the El Dorado Airport in Bogotá has high-end security in their baggage claim."

"But clearly not on their firewall," Jonathan quipped. "You never cease to amaze me with this stuff."

She gave a coy grin. "Oh, I'm just getting started. So, at the airport, every bit of luggage is tracked as a function of the passenger who carried it. Since we have fingerprints, we also have a ticket number. With the ticket number, we can know exactly what our guy was carrying on his direct flight from Washington."

She clicked again, and the screen filled with images of an unremarkable black nylon suitcase and an oversize hard-sided case that was double-sealed with a wrap-around strap. "Take a look at the big one," she said, "because I believe that it contains Evan Guinn. Notice the orange tag warning that it's overweight."

"I don't buy it," Boxers said. "It's too risky. TSA opens half the bags that get loaded onto a flight."

Venice clicked again. The screen displayed a close-up of

a TSA clearance tag. "I thought the same thing, so I enhanced this image and got lucky. I cross-referenced the number to the tracking database, and wouldn't you know it? There's no record of this particular piece of luggage being processed through TSA's Houston operation. It is a Houston tag, but it was cleared outside of normal channels."

Jonathan continued to be amazed, but right now he was confused. "Read between the lines for me, Ven. What are you telling us?"

"This is the same sort of thing that the government does when they transport items that they don't want to be opened in transit," she explained. "It looks to me like these skids are definitely being greased at a high level. I figure the guy with the grease gun must be in Houston."

Jonathan thought she was right. "I hope you're going to tell me where that big bag ended up."

Another smirk. Jonathan had learned over the years that this bit of theater was as important to Venice as the information she got to dig up. She pressed the button again.

Now they saw a still picture of Mitch Ponder at an airport luggage carousel, pulling the heavy bag off the turntable. "Prepare to be impressed," Venice said as she clicked through photo after photo. Each showed a still image, yet as she scrolled through, the photos left the impression of a movie on Jonathan's mind.

Together, they watched as Mitch Ponder left the terminal and wheeled his luggage to what Jonathan assumed was the Colombian version of short-term parking. "Notice how careful he is on the curbs," Venice said. She was right. Although for the life of him, Jonathan couldn't imagine how a bump on a curb could do anything to wake up a child that manhandling by baggage claim attendants hadn't done already.

The farther Ponder moved out into the parking lot, the wider and higher the angle became in the security camera photos, but they could easily make out the images of him wheeling the bags to a dark-colored SUV. The distances didn't allow for detailed viewing, but from the way Ponder squatted at the rear wheel well on the driver's side, Jonathan figured he had to be searching for a key. If so, he found it, because he stood again and loaded the bags into the rear compartment. From there, he backed out of his space and drove out of the frame.

"I thought for a second that we were going to lose him," Venice said, articulating Jonathan's thoughts. "But we lucked out." The image shifted again, this time to a split screen. On the left, they saw a head-on shot of the driver, unfortunately distorted by glare in the windshield, and on the right was an even more valuable prize.

"Holy shit," Boxers exclaimed. "Is that his license plate?"

Venice beamed. "The Holy Grail. Unless he changes it— and why would he?—we can use that number to track him through any number of databases. With any luck at all, he'll get pulled over for speeding or something."

"And if he doesn't?" Jonathan asked.

"Well, there's a little more," she said. She scrolled through a few more photos showing the SUV passing through various traffic cameras at intersections. "The complexity of their surveillance surprises me," Venice said.

"They're officially trying to beat down their drug industry," Jonathan said. "It's costing billions of dollars and thousands of lives, but—wink, wink, surprise, surprise—it continues to thrive. I'll bet you a thousand bucks that U.S. aid paid for that surveillance system."

Venice acknowledged him with a nod, but clearly she'd moved on in her mind. "These last two or three shots just show him driving into the jungles north of the city," she said. "I wish I had more."

"That's a lot," Jonathan said. "We know that Evan is alive—at least that Ponder thought he was. And we've got a positive means to identify his vehicle. Compared to other square-one intelligence data we've had, we're in a pretty good place." He turned to Boxers. "We need to get this info to Josie so he can start bribing the right people."

Boxers' expression showed disbelief. "I don't believe you're going to trust that son of a bitch again."

Jonathan recoiled. "Why shouldn't we? What did he do?"

"It wasn't what he did," Boxers said. "It's what he didn't do."

Jonathan rolled his eyes. "Don't dig all that up again. He was in self-preservation mode. He did what he thought was best."

"Since when did doing what's best involve throwing your ass under the bus?"

Venice cocked her head. "What are you talking about?"

"Nothing," Jonathan said.

"Fine. Have it your way. I just always promised myself that the next time I saw that son of a bitch I'd be pulling his liver out through his nose."

"Oh, now that's pleasant," Gail groaned.

"I've given Josie a list of what we need," Jonathan said, moving on. "He's going to meet us in the boonies at what he said will make a good base camp."

"You gave him the list of acceptable aircraft?" Boxers prompted.

"We'll exfil in a private jet, but only after a long hike and a car ride."

"No chopper, then?"

"No stealthy LZs," Jonathan said. "We can't afford to make noise."

"How do we get in?" Boxers asked.

"Commercial. Just like Ponder. The Colombian government is quick to shoot down anything these days."

"What about visas?"

"I'm going in as David Grossman. I've got you as Richard Lerner." Both names came from the lengthy list of fully vetted and documented aliases that Jonathan had collected for them over the years. If things went well, the aliases could be recycled, but if not, they could just as easily be tossed.

"I wish we had a third," Boxers mused aloud. "It's doable with just the two of us, but another face you know you can trust is always a good thing." He looked to Gail.

"No," Jonathan said before he could ask. "Gail has a job to do."

"Bruce Navarro has a sister," Gail explained. "Apparently, I'm considered charming enough to squeeze information from her. We've got to find Bruce. We'll never know it's over if we don't know why it started."

Boxers moved back to addressing Jonathan. "What are we doing for manpower there?"

Jonathan cleared his throat. This was the hard part. "Josie promised to raise an army for us."

"I'm not talking about cokeheads and farmers in green suits, Dig. I mean skilled operators. Shooters who are more likely to hit a bad guy than a good guy."

Jonathan set his jaw against the rising flash of anger. "Time is short, Box. We're going to have to live with a few shortcuts. Josie said he'd try to use as many familiar faces as possible."

Boxers scoffed, "Oh, now *that* makes me feel better."

Jonathan slammed the table with his palm. "Stop!" Everyone jumped. "Box. Gail and Ven. Let's be clear we understand what we're doing here. Look at the screen." He pointed, but they continued to stare at him, startled. "Look at him, goddammit."

Their heads all pivoted to the projected image of Evan Guinn. His face seemed small under his thick helmet of white hair. His blue eyes blazed. "Evan Guinn was my responsibility," Jonathan said. "He continues to be my responsibility. If Ven is right—and Ven is *always* right—that boy has just been folded into luggage. Luggage, people. Like so much dirty underwear. We need to fix this." He wondered if his hands might be trembling.

Heavy silence devoured the room. Boxers dared to be the

one to speak. "Calm down, Dig. We're all on the same team. We'll get the job done. This isn't the first time we've rescued a kid."

His anger continued to burn. "It's never been one of my own," he said.

CHAPTER TWENTY-TWO

Harvey Rodriguez made his way along the boat launch docks that ran behind and below Jimmy's Tavern. He'd exited the front door, but rather than walk directly back to the mansion, he'd hooked a right to track along the water for a while. He figured he was far less likely to run into the mysterious Bostonian here than up on the street. He'd wander among the yachts for a block or two downstream, and then cut right and meander his way back to where he wanted to be.

About fifty feet into his plan, Denim stepped around the corner and cut off Harvey's path. "Hi, again," the man said. "We need to talk." He held a pistol in his right hand.

Harvey reacted with the speed of a reflex, spinning on his heels and taking off at a dead run in the opposite direction. It's amazing how quickly the brain can process thousands of bits of information when it's fueled by raw terror. Denim needed information, which meant that he needed Harvey alive, which meant that the gun was purely a bluff. He couldn't afford to fire anyway. Here along the water, the echo would roll for miles.

Still, the skin on Harvey's back itched at the point between his shoulder blades where the bullet would hit if it was fired.

As his feet pounded along the dock's wooden planks, he both heard and felt the drumbeat of his pursuer's strides, but they sounded slower than Harvey's, reflecting the thirty pounds that separated them.

Harvey dug deeper with each stride and quickened the rhythm. Back in high school, this was how he'd competed in track meets, and later, in the Marine Corps, this was how he'd finished in the top rankings of his training unit. But that was back when he was in shape.

If he was going to win this race, he'd have to do it in the next few seconds, before reality overcame adrenaline and he started to lose steam.

Ahead and to the left loomed the steps that led back to street level, but the stairs would require even more effort than running, and they would shave distance off whatever meager lead he'd opened up against his pursuer. Steps were out. Running wouldn't be an option for long.

That left only a swim.

Navigating only by moonlight and the wash of light from the buildings up along the street, Harvey turned right at the next slip. When he caught a glimpse of Denim in his peripheral vision, his heart jumped. Harvey's lead, such as it was, had closed to about ten feet.

"Stop, goddammit!" Denim commanded.

Harvey poured on more gas. He was still running full tilt when the wooden decking below his feet became only air, and he launched the best racing dive he could muster. He hit the water palms first, and when he realized that he hadn't drilled himself into the mud and broken his neck, he scissor kicked hard and dove deep, fully expecting to be tackled from above or shot through the water, which was astonishingly cold for July.

Apparently, Fisherman's Cove was blessed with a deep-draft marina. He never did find the bottom. Instead, he found a forest of pilings and spiderwebs of rope, which in the inky darkness felt predatory, threatening to grab him and hold him under until he drowned.

He had no idea how long he stayed underwater or how far he swam—it felt like three slips, but how could you know?—but when the urge for a new breath hit him, it hit him hard. Harvey kicked again and pulled hard with his arms. His lungs screamed for relief, and it occurred to him in his disorientation that he could just as easily be pulling himself deeper as rising to the surface.

The new rush of panic redoubled his need to breathe. Now.

He kicked and pulled again, but as he saw the surface rushing to meet him, he aborted the effort, sculling madly to slow his ascent. If he exploded out of the water, he'd surrender any advantage that this swim might have bought for him.

He slowed to an easy float, again sculling to rise as slowly as possible. Just a few inches from the surface he saw a white fiberglass hull through the murk, and he rose to meet it with his hands, then used its support to hand-walk to the surface. Of the whole ordeal, the final five inches were the worst. The pressure in his lungs and the panic in his mind screamed at him just to give up and give in. He refused.

He broke the surface vertically, crown of his head first, then his eyes, and finally his nose and mouth. He pursed his lips to keep from exhaling with a burst of noise, gulped a new lungful of air, then took in his surroundings.

He had, in fact, swum under two slips and past four ranks of moored boats—maybe a hundred feet, farther in the water than he'd been since basic training. He allowed himself a moment of pride.

But Denim was still out there somewhere, armed with a gun and a plan that Harvey wanted nothing to do with. He couldn't see him and he couldn't hear him, but he was definitely there.

So, what to do next? Staying right where he was appealed to him for the time being, but that was ultimately self-defeating. Silhouetted as he was against the white fiberglass, he was nowhere near as invisible as he needed to be. Sooner or later, Denim would see him, and then Harvey would have no choice but to become a victim.

Harvey needed to get to the street. He needed witnesses—a crowd that would make it impossible for Denim to hurt him. Down here on the water, isolation worked to the attacker's benefit. Up there, the tables turned.

His mind conjured a memory of the long staircase that led to the street. Moving with excruciating care to remain silent, he pressed his hands against the hull to guide himself through the water toward the aft end of the boat—he figured it to be a twenty-eight footer, a speedboat—away from the dock, but toward the swim deck that he believed to be standard equipment on boats this size. Hey, if you can't ski or go tubing off the back of a speedboat, what was the point of owning one?

He wasn't disappointed. Actually, it was more of a shelf than a deck, slats of imitation wood hovering no more than eight inches from the surface. He faced the trailing edge of the deck, wrapped his fist around the closest plank, and did his first chin-up in a very long while.

As he strained to raise high enough to hook the deck with his leg, he realized for the first time that the night tasted like oil. A half-roll more and he was completely out of the water, watching the sky.

He didn't move. He couldn't afford to move. As long as his pulse was the only discernable sound, he'd be vulnerable to anything. He counted to sixty, and then he counted to sixty again. After two minutes, he felt in control again. At least a little.

Measuring every motion, Harvey gently rolled from his back to his stomach and pushed up to his haunches, where he froze again to reassess. Except for the slapping of the moored boats and the occasional sound of laughter from Jimmy's up the street, all seemed silent. All seemed normal.

The way things always seemed to victims in the moments before an ambush.

Where had Denim gone? Harvey had expected to find him two slips over, peering over the side into the water, waiting for him to rise and give himself away, but now he realized that it wouldn't make sense. Whole minutes had passed since Harvey's headlong dive. The smart move for Denim would be to pull back to a place that allowed the best recon and allowed him to set up the ambush that Harvey had been dreading. But where?

Careful to move only his head, Harvey scanned the marina, looking for any anomaly that might give away the presence of his enemy. But he saw nothing.

And then he did.

As if reading Harvey's mind, Denim had taken a position in the middle of the very stairway that Harvey had planned to use as his escape route.

Harvey cursed under his breath. When hunting, you wait at the spot where your prey must sooner or later go. He was screwed.

"Stop it," he said aloud. It was just a whisper, but the sound of his own voice startled him. "Grow a pair, pussy." The phrase made him smile. It brought him back to a memory of Mike Brown, one of his closest friends over in The Sandbox. He could almost hear Mike speaking the words.

Yeah, grow a pair.

He lowered himself back below the level of the rear gunwale and copped a squat. *Okay, we know what's broken*, he thought. *What's working?*

One: Denim clearly didn't know where he was. As long as Harvey remained invisible, he continued to have options—even if he didn't yet know what they were.

Two: Denim had taken a defensive position, betting that Harvey would ultimately make a break for it. If Harvey waited him out, maybe time would make it all go away.

Three: Well, he couldn't think of a third.

Harvey rose again for another peek, just to make sure that the status still remained quo. Sure enough, his enemy hadn't moved. He was ready to wait—

A steadily burning red LED light caught Harvey's attention. He saw it through a window to the boat's cockpit, which itself was locked up tight.

"Well, I'll be damned," he whispered. The boat had a burglar alarm. And why not? Sitting out here unattended, probably for weeks at a time during the slow months, you'd want to have some deterrent to keep kids from breaking in, wouldn't you?

Kids and homeless guys named Harvey. "Consider the pair grown," he whispered, smile blooming.

He pulled himself over the gunwale, grabbed the rail, and rolled on his belly over the rail onto the padded bench, and from there onto the wooden deck. It was all noisier than he wanted it to be—noisy enough that he feared he'd alerted Denim to his presence. He didn't dare peek to see if he had.

Instead, he started kicking the door to the boat's cockpit. On the first blow, everything held strong. On the second, he heard something crack, and on the third, it all came apart.

Then the alarm went off.

Oh, my, the alarm.

CHAPTER TWENTY-THREE

Jonathan kept his stride slow and casual as he made his way up the hill to Fisherman's Cove Police Headquarters. From the snippet he'd received over the phone from Chief Doug Kramer, there was a big-game hunter on the loose in their little town, and Jonathan was likely on the endangered species list. He'd learned a long time ago that the slower you moved, the more aware you were of your surroundings.

As usual, his .45 rode high on his hip, concealed by the jacket he wore specifically for that purpose, despite the withering heat.

The police station was an unassuming place, built of brick and taking up an entire short city block. It sported two stories above ground for offices and various administrative functions, and five basement holding cells that at first glance looked like throwbacks to Inquisition torture chambers. Jonathan had visited the cells a few times over the years, and he often wondered if a night or two in there wasn't enough in itself to put the common street criminal on the straight and narrow.

He let himself in through the door to the street and smiled

to Rachel, the civilian clerk who'd been in the job for at least twenty years. She smiled back through the bulletproof window and buzzed him in through the inner door.

"Hi, Digger," Rachel said with a cheery wave as he crossed the threshold. "I haven't seen you in a long time." She pointed to the far left-hand corner. "Chief Kramer's in his office. He's waiting for you."

On a different day, the station would have been empty at this hour; but on the heels of the kidnapping, the place was hopping, with starched and pressed strangers mingling among the familiar locals. Jonathan figured they had to be FBI. A few of them looked up as he entered the space, but went back to work after assessing him to be a nonthreat.

Jonathan wove his way through the jumble of desks and chairs and rapped on Kramer's door. He let himself in without hearing the invitation to do so. Doug held his telephone to his ear with his shoulder, but beckoned Jonathan closer. As he cleared the door, Jonathan saw that Harvey Rodriguez was in the room, too, seated in one of the folding metal seats that served as guest chairs. His hands were cuffed, and his soaked clothes stuck to his skin, but aside from that, he looked to be as comfortable as conditions would allow.

"I'm impressed," Jonathan said. "It didn't take you long to get in trouble."

"Better in trouble than dead," Harvey said.

Doug hung up the phone and stood to greet Jonathan with a handshake. "So, you really do know him?"

"He's staying at the mansion," Jonathan explained. "And he's safe enough not to need the cuffs."

"His court records say otherwise," Doug said. "He's not supposed to be within two thousand feet of a children's gathering place."

"He's my guest," Jonathan said.

"Doesn't change anything."

"Is that why you have him in custody?"

Doug hesitated. "No."

Jonathan held out his hand, gesturing for the cuffs key. "Let's take the offenses one at a time, then, okay?"

Doug screwed up his face and cocked his head. "Since when do you have a soft spot for child molesters?"

Harvey inhaled at that, but he didn't say anything. This was exactly the scenario he had predicted.

"I don't have a soft spot for child molesters," Jonathan said. "Which is why I'd like you to trust me on this and give me the key."

Doug held Jonathan's gaze, then begrudgingly fished the tiny key out of his pocket and handed it across the desk.

Jonathan unfastened Harvey's hands, and handed the hardware back to the chief. "Thanks, Doug. So, why *is* he in custody?"

"Well, according to Harvey, somebody's trying to kill him. When he got cornered down on the marina, he says he broke into a boat specifically to sound the alarm and bring attention. That last part worked. One of our patrolmen happened to be less than a block away."

Jonathan shot an admiring look to Harvey. "Yeah?"

Harvey shrugged and rubbed his wrists.

"Good thinking," Jonathan said. "And the bad guy?"

"Poof," Doug said. "No sign of him."

"Tell him the rest," Harvey prompted. "Your guy saw my guy running away after the alarm sounded."

Doug confirmed with a shrug and a nod. "Absolutely true." He pointed to one of the other metal chairs. "Have a seat, Dig. I've learned over the years that shit like this doesn't happen in this town unless your DNA is on it somewhere. Tell Uncle Dougie what's going on."

Jonathan sat, crossed his legs, and tried his best to look relaxed as he scoured his mind for a way to skirt what he knew was coming. "Doug, you know we've been friends for a long time—"

The chief laughed. "Oh, God," he said. "When you start down the friendship road, nothing good ever follows."

Jonathan remained serious. "We've always had an understanding about my business. You don't ask much, and I don't offer much."

Doug turned serious, too. "That was before people started shooting the place up and kidnapping children. That was before I had reporters climbing up my ass twenty-four hours a day and the FBI camped out in my squad room. Funny how stuff changes."

"You have every reason to be upset," Jonathan said. "If I were in your position—"

Doug held up his hand. "Save it. I don't need to be patronized or commiserated with. I need information, and I believe that you have it. I love you like a brother, my friend, but don't think I won't throw your ass in jail for obstruction. If that happens, I don't know how I'll be able to stop the leaks to the press about your little sideline business. I don't know the details, but I know enough to make your life difficult. What I haven't figured out yet, I'm sure that the press could stitch together in time. So, tell me, Dig. How fast do you want the pitches to come in this game of hardball?"

Jonathan felt stunned. "You're *threatening* me?"

Doug threw his hands in the air in frustration. "What the hell else can I do? Look, I know you see Resurrection House as your pet project run by your pet charities, but the reality is, it's in *my* town, and that janitor in the hospital—Alvin Stewart—is a neighbor of *mine*. Now, I know you're not real keen on some of the laws of this land, but you've got to live by them just like everybody else. At a *minimum* you've got to share specialized information with the people who are paid to enforce them."

Harvey Rodriguez watched the two of them as if they were a tennis match, his head turning from one to the other.

"You don't want to know some of these details, Doug."

The chief slammed his hand down on the desk. "Don't *tell* me what I don't want to know. I'm a big boy, Digger. I'm smart enough to sift details."

Jonathan had never seen him like this. Of all the people
he'd known over the years, Doug Kramer had always been
among the most staid. It was unsettling to see him this far
out of control. But he had a point. The chief had a job to do,
and to the degree that his job involved protecting the children at Resurrection House, they should be in lockstep. As
he made up his mind what he was going to do, he could almost hear Boxers screaming in protest. The big guy always
worried that he played fast and loose with OpSec—opera-
tional security—and to tilt his hand to the chief of police,
even one who'd been a friend since childhood, crossed all
reasonable lines.

Jonathan sighed. "I'll share what I know, but not what I
suspect," he said, "but on the condition that you don't ask me
to reveal my sources. You'll either believe me or you won't,
but I won't discuss anything about how I came upon the details. Fair enough?"

Kramer showed nothing. "I guess we'll see."

Jonathan stacked the various elements in his mind, then
decided to drop the biggest bomb first. "Jeremy Schuler is
alive and well, and in hiding across the street in the mansion."

Doug looked like he'd been smacked. "Jesus, Digger. Do
you know—"

Jonathan cut him off. "I'm not going to be lectured,
Doug. Listen or don't listen, but don't make any speeches,
okay?"

He waited for the nod.

"We know that Evan Guinn was taken as leverage against
upcoming testimony from his father against the old Slater
crime family. That begged the question of why they took Jeremy Schuler, and we found out that he was to be murdered
outright. Our friend Harvey here was able to rescue him and
save his life."

Doug's face remained blank as he turned to look at his
former prisoner with renewed interest. Harvey smiled and
waved.

Jonathan continued. "It gets deeper. We have very good reason to believe that the mission to murder Jeremy was launched by someone in the government."

"Which government?"

"The one in Washington."

"Oh, for Christ's sake, Dig. Why—" He stopped himself and retreated from Jonathan's glare.

"Like I said, I'm only telling you what we *know* to be fact. Once we found out that important people were after the boy, we thought it best to hide him. We kept it a secret on the off chance that the bad guys don't know that they missed, and we didn't want the press telling everyone that there was still a viable target."

Doug sat back heavily in his chair and rubbed his forehead. "Jesus, Dig. Do you know how many people are out there looking for that boy?"

"I hope it's a cast of thousands and getting bigger by the minute. The more they're committed to finding him and his kidnappers, the less likely they'll find him across the street."

Doug stewed on that for a couple of seconds and then laughed. "Goddamn, you are a piece of work. So what's with the guys who are chasing you, Mr. Rodriguez?"

Harvey started with a deer-in-the-headlights stare, then deferred to Jonathan with an upturned palm. "He's doing just fine. I think I'll let him talk about that."

Jonathan squirmed in his chair and cleared his throat. "That gets close to revealing sources," he said. "I believe that the bad guys might be missing a couple of their companions."

"Missing?"

"Move on, Doug. We're not going there."

The chief conceded. What choice did he have? "So now I guess all you have to do is find the missing boy and bring him home." He'd meant it as a joke, but when he saw Jonathan's expression, the shock returned to his face. "Holy shit. You know where he is?"

Jonathan shrugged. "More or less," he said.

"Where?"

"I can't tell you."

"Goddammit, Digger—"

"Under orders from the FBI, I can't tell you."

That took the wind out of his sails. "Our FBI? The ones out in my squad room?"

"Our FBI, yes. But definitely *not* the ones in your squad room. I need you to keep all of this from them, Doug. Not a word. Lives depend on it. Including mine."

"That doesn't make any sense," Doug countered. "You want me to believe that the FBI is keeping secrets from itself?"

Jonathan said nothing. Doug could believe what he wanted to, but there'd be no more details from Jonathan on the information shared by Irene Rivers.

"So what the hell am I supposed to do?" Doug said. Exasperation had driven his voice an octave higher.

"He did tell you that you wouldn't want to know," Harvey said.

"You shut up," Doug snapped, aiming a forefinger at Harvey's nose.

"I can't tell you what to do," Jonathan said. "You're welcome to check in on Jeremy if it's important that you know for yourself that he's safe, but please remember that whoever wanted him dead in the first place probably still does."

"So you want *me* to obstruct justice in my own town, letting the Fibbies chase their tails while I know full well that it's a false mission."

"It seems harsh when you put it like that," Jonathan said.

"How is that going to make me look when the word finally leaks out?"

Jonathan felt a rush of disappointment. "Since when did you start worrying what people think of you? The Doug Kramer I grew up with worried only about doing the right thing."

The chief flushed. "You know what I mean."

"No, I don't think I do. When I talk about protecting the life of a child, you counter with protecting the legacy of your career. As if the two are remotely equivalent."

Doug laughed derisively. "Ah, the ambiguous moral code of Digger Grave, Lone Ranger, ever perched atop his personal pedestal. You must tell me one day what the world looks like from up there."

Jonathan couldn't believe what he was hearing. This was the same man who not too long ago offered to suborn murder in the name of justice. "Who am I talking to?" he asked.

Doug locked his jaw and glared through the back of Jonathan's head.

"Step outside, Harvey," Jonathan said.

"What?"

"Just wait in the squad room for a few minutes."

"With the FBI?" Jonathan might as well have asked him to set himself on fire.

"Don't say anything to anyone, and don't wander off. Just wait."

Harvey looked to Chief Kramer for an appeal, but Doug was studying a spot on his desk blotter.

"It won't be long," Jonathan promised. His tone found the perfect balance between request and demand.

Harvey left.

"Talk to me, Doug," Jonathan said. "What's happening?"

The chief continued to stare at his blotter, clearly intending to say nothing; but when the silence did not relent, he rocked his eyes up. Somehow, he'd aged ten years in two minutes. "Don't you get what an incident like this does to a town like ours?" he said. "Don't you get the collective loss of innocence? This isn't a war zone, Dig. Hell, it's not even a city—not really. In New York and DC the place gets shot up, and once the media gets past it, so does everyone else.

"It's not like that here. This kind of violence erodes the very heart of this town. There's no getting past it, because the way things used to be doesn't matter anymore."

Jonathan scowled. "But what—"

"Hush. Just listen. For once in your life, just listen. With all your running around these past couple of days, I don't suppose you've had a chance to read the newspapers, but maybe you ought to. There are a lot of harsh words being thrown around—chief among them the *I*-word. *Incompetent.* That would be me.

"I've dedicated my life to this little burg. While you were off touring the world and defending our freedom, I was busting my balls for nothing an hour, keeping Fisherman's Cove from caving in on itself. And you're right, I was never in it for the legacy, or even the praise. I'd have been perfectly happy to remain anonymous, but I'll be goddamned if I'm going to be judged as *incompetent.*"

A pause followed, during which Jonathan thought his friend had finished. He had not.

"I've been with you every step of the way on everything you've ever done, Dig. I know what a shit life you had as a kid, and I know what a good friend you are to everybody in this town. But there's got to be a limit to this secrecy shit. Your neighbors are in tears in their homes, praying for the safety of a boy who is already safe. It would mean everything for them to know that their prayers were working."

"And soon enough, they will," Jonathan said. He leaned forward and rested his forearms on the edge of the desk. "But not until his safety is guaranteed. Doug, when all this settles out, I fear that it's going to be much, much bigger than a simple kidnapping. There's violence coming, one way or the other, and until we really know what it's all about, we've got to keep the lid on."

Doug sighed deeply and stretched his neck muscles. "I know you're right," he said, his tone again soft and sane. "I don't like it, but I do know it. It's just not the way things are supposed to be."

Jonathan smiled, happy to see the return of the man he knew. "Nothing about any of this is the way it's supposed to be," he said. "I'll fix it, though."

"Do you really know where the Guinn boy is?"

"I think so. We're pretty sure we do."

"And you're going to go get him?"

Jonathan nodded. Ordinarily, he would not have responded to that question at all. But he owed Doug that much.

The conversation became awkward, as if they'd burned through all the available words.

"I'd tell you to be careful," Doug said, "but I know how much you hate that."

Jonathan did indeed hate it. In his line of work, careful people died young, just behind the foolish ones. Aggressive and smart won the day every time. "Are we done here?" he asked. He started to stand.

"Actually, no." Doug hadn't moved, and his expression remained stern.

Jonathan settled back into his seat and waited for it.

"Your friend Harvey. There's the not-small problem of his parole. I'm willing to forgive the violation because you vouched for him, but what am I going to do with him? I can't let him hang around. Your vouching for him doesn't take away the judgment against him. And since you're going away, even that is moot. He's got to go."

Jonathan hadn't anticipated this. "Even though people are looking to kill him."

The chief shrugged. "I could put him in protective custody."

"There's no way he'd tolerate that."

"I'm just presenting options. Turns out it's a damn short list."

Jonathan stewed on that. It was a good point, well-made. While he trusted Harvey to be the person he said he was, he had to confess that his opinion was more gut than fact. There were limits to what he could ask even from a friend as close as Doug Kramer.

He shrugged. "I've got to convince him to come along."

*   *   *

Harvey stopped dead in the foyer. "You're out of your mind."

"It's not as if you have a lot of options," Jonathan argued. He'd had Doug drive them back to the mansion just in case the guy in denim was still lurking in the shadows waiting to take a shot.

"How about living? I've always been partial to that one."

Jonathan laughed. "How's that working for you so far? You still haven't dried out from your dive to dodge a killer. Where are you going to dive next time?"

"Nowhere in Colombia, I can tell you that. I hated the desert, and that was a dry heat. You're talking fuckin' jungle."

Jonathan laughed. "The issue remains that you don't have a lot of options."

Harvey gaped, trying to think of something—anything— to toss out as an alternative to exposing himself to gunfire again. "Were you not listening when I told you about my PTSD? I'm crazy."

"Crazy's a continuum," Jonathan countered. "You've met my friend Boxers, so you know that. You handled yourself really well back there at the marina. That was good thinking. And young Jeremy is perfect evidence that your medic chops are still good. Add the fact that I could use an extra hand, and I think this is a good opportunity for you."

"Opportunity." Harvey tasted the word. Didn't like it. "Is that what you call it? An opportunity to do what, other than dying?"

"To regain your self-respect," Jonathan said.

Harvey blushed.

"I don't mean to presume," Jonathan continued, "but I've been watching you. You're nowhere near as crazy as you pretend to be. You've had some hard breaks, and you've been aggressively screwed by the system, but I think that even you see the difference in yourself over the past couple of days."

Harvey blushed redder. "Now you're a psychiatrist in addition to all of your other superhuman skills? Can you see through walls, too?"

"Scoff if you want," Jonathan pressed. "I'm just telling you that the way things have been for you doesn't have to be the way it is from now on. What are you going to do? Go back to your tent? How do you expect to watch your back at night? How do you really ever sleep again?"

"Because you killed those guys! Thanks a lot."

"No, no, no. Don't you lay that all on me. I was there, remember? You were the point on that spear. You *chose* to help Jeremy Schuler. You *chose* to nurse him back to health."

"What was I supposed to do? He was dying."

Jonathan cocked his head. "Are you going to tell me that you weren't tempted to just pull out and go the other way?"

Harvey looked at the floor.

"It shows that you made a choice," Jonathan pressed. "You could have walked away, but you didn't. You could have sold the boy out in the bar, but you didn't, and by remaining quiet you almost got yourself killed. Like it or not, that's heroic behavior. Somewhere out there, there's a drill sergeant who's damn proud."

Harvey wanted to argue. You could see it right there on the front of his face. His mouth worked to form words, but none flowed.

"Come on, Harvey," Jonathan said, moving to seal the deal. "When was the last time you got the opportunity to do something noble?"

He was close. So close. "Why me? There must be a hundred eager soldier wannabes who'd piss all over themselves for the opportunity to shoot up a jungle."

"Because I don't have time to recruit. And because once you walked into this thing, you got skin in the game. You're a native Spanish speaker, right?"

Harvey shrugged.

Jonathan tapped a point in the air. "I thought so. Deep down inside, you're thrilled to be involved."

Harvey smiled. "I am, am I? How deep down inside?"

"Actually, not deep at all."

They shook on it.

CHAPTER TWENTY-FOUR

Jersey City was nowhere near as terrible a place as Gail had thought it would be. Nestled up next to the Hudson River, with some of the best views possible of the Statue of Liberty, the rows of well-kept town houses and the forests of neat single-family bungalows reminded her of the working-class neighborhoods of Chicago that housed her youth.

Her GPS had taken her directly to Wilkinson Avenue—in fact right to the front door of the house she was looking for.

Gail climbed out of the rented Celica, closed the door, and scanned the neighborhood for trouble, just in case. Some habits were too ingrained ever to be broken. Outside the protection of her vehicle, the neighborhood looked less inviting. Perhaps it would have been a better idea to make this visit during the day. Tucking her purse under her arm, she walked over the curb and toward the rotting steps that led to Alice Navarro's house.

She'd paid calls like this a thousand times over her career as a cop and an FBI agent, but it had only been since working with Security Solutions that she'd been paying them solo. A badge bought the luxury of backup. In the private sector, the best you could count on was your weapon and the skill to use it. In her case, she carried two: a Glock in her purse, and a backup .38 snub nose strapped to her ankle. In New Jersey, the mere presence of either one could get her put away.

Better to be tried by twelve than carried by six. Clichés become clichés for a reason.

The Navarro house was every bit of seventy years old, its façade built of brick, including the pillars that supported the porch roof. The screen door was locked. She rapped with her middle knuckle on one of the glass panes that flanked the door.

Fifteen seconds passed before a shadowy hand parted the sheer curtain and the worried face of an old man appeared. "Who are you?" He shouted much louder than was necessary to be heard through the door.

"My name is Gail Bonneville," she replied. She tried to gauge her own tone to be loud enough to be heard, but not so loud as to involve the neighbors. "I'm here to speak with Alice Navarro."

"Why? What do you want?"

Both reasonable questions, she thought. "Can you open the door please, sir?" she asked. "It's an important matter."

"I don't open the door after dark," the man said.

"I understand, sir. But again, it's very—"

"That's the second time you called me sir. Are you a cop?"

Gail had to smile. "No sir, not anymore. But I used to be. I'm a private investigator now."

"What do you want?"

A set of curtains pulled away from the front window next door. "It's about Alice's brother, Bruce," she said.

Two locks turned, and the door flew open, quickly enough to make her gun hand twitch. He fixed her with a furious glare. "Step inside." He swung his body like a gate—like an extension of the door—and ushered Gail into the foyer.

The décor was old and boring. Dark wood flooring had worn yellow in the front hall. Dark wood molding outlined the staircase, and the large flowered pattern of the wallpaper reminded her of the eighties.

The living room sat to the left of the foyer, bathed blue in the light of the muted television. Cast in that flickering light, the woman Gail presumed to be Alice Navarro looked terribly pale.

"Do you have some kind of a badge or something I can see?" asked the man who had let her in as he pushed the door closed and locked it. He looked younger in real life than he had through the window. She pegged him to be around fifty-five. He wore the wife-beater sleeveless T-shirt that seemed to be the universal working-class lounging uniform, but his muscular arms made it look good on him.

Gail pulled a silver business-card case out of her pocket and opened it. The lid bore the official seal of the Samson, Indiana, Sheriff's Department—her only parting gift from her previous employer. She saw her host's eyes catch the emblem as she slid a card out of the slot and handed it over.

She offered her right hand as a greeting. "Gail Bonneville," she said.

He scowled to read the card as he shook her hand. "Ken Harper. Says here you're a 'lead investigator.' What the hell is that?"

He'd pronounced it as "led"—like the metal. She corrected him. "It basically means that I have a senior position within our firm."

The woman from the living room materialized in the archway to the foyer. She, too, looked much younger in the full light, though during the day Gail was pretty sure she'd do something with the disheveled mop of brown hair on her head. She looked as if she'd been sleeping. "Did you say you have news about Bruce?" the woman asked.

"Are you Ms. Navarro?" Gail asked, proffering another business card.

"Mrs. Harper now," she said. "Call me Alice. Keep the card. One will do. No sense killing more trees than we have to."

Gail slid the case and its contents back into her pocket. "Can we please sit for a moment?"

"You're lucky you're inside," Ken said. "Don't push your luck. If you've got news about Bruce, just say it."

Gail winced as she tried to figure out how best to put it. "I didn't say that I *have* news, sir. I couldn't because I don't. I'm here to see if you can help me find him."

Ken's ears flushed. He reached for the doorknob. "That's it," he said, sliding the locks away. "Get out."

"But I—"

"Now."

He was clearly angry, but nowhere near to the point of violence. If Gail judged the expression correctly, he was embarrassed. She shot a pleading look to Alice. "It's to save a life," she said quickly. "A child's life."

They hesitated. Neither was sold yet, but she had a window, if she worked quickly. "I represent Resurrection House," she said. "That's a school down in Virginia, where—"

"The kidnapping," Alice said. "I heard about that on the news. An orphanage, right?"

Gail hemmed. "Well, no, actually, but it's okay to think of it that way. One of the kidnapped boys has ties to your brother."

The final lock turned. "No more of this," Ken said.

"No," Alice interrupted. "No, I want to hear what she has to say."

"Alice, no," Ken argued. "There's no good that can come of this."

"There's good if a child's life can be saved," Gail snapped. "With all respect, Mr. Harper—"

"Call him Ken," Alice said. "We like first names around here."

"With all respect, Ken, I've come a long way, and the stakes here are very high. Would a few minutes really kill you?"

Ken seemed startled by the outburst, maybe even slightly amused. "Funny you mention killing," he grumbled.

Gail's warning radar pinged. "What do you mean?"

"He doesn't mean anything," Alice said. She pushed herself away from the wall of the archway and gestured toward the dark living room. "Come on in. Have a seat. The place is a bit of a mess, but we weren't expecting visitors." She reached under the shade of a floor lamp and turned a switch, launching a pale yellow glow.

"Bit of a mess" didn't touch it. Apparently Ken and Alice were collectors. Every horizontal surface was covered with trinkets and knickknacks. Little people and little houses and little glass fish and little porcelain horses. Little everything. Hundreds of them. Maybe thousands. If you wanted a place to rest a drink, you were just plain out of luck. Then there was the floor. Stacks of glossy magazines lay positioned throughout the small room, all of them carefully and tightly bound by bright white twine. The one closest to the chair where Alice had been sitting actually had a drink glass sitting on top of it, proving in a glance that you weren't plain out of luck after all. For all the clutter, though, there seemed to be some underlying order to it.

Gail knew without asking that the other chair, separated from Alice's by a table dedicated to porcelain cats, was Ken's so she didn't bother to veer in that direction. She assumed that she was their first guest in a very long time. There was no place for her to sit.

"Guests get the chair," Ken said, pointing with an open hand to blue La-Z-Boy. The tone was one of resignation.

"No, I couldn't," Gail said.

"Sure you could," Alice said, settling back into her spot. She produced a remote from the seat cushion and put it on the table.

"But what about Ken?"

"Ken's perfectly comfortable on the *New Yorker*," Ken said, dragging the three-foot bound stack a little closer to the chairs. When he saw that Gail was still standing, he pointed with his chin. "Seriously, sit. Say what you got to say and let us get on with our lives."

"Ken!"

He rolled his eyes at his wife's scolding tone.

Alice said, "How can we help you, Ms. . . ."

"Gail. First names are fine with me, too."

Alice smiled. Perhaps that had been a test.

"Do the names Frank Schuler or Jeremy Schuler mean anything to you?"

"Are they the boys who were kidnapped? The ones in danger?"

"One of them is. Jeremy. Frank is his father. He's in prison now for killing his wife, Marilyn, who worked for your brother."

"Who once worked with a person who dated a girl who cleaned Kevin Bacon's windshield," Ken scoffed. "This has no relevance to us at all."

He was starting to piss Gail off. Every time she got close to starting a useful conversation, he was stepping in to derail it. "Ken, if you could just—"

He shot up his hand for silence. "Don't even think about lecturing me," he said. "If you've done your research, then you know all the shit that man has put us through over the years. We've had mobsters threaten us, and we've had FBI agents threaten us about not telling them about the mobsters. Look, we know he took a lot of money, and we know that he's probably living the high life somewhere, but that's neither our business nor our problem. So whatever platitudes you're about to drool out of your mouth, let me tell you loud and clear that I don't give a shit."

Gail stared as she stalled for time. She'd just learned new information, and she didn't know how to play it. She decided to try full disclosure. "What money?" she said.

Ken scowled, shot a look at Alice, and then came back to Gail. "Bullshit," he said.

"Excuse me?"

"I said bullshit. You're going to tell me you don't know about the money?"

Gail shrugged. "I guess I am, because I don't."

Another glance to Alice, and this time, Gail followed him. "I don't know anything about money, Alice. All I know is that Marilyn Schuler worked with your brother."

Alice wasn't buying. "Why does that matter? I'm sure she worked with a lot of people. She probably had good friends and brothers and sisters. Why come to us? Why is my brother more important than the others?"

"Because your brother was an attorney for crooks and murderers," Gail said. Her inner police officer had bloomed, and she was tired of walking carefully. "Given the brazenness of the kidnapping, it wasn't that big of a stretch to think that the mob connection might be relevant."

"I had nothing to do with that nonsense," Alice said, appropriately defensive. "Neither one of us did."

"I'm not suggesting you did," Gail assured. "But I'm hoping that you can help me find your brother."

"You and everybody else with a cause or an empty wallet," Ken grumped.

Gail took a deep breath. Settled herself. "Look, I'm sorry if I came on too strong, but a little boy's life hangs in the balance here." She dug into her pocket and found the picture she'd planted there in anticipation of a moment like this. Jeremy Schuler's smile carried an all-American wholesomeness that would melt anyone's heart. "I think your brother has important information that will help us identify the people who kidnapped this child."

"It's not our responsibility to protect the world," Ken said.

"He's only thirteen," Gail said. She turned in her chair to face Alice, betting that a maternal instinct burned inside every woman. "If you have any clue where your brother might be . . ." There was no need to complete the sentence.

"Don't say a word, Alice," Ken warned. "This could very well be a trick. How many times have they tried this in how many ways? If anyone so much as thinks that we know anything about Bruce—and I'm not saying we do—we'll never be left alone. If the feds don't put us in jail, those mob assholes will put us in graves."

Gail raised a hand this time. "Why would they do that?" she asked. "What am I missing here? Is this about the money you were talking about?"

"Do you really not know?" Alice asked.

"Alice, don't," Ken said.

"I really don't," Gail said. "Things are happening so quickly now that I haven't had a chance to do the kind of research I need to. Eight hours ago, I was visiting Frank Schuler on death row in Virginia. He mentioned the connection with your brother, and a colleague was able to get me your address. I found a plane, and here I am. Please share with me what you know."

Ken leaned in closer. "Alice, you don't have to say anything. I still say this could be a trap."

Gail snapped, "Of course it could be a trap. I could have been an assassin with orders to kill you all. I could have been here with a surprise inheritance. There are any number of things that I *could* be, Ken. But the fact of the matter is I'm a former police officer and a former FBI agent, and right now I'm doing my best to save a little boy's life. You can believe whatever you want of that, but why don't you try—just try—to believe the truth and help me do my job?"

"You're not the first, you know," Alice said, her tone soft. She waved for Gail to put the picture of Jeremy away. "Everybody assumes we know where Bruce is, or if we don't, that we know where the money is, but it's been long enough that they're convinced that we're not lying."

Gail heaved an exasperated sigh. "What money? What was it for?"

"It was mob money," Alice explained. "Bruce was the middleman. That's what he did. There was a payment supposed to be made, but it never arrived. It was a lot of money—a couple hundred thousand dollars. He says he never got it, but he had to run because the mob would assume that he had, and they'd come after him."

Ken chimed in, "So instead, the asshole just runs away

anyway, confirming in their minds that he did exactly what they thought he did. The feds think it, too."

"What was the money for?" Gail asked.

"I don't know, and I don't want to know," Alice said. "I'm ashamed that he would have anything to do with such things."

"But you know where he is," Gail guessed.

"I don't."

"Then how do you know that he didn't, in fact, take the money? How do you know he was the middleman?"

Alice gaped.

Gail closed the noose: "You said, 'He says he never got it.' That means you've talked to him since he disappeared."

Ken growled, "Damn it, Alice, I told you that we never should have answered the door."

Alice looked stunned. Her mouth worked as if to speak, but she produced no words.

Gail moved to seal the deal. She leaned forward and put her hand on Alice's knee. The other woman jumped, but Gail kept her hand in place. "I swear to you that I am exactly who I say I am, and whatever you tell me will remain in the strictest confidence."

Gail thought she saw cracks in the wall. "Sooner or later, you have to trust *someone*. Everybody does. Given the stakes—a child's life—don't you think that this might be a good time to start?" As she invoked Jeremy Schuler yet again, her thoughts went back to the anguish in his father's face as he envisioned a scenario that was far worse than the reality, and she again fought a pang of conscience. Manipulating the truth to gain a greater truth was a part of her job to which she would never fully adjust.

Ken stood. "It's time for you to leave."

Gail kept her eyes on Alice. "You know what's the right thing to do. Just let yourself do it."

"Don't make me throw you out," Ken said.

That got her attention. Gail eyed the man with gentle

amusement. Ken, with all respect, if you lay a hand on me, I'll put your head right through one of these plaster-lathe walls. Please sit down." One thing about being a woman on the FBI's Hostage Rescue Team: you learned how not to get pushed around by people who were bigger than you. The only hyperbole in the threat was the part about sending his head *through* the wall. Chances are it would have gotten stuck somewhere in the middle.

Ken looked like he'd been smacked. He looked to Alice for backup, and when it didn't arrive, he turned to huff out of the room.

"Please stay with us," Gail said. Her tone made it clear that the word *please* only softened a stark command. "You're upset. I don't want to worry about you going to get a weapon and sneaking up on me."

He hesitated.

"I'm almost done," she promised. She gestured back to his pile of magazines.

He hesitated, and then he sat.

Gail turned to the woman on her right. "What do you say, Alice? Are you willing to share what you know?"

Alice's face was a mask of conflict, that mantle of troubling self-doubt that precedes every confession in every interview room in every police station in the world.

When she finally started talking, it turned out that she knew a lot.

CHAPTER TWENTY-FIVE

Brandy Giddings needed rest. Lack of sleep was part of it, but the kind of rest she needed went far beyond going horizontal and closing her eyes. She craved a few consecutive weeks—even a few consecutive minutes would be a nice start—when her mind could be free of the terrible things that had been polluting it these past few days. She found it all debilitating, and the fact that she felt that way made her feel inadequate—like she was failing the secretary.

She worked for the man who told the president how to fight wars. Violence was supposed to be a part of her psyche. She knew every military branch's chief of staff by name. She should be tougher than this.

Still, when the phone on her desk trilled, she jumped. The caller I.D. confirmed that it was Pat Bachelor, SecDef's executive assistant, and her stomach fell. She'd asked to be put onto Secretary Leger's schedule as soon as possible, but that had been three hours ago.

"Secretary Leger can see you now," Pat said. "But I warn you that he has tickets for the Kennedy Center tonight, so you'd best be quick." Washington was chock-a-block with official reporting chains and protocol-driven rules of propriety, but in the Pentagon, everyone knew that Pat Bachelor outranked everyone but the Secretary himself. She'd never actually ordered anyone into combat, but Brandy had no doubt she could pull it off if she tried.

The source of her power had nothing to do with her ties to Washington. Rather, her loyalty lay exclusively with Jacques Leger, whose assistant she had been since the invention of the wheel.

Pat didn't like Brandy much; if there'd been any doubt in the past, the leer she delivered as Brandy walked by her desk made it clear today. Brandy wrote it off as old-and-fat dismissing young-and-beautiful, but she could never say it out loud.

The lock on the heavy mahogany door buzzed as Brandy approached, and she stepped into Secretary Leger's elaborate ceremonial office. It was in here that medals were occasionally pinned, and reporters were occasionally feted, but the real inner sanctum was nestled on the far side of the ceremonial space. She knocked, and when the secretary's muffled voice told her to come in, she opened the door and stepped into what was regarded throughout Washington as one of the most beautiful offices in all of government.

Secretary Leger's office presented a commanding, unobstructed view of the Potomac River in the foreground, and the famous monuments of the nation's capital beyond. Intricate moldings inlaid the twelve-foot ceilings, and the walls displayed a collection of Copleys and Sargents from the National Gallery of Art.

Conspicuously absent from Leger's personal office, Brandy thought, was any significant homage to the armed services. Having never served himself, he'd said that he wasn't comfortable choosing favorites, and to include every branch would make the place look, in his words, "like a castle keep." Instead, he surrounded himself with landscapes and still lifes that brought him a sense of peace.

"What can I do for you, Ms. Brandy?" Leger asked, looking up from the work on his desk, but not rising to meet her.

Navigating her way across the carpet was like walking on a cloud. "Good evening, Mr. Secretary. It's, um, about that matter we've been discussing."

She though she saw the secretary's shoulders stiffen as he turned back to the work on his desk. "I trust that it has resolved itself?"

When he moved his eyes away, she stopped advancing on his desk. She clasped her hands in front like an errant schoolgirl and shook her head. "No, sir," she said. "There's actually been some more information." She paused, hoping that she might pique his interest enough to look up again. When he did not, she added, "We've found Bruce Navarro."

That did it. "*The Bruce Navarro? He of the nine-year disappearing act?*"

She came close enough to hover near the guest chairs in front of his desk, but knew better than to sit without an invitation. "Yes, sir, the very one."

He scowled, clearly trying to decide whether or not to believe her. Finally, he gestured to a chair with an open palm. "I'm all ears," he said.

You can't sit in the presence of that kind of power and not be jostled by the wave of awe that comes with it. Brandy was speaking one-on-one with one of the most recognizable faces in the world—a man who held one of the planet's most important positions. She took a deep breath to settle herself.

"I received notification several hours ago from a company called Triple-S—Special Surveillance Specialists. They said that a long-dormant listening station picked up key word combinations and kicked back into active mode. They monitored a lengthy conversation from an address in Jersey City, New Jersey." She opened a leather portfolio and handed him the twelve-page transcription of the conversation. "That's the address right there at the top of the page."

Leger shushed her with an abrupt wave of his hand, giving himself time to read through the document.

Brandy had only recently learned that "bugging" a residence or a business was a nuanced task. It had never occurred to her that a listening device could live forever. Of course, it would be impractical to have a live person perpetually on the other end, twenty-four-seven listening to every word, so instead, smart devices could be programmed to "listen" passively for a certain combination of words, and then awaken itself to active mode. She imagined in this case that "Bruce Navarro" was the key phrase, but she had no way of knowing that for certain.

"Well, I'll be damned," the secretary said, looking up from the report. "Who's the person on the other side of this conversation?"

"We don't know for sure. Apparently, introductions were finished before the device went active. I have to assume, though, that it's Gail Bonneville, the private investigator who visited Frank Schuler in prison. It doesn't appear as if they were friends."

Leger laughed. "Hardly. It looks like the husband was ready to throw her out on her ass." He glanced through the pages one more time with an expression of mild amusement. "All these years of stonewalling, and it all comes down to one stranger promising to save a life. I'll be damned."

"The level of knowledge shown by the visitor is concerning," Brandy said.

Leger's look of amusement continued. "Concerning," he repeated. "How about damned troubling? The population of knowledgeable parties is multiplying like rabbits." Something arrived in his face behind the amusement. Fear, maybe? His eyes bored through Brandy as he waved the sheaf of papers. "Who else knows about this?"

"From me? No one. Just you."

He continued to stare, gauging her. Then he started through the papers again.

"There's more, sir," she said.

"From the look on your face, I was guessing there might be." He continued to read.

"It's about the investigator, sir."

"The one who works for the company that somehow continues to get the better of us."

"Yes, sir."

Finally, his eyes rocked up to see her. "Despite the fact that we have access to some of the best talent in the world."

Brandy's stomach flipped. "I suppose so, sir." If she layered the "sirs" on thickly enough maybe he wouldn't explode in his chair.

Leger waited for it.

"Well, Mr. Secretary, at first we thought she was a nobody, you know? A retired sheriff from somewhere in the boonies of Indiana. Well, then we looked a little deeper and we found some disturbing facts. For example, she's retired FBI. And she was tangentially involved in that big terrorist raid last year in Pennsylvania. You know, the one that involved the chemical weapons?"

The secretary's shoulder sagged a little. He recovered quickly, but not in time for Brandy to miss it. "What does 'tangentially involved' mean? And we both know that that incident had nothing to do with terrorism."

Brandy felt herself blushing. "Yes, sir," she said. That incident had occurred during the early days of the transition between the past administration and the current one, and it had exposed the Department of Defense to huge embarrassment. "By tangentially involved, I mean that she was there at the farm in Pennsylvania. The original terrorist raid—excuse me, you know what I mean—happened in her jurisdiction."

Leger's face formed a giant question mark. "That's tangential? What does direct involvement look like in your world?"

Brandy pretended that she didn't hear. "Well, the firm she works for in Fisherman's Cove is solely owned by a man named Jonathan Grave, who himself is former Special Forces. Frankly, I was unable to obtain any records on him, which leads me to believe that whatever he did was very, very black."

Now Leger seemed stunned. "I'm the Secretary of Defense, for God's sake. What records are sealed from me?"

"Jonathan Grave's, apparently." She heard the bite in her tone, and on a different day it would have bothered her. But today, when Jacques Leger was being a certified asshole, she didn't much care. She continued, "When Gail Bonneville was with the FBI, she was part of the Hostage Rescue Team. There were some career difficulties along the way, and some job-hopping, but the fact that she landed at a company run by somebody who I assume was a Delta Force operator—or maybe something even blacker, although I don't know what that might be—raises some major flags with me."

Leger looked tolerant at best. "And what might those flags be?"

Brandy couldn't believe that the secretary hadn't already pulled ahead of her. "What do HRT and Delta have in common?" She actually waited for an answer, but only for a couple of seconds, before she realized that SecDef probably did not like being quizzed. "Hostage rescue," she said, answering her own question.

She waited for him to connect the dots, but when he didn't, she pressed harder. "The church that owns the school where Ponder's men snatched the children is literally next door to Jonathan Grave's home. He spent a career rescuing people, and Gail Bonneville now works for him. Isn't it obvious that they're planning to rescue the Guinn boy?"

As she watched Secretary Leger decode it for himself for the first time, she saw the physical burden consume him. He pushed some papers around on his desk, then cleared his throat. "My, but you *are* full of news, aren't you?" he said.

He thought for a moment. "Well, clearly we have some things to do," he said after clearing his throat again. "The Guinn boy is not our concern. We'll pass along what we know about him to the right people, and that will be the end of our involvement there. I want to concentrate on this Navarro business." He avoided eye contact as he said, "Talk to your friend from New England. Tell him he now has the green light to do whatever he needs to do, to whomever it needs to be done in order to eliminate Bruce Navarro and the investigator woman."

Brandy felt her skin go cold. "Eliminate, sir?"

A beat. Leger made a show of sitting up straight and crossing his arms. "That's not too big a word for you, is it, Brandy?"

She gaped back at him. No, there was nothing big about the word. The *word* was easy. It was the murders that came with it that were difficult to comprehend. She squirmed in her seat. "Sir, if you're talking about killing people . . ." She let her words trail off.

Leger laughed. "Oh, for God's sake, Brandy, grow up. This has been about killing from the very beginning. Welcome to the big leagues. Only at this level, we don't think of it as killing. We think of it as problem solving."

She felt sick to her stomach. First the child and now this. "I, uh, I don't think I can do that."

"Of course you can't. That's why I would never ask you to. I never *have* asked you to. We have people who do that for us. Tell our Boston friend what we need, and he'll take care of the rest. You never even have to mention the *K*-word, if you don't want."

Brandy felt somehow heavier as she sat there. Would this never end? She found herself nodding in agreement before she'd even thought it all the way through.

"Good," he said. "And on the other thing, I want you to be my messenger. Go home and pack for a warm climate."

"Sir?"

"Someone will contact you with the details in a couple of hours."

It felt as if she'd slept through a part of the movie of her own life. "I don't understand."

Leger gave her a little wave. Of course she didn't understand. "We're going to get you down to Colombia," he said.

Evan Guinn had fallen asleep in the back of the SUV, lulled by the never-ending bouncing and rolling along the trails that doubled for jungle roads. When the jostling stopped, he awoke, confused about where he was. The nap had allowed him to forget. Now reality returned.

They'd reached a small clearing, about a quarter of the size of a football field, where the trees had somehow been removed, leaving only a green ocean of low-growing ferns and bushes. A few bore flowers, but most did not. On a different day, it would have been beautiful. As it was, Evan was overrun with the sense that he was going to die out here and no one would ever find his body.

As a lump grew in his throat, he refused to let himself cry again. He'd already been a pussy for running after the car. And what had that gotten him? If this was where they were going to drop him off, it had bought him nothing. Maybe less than nothing.

"Stay here," Mitch commanded. Without waiting for an answer, he pulled open his door and stepped out. He crossed in front of the vehicle and strode to the center of the clearing, where he stopped. With his arms outstretched and his legs spread to shoulder width, he slowly pivoted 360 degrees, and then stopped.

"What's he doing?" Evan asked the driver. He craved someone talking to him, but he wasn't surprised when the driver remained silent. He probably didn't even understand.

After maybe thirty seconds had passed, the surrounding jungle squeezed out four dark-skinned men armed with rifles—Evan thought they were M16s based on what he'd seen on the History Channel. The men were dressed like soldiers:

camouflaged uniforms that hadn't been washed in a very long time, which, he thought, matched the appearance of the men wearing them. For a second, he thought they were going to shoot Mitch on the spot, but then they approached him.

As they got closer, three of the four men held back, while the fourth approached Mitch like an old friend.

Mitch and the other man chatted for a couple of minutes. They shared a laugh, and they shook hands again before walking together toward the SUV. Evan's heart jumped as his stomach cramped. They were coming for him. He crab walked to the far side of the backseat, adding space between him and the approaching kidnappers.

This was his last chance to get away. He turned to the left-side passenger door to pull the latch and yelled at the sight of another soldier standing on the other side. He had no idea where he'd come from.

Mitch and the other man were here now, and both back doors opened simultaneously, a stern-faced soldier on his left, and coldly smiling Mitch on his right.

"Don't even think about it, kid," Mitch said. "You've got a long hike ahead of you, and it'll be a lot harder with your hands tied. Make us do it, and we will. It's your call."

He had no choice. This was why it was better to fight to the death before being taken. After that first moment, all the options were shitty ones.

"Allow me to introduce myself," said the soldier that Mitch had been talking to. "My name is Oscar." He reached a hand into the car, and Evan recoiled, almost falling out the other door on the far side.

The soldier closest to him reached out to catch him, but it wasn't necessary.

"Why are you doing this?" Evan asked. He heard the whiny tone in his voice, but he couldn't help it.

Oscar's features softened. He didn't smile, but it was close. "I realize that this must be frightening for you," he said. "How could it not be? You go to bed one night, and then in so short a time, you're in so strange a place. I'm sorry that it had to happen this way."

"What *is* happening?"

"You're embarking on a new adventure," Oscar said. His eyes didn't frighten Evan as much as Mitch's did.

"I don't need a new adventure. I don't *want* a new adventure."

Oscar smiled gently. "I understand. Unfortunately, we don't always get to choose the events in our lives. You need to come with us, Evan. No one means to harm you. In fact, these guns are intended to protect you."

Evan looked to the soldier who'd tried to catch him. The soldier gave him that quick smile that adults always give to kids when they make eye contact. The one that was meant to say that they were not a threat. It was also the smile of every child molester. *Can you help me find my lost puppy?*

"We have a long way to go before dark, Evan," Oscar said. "We need to get moving."

His mind raced for a way to stall. "Where are we going?"

Oscar cocked his head. "Does it matter? One way or another, I have to deliver you. As my friend Mitchell here said, it will be so much easier if you come along easily." He let that sink in, then motioned with a flick of his fingers for Evan to join him. "Let's get started, shall we?" He stood to his full height, and pivoted to the side of the door, opening a corridor for Evan to step outside.

In the end, he had no choice. He scooted on his butt across the bench seat and out into the weeds. They stabbed at the soles of his feet and tickled his legs—not in a way that made you want to laugh, but in the way that made you want to take a shower.

"Good for you," Oscar said. "You chose well." He extended his hand again. "Let's make it official. I'm Oscar, and it's nice to meet you."

Evan stared at the hand for a few seconds, and then he took it. "Evan Guinn," he said. Oscar's palms were as rough and hard as granite. He stopped short of saying that it was nice to meet him.

Releasing Evan's hand, Oscar turned to Mitch. "We'll take good care of the boy," he said. "Rest assured."

Mitch clearly didn't care one way or the other. He climbed back into the truck. The last thing Evan heard before the door closed was, "Let's get the hell out of here."

As the truck's engine revved, Oscar gently pulled Evan out of the way. The SUV drove in a wide circle through the clearing to turn around, and then it was gone.

He was alone now with his new captors. Evan became aware of Oscar's rough hand on his bare shoulder.

"Try not to be afraid," the man said.

Evan fought to control his breathing, which had started to chug like a train as he fought back the tears.

"I promise that no one wants to hurt you. I know that there's been some of that in your past, but you'll find none of that here."

Evan scowled and looked up at the man. What did he know about his past?

"We know a lot about you, Evan. I am not in a position to explain these things to you, but it's very important to us that you remain safe. That can be difficult in this country, and that truly is why I am accompanied by these gentlemen with the guns."

Evan's vision blurred with tears, and he swiped them away. People who didn't mean harm didn't kidnap people.

"The man who just left," Oscar went on. "That was Mitchell Ponder. He is a very, very dangerous man. Now that he has left, I promise you that you are safe."

"But why am I here?" If he could just know that one thing, then maybe something would start to make sense. Just that one bit of information might make him relax. Just a little.

Oscar sighed and cocked his head. It was a look of genuine sympathy, Evan thought. "Tell you what," he said. "Let's start walking so that we don't waste any more daylight. I'll try to think of a way to tell you something without betraying the confidences that I have pledged to honor. I know it's not really the answer you're looking for, but will it make do for a while?"

Again, there was no choice. Evan nodded.

They walked in single file, with two of the armed soldiers in the front, followed by Oscar and then Evan. Three soldiers brought up the rear.

The jungle swallowed them all.

CHAPTER TWENTY-SIX

Jonathan's team arrived in Colombia by flying to different cities on different airlines with flight times scattered across the clock. Boxers had left first, through Miami to Panama City and on into Cartagena. Twelve hours later, Jonathan and Harvey flew on different flights that took labored routes to Santa Marta, arriving within ninety minutes of each other. Jonathan made sure his was scheduled to arrive first, just in case Harvey needed additional encouragement after he'd touched down.

They found each other in baggage claim, then headed out into the thriving sauna that was Santa Marta. "I'm hating this already," Harvey said. "In case you were wondering." He ran a finger under the collar of his T-shirt.

Jonathan opted not to tell him that as hot as it was here on the coast, it was going to get a hell of a lot hotter in the jungle. Here, at least, they had a breeze.

"Are we winging it now, or do we have a plan?" Harvey asked.

Jonathan didn't honor the question with an answer. "We need to visit a friend," he said.

They grabbed a cab, and Jonathan directed the driver to a

hostel downtown that was known to cater to American college students on their obligatory narcotics pilgrimage. Even by the squalid standards of the neighborhood, the hostel was a dump.

"Oh, yeah," Harvey groused. "This just gets better and better."

Jonathan silenced him with a glare and paid the driver. He added a generous tip, which, at least in the old days, was the equivalent of buying blindness and deafness, in case anyone asked questions.

Together on the street in front of the entrance, Jonathan placed his palm on Harvey's chest to get his attention. "I need you to be my silent partner in here. Felipe is an old friend, but a suspicious one, out of necessity."

"How do you know each other?"

Jonathan answered with arched eyebrows.

"Oh."

"No names, either. If pressed, you're Mr. Smith."

Harvey's shoulders sagged. "Smith? That's the best you could come up with? Why not Jones?"

Jonathan smiled. "Because it's already taken."

The hostel was less shoddy on the inside than it was on the outside. More house than hotel, the place had the well-worn look of too many parties thrown by too many young people, of whom none were visible at the moment.

Jonathan called, "Hello?"

An ancient raisin of a man stepped in from what Jonathan knew to be the kitchen, and the mutual recognition was instantaneous.

"Hello, Felipe," Jonathan said in English.

"Señor Jones!" the old man exclaimed. A snaggletoothed grin consumed the lower half of his face. He shuffled over, his arms outstretched to enfold Jonathan in a bear hug. Given his five-foot-three stature, it was really more of a cub hug, but the thought was there. "It has been too long!"

Jonathan had never adjusted to the Latin American

abrazo—the man-hug—but he did his part by patting the old man on the back. "Too long," he agreed.

"You look good," Felipe said as they broke the embrace. He patted Jonathan's chest. "You skinny. You have neck now." The old man laughed.

Jonathan laughed, too. The last time the two had seen each other, Jonathan had been part of a Unit operation in which he and his squadron mates were supposed to disappear among the locals to gather intelligence against the drug cartel. Felipe had been an important link in the communication chain, and he had always teased Jonathan about being in far too good shape to ever blend in.

"I'm getting old and soft," Jonathan conceded.

Felipe pinched his cheek. "No, you look good. You look healthy." He turned to Harvey and extended his hand. "Who is your friend?"

"This is Mr. Smith," Jonathan said. "He's a business associate. He doesn't say much."

Felipe enfolded Harvey's hand in a friendly double grip. "Think of the coincidence," Felipe said. "Yet another business associate named Mr. Smith."

Harvey grinned. "Seems we're a dime a dozen," he said.

Felipe turned toward the back of the building and beckoned his guests to follow. "Come, come. We catch up." As he passed the tiny front desk, he leaned across the counter and produced a tent-card that read CLOSED. In English.

Felipe caught the knowing glance from Jonathan. "Yes, the American dollar is still good to me," he said. He beckoned again and led the way out the back door into a tiny courtyard that truly hadn't changed a bit in the decade-plus since Jonathan's last visit. The same tufts of grass peeked through the same spaces between the same broken bricks. Even the aluminum lawn chairs looked as rickety as before.

Felipe lifted two of the chairs a couple of inches off the ground and rattled them against the bricks. "Have a seat. I'll get us some coffee."

Jonathan gasped, "Coffee! Jesus, Felipe, it's a hundred and ten degrees."

"Only thirty-eight Celsius," he said with a grin. "Sounds much cooler."

"Thanks anyway," Jonathan said, waving the offer away.

"Beer then," Felipe said. "Or tequila. Whiskey?"

Harvey started to take the beer bait, then retreated from Jonathan's glare.

"Nothing, really," Jonathan insisted. "Thank you very much, though. *Muchas gracias.*" Jonathan sat in the proffered seat, and gestured to the other one. "Please, Felipe. Sit with us. Let's just talk."

The old man's smile gave way to a look of concern. "I don't like that tone, my old friend. I've heard it before. Soon I fear you will tell me that this is not just a pleasure trip to revisit the goods times with Felipe."

They shared a smile. Both were fully aware how much Jonathan despised this part of the world. Heat, corruption, violence, and poverty combined to form a perfect storm of misery for which Jonathan had no tolerance.

"My mission is nowhere near as large or difficult as in the past," Jonathan said. "If that makes you feel any better."

Felipe settled himself into his seat and crossed his legs. For a man of his apparent age, he'd always moved with considerable grace. "I hear you're working with your old friend José," Felipe said. He noted the startled look and added, "What, you think I don't have ears anymore?" Clearly, he wanted Jonathan to know that he was still in the loop.

"So how is Jammin' Josie these days?"

"He's hungry. Just like all of us."

"Is he still trustworthy?"

"Was he ever?"

Jonathan made a rocking gesture with his hand. "I never had a problem with him. At least he never betrayed me."

"That's because he feared you," Felipe said with a wry smile. "That makes you different. If he still fears you, then I suppose he is still trustworthy. Your big friend—what was his name?"

"Mr. Smith," Jonathan said. As if Felipe didn't already know.

"*Sí*. Señor Smith. What ever came of him?" He looked to Harvey. "I hope he is well."

"Oh, he's fine," Jonathan said. "We still work together. In fact, the plan is for me to join up with him tonight."

"Does José know?"

"Not yet."

Felipe laughed—a deep-throated peal that came from his soul and brought tears to his eyes. "Well, once José learns that the other Mr. Smith is with you, he'll be very, *very* trustworthy."

Jonathan joined him in the laughter. Throughout the world—from Cleveland to Samoa—Boxers was a big man. In South America he made Gulliver look short. Jammin' Josie was afraid of him at a level that made "terrified" seem like a small word. Boxers had always relished it, and Jonathan had always used it to his advantage.

As the laughter settled, Jonathan killed the frivolity. "We make light of Josie's shifting loyalties, but I need to know for real if he has gone bad. A child's life lies in the balance."

In South American culture, family meant everything, so Jonathan knew that Felipe would understand the urgency.

Felipe's expression wrinkled. "Your business here is not about drugs?"

"In Colombia, my friend, I'm afraid that everything is ultimately about drugs. First and foremost, though, my business is about a kidnapping."

"For ransom?" Felipe had been around long enough to understand that not all abductions are created equal.

"Not this time. For controlling information."

Felipe showed his palms, his fingers pointing down. "What could a child know?"

"I can't share the details. But I can't afford betrayal."

Felipe raised his hand, as if taking an oath. "On my mother's grave, José mentioned your coming only to impress me. For all I know his intentions are good." He paused. "He just talks too much. Is there a way I can help you?"

"Does the name Mitchell—or Mitch—Ponder mean anything to you?"

Felipe's eyes darted to the corners of the courtyard. He tried to cover his fearful twitch, but it was too late.

Jonathan smiled. "Felipe, it's me. You know that I'll die to protect your secrets." He said this without hyperbole, and Felipe knew it.

"Señor Jones, I hope that we have been friends long enough for you to know that I do not frighten easily." This from a man who'd pointed a finger in the face of Pablo Escobar, the mass murderer in charge of the Medellín drug cartel that Jonathan had personally helped to dismantle in the nineties.

"You're among the bravest men I know," Jonathan assured.

Felipe said, "This man Ponder frightens me. Because you mention him, I assume he is involved in what you must do."

"He is."

"Then be careful. Extraordinarily careful. This man is known here as *El Matador*. The killer."

Jonathan made a face. "That's a little dramatic, don't you think? With all respect, your country is full of matadors."

Felipe shook his head emphatically. "Not the same. Not like this Ponder. He reminds me of Pablo. He is that—how do you say it?—ruthful."

"Ruthless," Jonathan corrected. "After taking down the original Pablo, I'd think that the wannabe Pablo would be easy."

"We had two governments and thousands of people working to take down Pablo. Things are different now, no?"

Jonathan didn't bother to point out that elements of the Colombian government was more hindrance than help the first time around.

"Ponder is a gringo," Felipe continued. "You know how we Latinos are. Gringos lead, we follow. Ponder has paid the politicians well to allow him to make his cocaine in the jungle. The *policía* and the *politicos* all say that they are running the drugs out of our country, but they only care about the makers who do not pay well enough. Ponder, he pays good. Very, very good."

Jonathan was confused. "So if the pockets are all fat, what's the killing about?"

"Farmers and villagers who resist are killed in the worst ways. He hacks off hands and feet, then arms and legs as people watch. He makes people suffer horribly before he cuts their throats. He takes villagers' children to labor in the coca fields. Many parents never see their *hijos* again."

A bullshit bell rang in the back of Jonathan's head. "Come on, Felipe. You make Ponder sound like a monster from a bedtime story."

"Those stories all come from someplace. I'm telling you, he is the man that children of the future will learn about from their grandparents."

"It doesn't make sense, though. You terrorize the people, and they start to plan their retaliation."

Felipe made a puffing sound and threw up his hands. "It might not make sense to you, but it is always the way things are done." His eyes twinkled. "When there is no Señor Jones on your side, fear is all that many people have."

Jonathan caught the barb, but he wasn't sure how to interpret it. Was Felipe suggesting that he liberate entire villages while he was liberating the Guinn boy? Surely not.

Felipe said, "I still do not understand why a man like *El Matador* would come all the way to America to kidnap a child."

"That's the million-dollar question for us, too," Jonathan confessed. "But his is the name that keeps popping up. Tell me about these coca fields. Where are they?"

"Places where you have been before, I suspect. In the

Sierra Nevada de Santa Marta. No better farmlands to be found in all of Colombia."

Jonathan had indeed been there before. He recognized the Sierra Nevada de Santa Marta as some of the most punishing terrain in the world, where jungles were impossibly thick, and where Indian tribes lived undiscovered until the early 1970s. The mountain range ran north-to-south just east of the city of Santa Marta and featured Pico Cristóbal Colón, which, at 18,000 feet, was the fifth most prominent in the world. Back in the day, it was as lawless a place as any on earth.

Funded by billions of U.S. dollars, the paramilitary groups of the 1990s had been driven out by the Colombian government, but the open secret that no one wanted to acknowledge was that a drug war that attacks only the supply side of the equation is doomed to failure. As long as U.S. senators and their aides continued to party in their private offices on the products that they pledged to eradicate, a native population for whom cocaine is the sole source of income will find a way to keep the manufacturing chain going.

And where incomes are made by breaking the law, there's always someone smart enough to hijack the process through graft. Political corruption was a constant throughout the world.

Felipe poked the air in Jonathan's direction. "You need to be very careful, my friend. No one will want you there. And it's not just *El Matador*. Heaven only knows who the DAS is working for today—and whoever it is, it could change tomorrow—and the Indians don't like anyone."

Jonathan had to laugh at the ridiculousness of it all. Truly, Colombia's national security apparatus—*Departamento Administrivo de Seguridad* (DAS)—had been more or less up for bid since the 1960s. Every time they'd seemed to find some measure of stability over the years, someone would assassinate someone else, and then it would be time to spin the loyalty wheel again.

The native tribes, meanwhile, had grown weary of being

pushed around over the past four hundred years, and they'd become famously distrustful of everyone. Literally, *everyone* who was not a member of their immediate tribe.

"As long as I sleep with my eyes open and develop three-sixty peripheral vision, I should be okay, right?"

"You make light, Señor Jones."

"What choice do I have? Unless, of course, you would like to join my team and give me guidance along the way."

It was Felipe's turn to laugh. "I will show you a map. I'm not a warrior anymore. I've seen too much death. I've caused too much of it. I cannot do it anymore." His eyes narrowed, and he regarded Jonathan with a fatherly glare. "I am surprised that you still can."

Jonathan didn't like the dip toward sentimentality. "I don't kill," he said. "I save people."

"I mean no offense, Señor Jones." He looked to Harvey. "You truly are a man of few words."

Harvey shrugged. "But once I start talking, I'm freaking brilliant."

Felipe clearly didn't understand the humor, but he smiled anyway. To Jonathan: "So, short of putting myself in danger, how can I help you?"

"I need supplies," Jonathan said.

The old man cocked his head. "The kind of supplies you used to need?"

"More or less."

"Paper or hardware?"

"Both, actually. But in nowhere near the old quantities."

Felipe's eyes narrowed. "José said that he would provide these things."

Jonathan leaned back in his chair and crossed his right knee over his left. "Being cautious has always served me well," he said. "Besides, I have my share of enemies here in Colombia, and I'm more than a few hours away from my reunion with Josie."

"I see," Felipe said. "So, weapons for you and Mr. Smith. And one for the other Mr. Smith, just in case?"

Jonathan nodded. "Exactly. And I don't have much time. What do you have in stock?"

There was that smile again. "Come. I'll show you. You can shop for yourself."

Felipe led the way back into the house, past the kitchen on the left, and into a back bedroom that was far better kept than the rest of the rooms they passed along the way.

"This is your room?" Harvey guessed aloud.

"It is not much, but it suits me," the old man said. "I'm sure your home is much nicer."

Harvey was about to say something about his tent, but opted not to. The building that housed the hostel was bigger than it looked from the outside, comprising two connected structures to form one. Felipe's room was at the very end on the back side.

The old man beckoned them all the way in, and then closed and locked the door behind him.

"You're going to like this," Jonathan said. Obviously, he'd been here before.

A large wooden chest rested against the back wall under the window that looked out onto the chairs where they had just been sitting. On either side, at about head-height, very Mediterranean candle sconces flanked the window. Felipe pulled the curtains closed, then opened the chest and transferred three armloads of clothing and blankets to the bed. That done, he lifted the candle off the sconce on the right and handed it to Jonathan.

"If you don't mind?"

"Not at all," Jonathan said.

The old man then took down the entire sconce. He unscrewed the flat platelike candle holder from the wrought-iron curlicue that supported it, then rehung the sconce and brought the disk to the chest. He peeled up a corner of the wooden bottom to reveal the male end of a bolt poking straight up. Felipe screwed the disk onto the bolt. When it seated, something clicked under the floor, and he was able to

lift the entire bottom out of the chest, revealing a fixed lad-
der that reached straight down into a lightless shaft.

Jonathan grinned at Harvey. "Didn't I tell you you'd love
it?"

Felipe found three flashlights in the top drawer of his
dresser and handed one to each of them. As Harvey reached
for his, Felipe hung on to it for a second longer than necessary. "I trust you because Señor Jones trusts you," he said.
"Don't disappoint me. For your own sake."

Jonathan kept his expression light, but he'd never heard
that level of threat from the old man before. "I vouch for him
in every way," he said.

In his own time, Felipe let go of the flashlight, then led
the little parade down into the ground.

The first time Jonathan had seen Felipe's underground
storage tunnel, he'd been nearly speechless with admiration.
He was so impressed, in fact, that he would later create a
similar facility in his own home. His would be bigger, of
course, and it would feature state-of-the-art temperature and
humidity controls.

Felipe did the best he could with what he had. The underground chamber measured maybe twelve feet square, and it
was filled with all manner of weaponry, most of it still in its
original containers. Back in the day when they were fighting
Pablo, Jonathan had spent tens of thousands of Uncle Sam's
dollars in this very basement, arming citizenry to rise up
against the drug lords.

Without asking, the old man walked to one of the smaller
crates and opened it. He pulled out a Colt Model 1911 .45
caliber pistol—long Jonathan's preferred sidearm. He
dropped the clip out of the grip and jacked the slide back to
lock it open, then presented it to Jonathan for inspection. He
smiled broadly. "I don't forget, Señor Jones."

Jonathan had to chuckle. "Indeed you don't, my friend."
He released the slide lock and cycled it a couple of times. It
seemed to be well lubricated and in good shape. He would

tinker with it later, of course, but for now it seemed fine. He loaded it again, jacked a round into the chamber, then left it cocked as he stuffed it muzzle-first into the waistband of his trousers at the small of his back. It felt great to finally be armed again.

"You'll shoot yourself in the ass keeping it cocked like that," Harvey said.

Jonathan gave a tolerant smirk, then told Felipe, "My friend here was a Marine. He needs a dainty little pistol. Something with three safeties and a trigger lock."

Harvey bristled. "Hey, fuck you, doughboy. I'm just trying to keep you from getting a bullet in your GI GI tract."

Jonathan laughed. He actually had nothing but undying admiration for Marines, but man was it easy to spin them. And fun. "You a Beretta man?" That was the new standard-issue military sidearm—the one that replaced Jonathan's beloved .45. The 9-millimeter Beretta was widely accepted as having better range and accuracy than the .45, and it was certainly more user friendly. The problem with it, Jonathan thought, was that the people you shot with the thing didn't fall down nearly fast enough.

"I'm here as a medic," Harvey said. "What've you got in the way of Band-Aids and iodine?"

Felipe looked confused.

"He's kidding," Jonathan said with another glare. "Josie will be getting that for us. Pull a Beretta sidearm for my friend, and another for the other Mr. Smith. How about long guns?"

"I have MP5s, one or two M4s and a lot of AKs."

Jonathan grimaced at the mention of the AK-47. With tens of millions of the damn things in circulation, they were a perfectly acceptable assault weapon, but they weighed too much, and he'd be goddamned if he was going to look like a terrorist.

"I'll buy you out of M4s, and I'll take two MP5s. Let me have five hundred rounds for each of the rifles and a hundred apiece for the pistols." Felipe shuffled as Jonathan spoke, fulfilling the orders on the fly. "What do you have in the way of night vision?"

The old man stopped short and looked embarrassed. "Nothing, I'm afraid."

"Not a problem," Jonathan said, even though it was concerning. The ability to operate effectively at night was a huge force multiplier, especially in a jungle environment. He hated having to trust Jammin' Josie to be the sole supplier for something so important.

"While you're doing this," Jonathan went on, "I need to buy a car. What do you recommend?"

The smile returned to Felipe's face. "I recommend that you let me sell you a car."

CHAPTER TWENTY-SEVEN

It wasn't until she'd arrived in Colombia that Brandy Giddings realized her entire notion of what the country would look like had been shaped by the movie *Romancing the Stone* with Michael Douglas and Kathleen Turner. She'd expected muddy streets teeming with chickens and goats. She'd expected scary people on every corner and motor vehicles that were thirty years out of date.

What she got instead with Santa Marta was a modern if slightly threadbare city on the seashore that housed the Hotel Santorini, which itself sported perfectly acceptable air-conditioning, and whose bartender knew his way around a good caipirinha. And why not? She was a heck of a lot closer to the birthplace of the national drink of Brazil here in Colombia than she was in DC, where she'd first tasted the concoction.

Brandy sat in the lounge near a window that gave her a panoramic view of the Caribbean, watching the street vendors hawking their wares to tourists whose pockets were the targets of roving street urchins. She found comfort in the two beefy soldiers guarding the front doors. Actually, maybe they were policemen; they all wore the same uniforms in this part of the world. Either way, their presence put a lot of brawn and bullets between her and any of the criminals out there.

For the thousandth time in just a few days, she had to pinch herself to believe that she was actually here doing this. After she'd gone home from her last meeting with Secretary Leger, her doorbell had rung, and when she'd answered it, there was a young man in a crisp white Navy uniform, absent the ubiquitous white-on-black name tag. His equally white hat sat at a studied angle over his brow.

"Ms. Giddings?" he'd said. He had that sunny-but-tough Academy look.

"I'm she," she'd said, and instantly she'd regretted the Wellesley grammar.

He presented an eleven-by-seventeen-inch manila envelope. "I've been ordered to deliver this to you personally."

She took it without thinking. "Ordered by whom?"

"You're to read it carefully and speak to no one."

She'd actually giggled at that. It sounded like something out of a movie. "Is this from—" She cut herself off, just in case. "Who sent it?"

The young officer grasped the visor of his cap with his thumb and forefinger, a gallant tip of his hat. God, he was gorgeous. "Have a good day, ma'am," he said.

The envelope contained a second envelope, along with a U.S. passport with her picture but a new name, plus unsigned instructions for her to appear at Andrews Air Force Base in less than three hours, prepared for several days in a warm climate. She was to tell no one of the correspondence, and she was to make no unusual preparations before leaving.

The Andrews flight had taken her to Hurlburt Field in Florida, and then onto a commercial flight under her new name to Santa Marta. At a precise hour, she was to be sitting at this bar in this hotel, with but one mission: to hand the second envelope to a man who would come by and speak to her.

It was like being a freaking spy. It took everything she

had just to keep her hands from shaking. Could it possibly get any cooler than this?

Five times now she'd identified men in the crowd who she knew—absolutely *knew*—would be her contact, only to be disappointed as they glided past her to either meet someone else, or to get a drink, or to do whatever else they did instead of proving her right.

She needed to settle down. If she made eyes at any more men, she was going to get thrown out on the suspicion of being a prostitute.

Without conscious thought that she was doing it, Brandy repeatedly stroked the envelope she'd been dispatched to deliver, tracing her finger along the line where the flap sealed against the paper back. She'd been unable to contain her curiosity on the plane, and while in the lavatory she'd sneaked it open to take a look inside. She wasn't at all surprised by what she'd found. What did surprise her was how little emotion she felt when she realized that because of her actions people would soon be dead.

Commotion to her left drew her attention to the front door, where one of the soldier-policemen seemed to be having a dustup with someone. When she craned her neck for a better angle, she nearly laughed out loud when she realized that the other side of the confrontation couldn't have been more than twelve years old. If she wasn't mistaken, it was one of the boys she'd seen trying to score on the tourists just a few minutes ago. Poor kid probably tried to pick the wrong pocket and got caught.

Did they cut off people's hands for stealing in Colombia, or was that somewhere else in the world?

Brandy tired of watching the show, but as she was turning back to her drink, the strangest thing happened. The policeman stood straight and looked directly at her. Then he pointed.

She instinctively turned in her seat to see who was standing behind her. No one. Her stomach flipped.

She turned back around, and sure enough, the man in the

green camouflaged uniform was walking right toward her. He had the urchin with him, his fingers clamped on the boy's ear. The kid walked cockeyed with oversized strides to keep up.

Brandy felt an inexplicable urge to hide the envelope. She couldn't do that, of course, because it would call attention to the very thing she was trying to conceal. What on earth could be going on?

The officer brought the boy close enough that they could speak softly. "Excuse me, *señorita*," he said in a heavy enough accent that she could barely understand his words. "Are you . . ." He let go of the boy's ear, and gestured for him to complete the question.

The boy cleared his throat. "Hello, Mrs. Chalmers," he said in far better English than his escort.

Brandy stiffened in her seat, her skin electric with chills. That was precisely the sign she'd been waiting to hear. Her mind raced for the countersign. *Jesus, don't blow it now.* "Hello, Peter," she said. "How is Aunt Consuela?" It had seemed like such an odd patter when she was memorizing it, but now she realized that the boy had been part of the plan from the beginning.

"She is ill," the boy said. "She wants to see you."

That was it. The entire countersign had been completed. The chances of it being an accident—that a random conversation could follow the same pattern—were zero. But what was she supposed to do now? Just hand the package to a boy?

The kid seemed to be reading her mind because he glanced at the package, and then very subtly shook his head no. Without moving his head, he eyed the policeman.

"You know this boy?" the officer said. "He is bad boy. Very bad boy. Thief."

Oh, great. Now she was going to have to pay a fine for him or something. "No," she said, hoping that her smile looked genuine. "He's a friend of mine."

The cop looked *very* confused. "He is friend? *Está un amigo?*" Apparently he thought it might make more sense if he heard it in Spanish.

Brandy nodded and smiled more widely. "*Sí.* Yes. He's my amigo."

Definitely a cop, Brandy thought, not a soldier. He was examining her. "But you not from Colombia," he said.

Oh, shit! She drew a quick breath, and her heartbeat doubled. Truly, she was not cut out for this line of work. What was she supposed to say to counter that?

The kid took care of it. He darted the two-step distance that separated them and sat on her lap, wrapping his arms around her neck. "Don't let him hurt me," he said a bit too loudly, drawing attention from others in the lobby. "He hits me and kicks me. Don't let him!"

The move startled Brandy, but nowhere near as much as it startled the cop. He seemed keenly aware that he was being watched.

"We'll be okay," Brandy said to the officer. Then she gave a little wave to the others in the lobby. "Really, we're fine."

The cop hesitated, but in the end had little choice but to slither away.

When it was just the two of them again, the boy released his death grip and eyed Brandy's chest. "Nice boobies," he said.

A laugh escaped her throat before she could stop it. "*What?*"

He pointed. "Boobies. A-okay." He gave a thumbs-up and beamed a brown-eyed smile.

She laughed again. "Why, thank you."

"Can I see them?"

"No!" Brandy felt herself blushing as she glanced around the room to make sure they weren't still being watched. "How old are you?"

"I'm eighteen," he said.

Uh huh. "In that case, I'm seventy-three and way too old for you."

The boy gave a resigned shrug. "Okay. You need to follow me."

Brandy scowled. "To where?"

He nodded to the envelope. "To where that needs to go."

The boy stood and without looking back, started walking back toward the main door.

Brandy struggled out of her chair, bumping the table and spilling some of her drink. "Wait!" she yelled at a whisper. Who the hell was this kid? By the time they reached the door, they were walking together, and the boy seemed more than happy to be holding her hand.

Her hours in the air-conditioning had allowed her to forget just how impossibly hot it was outside. She'd worn cotton capris and a lightweight blouse, thinking that they would fit the bill for "dressing for a warm climate," but she realized after just one block of walking that she in fact did not own a wardrobe that would make this kind of peanut butter–thick humidity anything but oppressive. She was sweating, for heaven's sake! That's okay when you're in the gym, but out here on the street it was humiliating. She was soaking her blouse. And just what are you supposed to do with a sweat-soaked blouse when you're in a foreign country?

Two blocks away from the hotel, they turned right to head farther away from the water and the breezes it provided. "Where are we going?" she asked again.

The boy shot a smile over his shoulder. "Not far. We'll be there soon."

"What's your name?"

"Soon," he said, pointing to a spot somewhere up ahead.

As the water fell farther away and the temperature rose, so did the terrain, and there was nothing subtle about the hills. To think that she'd thought Rome was exhausting! That was like a basketball court compared to these hills.

Brandy tried her best to keep up with the boy who was her guide, but he inevitably pulled away—in one case as far as a half block ahead—before turning around and waiting for her. She felt an odd urge to apologize to the kid.

Farther still, and higher still. The street started to take on that old Europe look with narrow roadways and unbroken walls of building facades. Fifteen minutes into their sojourn, Brandy began to have second thoughts. The neighborhood was not a place where she would feel comfortable walking alone, and the presence of a twelve-year-old who featured himself a real man did nothing to make her feel safer.

Come to think of it, what kind of fool follows a kid whose name she doesn't even know? For all she knew, she was being set up for a mugging or a kidnapping. But if that had been the case, how would he have known the signs and countersigns?

No, this was the real deal. What had Jerry Sjogren called it? Tradecraft. This was real tradecraft—the life of a covert operator. And let's be honest, it didn't get a lot better than this.

The boy had stopped again, but this time only four or five doors ahead of her. That smile beamed again, and he pointed to a doorway. "We are here," he announced.

He pointed at the pink façade of a row house that might once have been grand, but now sagged with age. It occurred to her that this is what San Francisco neighborhoods might look like if no one painted or did repairs for twenty years. The heavy wooden door used to be purple. It was equipped with a substantial old-style knob that looked to be made of brass. Brandy wondered if she would be able to raise a high gloss from it if she polished it aggressively.

She stood in front of the door on the crumbling brick sidewalk and shot a glance to the boy.

He smiled.

"Should I knock?"

He jabbed a finger toward the door. "Just go in," he said.

Brandy hesitated. This didn't feel right at all. Why was he making such a point of her going first? Was this some sort of a trap?

"It's okay," the boy said. "I am not allowed."

Oh, now that made sense, didn't it? When you're arranging to have someone killed, you didn't need nosy street urchins hanging around to witness the event.

"The man is waiting for you inside," the boy said. He sealed the deal with that magnificent smile.

For crying out loud, what was she so nervous about? She was meeting an envoy of the secretary of defense. It was as if she were walking into a meeting with Secretary Leger himself. There could be no safer place in the world for her. This was what tradecraft was all about.

There'd be no doing it slowly, though. She needed to proceed with the commitment of pulling off a Band-Aid. She climbed the stoop, turned the knob, and pushed the door open.

In the transition between the bright sunlight and the darkened interior, she felt completely blinded.

She called, "Hello-oh!"

What the hell was that? The second syllable of hello escaped without her thinking, driven by a piercing pain above her right breast. For half a second, it registered as a thick pinprick, but then in the next half second, she realized that it was growing in intensity. She brought her left hand up to touch the pain, and then another jolt struck her again in the chest. This one hurt ten times worse than the first, and though she wanted to yell, she could produce no sound.

The agony was exquisite—completely off the scale. It caved her in in the middle, and as she doubled over, she got the first glimpse of blood on the floor. How about that? There was blood on her hand, too. And on her blouse. She felt the world spin, and as she struggled to steady herself against the wall, she lost her grip on the envelope. She saw it slipping through her fingers in slow motion, and while she tried to reach for it, nothing about her body was working right anymore. She had no choice but to watch it sail across the filthy linoleum.

As she slid down the wall to join the envelope on the floor, she saw a form step out of the shadow on the side of the center staircase. He carried something at his side. Something in his hand. As he closed to within a few feet, he raised the object at arm's length and pointed it at her head.

Brandy gasped. "Please don't——"

Three bullets for a single kill was embarrassing, but there was no other way. True silence was a necessity in the middle of the day, and that meant using subsonic loads to launch a bullet through a suppressor at a slow enough speed that the round would not create its own sonic boom in flight. For light loads like that, Mitch Ponder used a .22 with a full copper casing. If he could have gotten close enough to guarantee a one-shot kill, he might have used a fully suppressed .45, but by the time the combustion gases made it through the baffles of a .45 suppressor, there was never enough left to eject the round. If he'd wanted to live in a world where you only get one shot at a target, he'd have been born in the nineteenth century.

Silhouetted as she was against the sunlight, a head shot was out of the question, so he'd gone for center of mass. Even then, the distortion of the light caused him to miss the heart twice. Just as well, he supposed. If he'd hit the sternum, the slow, light bullet might not have penetrated the chest cavity at all.

"Please don't," she said.

Mitch hated it when they begged. No matter how small and underpowered the weapon, a bullet through the eye at close range always made it to the brain. Finally, she lay still.

Mitch stooped to pick up the envelope his target had dropped and gave it a quick glance to make that no blood had splashed that far. He wasn't sentimental about these things, but in his line of work, you didn't want objects in your possession to be spattered. He smiled. Another advantage to using small rounds.

He saw a shadow on the floor and recognized the silhouette as Jaime, the boy who'd been his legs for this job.

"Did I do good?" the boy asked. His tone brimmed with pride.

Mitch stayed on his haunches and pivoted his head. "You did *very* good," he said.

"Then pay me now?" Jaime held out his hand, palm up.

Mitch smiled. "Absolutely."

He proved yet again that a bullet through the eye always made it to the brain. The boy was dead before his knees buckled.

CHAPTER TWENTY-EIGHT

According to the meticulous research package that Venice had assembled, at the height of his career, Bruce Navarro had lived the life of the privileged. Big house, expensive cars and mistresses on both coasts, with a couple more rumored to be ensconced in Europe and Asia. On his tax returns, he reported an annual income north of two million dollars. The bulk of it came from perfectly legitimate clients as the result of legitimate and capable legal work. Nothing in the record proved that Sammy Bell or the old Slater crime syndicate had any direct connection to The Navarro Firm, but Venice had been quick to point out that in her haste she might easily have overlooked a "legitimate" client that was in fact a cutout for a criminal enterprise.

The information provided by Alice Navarro Harper turned out to be invaluable. The man once known as Bruce Navarro was now Tony Planchette, and his new address was Standard, Alaska, twenty miles or so west of Fairbanks. He'd stayed in reasonably steady contact with his sister over the years, despite the continuing surveillance from both sides of the law, by blanketing Jersey City with junk mail advertising whatever bogus product best served the coded messages on the cards. Technically it was mail fraud, but Gail thought it was a brilliant—albeit expensive—means of covert communication. He mailed thousands of cards so he could communicate with his one sister.

When Alice shared the stack of coupons she'd accumulated over the years, Gail realized that the accumulated newspapers and magazines in the house were a ruse to camouflage the stack of messages in the minds of anyone who might want to conduct a search. Bruce used a random rotating cipher, the key for which was embedded in the numbers under an otherwise meaningless bar code. The text itself often read as gibberish that must have annoyed the crap out of some of the recipients, but at the rate of one every six or eight weeks, apparently no one ever got angry enough to call the authorities.

Besides, this was America. If you wanted to pay the freight to post gibberish to the community, it was your God-given right to do so.

The essence of the various messages was fairly chatty, offering details on how he was adapting to an invisible life. Gail got the sense that they were as much a reassurance to his sister that he was still alive as they were any real communication.

And, unless Alice was concealing something, there was no mechanism in place for Bruce to get any information in return. For Bruce's safety, Alice had to assume that all of her outgoing communication was carefully monitored, and all it would take to raise the heat to intolerable levels would be for them to suspect that she was corresponding with Bruce. That alone would confirm that he was alive, and from there, nothing good could possibly follow.

This was Gail's first trip to Alaska, and as she drove her rented Jeep away from the airport parking lot of the Fairbanks airport, she was surprised how featureless an area it was. No hills to speak of, lots of trees and squatty construction that looked as weather-ravaged as any she'd ever seen. It wasn't that the place was ugly; it just wasn't as exotic as she'd wanted it to be.

Gail had spent the final two hours of her flight from Dulles studying the satellite photos that Venice had been able to download for her, showing the location of Bruce Navarro's home and the geographical features that surrounded it. It had taken some doing, too, since the public satellite mapping sites don't have a lot of detail of this part of the world. Venice had had to enlist the aid of SkysEye, a private satellite mapping company owned by Lee Burns, a longtime friend of Jonathan's. For a ridiculous annual subscription fee plus even more ridiculous tasking fees, Lee Burns's orbiting spy network could accomplish amazing things.

Navarro's change in lifestyle had been huge. He went from manicured acreage with horse stables and a swimming pool in the midst of unspeakable wealth in Great Falls, Virginia, to a foundation-mounted double-wide in the middle of nowhere.

Standard, Alaska, turned out to be less a town than a navigational benchmark along the Alaskan Railway north of Goldstream Creek. If you wanted to disappear from the face of the earth, this was a good place to go.

Navarro would be armed, she reasoned. Certainly he had firearms at his disposal. Out here, he'd be out of his mind not to, just to take care of the occasional marauding grizzly bear. Plus, he'd assumed the mantle of a loner specifically because people were hunting him with the intent to kill. If that didn't make someone quick to the trigger, she didn't know what would.

Gail opened her door and stepped out into the pleasant fresh air. She pegged the temperature to be somewhere in the mid-seventies; perfect weather, complete with a pleasant breeze that would help mask the noise of her approach.

Close up like this, the house was more substantial than it appeared to be from the satellite photos. The footprint of the building was the same as a double-wide trailer, but it had clearly been built in place. The weathered clapboard siding appeared to have once been dark green—forest green, she supposed—but unrelenting heat, cold, wind, and rain had taken the luster away.

Nerves kicked in as she climbed the three steps from the ground onto the covered stoop. She fought the urge to draw her weapon as she rapped on the door.

Through the open window on her left, she heard movement—a lot of movement, in fact, as if someone had jumped from height onto the floor. The noise was followed by mild cussing, and then silence.

"Mr. Planchette?" Gail called. "Are you all right, sir?"

No words, but more movement.

"Please don't be frightened," she said. She stepped away from the door and back to the front edge of the stoop, where she could have a broader view of the window. "I'm not with the police, I'm not with the government, and I'm not with Sammy Bell. I'm here because I need help. It's important enough that your sister Alice told me where to find you." She hoped the data dump would establish her bona fides with him. She decided not to use the word Navarro, however, because she worried that it would spook him.

"Are you armed?" a voice asked from the darkness behind the window.

"Yes. Isn't everybody out here?"

"You're not from around here."

She smiled. "No, sir, but you are." She let it go at that. She didn't venture to interrupt the long silence that followed. This would be difficult for him to process.

"Is Alice all right?" he asked, finally.

"Yes, sir, she is. She sends her regards. Not being able to communicate with you has been a terrible burden. But I have to say that the whole coupon plan is brilliant." *Keep throwing stuff out*, she thought, *and sooner or later he'll relax. Right?*

"Step out into the yard and put your gun down," the voice ordered.

"I don't think I'll do that," Gail said. She'd learned a long time ago that in tense negotiations, stating the truth as matter-of-factly as possible—even when denying a request—served to put the other party at ease. "If I were any of the people you fear that I might be, we wouldn't be talking right now. We'd already be shooting at each other. Just the same, I'd rather not make myself any more of a target than I already am."

The sound of more movement made her tense, and then the door opened. The man on the other side bore the same features as the photos Gail had studied, but all semblance of polished corporate lawyer had eroded away, leaving a much thinner, more drawn and haggard-looking alternate version. He wore blue jeans and a gray sweatshirt, and if anyone had asked, she would have said that this man was more attractive than the softer one from the past. He stared at her, cradling a sawed-off side-by-side shotgun in his arms. His finger lay poised outside the trigger guard, and the muzzle was not threatening her.

"Say what's on your mind," Navarro said.

"I'd like to come inside."

"I'd like to be twenty again," Navarro replied. "Which do you think will happen first?"

Gail smiled. Good guy, bad guy, or somewhere in between, you had to admire a sense of humor. "I'm going to reach around to my back pocket," Gail said. "I have a note from Alice. I'm hoping it will put your mind at ease."

Navarro nodded.

Avoiding any jerky motion, Gail reached with her left hand to her pocket, where her fingers found the edge of the invitation-sized envelope. She withdrew it and handed it to Navarro.

He accepted it, then appeared hesitant to look away from her.

"I'll wait in the yard," Gail said. She walked back down the steps to the lawn. She figured the distance would make Navarro feel less vulnerable.

The envelope appeared sealed, but of course she'd already read the contents—it would have been foolish not to verify that Alice hadn't given her brother an order to kill Gail on the spot. The note was short and sweet, oddly devoid of personal information despite the years. Perhaps the separation hurt less if the communication stayed businesslike. That it took Navarro over a minute to look up from the note told Gail that he must have read it several times.

When he was finally finished, he turned on his heel and disappeared into the house, leaving the door open behind him. Gail took that as her invitation to enter.

The interior was every bit as well-groomed as the yard. Navarro had decorated the place as if it were a New York apartment, in stark colors with minimalist furniture that must have cost a fortune to begin with, and then another fortune to have delivered. At first glance, the place was very dark, but as Navarro walked deeper in, he flipped wall switches that bathed each room with light that seemed to emanate from behind the walls. Maybe *through* the walls. Overall, it was a stunning effect.

"Your home is lovely," Gail said, perhaps for no other reason than to say something.

Navarro stopped in front of a conversation cluster of two chairs and a love seat near one of the front windows. "I believe it's best to make do with what little you have," he said. He gestured to one of the chairs. "Please," he said. He took the love seat, clearly the most worn piece in the room, for himself. The dent in the pillow confirmed for Gail that he had been sleeping when she knocked on the door. He never relinquished the shotgun. On the other hand, he never menaced with it, either. It was just there in the crook of his arm if he needed it. Behind him sat a rack bristling with firearms. It said something about Navarro's personality that he chose the shotgun over the others. She wasn't sure exactly *what* it said, but there was definitely a conclusion to be reached. Maybe he just wasn't a very good shot.

The cushions crinkled as Gail sat on them.

"They don't get sat in very often," Navarro said, reading her thoughts. "Under the circumstances, I'm not all that fond of visitors."

Gail gave a pleasant smile.

"You must be proud of yourself for finding a man so many have been hunting for so long," Navarro said.

"I had certain advantages," she said. "It helps to be doing the right thing for the right reasons."

Navarro nodded. "My sister's note mentioned something about a kidnapping."

Gail revealed the details of the assault on Resurrection House and the information they'd learned since. As she laid out the story, the lines in Navarro's face grew progressively deeper.

"Mr. Navarro," she concluded, "you are the common denominator in this story. Arthur Guinn is being threatened in order to silence his testimony against Sammy Bell and the Slater syndicate, Marilyn Schuler worked for you, and you worked for Sammy Bell. The smart money says you're the one who can untie this knot."

For the longest time, he just sat there, mulling over the story he'd just heard. Gail gave him space. After a minute or so, she saw the shotgun lift out of the crook of his arm, and she went to high alert—but only for an instant. He swung the weapon in a wide arc, the muzzle never in play, and set it down on the coffee table in front of the love seat.

He stood, shoved his hands into his trouser pockets, and turned to look out the front window.

"Life never ceases to surprise me," he said, his back turned to Gail. "You don't get into the kind of trouble I'm in and expect to survive all that long. It's been a good run for me—nine years is about ten years longer than I had a right to. I always figured that when I was finally busted, there'd be a lot more violence."

He turned to make eye contact, and Gail tried to conjure her most pleasant smile.

"If I tell you this, what happens to the information?"

"We use it to rescue a child."

Navarro thought for a moment more, then resigned himself to the inevitable.

CHAPTER TWENTY-NINE

They walked for a long time. Evan guessed it was three hours, but it could just as well have been two or five. The jungle never changed. The heat never cooled. A foul smell filled the air at every step, as if everything around them were rotting in the heat. At first, he'd wished that he had boots like Oscar and the soldiers did, but after walking over and over again through shin-deep water, he bet they wished that they were barefoot like him. He saw a show on History Channel on trench foot, and given the shit they'd had to wade through, his guards would be lucky not to pull their skin off when they removed their socks.

No one spoke during the walk—certainly, no one spoke to him—which was fine with Evan, because he'd promised himself not to say anything to anyone until someone had answers. So he just walked. One foot in front of the other, hoping, even though it was ridiculous, that his footprints might leave a clue for someone to come and rescue him.

No one could find him out here. No one except God, of course, and as he slogged along, he offered up a continuous prayer that maybe He would at least tell Father Dom that he was okay. Father Dom would worry about that sort of thing.

It's funny how your mind shifts into neutral when there's nothing to say and nothing to see. It occurred to him that despite the hours spent marching along like this, he had no real memory of any of it. There were no special plants or flowers that stuck out to him—although he knew that he had seen some beautiful ones. It's as if the sameness just attracted more sameness, and in the end it all translated into nothingness.

He was mentally entrenched in that sameness place when he became aware of a new aroma. He didn't know where it was coming from, but it was as if something pleasant were struggling to push away the constant fart smell of the jungle. Could it be food?

He told himself that he was just getting hungry, and that he was imagining things; but within a dozen steps or so, he changed his mind. He was definitely smelling food. His stomach rumbled.

Apparently the others smelled it, too, because the whole line picked up its pace. By Evan's estimation, they'd been doing about one step per second, and now they were doing like twice that. Would they let him eat?

His heart skipped a beat as he had a wild thought: Maybe someone in whatever place was cooking food would help him get away. Was that too much to ask? He didn't need a big break—a little one would do. *Any port in a storm*, as Father Dom used to say.

The parade picked up the pace even more as the terrain became steeper. Evan didn't have to run, exactly, but he had to move quickly to keep from getting run over by the soldiers behind him.

The ground was hard and dry here. The hard-packed dirt felt good against the soles of his feet. And the food smelled fabulous.

Without warning, the jungle gave way to a clearing that was lined with huts that were not dissimilar to the one he woke up in yesterday. That *was* yesterday, wasn't it? Maybe two days ago? A week? God, what was happening to him?

Evan didn't know what he was expecting to see when they entered the village, but it was miles away from the fear he witnessed. Soldiers waved their rifles in the air and shouted words he didn't understand.

As the villagers scattered, there was no way to count them all, but Evan thought that there had to be forty or fifty of them at least. He noted, too, that they seemed either to be young or old, with few in between. Certainly, there were no young men. In fact, if you discounted the soldiers in their little parade, Evan was the oldest boy in sight. Even without thinking it all the way through, he knew there was no way for that to be good news.

The two soldiers in the front of the line took off at a run, chasing villagers who seemed to be running for their lives. The one who caught Evan's eye just because he was closest seemed focused on one of the girls in the crowd, and she seemed equally intent on staying away from him. The soldier chased her at a dead sprint. At the last second, just as he was about to catch up, she cut hard to the right and evaded his grasp.

The soldier shouted at her—bitter staccato syllables that could only be cursing. The girl ran faster. The soldier stopped abruptly, stooped, and snatched a baseball-size rock from the ground and hurled it at her. From ten yards away, the rock sailed with no arc and caught the girl in the back of the head, sending her sprawling face-first into the dirt.

She screamed as she fell and clutched her head with both hands.

Evan saw a flash of red through her fingers. All around him, the other villagers had stopped running. Many stood and watched the attack, and Evan couldn't believe that no one was doing anything to intervene.

The soldier wasn't running anymore. He walked with long strides up to the girl and shouted at her. When she curled up tighter on the ground, he bent at the waist, grabbed a fistful of hair and pulled. She screamed louder, and he yanked, lifting her to her feet. When she tried to wriggle free, the soldier hit her across her face with an open hand. The blow seemed to stun her, and as she stood there, the soldier ripped open her shirt and yanked it down off her shoulders, exposing her breasts. She made a tired gesture to cover herself up, but when the soldier slapped her hands away, she surrendered the effort.

The soldier bent and kissed a breast, then turned back to face the rest of the soldiers, displaying the girl like a trophy, with one hand draped over her shoulder and the other rubbing his dick through his pants. He gave a thumbs-up sign, then shoved the girl through the door of the nearest hut. Three seconds later, an old woman and a little boy hurried out through the same door.

"A young man has needs that cannot be denied," Oscar said from very close by.

Evan turned to see him standing at his side. The boy just stared.

"I could have them provide for you, too, if you would like," Oscar said. He winked.

Evan backed away.

"Don't wander far," Oscar said with a smirk. "What the jungle takes it rarely gives back." Behind him, the girl screamed from inside the hut and then fell suddenly silent after the scream was cut short.

Evan's head swam with confusion. Where the hell was he? What was going on? Why were all these people just standing around as a girl was being raped? Yeah, he knew that's what was happening. You don't live the kind of life he'd lived and not know what a rape looks like when you see it.

The villagers outnumbered them ten-to-one. Why couldn't they—

A hand landed on his shoulder. Evan jumped as if shot with electricity and whirled to see an old woman very close by, reaching out to touch him. He stepped to the side, the only way to distance himself without stepping closer to Oscar and the soldiers.

The woman smiled, revealing kind eyes and a mouthful of half-missing teeth. "Boy," she said. She beckoned him with a gnarled old hand. "Wheat boy. Comb."

She meant no harm, he knew. He recognized the friendliness in her eyes. In fact, she might have been trying to protect him, but it was hard to walk toward someone so . . . well, ugly.

"You. Wheat boy. Eat?" She pantomimed putting food in her mouth and smiled again.

Food. His awareness of the cooking smell returned, and with it his stomach rumbled. God yes, he'd love some food. He nodded.

The woman beckoned more broadly. "Comb." She walked toward the open door to one of the huts, checking over her shoulder with every other step to be sure Evan was following her.

He was. Part of him said he was crazy for doing it, but that wasn't the part that was screaming for food. For a fleeting moment, he thought of Hansel and Gretel, but he pushed the images away. He was definitely staying away from any cages, though.

As the old woman got closer to her doorway, she beckoned more aggressively. "Comb, comb, comb," she said.

In that moment, Evan realized that she was saying *come* not *comb*. She was trying English, and the effort made him feel warm inside.

"*Gracias,*" he said, hoping that it was the right word for *thank you*. He followed the woman through the open door and into a cramped living space that looked more like pictures he'd seen of teepees in the Old West than of any modern home. There was no real furniture—just some rough-looking wooden chairs—and the floor was made of the same dirt as outside, but somehow felt cleaner against his feet. Certainly drier.

Eight people—six of them old and two of them under five—filled the single room to capacity, yet they all stood as he entered. The old woman spoke a mile a minute, and the people in the room seemed to be pleased by what they were hearing. They pulled away from their tight circle in the middle of the room and made room for him at a table that was otherwise invisible. Just beyond the table was a pot of some kind of stew that smelled like heaven. One of the adults pulled a bowl away from one of the children and placed it on the table in front of Evan. She said something to him that he didn't understand, but the accompanying smile reassured him that he was being welcomed as a special guest.

As Evan took a seat in the middle of a long bench, a different old woman leaned to the center of the table and ladled out a generous helping of the stew. Evan had no idea what it was, but because the broth was brown and there were green vegetables mixed in, he told himself that it was beef stew. The first sip blew that out of the water, but he refused to think about it. Whatever it was tasted good, and for now, that's all that was important. That and the fact that it put food into his belly.

After two or three more spoonfuls, Evan realized that he was the only one eating. He looked up at the old woman who had brought him in, and he gestured with his forehead toward the pot. "Please," he said. "Eat."

Apparently, those were exactly the words they'd been waiting for because they wasted no time diving in and ladling stew into their own bowls. Conversation he didn't understand roiled all around him as they crammed onto the benches hip to hip. They all seemed happy, and Evan didn't understand how that could be the case when one of their tribe—if that's what you called them—was being brutalized nearby. For all he knew, every one of the soldiers was out there raping someone. Yet the people in here were laughing and having a grand old time. It didn't seem right.

But the stew was great. He ate like the starving young man he was, slurping spoonful after spoonful down his gullet, barely pausing to chew the vegetables and the occasional hunk of meat that tasted different than anything he'd had in the past. It wasn't till he'd emptied his bowl that he realized that the others were all way behind him. They were watching him, and whatever expression crossed his face made them all laugh. He felt his ears turning red, and then they laughed some more.

But it was friendly laughter. He smiled along with them and even got the feeling that he probably would have been laughing with them if only he'd known what was so funny.

The lady who'd brought him in leaned close and said something he couldn't understand. It sounded like *blahn key roho.* When he shrugged to tell her that he didn't understand, she repeated it. He still didn't get it.

She held out her hand palm up, and he gave her his, palm down. She gently lifted his arm and ran her fingers down its length. She fingered his long blond hair. "Wheat," she said. "*Blanco.*" Then she brushed his cheek and ear. "Roho." She paused as she searched for a word. "Red?"

Then he got it. She hadn't been saying *wheat* all this time. She'd been trying to say *white.* White boy. White arm, white hair, red face. Evan smiled. He rubbed his own cheeks with his other hand and said, "Blushing. White skin and red face means 'blushing.'"

She repeated the word, and he didn't correct her when it sounded more like *blooshing.* Then they all tried it, and they all laughed. There was some more small talk and laughter, and then the faces of the people across from his turned suddenly fearful.

Evan felt Oscar's presence before he heard anything. "Kid!" he boomed. "You ready?"

The boy felt his shoulders sag, and the instant it happened, he knew that he'd just telegraphed weakness. "No," he said. "I like it here."

Oscar laughed. "Two minutes," he said. "*Dos minutos.* Don't make me drag you out of here. It's tough to walk on a broken leg." Two seconds later, he was gone.

The mood in the hut turned black. His hostess stood, and the others followed. She hooked her arm in his armpit and gently lifted him. When he got to his feet she cupped his chin in her palm and said something to that he couldn't understand, but the tone of her voice clued him in that it was important.

He shook his head. "I don't know what you're saying." Fear rose in his throat.

The woman looked to the others for help, but there was none to be found. Her eyes brightened, and she held up her forefinger as an idea struck her. She hooked her arm around Evan's shoulder and moved quickly across the room to a primitive set of shelves that was packed with all kinds of crap. Talking a mile a minute, she tore a small piece from a sheet of paper and then shaped into a rough oval. She held it up for him to see, nearly pantomiming Father Dom's pose when he offered up the Host during Holy Communion.

Whatever she was trying to tell him, it was all about the slip of paper. Apparently it was a very *important* piece of paper.

"I don't understand," Evan said with a full-body shrug.

The woman shook her head emphatically and tapped his lips with her fingers. She wanted him to be quiet and listen.

That'd be great if only he knew what the *hell* he was listening to.

"Evan!" Oscar boomed.

The sound of the man's voice made the woman double her pace. Still yammering about whatever, she gestured one more time with the piece of paper, put it in her mouth, then violently spit it out.

Evan reflexively jumped back, but the old woman grabbed his hand to keep his attention and spat again, three times for added effect.

"I'm supposed to spit?" he asked.

She nodded enthusiastically. "*Sí, sí.* Speet."

So he spat. No wad of goo; just, you know, spit.

"No, no, no, no." She let him have it with another long string of Spanish. Or maybe Martian. He didn't understand one any better than the other.

"Evan!" Oscar reappeared in the doorway. "Right now. *Ahora.*"

All of the animation drained from the woman. She exhaled heavily, then gave Evan a quick hug. "*Vaya con Dios,*" she said.

Evan knew what that one meant, though he wasn't sure why. She'd said, *Go with God*. He smiled even though he inexplicably wanted to cry. "Thank you," he said. "*Gracias.*"

The woman smiled, then turned him around and swatted him on the ass. "Bye-bye, blooshing boy."

He turned to smile at them, but they seemed to not want eye contact.

"Come, kid," Oscar said. "The boys are refreshed, and we've got a long walk."

The little parade reformed outside, and Evan fell in line. He looked away as they passed the hut the girl had been dragged into. He might have been imagining it, but he'd have sworn that he could hear crying from inside.

CHAPTER THIRTY

Navarro seemed incapable of sitting. He walked to the rear of the house, to the kitchen, inviting Gail to join him. "Would you like some tea?" he asked.

"Yes, please," she replied with a smile. She hated tea. It reminded her of childhood sickness, when her mother used hyper-sweetened tea to mask the flavor of whatever foul home remedy she might have concocted. Still, an affirmative answer seemed like the best way to keep Navarro talking.

He filled the copper teakettle from the spigot over the stove and settled it on a front burner. He turned the knob and bent at the waist to verify that the blue flame was exactly right; then he turned to face Gail.

"I was their attorney," he said, getting right to it. "I dealt mostly with a man named Arthur Guinn, but I did meet Mr. Bell a time or two. They were surprisingly nice people. Very cordial, always dignified. Not at all what you'd expect from people in their line of work. If you didn't know they were mobsters, you'd have thought they were Ivy League country clubbers."

"So you knew they were mobsters when you went to work

for them?" Gail pulled a chair away from the kitchen table and helped herself to it.

Navarro turned on the sink spigot and pushed the lever all the way to hot. "Of course I knew. The whole world knew. But when I started, I just did corporate work for their legitimate covers." He filled the teapot with hot tap water and set it aside. "Preheating the pot is very important," he said.

"Excuse me?"

"When making tea. Too many people make the mistake of pouring the heated water directly into a cold pot. Ruins the tea."

"I've always just put a tea bag in a cup of hot water," Gail said.

Navarro shivered. "Might as well drink from a mud puddle." He withdrew two cups and saucers from a cupboard over the stove and started preheating those, as well. "Tea drinking and pipe smoking are both as much about the fussbudgetry as they are about the final reward."

Gail didn't care. But she didn't want to push too hard.

Navarro leaned back against the counter and crossed his arms and legs. "I remember when I was in law school a professor told us how fragile one's ethics can be. He was an absolutist. His favorite expression was, 'You can't be just a little bit dirty.' It made sense in the classroom, but in practice it's a hard lesson. Rationalization is a tricky thing. You know you're working for a criminal, but you justify it by telling yourself that even criminals need legal counsel. It's the way our system of justice is built. I was working just for the legal side of what they do. After a dozen years or so, the blurry line gets fuzzier and fuzzier. Before you know it, you're seeing the line for exactly what it is, but you look the other way. In the end, you're in so deep that it doesn't matter anymore where the line is."

The teakettle whistled, and he turned to tend to it.

"What sort of things did you end up doing?" Gail asked.

He killed the flame under the kettle and let it sit while he dumped the water from the preheating pot and cups. He wiped them dry with a dish towel and then measured two teaspoons of loose tea from a tin into the dried pot.

Gail had never seen all this pageantry for a cup of tea, and she found herself oddly fascinated.

Navarro poured water from the kettle into the pot and put the lid in place. "Three minutes," he said. "No more, no less. In America, we tend to oversteep our tea. Where were we?"

"You were about to tell me what sort of services you performed for Sammy Bell and company."

"Ah. Well, toward the end, I was the handler of cash. The trusted middleman."

"For what?"

"I didn't ask."

"But you knew."

"I *suspected* at first; but yes, sooner or later I knew. I handled payments for services rendered. With my fingerprints on the transaction—literally and figuratively—it all became subject to attorney-client privilege, and therefore untraceable."

"What was the money for?"

He hesitated. "Just about anything you can think of." He busied himself with a search of the kitchen drawers.

Gail sighed heavily. "Please don't make this more difficult than it has to be."

His head snapped up at that. "It *is* difficult, Ms. Bonneville. It is extremely difficult, and I'm doing my best not to just shut up and send you on your way."

Gail looked away, inexplicably embarrassed.

He wasn't done. "Have you ever done anything you're ashamed of?"

She felt heat rising in her ears. *Lord yes*, she thought; but she would never share the details with others.

"If you have, then you know how easy it is to push the awfulness aside." He closed one drawer and opened another. "I've built myself a cozy little life here in exile. I have very nearly reached the point where I can look at myself in the mirror and not feel nauseated." This time he slammed the drawer in frustration, and went for a third. "So if I am some-how frustrating you by not baring my soul quickly enough, I'm afraid I'll just have to beg your pardon."

This time, he slammed the drawer hard enough to shake the floor. "Where the *hell* is my tea strainer?"

Gail stood to help and saw it right away. "Is that it? There on the counter?" She pointed next to the sink, to a spot in plain sight.

He followed her finger, and his shoulders slumped. "Yes," he said. "Thank you." He picked it up and rinsed it in the sink. "As I'm trying to introduce you to the wonders of tea, I can't very well leave it unstrained, can I?"

His voice cracked at that last part. Gail returned to her seat and just watched while he finished the pomp and cir-cumstance. He carried the cups easily, each balanced on its saucer with a spoon on the side. "Sugar's on the table," he said. "Would you like lemon or cream?"

I don't even want the damn tea, she didn't say. "No thank you." She opened the sugar bowl and was not the least sur-prised to find cubes. She helped herself to two lumps and stirred them in, while Navarro took three. She sipped, and was delightfully surprised. The flavor was like no tea she'd ever had. "This is good," she said, the surprise evident in her voice.

"Let this be a lesson," he said. "Life is too short and filled with disappointments to deny yourself the best." He took a sip of his own and savored it. "Tea bags are a sin."

Gail laughed. She felt as if she'd stepped through the looking glass, tea party and all. This man savored his brew as Jonathan savored good scotch. She allowed the moment to stretch a little more, and then came back around to busi-ness.

"A young boy is awaiting rescue, and people are trying to harm him," she said. "We have to get back to the subject at hand."

Navarro bowed slightly from the shoulders. "Please," he said.

"Tell me about Marilyn Schuler," Gail said. "How does she fit into all of this?"

Navarro sat taller in his chair and shifted his eyes to a spot over her shoulder. She followed his gaze, but there was nothing there.

"Marilyn was a lovely woman," Navarro said. "Lovely in every sense of the word." He looked back to Gail and made his eyebrows dance. "Perhaps too lovely for her own good."

Gail waited for it.

"You know she was having an affair with another young man on my staff."

She played dumb.

"A fellow named Aaron Hastings. I never did like him much. Never trusted him, really; but he was a recommended hire from my biggest client."

Gail's ears perked. "Sammy Bell?"

"The one and only. And it never behooves to disappoint one's largest client."

"Especially this one," Gail said.

"Indeed." He took another sip. "If only Mr. Bell knew the truth of his friend."

"What truth is that?"

Navarro looked concerned. "Alice didn't tell you?"

"You'd be shocked—or maybe pleased—to know how little she shared with me about anything." Gail told herself that she was going to have to reexamine her whole attitude about tea.

Navarro pushed his chair away from the table and crossed his legs. "I don't have any real proof, you understand. Common wisdom—now there's an oxymoron for you—has it that Marilyn's husband killed her because of her affair with Aaron, but I've always felt that poor Mr. Schuler was set up by that young man, and that the young man himself was Marilyn's killer."

Gail recoiled. "Why would he do that?"

Navarro's face twitched. It looked like equal parts smile and wince. "I hope you have time for a long story," he said.

As Navarro unfolded his tale, it seemed obvious to Gail that he'd been thinking a lot about this over his years in exile.

"Sometimes I found myself in the position of shuttling money," he explained. "I was never entirely sure what it was for, but you get a feel for these things over time. The amounts were always large. Tens of thousands of dollars. And of course nine times out of ten, the money was flowing toward Mr. Bell's operation. Rarely away from it."

Gail detected subtext. "Except sometimes?"

He stabbed a finger toward her nose. "Exactly. Except sometimes. Like, for example, the three days before my life as I knew it was forced to end. We handled an outgoing payment of two hundred fifty thousand dollars."

Gail gasped. "Yowsers."

Navarro smiled. "My thoughts exactly. We handled the payment in two parts, about a week apart. Half one week and half the second week." His eyes narrowed. "So, Ms. Private Investigator, what does that sound like to you?"

"Half on contract and half on delivery."

Navarro gave a conciliatory bow. "I left out a detail. There *was* no delivery of goods. Just a payment followed by another payment."

Something clicked in Gail's head. "A hit?"

He jabbed his finger in the air again. "That's what I concluded. It's the only thing that made sense. For that amount of money, it's somebody damned important. And it certainly makes sense to have a completion bonus. There's also the fact of the dead drop. I forgot to mention that, too. We weren't supposed to deliver either payment to a person. Instead, there was a dead drop at a rest stop along the Jersey Turnpike. Lots of money, anonymous recipient."

Gail found herself nodding. "Definitely a hit."

"Right. Murder. Cold blood and all that. Be honest with you, that was way beyond anything that I signed up for. Scared the bejesus out of me. It's one thing to risk disbarment and maybe a year or three in prison, but now we were talking big time."

"Did you say no?"

He gave her a don't-be-an-idiot look. "The 'say no' ship had sailed long before then," he said. "I was in far too deep to play that kind of game. So I swallowed hard and made the first payment. Then, on my way back, about three miles from making the drop, I got pulled over for speeding. Seventy-eight in a sixty-five. Funny how some details just stick with you, isn't it?"

Gail stole this thunder: "That created a record," she said.

"It did *exactly* that. It was just a routine traffic stop, I know. Nobody's going to think twice. But then if someone gets hit, they're going to start checking records."

That's exactly what they'd do, Gail thought. After a murder, one of the first investigative tasks is to check moving violations in the area. "Did you have a criminal record?"

"No, but I had a high profile. When you're a mobster's lawyer, people notice. You'd be surprised how many people are jealous, in fact. So that next week, I was a basket case. I scoured newspapers and the Internet looking for something about a murder, but I never saw it. Then I got the order to make the second drop."

"But no one was ever killed?"

"Not that I knew of. Still, I was spooked. I didn't want any more blood on my hands, so I sent Marilyn Schuler to make the delivery. She wouldn't do it unless I told her what was in the package, and when I did tell her, she sort of freaked out. She didn't know what it was for, of course, but it was still a lot of cash. She insisted that she'd only go if I let her boyfriend come along to protect her."

"That would be Aaron Hastings?"

"Right." He leaned forward. "Only the money never arrived. Marilyn and Aaron disappeared. I didn't realize that things didn't happen until over a day later when I got word from Arthur Guinn that there was one very pissed off, very bad man who wanted his money." Navarro closed his eyes and cocked his head, as if the memory had become painful.

"You didn't tell him about Marilyn?" Gail said.

He shook his head. "Looking back on it, it's hard to believe I was that stupid; but telling him would mean confessing that I had given the job to my assistant, and God only knows what would have come from that." He sat straight again and spread his arms wide. "Besides, I didn't think she could be so stupid as to steal from the Slaters. Then she turns up dead, and the money and Aaron are both missing. Only nobody knows about him. Just like that"—he snapped his fingers—"I've got the mob and this 'very bad man' looking for me, and I've got nothing to give them. So I disappeared."

Gail scowled as she listened. "You're a rich guy. Why didn't you just make up the difference out of your own pocket?"

"Because I was convinced that I was dealing with a professional killer. I'm *still* convinced that I was dealing with a professional killer. Every scenario I ran through my head ended up with me dead. Especially because I didn't come clean with what happened in my very first phone call from Arthur."

"So you panicked," Gail summarized.

Navarro shrugged. "I prefer to think that I reacted the only way that made sense at the time."

Gail took a moment to catch her notes up and then to review what she'd written.

"There's more," Navarro said, interrupting her thoughts.

He had her attention.

"I've had a lot of time to think through all of this," he said. "Thank God for the Internet. The amount of the payment I shuffled gnawed at me like an ulcer. That kind of money means something way bigger than any mob hit. That's special money, requiring the services of a special killer. Expertise is expensive in any line of work, right?"

Gail nodded. "So the Slaters wanted someone dead in a big way."

Navarro looked horrified. "The Slaters? Oh, lord no, this kind of hit wasn't ordered by the Slaters. They were merely the middlemen. Someone wants someone else dead, you go to your local crime family and you work out a brokered deal. I laundered the money that they had already laundered once. Presumably, the contractor on the other end of the transaction laundered it a couple more times to make it damn near untraceable."

Gail was lost. "So why are the Slaters even looking for you?"

"Well, they had to cover the loss, didn't they? They had to make good on the transaction, or else the very bad man would have an issue to settle with them, and no one needs that kind of heartache. But to cover their hind parts, they'd want to make sure that every stakeholder knew that I'd fumbled the ball."

Pieces still were not fitting for Gail.

"That's your government connection," Navarro said, as if it were the most obvious thing in the world. When she didn't get it, he sort of growled in frustration. "The government was the customer."

A glimmer of comprehension now.

"Well, not the government, per se," Navarro corrected himself, making a twitchy wave-off gesture. "More like a powerful individual within the government."

Gail found herself leaning forward in her chair.

"Remember when I said that when they asked for the second payment, no one had been killed? Well, I realized that I wasn't looking at a big enough picture. I'd been assuming that the hit would happen near the site of the money drop. Then I realized that for that kind of money it could have been anywhere. That's when it got scary."

Gail waited for it. The dramatic exposition was wearying, but given the man's years without human interaction, she tried not to show frustration.

"Do you keep track of Washington politics, Ms. Bonneville?"

"Quite the opposite, actually. I try very hard to avoid them."

"Then perhaps you don't remember the South Dakota

senatorial campaign from that year. The one between Lincoln Hines and—"

"Didn't he commit suicide?"

"So you do remember. Yes, the common assumption was that he had committed suicide, but there are those who say that he would never do such a thing. His family, for example."

Gail rolled her eyes. "Ah, conspiracy theories. You gotta love 'em."

"What was it that Henry Kissinger told Richard Nixon? Just because you're paranoid doesn't mean that people aren't trying to get you. You should look at some of the theories. Beyond what many say is a lack of suicidal motivation, there were issues with the positioning of the body, and with fibers found on his clothes and such."

"As is frequently the case," Gail said. Armchair detectives were the bane of every real investigator's life. "Trust me. If those fibers and the rest were relevant, there would have been a prosecution."

"How about if the prosecutor was of the same political party as the dead man's opponent? And the sheriff in charge of the investigation, as well."

Gail laughed at the absurdity of it. "So the opponent kills his competition and he just talks everyone into covering up his crime? Forgive me, Mr. Navarro, but it just doesn't work that way."

Navarro remained unfazed. "I'm not suggesting a conspiracy, necessarily. In fact, I'll stipulate that it probably *wasn't* such a thing. But perceptions inform assumptions, and assumptions drive investigations, do they not?"

"Of course, but—"

"Hear me out. People suggest that the candidate who officially died of a self-inflicted gunshot wound was in fact murdered. Among the most logical suspects would be the man who stood the most to lose. The incumbent, no less, whose departure would throw the political balance in the Senate to the opposing party. So, your highly placed, very dapper and charming suspect says that the charges are ridiculous, that he would easily have won the race, even though the poll numbers at the time indicated that such might not be the case. Besides, he had an ironclad alibi for the time of the killing. Under those circumstances, where would your investigative instincts likely take you?"

Gail inhaled deeply and let it go as a sigh. In every investigation, there are wild-ass theories that simply have to be discounted or ignored. Otherwise, no case would ever close. It happened, sometimes, that a discarded theory turned out to be the one that defined the actual events, but it was a rare occurrence. Still, more than a few innocents were paying undeserved penalties in American prisons, Frank Schuler among them, apparently.

Navarro smiled and pointed at her. "Not laughing now, I see. Think about what was at stake: A senator had killed his competition using the Slater organization as a go-between. Everything would have been fine. Only the deliveryman"— he raised his hand—"screwed up and left loose ends that needed to be tied."

"Which senator are we talking about?" Gail asked. "I don't remember which one's from where."

"Oh, he's not a senator anymore," Navarro said. "When the president was elected, the guy was selected to be secretary of defense."

"Jacques Leger?" Gail said.

"Exactly. See, you do pay *some* attention to Washington politics."

Gail paused. She didn't want to believe it; but Navarro's wild theories did explain some things. "So help me think this through," she said. "Would Arthur Guinn be in a position to know all of this?"

"Absolutely. All the way down to the little details. He wouldn't say anything if he hopes to see tomorrow, but he would definitely know."

Gail didn't share the fact that he would be sheltered by witness protection. "So, to keep him quiet—if only as added insurance—it would make sense to kidnap his child."

"Absolutely. That or just have him killed outright."

Gail nodded. "And Frank Schuler would have to be considered a loose end, too; just in case Marilyn had said something to him. Maybe they even think he has the money. But that's a loose end that the Commonwealth of Virginia will take care of in a week or so."

"That leaves his boy. Call it a long shot that he'd know anything, but in for a dime, in for a buck, right?" A shadow of concern fell over Navarro's face. "You know, that boy is probably dead. If we're right and this is the scenario, then there's no reason to keep him alive."

Indeed there wasn't, Gail thought. Thus the reason they left him for dead.

"So, do you think I'm right?" Navarro pressed.

Holy shit. Did she think that a sitting secretary of defense ordered the murder of his senatorial rival? Did she think that the cover-up could involve kidnapping and more murder? Did she think that ambition could bring such darkness into a public servant's soul? To think such things would sicken her.

"Yes," she said. "I think that's exactly what happened."

Navarro smacked the table with both palms, a gesture of triumph. "Yes!" he proclaimed. "So what are you going to do about it?"

Interesting question, to which there was only one appropriate answer: "We set the record straight."

The triumph drained from his face.

"We?"

Gail shrugged. "Okay. You, actually."

Navarro laughed. "Like hell. I've gotten used to living."

"The secretary of defense is a murderer. You can't live with that."

"What are you talking about? I've *been* living with it. He was every bit as much a murderer yesterday as he is today. The rest is not my problem."

"I can arrange protection," Gail said.

Navarro laughed harder. "Oh, you can, can you? That must be some private investigation firm you're with."

Gail didn't retreat. "It *is* some private investigation firm I'm with. Certainly different than any you've heard of. We have connections."

"Yeah, well, congratulations. I don't. All I've got is me. I've come to care about me a lot these past years, and the more committed to me I've become, the less I care about anyone else. I gave you what you wanted. Now you take care of the rest." He stood. The meeting was over. "Do travel home safely."

Gail didn't move. "Are you anxious to disappear all over again?"

He scowled. "What do you mean?" The way the color drained from his face, Gail figured he might have already figured it out.

"Mr. Navarro, there are some secrets that I just cannot keep. Not when the stakes are so high."

"You mean you'd rat me out."

"I don't want to," she said. She tried to keep a pleading tone in her voice. "But what choice would I have?"

"You could respect my openness and generosity and understand that I am in a very difficult position."

Gail cocked her head. Surely he had to know better.

"I could kill you," he said. "No one would ever find your body."

She smiled. "All respect, I'd make you dead three times over before you got your finger on the trigger."

"I could kill myself, then."

Gail shook her head. "You've had years to kill yourself. The time has come for you to do the right thing."

Navarro laughed. "Sure," he said. "At this stage in my life I'm going to start—" His expression changed to one of concern, and he cocked his head. "Do you hear something?"

Gail cocked her head, too. At first, the answer was no, she didn't hear a thing. Then she did—a very soft thrumming sound in the distance. In a city setting, it would have been inaudible, but out here, not only was it clear, but it was getting louder. "Helicopter?" she guessed.

Navarro shot to his feet, knocking over his chair. He snatched his shotgun from the counter with such speed that Gail found herself drawing down by instinct. "Don't!" she yelled.

"What did you do?" Navarro yelled. "Who did you tell?"

But he wasn't interested in an answer. He hurried out of the kitchen, through the living room, and up to the open front window.

"What is it?" Gail said, trailing after him.

"It's a goddamn helicopter!" Navarro exclaimed.

"So? Maybe—"

"No maybe," Navarro snapped. "What did you do?"

CHAPTER THIRTY-ONE

Jonathan had no idea how Felipe had been able to scare up a late-model Range Rover, but as the roads got progressively nastier, he was thankful for the wide wheelbase and the four-wheel drive. Given the bargain-basement price for the vehicle, the smart money said that Felipe had either stolen it from someone himself, or he'd bought it from someone who had. The leather interior and the air-conditioning, though, didn't exactly fit in with the nature of the cargo, or the mission that lay at the other end of their journey. Despite their best efforts to tie down their cargo, the weapons and equipment made a hell of a racket as they bounced along trails that only people in the third world would have the guts to call roads.

As they approached the rallying point—not a town or even a village, but rather the intersection of minutes and seconds of longitude and latitude—Jonathan told Harvey to stop the truck.

"Gladly," he said. "The instant you want me to turn around, you just say the word and we're out of here."

Jonathan ignored him. Their time together had been defined by three hours of endless bitching, and he'd grown tired of it a long time ago. He was giving the guy a shot at a new life, for God's sake, and all he could do was whine.

Jonathan lifted his portable radio from the center console and keyed the mike. "Big Guy, this is Scorpion. How do you copy?"

He'd expected a delay as the man on the other end of the radio scrambled to find the transmit button, so he was surprised when he heard Boxers' voice respond right away. "It's about time," he said.

"We're a half mile out," Jonathan said. "I didn't want to startle anyone."

"I was hoping that was you," Boxers said. "You make a hell of a racket. Come on in."

"On our way." Then to Harvey: "You heard the man. Tally-ho."

Harvey eased pressure onto the accelerator, and they were on their way. Less than a minute later, Jonathan pointed ahead and to the right, where he spotted the first picket. "See the guy in the trees up there?"

Harvey nodded. "I got him. What do you want to do?"

Jonathan repositioned the M4 in his lap so that he could fire left-handed if he needed to. "Just keep going. If he brings a weapon to bear, I'll take him out."

"I thought these guys were our allies."

"In an hour, maybe they'll be allies. Right now, they're just strangers with guns."

"There's another one on the left," Harvey said. When he pointed, he kept his hand low so no one could misinterpret the gesture as aggressive.

Jonathan appreciated the smart thinking. "I see him."

"How many directions can you shoot at one time?"

"When motivated?" Jonathan quipped. "You'd be surprised. Just keep going. Don't speed up, don't slow down. Nothing's pointing at us, so I guess they got the word."

"You have no idea how little comfort that gives me."

It had been a mistake to leave the windows up, Jonathan

realized. Shooting through glass was inaccurate at best. What he lacked in accuracy would have to be made up for in volume, and just to make sure he was ready for the possibility, he caressed the M4's selector switch with his left forefinger and verified that it was in the three-round burst mode. As long as he was alive and still had a trigger finger, there wasn't a target on the planet that he couldn't hit with six rounds.

Ten seconds later, they were past the sentries and closing in on the clearing that would be their base camp. Including the pickets, whom he could see in his rearview mirror following the Rover, Jonathan counted seven soldiers, all dressed in jungle camouflage, and all holding rifles. To the left of center, Boxers towered over the others, and next to Boxers stood an utterly unchanged José Calderón.

"Boy, you don't really get how friggin' huge he is till you seem him next to other people, do you?" Harvey said. "He looks like Frankenstein."

Jonathan pointed to a random spot on the ground beyond the front bumper. "Just stop anywhere in here," he said. "And Mr. Smith?" Jonathan was fanatical about not using real names on operations, even when outside the hearing of others.

"Yeah?"

"I'm gonna give you a literal life lesson right now. As in, a lesson that will lengthen your life. Big Guy doesn't like it when people call him names like Frankenstein. He doesn't like Lurch; he doesn't like Paul Bunyan. Frankly, he's not all that fond of Big Guy, but he puts up with it because it's his code name. In general, he doesn't tease well."

"A bit of a sociopath, is he?"

Jonathan's glare darkened. "That would be calling him a name, wouldn't it? As the man whose ass he's saved on more than one occasion, you're beginning to piss me off."

Harvey opened his mouth to say something, but Jonathan wasn't interested. He pulled the door handle and stepped out into the jungle sauna. By the time he got his door closed again, Jammin' Josie was already on his way over, his arms outstretched. Again with the *abrazos*. "Señor Jones, it's been too many years."

Jonathan held out his arm to stop the man. When he complied, the sign to halt became an offer for a handshake. "How are you, Josie?"

At first, José looked confused, but then he offered up a wide grin. "I forget that you don't like to touch," he said.

"I don't mind touching," Jonathan said. "I just don't like having to check for my wallet afterward."

José put a hand to his chest, feigning a wound. "Is that any way to greet an old friend?"

"Actually, it's not at all how I greet old friends. How many people know that I'm here?"

The wound grew deeper. "I have told no one, Señor Jones."

Sensing trouble, and no doubt welcoming the opportunity to settle it, Boxers moved closer. Behind him, Harvey stepped out of the Range Rover. José's troops sensed it, too, and several unslung their rifles.

"Don't be an idiot, Josie," Jonathan said. "Where do you think I got the Range Rover?"

The smile dimmed, and then returned. "Oh, well, Felipe knows, of course."

"Of course." He scanned the faces of the men who continued to close in, ever so slowly, and reflexively calculated lanes of fire. They still had time. "Tell your men to stand down," he commanded.

José said the right words in Spanish, and when the men hesitated, he repeated them more forcefully. His troops relaxed, but not entirely.

Boxers said, "You watching this, Boss?"

Jonathan opened his stance so he could keep a better eye on the crowd as he continued his chat with Josie. "Mr. Smith?" he called without looking.

Harvey said, "Sir?"

"Arm yourself, please."

Concern fell across Josie's face. "What are you doing, my friend?"

Jonathan dared a glance to satisfy himself that Harvey had picked up his weapon from the Rover's seat.

Josie said, "You seem to be expecting violence from me. I am your friend."

"Tell me how Felipe knows so much," Jonathan said.

José shuffled his feet and forced a smile. "Felipe knows everything, yes?"

Boxers made himself taller still, and Josie seemed to shrink accordingly.

"Who else knows?" Jonathan pressed.

The little man held his hand as if taking an oath. "On the grave of my mother, I have told no one."

Boxers growled, "Careful, Scorpion. Snakes aren't born. They hatch."

José turned on him, craning his neck to look Boxers in the eye. "I don't like you," he said. "I been nothing but nice to you all day, you been nothing but lousy in return." Then he faced Jonathan. "And then you come and treat me like I am traitor. I never betrayed you, Mr. Jones. Never once, not even during our fight with Pablo. I could have been a rich man if I had betrayed you, but I never do."

"You would have been a *dead* man if you'd betrayed us," Boxers said.

"Back then we all think we are dead men anyway," José countered. "I could have been much safer telling people about you, but I never do that."

Jonathan felt tension draining from his shoulders. Jammin' Josie was exactly right. During the shoot-'em-up drug war, there had been a time when the only safe people were the ones on the wrong side of the law. A man like Josie could have retired on the reward for betraying the good guys.

"You've always been a good friend to me," Jonathan said.

"But it's been a long time, and things are different now. Josie, right now is your one and only opportunity to tell me if your loyalty has been compromised. Tell me the details of what you've told others, and I promise that I'll let you all walk away. I won't come looking for you."

Something changed in Josie's eyes. A brief flash of panic, maybe. Boxers saw it, too, and he shifted his grip on his rifle, allowing his gloved finger to slip into the trigger guard of his M4.

"Oh, shit," he said.

Harvey sensed the tension between Jonathan and his old friend, but there was nothing about their interaction that seemed critical. The order to arm himself surprised him, but even then he didn't sense urgency. As ordered, he'd lifted out his MP5 machine gun, but he thought it was more a symbolic gesture than preparation for combat, so he didn't even bother to extend the telescoping stock. He stood, watching and doing his best to listen, with the weapon dangling from his hand like an overgrown pistol.

Such was his posture when one of the mercenaries on his left shouldered his M16 and brought it to bear.

Boxers said, "Oh, shit," and then the jungle exploded in automatic weapons fire.

Harvey dropped to the ground for cover, but by the time he rolled to a prone shooting position and brought his weapon up, it was over. None of the mercenaries remained standing. Most appeared to be dead, but the one closest to him writhed from his wounds, one of which pumped blood at a fatal rate.

Harvey whipped his head toward the spot where he'd last seen Jonathan and Boxers, and both of them had dropped to a knee. Barrels smoking, their weapons remained locked in on their targets. In less than five seconds, they'd cut down seven men. Harvey had never seen anything like it.

"Mr. Smith, are you all right?"

Harvey gaped. His ears felt like they'd been stuffed with cotton. "Yeah," he said. "Holy shit."

While Jonathan held his aim, Boxers rose to his feet, and with his weapon always at the ready, approached the bodies. "If you've got nothing better to do, how about giving me a hand?" the Big Guy said.

"M-me?" Harvey stammered.

"Y-yeah, y-you," Boxers mocked. "Disarm these men."

Harvey rose to his feet. "But they're dead. Jesus." Once he stood, he could see just how dead they were—every one a head shot.

"Disarmed and dead is better than just plain dead."

"No, Big Guy, I need him here with me," Jonathan said. He was kneeling over Jammin' Josie, his bloody hands pressed against the other man's belly. "Find the aid kit and bring it here."

The trauma bag lay on the top of the equipment piled next to one of Josie's Blazers.

Harvey knew it was bad the instant he saw pallor in Josie's face. The location of the bullet wound in the upper left quadrant of the abdomen, combined with the flow of blood, said that his spleen had been hit.

"He needs a surgeon," Harvey said.

Jonathan gave him a knowing look. Josie was not long for this world. "Do what you can."

A new kind of fear gripped Harvey's insides. He hadn't seen a bullet wound in years; and the last time he did, a medevac chopper was always a radio call away. He had no magical powers. This man was going to die, and Harvey was going to have to tend him while it happened.

"What's this all about?" Harvey asked. "What just happened?"

"You tend to the wounds, Doc," Jonathan said. "And we'll find out the rest together."

* * *

Jonathan helped Harvey strip Josie of his shirt, exposing the wound that had been inflicted by one of Josie's own—by accident, Jonathan assumed, but with mercenaries, you could never be sure. This man who'd betrayed him had a chest and belly much like Jonathan's own—less developed, perhaps, but equally disfigured by scars from previous wounds. This new one was a perfectly round hole in the front, about the diameter of a number-two pencil, while the exit wound in his back was a ragged avulsion three times the size of the entry hole.

While Harvey pulled HemCon packets out of his med kit and ripped them open, Jonathan said, "Tell me what you did, Josie."

"Am I shot bad?"

"Yes," he said. "You're shot bad." No matter what, Jonathan owed him the truth.

"Fatal?"

"Probably."

"Jesus," Harvey snapped. "Where did you learn bedside manner?"

Jonathan ignored him. "I need to know the details, Josie. You don't want to die with betrayal on your soul."

Harvey said, "This is going to hurt." He'd donned a pair of latex gloves and prepared to insert the HemCon pads into the wounds. Similar in appearance to standard gauze dressings, HemCon pads were soaked in a coagulating agent that was damned effective at stanching the flow of blood from traumatic injuries long enough to get the patient to a hospital.

"Wait a second," Jonathan said.

Harvey shook his head. "No."

No easy way existed to jam fabric into the ballistic pathway of a bullet. Josie howled like a tortured animal as Harvey stuffed first the entry wound and then the exit. The very thought of it churned Jonathan's stomach.

Josie lay soaked in sweat and heaving for breath when it

was all done. He'd nearly bitten through his lower lip. "*Dios mio*," he moaned.

Jonathan stroked his hair. "It's over now. That should slow the bleeding."

"Then maybe I can live?"

Harvey shot a glare.

"Maybe," Jonathan said. "But Josie, you have to tell me what you did. After you do that, we can give you a shot for the pain."

Josie locked eyes with Jonathan. They shimmered with fear and shame. "A man came to me," he said. "He knew of our work together in the past. He had pictures of you. All three of you."

Jonathan's heart skipped. No one knew they were coming. "Who was this man?"

"I don't know him."

"You know his name," Jonathan said, his heart heavy with disappointment. "I know it, too, but I need you to say it. Please don't lie to me. Not now."

Tears tracked from the corners of the little man's eyes. "I don't know how he found me," he said. "He approached me on the street, showed me a picture of my family, and told me that if I saw any of you—he showed me your pictures—I was to call him and tell him."

"Tell him what?"

"That I saw you, I suppose."

Boxers had rejoined them. He stood at his full height, allowing his shadow to keep the sun out of José's eyes.

"He threatened my family," José said.

Jonathan understood now. "What did he want?"

The last of the resistance went away. Jonathan saw real remorse. Genuine regret. "He knew that I was raising an attack force. He guessed that it was for you." He tried a friendly smile. "I'm not the liar I used to be. He wanted me to kill you."

Jonathan gave a wry chuckle. "With the people I hired to help me?"

Josie closed his eyes against another wave of agony. "It would have pained me," he said after it passed. "He had pictures of my family. He was going to kill them."

"What makes you think we won't?" Boxers asked.

Jonathan didn't like the question, didn't like the tone, and didn't like the implication. But he showed none of it.

José smiled. "You are here to rescue a child," he said. "People who rescue children don't kill them."

Bingo, Jonathan thought. In fact, a Silver Star citation posted on the wall at Unit headquarters at Fort Bragg gave testimony to the lengths Boxers would go to protect children.

Jonathan cranked his head to look up at Boxers' silhouette. "Get on the horn with Mother Hen and have her scan the screens. Make sure we're still alone."

Boxers backed off a few feet and keyed his microphone. Jonathan tuned him out. "I need to know everything, Josie. Every detail. Start with his name."

The little man squinted against the sun. "I knew who he was as soon as I saw him. They call him *El Matador.* He is very feared by the people here in the mountains, and he is allowed by the *policía* to do whatever he wants. He kills people, Mr. Jones. His last name is Ponder. First name Michael, I think. No, it's a different name that sounds like Michael. I don't know."

Jonathan didn't know what to say. This mission had barely begun, yet the battle plan had already been shredded.

"I did it to save my family," Josie repeated. Another wave of pain rolled through his gut. And he tensed against it. "It was never my plan to betray you, Mr. Jones. You must know that."

Boxers' shadow returned. "We're alone," he reported.

"Good to know," Jonathan said. To Josie: "Did you even look for the boy we're trying to find?"

José's eyes cleared. "*Sí.* I found him."

Jonathan shot a look to Boxers, and the Big Guy retreated to one of the ancient Chevy Blazers that Josie had brought for transportation. He returned with a plastic laminated map that was covered with grease-pencil markings. Jonathan unfolded the map and held it so Josie could see it. "Show me."

Josie took a moment to study it and orient himself. "We are right here," he said, leaving a bloody dot on the map. He pointed to another spot. "This is where the boy is. You cannot drive to it, and you cannot fly to it. You have to walk."

"How do you know this is the place?"

"The boy you are looking for has very blond hair, yes?"

"Yes."

Josie pointed to yet another spot on the map. "Everybody knows that Ponder has a permanent camp here. It's a—how do you say it?—stage area."

"Staging area," Jonathan corrected. "For what?"

"For food and supplies for his factories. They gather the materials there, and then move them out into the mountains to the factories."

"How many factories are there?"

José shrugged. "I don't know. No one knows. Many. But one of the men who works there is easily bought. He told me that a blond-haired boy was brought to this staging area two days ago. He was—how do you say it?—asleep, but not normal sleep."

"Unconscious," Jonathan helped.

"Yes, exactly. When he woke up, they put him in a truck and drove him into the woods."

"To one of the many factories."

"*Exactamente*. This one here." He pointed back to the spot where he said Evan was.

"How do you know it's this one?"

"Because of the white hair. Word of such things travels quickly among the Indian villages. This one here"—the spot he pointed to this time had no marking at all—"has been treated particularly badly by Ponder's men. Many rapes and murders. No men left in the village at all. No boys, even, beyond *ocho años*. They have all been killed or put to work in the factories. Slave labor. So when a boy who looks like the boy you seek comes through, he is noticed. He was there yesterday. Only one factory is close by. That is where you will find the blond boy." José gave a weak smile, clearly proud of himself.

Then it disappeared. "When Ponder discovers that you're still alive, he will kill my wife and children."

Jonathan sighed. "I'm sorry."

Harvey offered, "Lie to him. Call and say that you killed us. That would buy time."

"I wish it would," Josie said. He closed his eyes. "I was supposed to deliver your heads to him," he said.

Ten minutes later, they were ready to go. While Jonathan and Boxers managed the business of loading two vehicles, Harvey made final preparations with Josie. As gently as possible, he dragged the man to a shady spot and propped him against two rucksacks whose owners no longer needed them.

"Are you comfortable?" Harvey asked.

Josie looked terrified. As promised, Harvey had given him an injection for the pain, but it hadn't touched the man's fear of dying. "Please take me with you," Josie begged. "Don't make me die out here."

Harvey avoided eye contact. "Boss says no."

"Please. You can talk him into it. You look like a nice young man."

"Yeah, well, looks can be deceiving."

"Please."

Harvey's stomach churned. "I can't," he said. He stood.

"Then kill me," Josie said. "Give me another shot. Give me five shots. Make me go to sleep and—"

Jonathan stepped into Harvey's space. "We're not assassins, Josie," he said. "He won't drug you to death, and before you ask, I won't shoot you to death. It's not what we do." He put a hand on Harvey's shoulder. "Go ahead and mount up. We'll be in the Range Rover."

José tried to sit up more, but his body wouldn't cooperate. "Mr. Jones. All those years."

"They're all in the past. I'm sorry. I wish you hadn't done what you did."

"But my family."

"They'll be killed, I suppose."

"You could help them."

Jonathan paused. He didn't want to rise to that bait. The man was dying, for God's sake. He was desperate for some thread of hope. Behind him, one of the Blazers rumbled to life.

"Good-bye, Josie."

José took a huge breath and seemed to focus all his energy. "I don't want to die here!" he shouted.

Jonathan turned his back on his old colleague and walked away.

CHAPTER THIRTY-TWO

As the sound of the approaching chopper grew louder, Navarro pulled an AR-10 rifle off the rack and hovered it in the air for Gail. "You know how to shoot?" he asked.

Gail swallowed her annoyance. He had no way of knowing her past. "I'm actually pretty good," she said.

"I hope so," he said. "Take this."

Gail accepted the weapon. She recognized it for what it was—a 7.62-millimeter monster that would put a hole through anything. "Aren't we overreacting a bit?"

"Overreacting would be shooting at a news helicopter," Navarro quipped, reaching back to the rack. "Repelling an airborne assault is quite the opposite." He grabbed a pristine 1950s vintage M-14—the precursor to Gail's rifle, and by most estimates one of the finest weapons ever manufactured for the military.

"I need ammo," Gail said.

But Navarro was ahead of her. He handed her two full magazines. Including the one that was already installed, that gave her sixty rounds, plus the fifteen in her Glock. Add all of that to the sixty that Navarro took for himself and they could have themselves quite the war.

"We don't get traffic in this airspace," Navarro explained. "We don't get visitors, either. To get both on the same day means that someone's about to die. I don't want it to be me." He headed for the back door.

"Where are we going?"

"Out."

"Where?"

Navarro didn't answer, and Gail realized that she'd find out by keeping up.

Navarro moved with surprising agility as he made a bee-line for the back door, pausing only long enough to turn the three locks that kept it closed. Out here, the chop of the approaching rotor blades was louder, registering in Gail's chest as a deep thump that had a physical force to it.

"Definitely coming here," Navarro said, perhaps to himself, but loudly enough for Gail to hear. He seemed to know where he was going and what he had planned. And why not? He'd had enough years of solitude to plan for just about any eventuality.

From the back door, he picked up his pace toward the woods line, about seventy-five feet from the back wall. If he had, in fact, designed this property as a fortress of sorts, then he had obviously planned more for defense than offense. The wide fields of fire were great for fending off an attacking force, but they were exactly the wrong choice if you were trying to make a break without being seen. Ask any prison yard designer and he'll agree.

The rotor sound crescendoed at about the halfway point of their run for the woods, and Navarro really poured on the gas to get to the tree line before being spotted. With the carry handle for the AR-10 clutched in her right fist, and the spare mags in her left, Gail kept up step for step.

With ten yards left, she would have sworn the chopper was immediately overhead. As if to confirm her worst fears, the voice of God said, "Federal agents. Stop where you are."

For an instant—no longer than the width of a heartbeat—

Gail considered complying. Even Navarro slowed by half a stride. But this wasn't right. She didn't quite know why yet, but something about the scenario was wrong for an action by any federal law enforcement agency. "Keep going!" she yelled. "Go, go, go!"

It was all Navarro needed. He picked up speed again.

There's no way to accurately track time in stressful conditions, but in the seconds that separated them from some measure of shelter, the hairs on the back of Gail's neck went to full attention. Out of sheer instinct, she cut hard to her right, and then back to the left again to ruin any shooter's aim.

The first bullet didn't arrive until after they'd crossed into the trees, and at that, it went two feet wide, drilling a pine between the two of them.

Navarro dove to the ground for cover, and Gail was three strides past him before she realized what he'd done. "Bruce!" she yelled. They weren't deeply enough into the woods yet for adequate cover. Two more rounds screamed in, way too close to him. The shooter was getting better.

"Stay down!" Gail yelled. She took a knee behind a hardwood and brought her rifle to bear, trying her best to stay invisible as she searched the horizon for a target. The hammering sound of the rotors hadn't lessened a bit, but it seemed to be coming from directly overhead. She didn't have a clue what the shooters were up to, but she knew that if she couldn't see them, then they couldn't see her. "Bruce, get up now. Find cover."

Navarro reacted quickly, again surprising her with his lithe flexibility. He got his feet under him and more sprang than ran to a different tree. "What are they doing?"

The rotor noise had stabilized, as if they'd parked the chopper in the air overhead.

Directly overhead.

"Oh, shit," Gail breathed. "Run, Bruce!" she yelled. "We've got to move. Follow me."

She took off at a dead run, staying inside the tree line, but running parallel to the clearing, sprinting in the direction she thought they'd least likely anticipate.

Inside ten seconds, the grenades started falling through the canopy of leaves. The explosions were not as loud as she expected them to be—no louder, really, than the flash-bangs she'd used during her HRT days—but the fragmentation damage was staggering, obliterating bushes and smaller trees, and stripping bark and leaves off the larger ones. She knew for a fact that she heard three explosions, but after that it was just a cacophony that reduced their abandoned hiding spot to a lifeless crater. She ignored the two hornet stings in the back of her right leg, which she knew had to be grenade fragments finding their mark.

She drew to a stop behind another tree, the largest one she could find, and Navarro joined her. "Bombs?" he shouted, nearly hysterical. He'd lost his steely calm, and what had replaced it was not at all endearing.

"Hand grenades," she said. "I suspected they were going to drop something once they moved over the trees, where a sniper would have no shot. Then, when they went into a hover, I knew for sure. Are you okay?"

"They threw hand grenades at me!"

"Are you hurt?"

Navarro shook his head, then grew concerned as his gaze shifted to Gail's backside. "You're bleeding," he said.

"I'm hurting, too," she said. "Seems only reasonable." Now that they'd stopped running, she could feel the trails of blood running down the back of her right leg.

"Are *you* okay?"

"They dropped grenades on me!" Gail tried to match his incredulous tone, and succeeded in eliciting a chuckle. "I think I'm fine."

She forced herself not to look, deciding that as long as the pain was tolerable, and the flow was a trickle and not a gush, it was a minor wound. To look now and discover otherwise would help no one and change nothing. The bones were intact, and she was alive. In times like these, it pays to take things one step at a time.

The chopper was moving again, circling around to hover over the clearing between the house and the tree line. It was a fairly old-style Bell Jet Ranger, popular among police forces in the 1990s, and it had no markings that showed it to be anything other than a private aircraft. The chopper pivoted in the air, bringing its port side parallel to the trees, its nose pointed directly at Gail and Navarro.

She could see the pilots clearly through the windscreen—so clearly, in fact, that she wondered how they were not seen in return. Then she got it: they were surveying the damage they'd wrought.

Navarro raised his rifle. "Let's take them out."

"No!" Gail snapped. Her mind raced to review their options. This was their perfect moment of advantage. The aircraft was completely vulnerable. If they opened fire now, they could knock it out of the sky and neutralize the danger. Except they didn't have cause. They were not in imminent danger, and every professional law enforcement officer knew that in the absence of immediate threat, deadly force could not be used. It was always a last resort. That's the way things worked in an ordered, civilized society. There was *always* another way. *Always* a better option than killing, right up until the moment that those options proved impossible.

A man with a rifle appeared in the Jet Ranger's open side door. He raised the weapon to his shoulder and opened fire, blasting bullet after bullet into the smoldering, ravaged remains of what had been their hiding place.

Fuck it.

Gail brought her AR-10 to bear. "You take the pilots," she said. "I'll take the shooter." Without waiting for an answer, she steadied her rifle against the trunk of her sheltering tree and lined up for a slam-dunk fifty-yard sure thing. She double-checked the firing selector to make sure it was set to single-fire, she corrected for the downwash of the rotors, squeezed the trigger and—

Navarro opened up on full-auto, emptying his twenty-round magazine in less than two seconds, and filling the air with twenty deadly projectiles that hit nothing. Nothing! Jesus, how was that even possible?

Gail's shot went high and right, harmlessly shattering the window of the open sliding door.

The pilot reacted instantly, pouring on power and pitch. The nose dipped dramatically—perilously, Gail thought—as the rotor blades dug deeply into the air and pulled the aircraft up and away with amazing speed. Buffeted by the downwash, she tried to react, shifting her aim to the cockpit, but she wasn't fast enough. She fired three shots in their direction, but they were wasted. She was reasonably sure that she hit the chopper somewhere, but if she'd done any damage, it would have been from pure luck. As the aircraft pulled up and away, the pilot also slipped it sideways, a combat tactic that made even a relatively slow target like a chopper difficult to hit with ground fire. She considered firing again but decided against it. Chances of a kill shot had dropped to nothing, and even out here, all those bullets had to come down somewhere.

To her right, Navarro finished reloading and shouldered his rifle again.

Gail slapped the muzzle down. "What was that?" she yelled. "How do you miss something that big when it's that close?"

Navarro's face glowed an unnatural red as he shouted back, "I was a little stressed, okay? I've never tried to shoot anything down before. What about you, Miss Expert? You didn't do any better. I say we make a run for it."

"To where?"

"To anywhere. You've got your truck, and I've got mine. We just get in and drive."

"Not with them in the air," Gail said, rejecting the plan out of hand. "Any advantage we have is tied to our mobility. A car is dependent on roads, and roads bring predictability. That's the last thing we need."

"So what do we do?"

"We wait to see what *they're* going to do, and then react."

She led the way deeper into the woods, and then left, back toward their first hiding place. Drawing on her HRT counter-sniper training, she knew that that people on the move tend to stick to one direction, rarely doubling back.

"Why are we going back this way?" Navarro asked.

"Because we are," she said. Sometimes the simplest answers were the best ones.

They both paused and gasped in unison as they passed by the ravaged section of woods that had been ground zero for the grenade attack. The earth had been ripped open, and tree roots avulsed from the dark soil. Hundreds of white gashes showed the tearing force of the fragmentation explosives against the tree trunks. Looking at the damage made her leg hurt even more. It had gone from a searing sting to a dull vibrant ache. Almost without thinking, she dared to touch the fabric of her denim jeans, but regretted it when she saw her wet, red fingertips.

"We're not there yet," she said, and she nudged Navarro on with a gentle push on his shoulder.

"Where are we going?"

"I'll know it when we see it," she lied. What she meant was, *Anywhere but here.*

When the distance felt right, she turned to the left and moved to the tree line again. With great effort, she lowered herself to her left knee, and peered out from behind a sheltering oak. At first, it appeared that the chopper hadn't moved. It just sat there, parked in the air over the distant forest, well out of range. Were they radioing someone for instructions? Awaiting reinforcements, perhaps?

The thought of backup forces made her heart skip, but then she rejected the idea as unlikely. If they'd had more troops, they would have waited for them. No, whatever they decided to do, they would either do it alone, or they would do it another day.

"Okay, I'll come with you," Navarro said, a propos of nothing. "I'll testify."

Gail had almost forgotten he was there. "Yeah? Why the change of heart?"

He chuckled wryly. "I'd say my cover's kind of blown, wouldn't you?"

Gail didn't respond. There was more, and he'd either share it or he wouldn't, but that answer was too easy.

"Nobody should have this kind of power," he said. "Too much violence, all to cover up a murder."

Gail liked that. She acknowledged his decision with a nod.

"So, do you think they found me by following you?" he asked.

"Must have," she admitted. "I don't know how, but I guess that doesn't matter now."

He pointed. "I think they're coming back."

At first, she didn't see it, but then she did: the chopper was definitely getting bigger. It was keeping out of range, but it was circling in closer. It seemed to be on a course that would take them to the front side of the house. "What are they doing?" she wondered aloud.

"Maybe they're just looking for us. You know, cruising around to see if we're hiding out there."

Gail didn't like it. "No, they have to know we're still in the woods somewhere. If we'd crossed into the open, they'd have seen us."

"Even from that far away?"

"A clear day like this, you can see amazing detail when you're on the lookout for it." So, what could they be up to in the front of the house? When the shooter reappeared in the doorway, she knew exactly what their plan was.

"Oh, hell," she said. "They're going to take out my Jeep. Trap us here."

"But I have a truck of my own," Navarro said.

"Pray they don't know that."

A plan blossomed in Gail's mind. "Okay, Bruce, listen to me," she said. She spoke so quickly that her words ran together. In the distance, the Jet Ranger began its run. "When I say, I want you to do exactly what you did before. I want you to point that rifle directly at the chopper and unload it on full automatic. Then I want you to curl up in a ball behind that tree and not even peek out until the shooting is over."

His jaw dropped. "What—"

The door gunner started shooting at the front of the house.

"When I say," Gail reminded, and she sprinted ten strides farther to the right. Her leg screamed at her as she slid to a halt on her left hip, and she shouldered her AR-10. On the far side of the house, a column of smoke rolled skyward from the murdered Jeep.

"Now!" she yelled.

Her words had barely evaporated before Navarro unleashed another twenty-round string.

This time, the pilot had been setting a trap, and he was ready for it. Again with amazing speed, it pivoted in the air and raced sixty yards closer, presenting a broadside target. The shooter opened up on Navarro's hiding spot.

And Gail opened up on the shooter. With the selector on full automatic this time, she fired two three-round bursts. The first nailed the door again, but it startled the shit out of the shooter. He pivoted on his knee and pointed his weapon directly at Gail's muzzle flashes. Her second burst caught him as he was still moving. She noted the pink mist in the doorway, and was dimly aware of the man falling away from the chopper to the ground, but by then she'd shifted her target.

From this angle, she could no longer see the Jet Ranger's windscreen, but she could clearly see the bulkhead that separated the cockpit from the cargo section, and she knew that the pilots' seats were just on the opposite side. Even as the chopper's nose dipped and attempted to race away, Gail pressed the foregrip tightly against the trunk of the tree, and she squeezed the trigger, unleashing all her remaining ammunition in a single uninterrupted blast.

This time, not a single round was wasted. Fourteen, fifteen, whatever was left in the magazine plowed into the helicopter. The bird hesitated in midair, rocking slightly on its center axis as the pilots struggled to bring stability to the critically wounded bird.

As the receiver locked open, Gail dropped out the spent magazine, slapped in a second, and slid the receiver home. She braced against the tree, instinctively held her breath, and opened up again, pouring more bullets into that bulkhead. Only five or six rounds into the second burst, it was over. The aircraft wobbled, then heeled over to its starboard side.

Gail dove for cover, pressing herself into the dirt and covering her head with her arms. As if mere flesh and bones could protect her from the shrapnel of a disintegrating helicopter. The ground under her jumped at the impact, and an instant later, a searing wall of heat preceded a low-order explosion that was more a *whump* than a *bang*.

She pressed deeper into the ground as something whistled through the air over her head and then sheared off the tops of trees, creating a rainstorm of leaves and branches.

The heat bloomed painfully over the next three or four seconds, and then it retracted just as quickly. In Gail's mind, she could almost see the roiling fireball tumbling over itself as rolled into the sky. When she dared to raise her head, that was exactly what she saw.

That, and a world on fire. It had started with her truck,

and then the helicopter; but when the chopper fell out of the sky, it clipped the roof of Navarro's house, and now fire was consuming the building's roof, traveling from the far end to the near.

To her distant left, Navarro struggled to his feet, his rifle dangling from his hand. "Well," he said. "Shit." He turned to look at her. "Good thing I keep my keys in the truck, huh?"

CHAPTER THIRTY-THREE

The rain started to fall the minute Evan Guinn and his escorts arrived at the big camp in the jungle. And when it fell, it fell like a house. No little drip, drip followed by a patter that gradually increased. This rainstorm was born as a gulley-washer. That's what Father Dom called lots of rain. But even that dramatic description couldn't touch this deluge. No gulley could contain this rain, so thick and heavy that you couldn't see more than fifteen feet ahead. The flood of water turned the ground to an ankle-deep river of mud, and again, the boy was grateful not to be burdened with shoes.

This camp was a lot like the one where he'd first awakened, but many times the size, with probably ten times the people, many of them carrying machine guns, and more than a few wearing soldiers' uniforms. He saw more of those raised-floor huts, too, like the one where he'd awoke, but most had no walls. The roofs were made of weeds, but the sides were wide open. It was hard to know exactly how many there were through blinding rain, but he counted eight, and thought he could make out the outlines of several more.

As he passed the first building, the soldiers who'd been escorting him peeled off and disappeared into the rain. Evan started to follow, but Oscar cupped the back of his neck with his palm and moved him forward. Under different circumstances, it would have been a nearly playful gesture.

"Almost there," Oscar said.

The deeper they traveled into the camp, the barer the ground became, until finally, they entered what felt like the middle, where the mud was ankle deep. The trek ended at the base of a huge hut, at the bottom of a five-stair climb.

At shoulder height, the hut buzzed with activity and stank of gasoline and rotten eggs. A dozen or so half-naked people, a few not much older than he, moved about at a frenzied pace, clearly in a hurry to finish something, but Evan had no idea what the something might be.

Oscar nudged his shoulder, less playfully than last time. "Up," he said. "You first."

"Where are we?"

Oscar smiled, ignoring the water that cascaded from his nose and chin. "This is your new home."

Evan made a point of showing nothing. Shielding his eyes from the rain, he tilted his head to look up to the top of the stairs, and then climbed. He wasn't sure it made sense, but the higher he got off the ground, the less the place stank of gasoline. He was grateful for that, because it was a smell that made his stomach uneasy.

When he reached the top, the rain stopped falling, and he realized that he was under a roof. A second later, Oscar rejoined his side and craned his neck to look around, clearly searching for something or someone in particular. He made eye contact with a man on the far side of the enclosure and waved—a big wave, high over his head.

Evan followed his eye line and saw the man return the wave with a nod before turning back and finishing his conversation. The man looked angry, and the boy on the other end of the conversation looked frightened. When the man doing the talking punctuated his remarks with a slap against the side of the boy's face, the kid cowered long enough for the man to turn away, and then he went back to work doing whatever he was doing. Something that involved cloth suspended over a tub.

The angry man walked with long, quick strides directly at them—so sternly that Oscar took a step away from Evan, who took a step the other way. Evan was not going to let himself be slapped by a stranger. As he closed the distance even more, the man's pockmarked face drew back into a wide grin that looked more menacing than friendly.

"So this is the famous Evan Guinn!" the man proclaimed. "You look like crap." He turned to Oscar. "What the hell have you been doing with him?"

Oscar responded in Spanish. Evan couldn't understand the words, but the hand gestures said he was talking about a long damn walk through the jungle. The angry man just seemed to get angrier. He turned to the gathered crowd of workers and barked something at them. A few seconds later, someone hurried over with a white block in his hand. The man snatched it away.

He handed it to Evan. "Here," he said. "It's soap. Go use it."

Evan stared. He understood the words, but they didn't make sense to him.

The man took a step closer and shoved the bar at him again. "Take the soap and go wash all that shit off your face. Your hair, too. Before I cut it off with a pair of scissors."

"What's your name?" Evan asked.

It was the man's turn to look confused. Then he laughed. "My name? *Dios mio*, did I forget to introduce myself?" He bowed deeply from the waist. It was an exaggerated motion that Evan knew was designed to embarrass him in front of people. "*Me llamo* Antonio. But you can call me *jefe*."

It sounded like "heffay."

"Now, *por favor* Mister Evan Guinn, would you please be so kind as to wash that shit off your face and hair?"

Antonio had dead eyes that scared Evan. He decided it was not a time to argue. "Where?" he asked.

Antonio laughed again. He pointed out to the rain. "Welcome to the jungle," he said, "where you never have to find a bathtub because a shower finds you every day."

Was he kidding? He was supposed to just stand in the rain and scrub himself down in the middle of everyone?

Antonio leaned down to look Evan square in the eye. "I have a job to do, Mister Evan Guinn, and it requires you to be clean. If I have to do it for you, I will use a wire brush, and you will not like it." His breath stank with an odor that Evan had never smelled before—sort of like medicine, but not really.

Not seeing a choice, Evan turned. He walked back into the rain and down the stairs, the bar of soap clutched in his hand. *What the hell*, he figured. Water was water, right? He could keep his pants on like he did in the dorm showers at Resurrection House (okay, that was a swimsuit, but still) and wash around them. As he started scrubbing his chest and his face with the soap—it was Ivory, his favorite—it actually felt pretty good. He did his arms next, but decided to forgo his legs and feet. Didn't make a lot of sense when you were standing in a mud puddle. He finished by lathering up his hair, and then put the soap on the step while he allowed the rain to rinse him.

When he was done, the ground around his feet frothed white, and he felt a lot better. It wasn't until he started to climb the stairs again that he realized how many people were watching him, and how desperately filthy they all were.

Antonio noticed it, too, apparently, because when he barked out an order, they all went back to work.

Under cover again and out of the rain, Evan handed over the bar of soap and stood there, dripping onto the floor. "Better?" he asked.

Apparently not, judging from the look on Antonio's face. He barked another order, and a towel appeared—a ridiculous purple one with a picture of Mickey Mouse on it. "Dry yourself off," he ordered. "And come with me."

He led the way to the middle of the big covered platform, where an area had been cleared. Grateful for the opportunity to at least try to be dry, Evan employed the towel and watched as Antonio opened up a three-foot-long black tube and removed what looked like a stack of aluminum rods with black plastic on the ends. Evan was fascinated, in fact, as Antonio pulled on the rods and they expanded to form a tall framework of aluminum that stretched to six feet tall when it was set on its end. With the framework erected, Antonio reached into the tube again and unrolled a picture onto the frame. When it was all done, they had a tall picture of a seaside resort, with lots of buildings built into the side of a steep hill and impossibly blue water in the foreground.

"That's the Amalfi Coast," Antonio said. "Very beautiful."

With the picture set up, Antonio opened a padded envelope and removed a royal blue T-shirt with a Puma logo on the front, under an embroidered green, white, and red shield that sat dead center, just under the collar ring. The middle of the shield featured a stylized soccer ball with the letters FIGC in the middle.

"Put this on," Antonio said.

"Why?" As soon as the question escaped his mouth, Evan pulled it back. He slipped the shirt over his head.

"You recognize?" Antonio said. "That's the shirt for the national *fútbol* team of *Italia*."

Evan didn't care. He didn't even know that they played football in Italy.

Antonio pointed to a spot on the floor in front of the picture. "Stand there."

Evan did as he was told while Antonio produced a little camera and a newspaper from the padded envelope. The paper was called *Il Golfo*, and it featured a picture of a man Evan had never seen before.

"Hold the paper up next to your head and smile," the man commanded.

Evan remained stone faced.

Antonio's expression grew colder. "Mister Evan Guinn, we do not know each other good yet, but in the coming years, we will get to know each other very good, and as we do you will find that I am not a nice man. I am a mean man who does not mind hurting people. I do not mind hurting you."

Evan's stomach iced over. Did he just say *in the coming years*? Could that possibly be true?

"Evan Guinn, you will smile for this picture one way or the other, but I promise you that it is far harder to smile when you are in pain."

Evan stood tall, raised the paper next to his head, and smiled.

The camera flashed a total of five times as Antonio took the same picture again and again.

When he was done, he slipped the camera back into the envelope, and he snatched the newspaper out of the boy's hands. "Give me back the shirt," he said.

Evan nearly asked why, but stopped himself. He retracted his arms from the sleeves, then slipped the neck ring over his head and handed it back.

"Very good," Antonio said. He carefully folded the shirt and eased it back into the envelope, which he then placed on a nearby table.

"It's good to have that done," Antonio went on. "Now we put you to work."

CHAPTER THIRTY-FOUR

Mitch Ponder ordered a Modelo beer to go along with his fourth club soda and lime. With his guest running late and the restaurant filling up around him, he figured he had to order something with a price tag just to keep from getting thrown out.

The fact that he hadn't yet heard from José meant that the man had either had a change of heart, or he had gone to the other side. Either way, his family would be dead by morning. A promise is a promise, after all, and actions must have consequences. Mitch wouldn't handle the details himself, of course—finding street thugs willing to kill was not a challenge in this godforsaken country—but they would be handled. Mitch intentionally did not immerse himself in the minutiae. Whatever itch he had for taking lives was more than adequately scratched by people who were willing to pay for the service.

Continued good pay, however, required continued competent service, and by any measure he'd come up short of that on the Lincoln Hines hit. Who knew that something that happened so long ago could have legs for so many years?

It wasn't even a complicated hit. Sure, it was high-profile, the guy being a Senate wannabe and all, and the guy who paid for the hit was naturally the first suspect, but engineering a fake suicide was the easiest thing in the world. You plant a few distressed e-mails in the guy's past, establish a tawdry double life he never had, and then make sure that someone finds the bogus blackmail letters that drove him to do the dirty deed. With the pieces in place, you follow him closely enough to know when he's going to be alone, and then you pop him. People find the body, they find the fake evidence, they force two and two to equal four, and you're done.

The fact that the financier—Jacques Leger, in this case— was such an obvious suspect actually worked in his favor in the end. Everyone assumed that no one would be foolish enough to bring that kind of attention down on himself.

Mitch had been doing this shit for years, and he was damn good at it. Good enough that on the rare occasion when things went wrong, he readily and easily cleaned up after himself. Where third parties were involved—like today, for José's family—the hoods who jumped at the opportunity to work for *El Matador* were so paranoid about ending up on Mitch's shit list that they would figure out a way to violate the laws of physics and chemistry if they had to, to make sure that nothing went wrong.

Mitch had worked long and hard to establish his reputation as a harsh master. In his business, fear kept you alive. That universal business truth explained why he'd always been comfortable working for Sammy Bell and the Slater family. People were at least as afraid of them as they were of Mitch Ponder. With fear up and down the chain of command, things worked like clockwork.

Given all the moving parts that are involved in a hit, who would have ever thought that a smooth operation would break down at the payment phase? What special breed of idiot would a person have to be to abscond with money from a crime family on its way to a hired killer? And who would ever have guessed that that special breed of idiot could actually get away with it?

The Slater organization made good on covering the debt to Mitch, of course, but it was a stupid career decision on the part of the lawyer who took it. Bruce Navarro.

Except Navarro wasn't the thief.

The real thieves were Navarro's secretary and her boyfriend. Some bitch named Schuler. Mitch had deduced that connection within an hour of hearing that she'd turned up dead. The boyfriend killed the secretary and got away with the cash. In Mitch's book, the buck twenty-five wasn't nearly enough dough to sentence yourself to a life of looking over your shoulder, but he had to admire the boyfriend's originality. It was a pretty slick move how he pinned the murder on the husband. Damn good job, too, all things considered. Hubby got sentenced to death, for God's sake. How much better could you get? Having gotten away with murder, all the boyfriend had to do was try his best to prevent his own.

From Ponder's perspective, the whole cluster fuck had evolved into an amusing stability. Navarro kept his head down because of the active contract on it, the boyfriend was living the high life on the run, and Schuler's husband was going to be offed by the state. Jacques Leger's involvement was protected by an armored shield of secrets. Everybody could relax.

And then Arthur Guinn got himself arrested.

Good God almighty, of all the shitty luck. When old man Slater passed away in the late nineties, and Sammy Bell ascended to the throne of the organization, Arthur ascended to number two, the position originally held by Sammy. That made him heir apparent, and the fact of his arrest sent Sammy into a panic. He put out a contract on Guinn within two hours of him being taken into custody, but by then the window of opportunity had slammed shut. The FBI knew what they had in Guinn, and they knew how many people were gunning for him, so they made him invisible. When he moved from one place to another, the security was like something you'd expect for the president of the United States. They even shut down airspace, for God's sake.

Mitch had done a lot of business with the Slater family over the years—as he had done business with their competitors and, once upon a time, for the federal government—but he'd never seen Sammy Bell as shaken as he was in the months following Guinn's arrest. The details were none of Mitch's business, but it was clear that Guinn knew *everything*.

The silver medal for panic response came from Senator Leger. When you're a powerful man and you hire powerful criminals to do your dirty work, you expect absolute confidentiality. Mitch was sure that Leger paid dearly and regularly for that kind of confidence. It was no wonder that he went into orbit when he learned that Guinn was in custody.

But then absolutely nothing happened.

After the initial panic had gone unrequited, and no one else had been arrested in the next twelve months—and then twenty-four and thirty-six months—Sammy had begun to relax. He'd talked himself into believing that maybe Arthur would honor his friendships and keep true to his loyalties. Mitch had tried to believe it, too, even though he knew from experience what hard time can do to a man. Mitch had known all along that it was just a matter of time.

Then the new administration was elected into power, Leger became secretary of defense, the rise in profile started to make people nervous again.

Apparently Sammy Bell had good sources within the FBI or the prison system—maybe both—and about a week ago, those sources told him that Guinn was ready to cut a deal in return for protection. He was driving a hard bargain, too—he'd give everything if his conditions were met, and nothing at all if they weren't. Mitch had heard rumors that the ultimate decision went all the way to the White House, and part of him really hoped that Leger was in the room when the attorney general or FBI director made the pitch. That must have triggered a special breed of panic.

It certainly triggered an urgent phone call to Sammy Bell, who then passed the urgency to Mitch. At the end of the day, this mess was his loose end to be tied, and everybody expected him to finish his job.

So, how do you keep a man from spilling his guts to people who are willing to give him whatever he wants? You threaten his family. The tactic works just as well with big shots as it does with peons like José. Family in general—children in particular—are everybody's Achilles' heel, from hero to sociopath. The tricky part was to make the threat viable, and to keep it perpetual. It's the threat of violence that motivates silence in a case like this, not violence itself.

They knew that Guinn had a kid somewhere, and research led them to a school in a little Virginia town that no one had heard of. The most logical solution was to grab him and hold him hostage, but that strategy came with huge risks—not the least of which was the involvement of the FBI, whose mission it was to solve kidnappings. This one would be rendered even more challenging by the need to constantly remind Guinn of the stakes. Snatching someone and disappearing with him was difficult but doable. Keeping them disappeared while at the same time remaining in frequent contact raised the stakes enormously. Each new communication created an opportunity for the FBI to dial into the chain of evidence—and there was always a chain of evidence, no matter how careful you were to prevent one.

The solution came from Troy Flynn, the man who nominally succeeded Arthur Guinn after his arrest. (*Jesus, you think too much about this stuff, and it starts to sound like a royal chain of succession.*) Flynn suggested an offshore kidnapping. He said that he had assurances from very reliable sources that if they chose the country carefully, the FBI would be unable to follow, and if they did, they'd be unable to secure extradition.

And wouldn't you know it? One of the leading countries suggested was the very one in which Mitch Ponder had a number of existing business interests that were always looking to prosper from an addition to the labor pool.

Mitch read that as a guaranteed safe zone to spirit the kid off to after they snatched him. But first they had to get their hands on him, and for that Mitch needed a team. He hated working with teams. The extra players posed that many more opportunities to screw things up, and that many more people whose loose lips could sink the Steamship Ponder.

In this case, though, having a third party involved actually helped Mitch with another problem. Because of the complexity of what they were attempting to pull off, and the fact that Leger and his contacts were going to be giving him some backup, he needed a way to communicate directly with the secretary. Troy Flynn and Sammy Bell didn't want to be seen in the halls of the Pentagon any more than Leger would have wanted them there. For all the same reasons, the further away Mitch could stay from direct contact, the better off he was going to be.

Enter Jerry Sjogren, the hulking Bostonian who, as far as Mitch could tell, feared no one. Mitch had never worked with him before, but he certainly knew the name. Sjogren looked and sounded like a barroom bouncer. He'd approached Mitch, in fact, and, without actually saying the words, made it extremely clear that he considered himself to be Secretary Leger's go-to guy.

Sjogren was the one who'd first noticed that Marilyn Schuler's kid went to the same school as the Guinn kid, and brought word that his boss wanted the Schuler boy snatched at the same time. Mitch had argued against it if only because of the daunting logistics of snatching two at once and getting them out of the country. When you double the scope of an operation like that, you *square* the logistical hassles. To risk success with a high-value target like the Guinn kid by snatching a low-yield target like the Schuler boy—honestly, what were the chances that the kid knew anything that could hurt Leger?—was a special brand of foolishness.

But Sjogren had been firm. Besides, he'd argued, Mitch would never have to worry about the second kid because they were going to pop him after they snatched him. For Mitch's little corner of the operation, nothing would change.

Yeah, right. Never in the history of Murphy's Law had so many things gone perfectly wrong at precisely the worst moments. Everything Sjogren touched had turned to shit, up to and including the capping of a child. *Good God.* And he'd already been drugged, to boot.

The litany of things gone wrong swirled through Mitch's mind with such intense clarity that he nearly missed the arrival of his guest, who announced himself by casting a shadow over Mitch's untouched beer.

"Good evening," said the new arrival in heavily accented English.

Mitch looked up, at once pleased that his guest had finally arrived, and concerned that he had allowed himself to drift so far away from the present. Inattentiveness was a fine way to get yourself killed.

Mitch rose to greet the man and shook his hand. "General Ruiz. How are you sir? Thank you for joining me." He gestured to the seat across from him. "Please sit."

General Ignacio Ruiz was the head of the PNC—*Policía Nacional de Colombia*—the Colombian national police force. He had risen through the ranks, as had most of his predecessors except for a brief period in the late nineties and early 2000s, on the corpses of assassinated and disgraced former leaders. Given the brief tenure of most incumbents in his position, they tended to live large and fast during the time allotted to them. This evening, the general had shed his uniform in favor of beige linen pants and a white *guayabera*.

Ruiz looked around uncomfortably. "I think this is perhaps the wrong place," he said.

Mitch resumed his seat. "With all respect, sir, I think this is exactly the right place. You're not in uniform, we can converse in English, and I will remain in a public place during my meeting with a man who is so . . . *renowned* for his skills."

Ruiz hesitated a moment longer, then produced a smile as he lowered himself into his chair.

"State what is on your mind," the general said.

The waiter returned. The recognition was both instant and awkward. Having clearly been made, the general told the young man in Spanish to leave them. Two seconds later, they were alone.

"You were saying," Ruiz reminded.

Mitch smiled. "Yes, I suppose I was. I came here to alert you to an invasion that is ongoing in your country."

Ruiz's expression darkened. "What kind of invasion?"

"Small but important. It involves my business interests in the Santa Marta."

Ruiz's expression reflected a foul odor. "I'm not a fan of your business interests," he said. "They are ugly and violent."

"And profitable," Mitch reminded. "Profitable enough to be of great interest to your bosses." He let that sink in. He and the general had had this discussion before. While they stood on different sides philosophically, each understood that philosophy paid no bills. "If the businessman in you does not care, then I appeal to the patriot within you. Do you really want these invaders to return us to the nineties?"

"These invaders as you call them. They are Americans?"

Mitch nodded.

Ruiz waved his hand dismissively. "I do not believe it. We have assurances from the U.S. government that—"

"They still don't care about the factories, sir. Their official incursions are over. This is a smaller invasion than what you have seen in the past, but if I'm not mistaken some of the players are the same."

Ruiz shot annoyed glances over both shoulders, then leaned his forearms on the table. "You're speaking in riddles,

Mr. Ponder. I have neither the desire nor the time to figure them out."

Mitch gave an understanding nod. "Of course, sir. At one of my business establishments, I have some rather specialized business going on. Believe me when I tell you that you don't want to know too many of the details. This is above and beyond the manufacture of our usual product. It is for this expanded product line that these commandos are invading your country. They entered on commercial flights from the United States under false passports, but unfortunately, I don't know under what names they arrived."

Ruiz raised his hands palm up in an extended and exaggerated shrug. "If you know where they are going, surely you have enough men and weapons to take care of things yourself. What could you possibly need from me?"

Another thoughtful nod. "Well, sir, we have reason to believe that they have raised something of an army for themselves."

"Surely not an army bigger than yours."

"No, sir, probably not. But it's entirely possible that they are better skilled than mine."

Ruiz lowered his voice to a whisper and leaned in very close. Mitch joined him. "If you are asking me to deploy my soldiers into the mountains to defend your operations, then the answer is no. My God, you've been allowed to assemble—"

Mitch raised his hand to interrupt. "No, sir, I would never ask you to do that."

The general leaned back into his chair and crossed his arms. "What, then?"

Mitch laid out his entire plan in less than five minutes. After another ten minutes of questions and answers, it was a go.

CHAPTER THIRTY-FIVE

With the jungle this thick, satellite access was spotty at best—far too unreliable for Jonathan to track his own progress on the computer, or even on his GPS system—but compasses never lied, and his good old-fashioned land navigation training was so ingrained that he was almost pleased to have an opportunity to use it again. He found reassurance in the fact that their route was well worn by wide-wheelbase vehicles that clearly traveled heavy.

Thank God for Venice. By tasking the SkysEye network to scan the areas marked by Josie, she was able to confirm the presence of the villages and the mountaintop factory. With the current weather conditions, though, she'd only been able to use the thermal sensing capabilities. No visual confirmation of individual people would be possible until the skies cleared.

Venice also delivered the news that a new picture of Evan Guinn had been posted on the anonymous website that the kidnappers had established. Apparently, they were trying to sell the notion that the kid was in Italy—they'd even gotten their hands on yesterday's edition of a daily newspaper published for towns along the Amalfi Coast.

"The backdrop is just that, though," Venice had said. "A backdrop. A cheesy one at that. Evan could really be any-where. I'm trying to track down the location of the server they're using for the website. It should be a little easier if I assume that it's somewhere in Colombia, but so far I'm not having any luck. The people running this are very good."

"So are you," Jonathan had encouraged. "What do you hear from Gail and the Alaska connection?"

The pause before the answer had said it all. "I don't think it's good news, Digger. The satellite imagery there shows a lot of fire and smoke."

"You don't *think* it's good news? Jesus, Ven."

"I know, I know. But I haven't heard anything from her one way or another. Obviously, something went wrong, but I don't know that she's been harmed."

"How long has it been?"

"The screen showed nothing twelve minutes ago. Now, for the last eight minutes I've been showing the fire and smoke."

Jonathan ran the options through his head. Gail was smart, and she was resourceful. If she had survived, then she'd be in control. "What exactly is burning?" he asked.

"It's hard to tell from the steep angles," she said. The SkysEye network orbited close to the equator, so the images from the extreme north and extreme south were always dis-torted. "Certainly the house is burning, and it looks like the car she rented, but there's another big fire off to the north of the house itself." It was clear from her tone that she was ex-amining the images as she discussed them.

"I gotta tell you, Dig, it looks like burning gasoline, to me. You know, that greasy black smoke."

Jonathan's gut tightened. He knew exactly what she meant. It was the kind of fire that never occurred in nature, which by definition meant that it was caused by man, and the man who caused it meant to do harm. "Okay, here's what I want you to do," he'd told Venice. "Call Wolverine. Get her involved."

"With what?"

"With whatever is going on up there. This is half on her dime anyway. Have her scramble a medevac chopper or a local squad car or something. If Gail is up there wounded, I want her to get some medical attention right by-God now."

This was new territory for Jonathan. Until this mission into the jungles of hell, he'd never been in a position to divide his troops—at least not since leaving the Army. Before, it had always been just him and Boxers doing the covert side of the business, with occasional help from outside contractors. Throughout all those years, success had been dependent upon the effectiveness of his command abilities—abilities of which he was abundantly confident. Now, the sphere was expanding with the addition of Gail to the covert team, and the first time he'd taken his eye off the ball, something had clearly gone very wrong, and he was in no position to do anything about it. A knot of fear materialized in his gut and had started to metastasize.

When they'd hung up, Venice was supposed to make that phone call next. He hadn't heard from her since. That was over four hours ago.

Since then, they'd driven the Range Rover and the Blazer to the spot where the road ended and a trail began, and they'd been hiking since, mostly uphill. They'd taken their time dividing up the equipment. Jonathan had ordered, and Josie had provided the Marine Corps equivalent of rucksacks because, loyalties aside, he thought they were better than what the Army used. Made of the standard MARPAT camouflage scheme, they featured an abundant array of PALS straps for pouches, and they were specifically designed to accommodate modular tactical vests and CamelBak water bladders to keep them from sweating themselves dry.

Absent any reliable intel on the conditions in which Evan Guinn was being held, they had to plan for a number of contingencies. Boxers and Jonathan both carried M4 carbines combat-slung across their chests, plus twelve-gauge Mossberg shotguns bungee-slung under their armpits. Jonathan

had his Colt 1911 .45 in a tactical holster on his thigh, the
same spot where Boxers carried his Beretta 9-millimeter.
Each carried twelve spare mags for their rifles—three hundred sixty rounds—plus four spare clips for their side arms
and twenty rounds each for the Mossbergs—fifteen rounds
of double-ought buck and five Foster slugs for making big
holes. Add to that three fragmentation grenades and two CS
grenades, plus a couple of bricks of C-4 explosives and detonators, and each of them was carrying half his body weight
in equipment.

Okay, for Boxers a quarter of his body weight, but it was
still heavy. Jonathan drew straws with the Big Guy to see
who would carry the long-handled bolt cutters—in case they
had to snip a padlock—and the Big Guy lost. Jonathan almost felt sorry for him—*almost*. While Boxers was two
times stronger than Jonathan, he was also the only one
among them with a rod in his femur where there should have
been bone. Jonathan figured that that was countered by the
fact that he, Jonathan, had been gut-shot twice in his career
and therefore had fewer functioning viscera. He didn't know
what that meant, actually, but it had sounded good at the
time.

For his part, Harvey carried an MP5 machine pistol with
two hundred spare rounds, plus a sidearm and a shitload of
medical supplies. Jonathan had tried to talk him out of some
of them, but Harvey had ignored him. In fact, Harvey hadn't
said a dozen words since they'd left the scene of Josie's
shooting.

Finally, Jonathan had insisted that they "soldier up all the
way" for this mission, meaning mandatory body armor and
helmets. This mission nearly guaranteed CQB—close quarters battle—and he wanted them prepared. As he'd said, "It's
not about comfort, it's about professionalism. The only way
Evan Guinn finds freedom is if we stay alive. And if we have
to carry you, we won't be able to carry him if we need to."

Jonathan took point on the walk into the jungle, with Harvey in the middle, and Boxers in the rear. After an hour, Jonathan dropped back to walk alongside Harvey. In a real war zone in a real war, it would have been unforgivable, but out here he thought they could afford a little bunching.

Harvey's silence was bothering him. He seemed to be struggling with the emotion of the fight with Josie. Jonathan had discovered before that medics were wired differently than other soldiers, equally willing to risk their lives—perhaps even more willing—but oddly disconnected from the real business of war, which was killing. For medics, the line that separated good guys and bad guys was refreshingly blurred by the presence of beating hearts on both sides.

Harvey just walked. He kept his jaw clamped tight and his lips pressed into a thin line, as if forcibly locking his anger inside his head.

Finally, Jonathan had had enough. "Okay, Harvey, spill it. What aren't you saying?"

Harvey glanced at Jonathan, then returned his gaze to the road. "Anything, so far as I can tell."

Okay, he'd walked into that one. "I need you to tell me that you're mission capable."

Harvey cast him a sideward glance and smirked. "By 'mission capable' do you mean 'not about to wig out and frag the commander'?"

"That'll do as a start," Jonathan said.

Harvey took his time answering. "Don't worry about me knowing right from wrong," he said at last. "Killing's never been my thing, okay? If I've led you to believe otherwise, I apologize. I'm way more about hiding and healing, so if you're expecting me to do a lot of shooting, you might be disappointed. I might be disappointed. Who knows? And the part about wigging out? I just flat-out don't know. I hope not. But if I do, I don't owe you or anybody else an apology. You invited me to this party, remember?"

"I remember," Jonathan said. And he appreciated the candor.

"And about your leaving that guy to die, well, it's done. You didn't ask my permission, and you certainly don't need my forgiveness. There's a reason why I was never promoted to a position of leadership in the Marine Corps."

"Says the man who won the Navy Cross," Jonathan said.

Harvey laughed. "A fleeting bout of insanity, I assure you."

"I read the citation."

"Then you know for certain that it was a fleeting bout of insanity."

"I know that you repeatedly exposed yourself to heavy enemy fire to pull three critically wounded Marines to safety one at a time."

Harvey avoided eye contact. "I feel like I'm repeating myself now. Insanity."

Jonathan wasn't about to let him get away with that. "You're not in a Senate hearing now, Harvey. You're with a guy who's been there, okay? I know what you did, and I know what it took for you to do it."

"Well, that makes you one of about three in the world then. Congratulations." He fell into silence for a long moment, and Jonathan let him have it. He didn't want to be too direct in looking, but out of his peripheral vision, he thought he might have seen Harvey's eyes getting moist. No man wants that button pushed.

After a minute or more, Harvey said, "You know, I can point exactly to the moment when I realized I didn't give a shit anymore. Want to hear about it?"

If it were anyone else in the world, Jonathan's honest answer would have been no. All things related to touchy-feely and fully bared human emotion left him cold. But he was devoted to valor, and those who exhibited it. "Sure," he said.

"I had a buddy in boot camp—John Avery. We got really tight. After basic, we went to infantry training together, and in the last week, he blew out his knee in some dumb-shit PT exercise, so we got out of sequence, him six months behind

me. I'd finished my tour and was back in the States when I
got word that John had been killed by a sniper in Anbar
Province."

"I'm sorry," Jonathan said.

"So was I. That was at the height of my crazy period, you
know? Anyway, I wanted to go to his funeral. The docs
weren't sure it was the right thing to do, but I was pretty
firm, so they let me go."

He cleared his throat. "You know, he was a young guy.
What, twenty-three maybe? He had the kind of service
records that they make movies out of. Great guy, terrific
leader, and scared of absolutely nothing. So a sniper takes
him out while he's sipping out of a canteen at a roadblock.
The funeral was everything you like and everything you
dread. Lots of family, lots of tears, lots of townspeople, out
in Nowhere, Tennessee.

"The Marine Corps sent an honor guard, and they did their
best to make it feel military as they buried him in the yard
outside of the Baptist church where his great-grandfather and
everybody after him was baptized and married. It was kind
of beautiful in its own right.

"And then these war protestor assholes showed up to
heckle. At a fucking funeral, man. A fucking *funeral*. These
are third-generation hippie wannabes who've never fought
for anything, and while family and friends are trying to bury
a no-shit war hero, they're trying to make it about *them*. I
mean, this is what we fight for, right? So that everybody can
say whatever's on their mind? At John's funeral, the cops
who were originally there as honor guard escorts ended up
protecting the assholes who had nothing better to do than
ruin a mother's last memory of her son. Would you care to
tell me where the sense is in that?"

Jonathan shook his head. "I couldn't begin to."

"Well, you see, this is where it really helps not to be
crazy. 'Cause from where I sit it doesn't even make sense to
keep trying. Fuck 'em all. Then I got jammed up by some
adolescent bitch who knows how the news cycle works, and

I just sort of ran out of things worth dyin' for, know what I mean?"

Jonathan did know. He'd known for decades; but the mark of an American soldier was the ability to push aside the weaknesses of politicians and slothful do-nothings to accomplish the mission within guidelines established by the politicians and slothful do-nothings. Jonathan's years in the military had shaped his understanding of God and country. He believed with all his heart that civilians needed to be in charge, but he prayed for the day when those civilians would quit using people like him as political chess pieces.

The rain had slowed to an unpleasant drizzle by the time Jonathan and his team arrived at the village, which itself seemed strangely quiet. Clearly, the place was occupied, but the residents were apparently all inside. The three of them gathered in the center of what would be the town square if the village were in Ohio. A face appeared in the window of a nearby hut, and then disappeared.

"I'm taking theories," Jonathan said.

"Maybe they're all just staying in out of the rain," Boxers offered.

"Or maybe they're scared shitless because we've got enough guns and bullets to take over the country," Harvey countered.

Jonathan leaned more toward the latter than the former. He shouted, "*Hola! Hay alguien aquí?*" He meant that to be, Hello, is anyone here?

More faces appeared in windows, but no one stepped out to greet them. Jonathan tried again. "*Me gustaría hablar con su líder, por favor.*" I want to speak to your leader. "*Somos amigos.*" We are friends. Then, to drive the point closer to home: "*Estamos aquí para herir sus enemigos!*"

Boxers chuckled. "We're here to hurt your enemies," he translated. "I like that."

And so did the villagers. Two and three at a time, they

wandered from their huts to see. They didn't draw closer, but they didn't run away, either. They gathered in clusters, talking among themselves but watching the newcomers.

"There are no men," Harvey said.

Jonathan called out again, *"Me gustaría hablar con su líder, por favor."*

A woman stepped forward. She could have been fifty or eighty. "Our leaders are dead," she said in Spanish. *"El Matador* killed them."

Jonathan removed his helmet and offered his hand. "How do you do?" he said, also in Spanish. "My name is Jones. I'm sorry for your loss."

"Many losses," she corrected. "I am Isabella. Is that man a doctor?" She pointed to the medical emblems on Harvey's equipment pouches.

"Yes, ma'am," Jonathan said.

Harvey doffed his helmet and tucked it under his arm. "Hello."

"They attacked my daughter today," Isabella said. "I think she needs a doctor."

"Show me where," Harvey said. "I'll be happy to help."

Isabella led the way back to her hut, the one from which she'd just emerged. Jonathan held back while Harvey led and Boxers stayed in the middle of the yard, looking scary. *Hey, do what you're good at.* Isabella stopped at the doorway and motioned for Harvey to go in first. As they approached, Jonathan heard moaning, and then caught a glimpse of movement inside. It had the look and feel of a bedside death watch. Harvey must have caught the same vibe, because he shot a concerned look back at his boss before stepping across the threshold. Jonathan started to follow, but Isabella held up a hand to stop him.

"Not you," she said. And then she shouted something to the gathered villagers in such quick dialect that Jonathan caught very little of it. He heard the words for *welcome* and *food*, though, so he had a good idea what the intent was.

Moving as one, the villagers closed in. Instantly friendly,

they surrounded Jonathan and Boxers like they were family, flooding them with offers to sit and relax. Benches appeared in the middle of the compound, and then some tables, and within a couple of minutes, food started to arrive. Jonathan had no idea what it was, but the enthusiasm with which it was presented told him that he was receiving special treatment.

Following Jonathan's lead, Boxers slipped out of his gear and helmet, but kept it all close by. Neither of them removed their weapons. This was a party, and they were the guests of honor. The villagers seemed fascinated by Boxers' size. Jonathan took odd pleasure in the Big Guy's obvious discomfort at being scrutinized.

Jonathan had positioned himself in a way to be able to watch the hut that had swallowed the third member of his team. Thirteen minutes into the party, Harvey reappeared, absent all of his equipment but his sidearm. He looked shaken, and there was blood on front of his uniform.

"Excuse me," Jonathan said, and he rose from the table.

Boxers mimicked the action, moving like Jonathan's reflection. "What's up?" Then he turned and saw it, too. "Oh, this can't be good," he mumbled.

Jonathan closed half the distance and waited for Harvey to join him. "Are you all right?" Jonathan asked. "You look terrible."

"We're hunting animals, Boss," Harvey said. "Fucking animals. You should see what they did to that little girl in there. She's fourteen, for God's sake."

Jonathan felt the heat in his neck. He had no desire to see. He'd seen enough and lost far too much to the kind of human predators that Harvey described. Everything that Felipe had told him was turning out to be true.

"Will she be okay?" Jonathan asked.

"I think she'll live," Harvey replied. "Being okay is a little too vague. A little too relative."

"Where is your weapon and equipment?" Boxers asked.

Harvey pointed back to the hut. "I'll get them in a minute."

"What, are you crazy?" Boxers said. "You can't just—"

"Hush, Box," Jonathan said.

"And what's with the real names all of a sudden?"

"What part of 'hush' confused you?" Jonathan grumped. To Harvey: "Are you okay?"

Harvey shifted just his eyes to look at him. "She's fourteen," he repeated. "Yeah, I'm fine. It's just been a long time." He pivoted on his heel to return, then stopped and looked back. "More and more mission capable every minute."

Navarro drove a twenty-year-old Ford Bronco with enormous knobbed tires and more rust than paint on the body. "Buying vehicles is one of the toughest parts of living an anonymous life," he explained to Gail as he carefully piloted the vehicle onto the main road off his potholed driveway. The attackers were all dead, and everything he owned was on fire. They'd hung around checking things out for about fifteen minutes, but then knew it was time to get going before emergency vehicles started responding to the smoke.

Bruce hadn't so much as cast a longing glance at his blazing home as they drove away. "If your car's not a piece of crap that you can pick up for a few thousand bucks, you're either going to leave a paper trail, or people are going to notice. That was hard for me, getting over the need to be noticed."

They drove in silence for a while. "Think I'll see jail time?" he asked.

Gail looked at him and gauged her answer, which could not have been more different than the one she would have given a year ago, when she was still a cop. "Not if you play your cards right."

She had his attention.

"Think about it. You've got the kind of information that will make a prosecutor's case. You can make them heroes.

That kind of information comes with a price." She let it settle on him. "If I were you, I'd hold out for immunity and a new identity."

"They'd give that to me, you think?"

Gail shrugged. "Play a little poker. Lawyer up first chance you get, and then make your conditions clear. I happen to think they'll roll over."

Navarro smiled, then chuckled. "Wouldn't that be a kick in the—oh, shit."

Gail saw his eyes locked on his rearview mirror, and turned in her seat to see a sedan with a light bar pulling him over. "Do you know the car?"

Navarro slapped his blinker and drifted to the right shoulder. "I know the *guy*. It's Jerry Soaring Eagle. He's sheriff around here."

Gail's mind raced, but came up blank. What else was there to do but pull over? "Do you like him?"

He gave her a look. "He's the sheriff. It's his job to know everybody. Mine was to keep from being known. We're not buddies, but I think he's a decent fellow." Bruce rolled down the window and waited for the sheriff to arrive. "I left my wallet inside the house," he mumbled.

Gail turned in her seat to watch the cop approach. She noted that his weapon was holstered, and that his gait was easy. He didn't have a face from her angle—not until he got to the driver's window and bent at the waist to look in.

"Mr. Planchette, how are you?" the sheriff asked. Gail had almost forgotten Navarro's alias.

"I'm just fine, Sheriff," Navarro said.

The sheriff looked beyond the driver to lock eyes with Gail. His Indian blood was obvious in his features, and his face was set hard. "That so? I think if everything I owned was on fire, I'd be a little, I don't know, something other than 'just fine.'"

Navarro paled and shot a look to Gail.

Before she could say anything, the sheriff asked, "Are you Gail Bonneville?"

Her jaw dropped. "I, uh, yes."

He fixed her with a stare. "Uh-huh. Well, could I ask you both to step out of the car?"

Gail's stomach tumbled and her mind raced, but options still evaded her. Obviously, the guy was really a cop. But how could he know who she was? She pulled the door handle as he opened Navarro's door for him. "Sheriff, I need to tell you that I'm armed," Gail said.

"I figured as much," the cop replied. "Don't touch yours, and I won't touch mine. How's that?"

Oh, this wasn't right at all. At the very least, he should have asked to see a carry permit. She let Navarro leave the car first and then took her turn, so as not to overload the cop's senses. Her door opened over a ditch, so she lost six inches in height on her first step. She walked around the right front fender and positioned herself directly in front of the worn Ford medallion. Ahead and to her right, Navarro looked terrified.

The sheriff looked from one of them to the other and winced a little as he shook his head. "You know," he said, "I just got the damnedest phone call about you two."

Navarro shot her a panicked glance. "Is that so?" Gail asked, trying her best to look unmoved.

"It is, indeed," the sheriff said. "I've been in this business for a long, long while. I've seen and heard a lot of strange things. After a while, given the nature of the job, you get used to being surprised. But this phone call beat everything else combined."

He took a deep breath, and his scowl deepened. "It's just not every day that you get a call from the director of the FBI."

Isabella reemerged from the hut with Harvey and joined the others in the center. He had his helmet crooked on his head, his MP-5 in his hand, and his pack slung over his shoulder. He looked like he needed a very long nap.

Isabella made a shooing motion with her hands—the exact same gesture Mama Alexander would use to chase away pigeons when Jonathan was a boy—and the villagers dispersed, leaving the table for Jonathan's team and Isabella.

"I'm sorry for your daughter," Jonathan said in Spanish.

"She is just one of many," she said. "The soldiers are very bad men." She looked uncomfortable. "Not you. Them. You saved my daughter. I am very thankful. Are you here for the white-haired boy?"

The directness startled him—more so because this was a culture known for obfuscating everything from the weather to the color of the sky. Slipping a question like that into an unrelated discussion was an old interrogator's trick, and Jonathan was pissed at himself for showing a reaction. With the option of a bluff gone, he said, "Yes. What makes you ask?"

Isabella smiled ruefully, exposing a set of well-worn teeth, from which several were missing. "I notice things," she said. "Sometimes those things are hard to see, sometimes they are easy. A white boy with white hair is easy to see. Soon after, white soldiers with guns are easy to see. I think maybe one has something to do with the other."

"His name is Evan," Jonathan said. "He was taken from his home, and we are here to take him back."

Isabella's eyebrows scaled her forehead. "Just three people?"

Jonathan shrugged.

"They are many," Isabella said. "Thirty, maybe forty."

"Holy shit," Boxers grunted.

Jonathan ignored him. "Thirty or forty total, right? Not thirty or forty soldiers."

Isabella nodded. "Twenty soldiers. But many people with guns. Men and boys with guns keep men and boys without guns from running away. Keep enemies out."

Jonathan and Boxers had seen it before throughout the world. Young men with nothing to lose confuse firearms with manhood. You see it on the streets of the United States, too, but in the third world, those young men with guns had jobs to do, and they were handsomely rewarded for them. In his experience, the average age of guards and terrorists and pirates all hovered in the mid-teens. Like teenagers everywhere, they were genetically wired to be fearless. Combined with indoctrination to kill without hesitation, that fearlessness made them fierce warriors.

Sensing the pall in the air, Jonathan changed the subject. "You say that Evan was here yesterday? How long ago?"

Isabella nodded. "Five, six hours. Maybe longer. With the men who hurt my daughter." Her eyes hardened. "With the *boys* who did that to her." Clearly, she'd sensed their discomfort in engaging young people in combat. "The *boys* who do that to many of the women in the village. At fifteen, sixteen, seventeen years old, they are already devils. Do not pity them."

"How was Evan?" Jonathan pressed. "Was he in good health?"

A sudden wariness changed Isabella's face to a mask of suspicion. All trappings of hospitality evaporated. She seemed suddenly angry. "Leave now," she said; but she didn't rise.

Jonathan recoiled. He looked to Boxers and got the shrug he knew he was going to get before he looked. "Have I done something wrong?" he asked.

"Leave," she said again. "I want no part of this."

Jonathan made no effort to comply. In fact he leaned closer and lowered his voice. "Isabella, if I have offended you, I apologize."

She glared. "You offend me by being here," she said. "You see my daughter, I tell you about the devils on the hill, and all you care about is the white boy. The American. The gringo. My son is dead. Many sons are dead because of the devils, but no one cares. The white boy—your Evan—is another mother's son. I help you help him, and I bring danger to all the people of my village. You don't care about my people, I don't care about yours. You must leave now."

Harvey cleared his throat, drawing all eyes around to him. "Where are the men?" he asked.

"Dead," she replied.

"All of them?"

"All who were old enough to fight. The others work up there." She pointed toward a spot in the air that only she could see.

"What work do they do?" Jonathan asked. He knew the answer, but he wanted to hear it from her.

"Coca drug," she said. "They have a factory up there. Young men and boys put to work up there. We stay here and bring them food." She looked away as she said the last part, and Jonathan interpreted that to imply other services that one would expect from a village of slaves.

"Why don't you leave?" Harvey asked.

"They are our sons," she said, as if it were the most obvious thing in the world. "They work or they die. We stay or they die. If they try to escape, then we die. That's why they work for the devil."

"Jesus," Harvey breathed.

Jonathan had seen it before, in all corners of the third world. The average American, accustomed to twenty-four-hour cable television and air-conditioning on demand, found it impossible to comprehend the suffering endured by the other eighty-five percent of the world's population. While we prosecute hate speech, the rest of the world enslaves their enemies.

Jonathan sighed noisily. "If you help us, we will fix it for you," he said. "If you can help, we can make them stop hurting you."

Boxers got squirmy in his chair. "Um, Scorpion?" he said in English. "What are you doing?"

Isabella looked interested. "I don't think I understand," she said.

"We'll kill some, and make the others too frightened to ever hurt you again."

"We need to talk," Boxers said in English.

"There are only three of you," Isabella said.

"But we're very good at what we do," Jonathan countered.

"Scorpion, stop!"

Jonathan slammed the table with his hand. "Quiet!"

"Are you listening to what you're saying?" Boxers railed. "Do you think maybe a team meeting is in order?"

Jonathan's eyes flared. He shifted to English. "What's the alternative? What would you have me do? We're just going to sneak in, take our one precious cargo, and then leave the rest for these people to live with?"

"That's exactly what I'd have you do," Boxers fired back. "That's the mission. We're surgical, remember? Not tactical. In a perfect world we sneak in and sneak out and never fire a shot. You're talking about going to war."

Jonathan cocked his head. "Since when did you start backing away from starting wars?"

"When I learned to count and discovered that three against a lot was really bad odds. What they have going here is not our fight. It's their fight."

"But our fight is going to make it worse for them."

"So? Our fights *always* make things worse for *somebody*. It's what we do."

"It doesn't have to be." Jonathan stood. He thought more clearly when he paced. "Just once, wouldn't you like to actually finish the job we started? Just once, wouldn't you like to solve the problem behind the problem and bring justice to everybody?"

Boxers looked confused. "Are we still talking about Evan?"

"Think about it," Jonathan went on. He was on a roll. "Vietnam, Grenada, Mogadishu, Heavy Shadow, two Gulf Wars. Hell, Afghanistan. We moved in, we did what we had to do, and then we left a mess behind. We told ourselves we were successful because we achieved our objectives, but then we left misery behind."

"What's this 'we' shit? *We* did our jobs. *We* would have stayed for as long as it took. But *we* were just the muscle for the assholes in Washington. Don't lay their shit on me."

Jonathan opened his palms, as if balancing an invisible tray. "But don't you see? You just made my point. Washington isn't in on this. This one is all *us*. The scope of what we do is our design. What we do or don't do is all on us. We can do this right."

Boxers rose, too, and when he did, Isabella and Harvey both stirred uncomfortably. If this came to blows, it'd get real ugly real fast. And no one in his right mind would put a dollar on Jonathan to win. "Jesus, Scorpion, why do you always pull this shit? Why is there always some fucking moral dilemma to lay on me? These people were born badly, okay? Whoever spins the luck wheel before we're born let it stop a tick or two early for all these poor fucks. But we can't fix it all. Even if we had enough ammo, we couldn't carry it, and sooner or later some lucky fucker is going to drill me. Again."

Harvey raised a finger to interrupt. "Are you saying—"

"You shut up," Boxers snapped, thrusting a finger in warning. If it had been a gun, Harvey would have been dead.

Jonathan nodded that it was a good time to sit quietly. He wanted to hear Boxers out. He valued the Big Guy's input on his occasionally quixotic plans.

"And what about the Guinn boy?" Boxers said. "You're going to risk his life while you're saving the third world?"

"His life is already at risk," Jonathan said.

"Which is why we're here. How do you think he's got a better shot at getting home? By us sneaking him out under cover of darkness, or by touching off a running firefight?"

That point scored. Jonathan wanted to argue. He wanted Boxers to be wrong, and he wanted to fight for these people. But Big Guy was right. Evan Guinn was the target of this op. It began and ended with him, and whatever resources they expended needed to be expended exclusively for the mission. On another day, under different circumstances, or maybe even with more manpower, this was a fight they could afford to wage.

But not today.

"We could give them the extra weapons," Harvey said, flouting danger and daring to speak.

The others turned in unison to face him.

"The weapons we left behind at the bottom of the hill. The ones that Josie's guys surrendered. We could leave them for the villagers to fight back. They won't need us."

Boxers stood a little taller and planted his fists on his hips. "Just like that, huh? Just give 'em to the locals and leave? No training? Is that the way y'all did it in jarhead school?" He snorted a laugh. "Explains a lot of the Marine marksmanship I've seen."

"They'll be as trained as the people they're shooting at," Harvey said, ignoring the interservice dick-knocking.

"Or they'll end up providing additional weapons to the bad guys," Jonathan said. "Either on purpose or otherwise." He shook his head. "I was wrong," he said. "It was a stupid idea."

Harvey stood. "No, it wasn't. It's the right thing to do."

"Says the medic," Boxers scoffed.

Harvey took two steps closer to the Big Guy, craning his neck to stare him down. "Exactly, says the medic. The very same medic, in fact, who just did his best to repair what may be irreparable damage. Chances of bearing children maybe five in ten. Then there are the facial cuts. You want to see?"

Boxers tossed his do-you-believe-this-guy smirk to Jonathan, but Jonathan wasn't receiving.

"Come on," Harvey pressed, grabbing Boxers' sleeve. "Come on in and take a glance. See if it's worth fighting for."

Boxers yanked his arm away. "I don't need to see what I already know," he said. "I've seen it before. Don't care to see it again."

"But you don't mind letting it happen some more, right?"

"It's not our *job* to stop it. Our *job* is to rescue a little boy who needs rescuing."

"A white boy," Harvey mocked. "Just like Isabella said. We love 'em if they're white, but put a little color on 'em and we don't care so much."

"Who the *fuck* are you to lecture me?" Boxers growled. "You've got no idea what I got in my heart. You've got no idea what I want to do and what I don't. What I'm telling you is that professionals don't think with their hearts. They think with their heads. I don't know where jarheads come from, but where I come from, it's a professional's job to push all that shit aside and concentrate on the fucking mission. If I'm gonna die in some fuckin' stink hole like this place, it's gonna be because I was trying to do my job."

"And these people?" Harvey made a wide sweeping gesture with both arms. "What about them?"

"They are *not* my job. Not this time, anyway."

Harvey gave up that fight and turned to Jonathan. "Boss, don't back down. You were right the first time. We've gotta do what we came to do up there at the top of the hill. That's a sure thing. But after we do, what about all these villagers? They're going to pay the price for our success."

"You make like they're innocent," Boxers said, reengaging. "That's bullshit. Where I sit, these villagers might not be the monsters that the others are, but their fingerprints are on this business, too. They know what's going on up there, and they let it happen every single day."

"They're powerless to stop it!" Harvey yelled.

Jonathan held up a hand for his turn. "Not entirely," he said. "Big Guy has a point. In World War Two, Eisenhower held townspeople accountable for the concentration camps. They accepted soldiers' business in their shops, and they kept roads clear for the shipment of people to the death camps. Wasn't it Edmund Burke who said, 'All that is necessary for evil to triumph is that good men do nothing'?"

"Exactly," Boxers said. "Thanks for seeing my side."

Jonathan gave him a hard look. "We're good men, Big Guy," he said with a wink. "We've gotta do *something*."

CHAPTER THIRTY-SIX

After taking Evan's picture, El Jéfe assigned a new guard to escort the boy farther into the jungle, past the cluster of huts that he presumed to be the headquarters for whatever was going on.

Evan had never been so exhausted—never in his entire life. Every muscle ached, and every square inch of skin screamed from the onslaught of God only knew how many different varieties of bugs. He'd known from the History Channel and Discovery that prehistoric times still reigned in the jungles, with man-eating plants and insects, but Jesus. How did the people who lived here get anything done when three-quarters of every calorie was burned up by either slapping something or scratching the bite that an unslapped something left behind?

Only a few minutes into the hike, they emerged over the crest of a hill onto a rolling vista that might once have been beautiful. There were fewer trees here, affording a view of thick ground foliage that swept downhill from where he stood to a little valley, and then uphill again on the other side. Evan wasn't good at judging distances, but he guessed that it had to be a half mile or more between where he stood and the opposite peak.

The field of bushes had an undulating feel to it, as if it were alive. For an instant, Evan thought it might be the wind, but the rhythm wasn't right. It wasn't natural. When he realized the truth of it, his heart skipped a beat. The place was alive with children scattered among the bushes, working their asses off stripping leaves from the branches and stuffing them into sacks that were slung over their shoulders.

He saw only boys among the workers and only men—some of them teenagers—among the guards who watched over them. The children all wore tattered remnants of what had once been poor people's rags, though some wore nothing at all. Evan pegged the workers' ages at somewhere between eight and maybe fourteen years old.

Evan's arrival startled a soldier who looked like he might have been sleeping. He jumped when one of Evan's escorts called his name, and he fumbled with his rifle—an AK-47, Evan thought—but then stopped when he recognized them. The guard who called his name had been part of Evan's parade ever since he'd first met up with Oscar in the field. He spoke with rapid words and an angry tone to the man who'd been sleeping, and the guilty guard looked more terrified with every word that was being fired at him.

Evan's guard finished his diatribe by shoving the younger man in the chest hard enough to make him stumble over his own feet and fall backward into the undergrowth.

Evan didn't understand a word of it, but he was pretty sure he got the gist. "*Estúpido*" probably meant in Spanish more or less what it sounded like in English.

It wasn't lost on him that his captors treated everyone else much more harshly than they treated him. It's not that they were nice—far from it. It was more as if he weren't even there—better still, as if he were a dog or a piece of furniture. Whichever, he was obviously a valuable dog or piece of furniture.

Finished with delivering his tongue-lashing and obvi-

ously pleased with himself, Evan's guard led the way into
the endless field of bushes. He said something into his radio,
and then they stopped again. A couple of minutes later, a
man emerged from the brush. He was very tall, very black,
and wore more or less the same tattered-shorts uniform as
the workers. On his belt, though, he carried a coiled whip; in
his hand, a well-worn Louisville Slugger baseball bat.

Evan's stomach knotted in fear. This man with the glistening skin and powerful muscles was bad. Evil was written
all over him just as surely as if it had been drawn with Magic
Marker.

The presence of the new man transformed Evan's guard
from abusive bully to timid wimp. As the two of them spoke,
it was clear that Evan was the topic of conversation, and the
angry set of the black man's face told the boy that he wasn't
welcome here.

When their brief conversation was done, the guard put a
hand on Evan's shoulder and pushed him closer to the black
man. In the staccato conversation that accompanied the
push, Evan heard his name.

"Ah, so you are the prince," the black man said. His tone
was leaden with sarcasm. "Welcome to your new home." He
held out his hand.

Evan took it. He was going to say, "Pleased to meet you,"
but before he had the chance, the man's grip closed like a
talon.

"My name is Victor," he said. "You are mine. You will do
what I say. If you are too slow or if I am in a sour mood, I
will hit you with my whip. If you try to run away, I will
break your legs with my baseball bat. Do you have any questions?"

Evan found himself transfixed by the way the man handled the bat. When he talked about breaking his legs, he
twirled it in a manner that projected perfect intimacy with its
potential to inflict damage. Evan shook his head no—a silent
lie. He was filled with questions—consumed by them—but

nothing was more clear to him at the moment than the fact that the correct answer was no, he had nothing to ask.

"*Bueno*," Victor said. He then spoke rapidly to the guard, who laughed and walked away after giving Evan an angry glare that the boy felt he hadn't earned.

Victor poked at Evan's belly with the baseball bat, but he bent in the middle and jumped back, avoiding contact. Victor laughed. "Good reflexes," he said. "They will serve you well among the other workers. Come."

He led the way down the hill into the thickness of the bushes. As if it were even possible, the heat and the humidity both doubled. Most of the bushes were taller than Evan, and the height of the foliage blocked whatever semblance of breeze there once had been. Within a minute, his skin was slippery with sweat, which in turn summoned more insects.

"What is this place?" Evan asked.

"Your home."

The answer was intended to frighten him, and it succeeded. But Evan wasn't going to give his captor the satisfaction of showing it. "I meant the bushes," he said. "What are they?"

Victor scowled. "You have hair like a girl."

"That's not an answer."

"Perhaps I should cut it off."

Evan looked him straight in the eye. "If you want to, you will. I'm not big enough to stop you." Actually, right now, in this heat, he sort of hoped he would. He'd have welcomed a buzz cut. But he sensed that these people wouldn't let him cut his hair even if he begged for it. Whatever this was about, taking his picture was an important part of it. Since they'd already shot his photo twice in the last couple of days, it only made sense that they'd want to take it again, and if that was the case, they'd want him to look like himself.

Victor asked, "Have you heard people say that money does not grow on trees?"

Evan nodded.

"These bushes"—Victor brushed them with the tip of his bat—"prove that to be wrong. These leaves are U.S. dollar bills. Over there are Euros. And rubles and rupees and pesos. The work we do here makes people very wealthy." He plucked a few leaves from one of the bushes and offered them to Evan. "Here."

Evan took them, held them in his fist. They looked like any other leaves, green and oval-shaped. He looked at Victor.

His captor stripped a few leaves for himself and tucked them between his cheek and lower gum, the way people back home dipped snuff. "You chew the leaves. Suck on them. Make you feel happy. Make you feel strong."

Evan remembered the nice old lady from the village spitting out the bits of paper that looked very much like these leaves. He handed them back. "No, thank you."

Victor looked offended. "Coca leaves. Very good for you. Like Coca-Cola."

So that was it. They're making cocaine up here. Evan had watched a documentary once about the development of soft drinks, and he remembered that early on, Coca-Cola had cocaine in it. They'd removed it years ago, but apparently, a hundred years later, Victor still hadn't gotten the word.

Evan dropped the leaves onto the ground and brushed his hands together. "No, thank—" A flash of light behind his eyes and an explosion of pain cut off his words as Victor knocked him on the back of the head with his bat. The boy yelled and bent over as he grabbed the wound. A second, harder blow to his right hip dropped him to his knees. From there, he curled into a protective ball, terrified of where the next hit might land.

"Stand up," Victor commanded.

Sensing another blow, Evan raised a protective hand blindly, not daring to look where it might be coming from.

"On your feet now, *chico*, or I will truly hit you. Those were only light taps." He poked him with the end of the bat, eliciting a yelp. "Stand now, or get hit again."

Stunned by the suddenness of the attack and aching from the points of impact that were already starting to swell, Evan scrabbled to get his feet beneath him. He stood, his hand still pressed to his head.

"When I say to do something, you do it," Victor said evenly. His tone made him sound like the voice of reason. "Now pick up those leaves I gave you."

Luckily, they'd fallen in a clump on the dirt path where they'd been walking. Unluckily, they'd fallen in mud. As Evan picked them up, he noticed how filthy his hands were. He might as well never have washed. Perhaps that's why no one else did.

He displayed the three leaves for Victor, spreading them in his fingers as you might show a hand of cards.

"Put them in your mouth," Victor instructed, and he watched as the boy complied. "Chew them a little to get them soft, then settle them here." He pointed to the dip-spot in his own mouth.

Evan chewed as instructed, in spite of the terrible, bitter taste. In seconds, he could feel his tongue going numb—not as thoroughly as with Novocain at the dentist's, but that same sort of feeling.

"Be sure not to swallow them," Victor said. "It should be okay to move them to your cheek now."

Again, Evan followed directions and this time Victor watched expectantly. "How do you feel?"

"My mouth feels numb," he said. "I don't like it."

"But how does your head feel? And your hip?"

Holy crap, the pain was nearly gone. He didn't say anything, but apparently his expression spoke for him.

"See?" Victor said, smiling. "I told you the coca was good for you. Come."

The walk continued. After a minute or so, they started to pass other people at work. It was as he'd suspected. The workers were all boys, and he was among the oldest. Most didn't even notice him passing, but those who did registered a curious glance quickly and then went right back to strip-

ping the leaves off the branches. Off to the left, Evan saw
one kid squatted with his butt close to the ground taking a
dump right in the middle of everything. Curiously, the smell
of his shit was lost in the general atmosphere of rot and
decay.

Victor bellowed, "Charlie! Where are you, boy?" Evan
wouldn't note it until later, but he shouted in English. After
he didn't get an immediate answer, Victor poked another boy
with his bat. "Jesús," he said, and the boy jumped. Victor
asked him something in Spanish, and the boy pointed behind
them.

"You stay here," he said to Evan, and then he retraced
their steps back a dozen yards. "Charlie!" he yelled, clearly
finding the face he was looking for. "Come out here."

A boy of about twelve emerged from the bushes, and
Evan's heart fell. It was the one he'd just seen taking the shit.
He was nearly as dark-skinned as the others, but his hair was
brown, not black, making Evan wonder if maybe genetics
had less to do with his skin color than sun exposure. He was
skinnier than the others, too. A rope kept his tattered shorts
in place. He was beyond filthy, and his eyes had a dull look
about them. Evan instantly disliked him.

"Look what I brought for you, Charlie," Victor said as he
brought the boy closer to Evan. "Another English speaker."
They were very close now. "Charlie, shake hands with
Evan."

The other boy dutifully raised his hand in greeting, but
Evan hesitated. The kid had filthy hands, and there was no
toilet paper out here. Figure it out.

He offered a fist for a knuckle-knock, and Charlie took
him up on it.

Victor said, "Charlie, I want you to take charge of Evan."

Charlie didn't like the idea at all. He said something to
Victor in Spanish, and Victor responded in a harsh tone.
After a pause, Victor unleashed some more words, and Char-
lie caved.

Victor explained, "For the first few days, you work the

same bag. Today you will learn, Evan. Tomorrow, you are half responsible for Charlie's double production. You don't want to fail. Show him, Charlie." Victor made a spinning motion with his forefinger, and Charlie turned to display crosshatched scars on his lower back. He showed them just for a few seconds, and then he turned back.

"Tell our new friend how you earned those," Victor encouraged.

Charlie cleared his throat and spoke to Evan's feet. "From the whip," he said. "Because I didn't work fast enough."

"*Exactamente*," Victor said, smiling. "There are many scars here. I like giving scars." As if reading Evan's mind, he bent low till he was face to face with him. "And no matter how badly I make your back bleed, the pictures will always look just fine."

Jonathan and his team gathered around the computer screen, examining the satellite imagery that Venice had gotten them via an encrypted sat link. "Mother Hen, those are some great pictures," Jonathan said into the radio. "I don't suppose you see any blond-headed kids on your screen, do you?" Back in the War Room, Venice would have these images displayed on the ninety-six-inch high-definition screen.

"I'm looking," she said. "I haven't had access to the sat link for much longer than you have."

The imagery they were looking at now was just a few minutes old, and it showed a cocaine factory of a scale that Jonathan had never seen before. This one stretched for dozens of acres across difficult terrain, and showed a level of organization that Pablo Escobar could only have dreamed about. No longer burdened with the need to hide their activities from the government, they could incorporate efficiencies that were normally reserved for legitimate manufacturing. There appeared to be a central headquarters area, the details of which were difficult to discern because of the thick jungle canopy, but with penetrating imagery technology, they could clearly make out fourteen covered structures of various sizes, thirteen of which were built in a rough rectangle around a central structure that was four times larger than the next largest building.

Southeast of the city—why not call it what it looked like?—stretched the acres of coca bushes and the teeming population of workers, several dozen in total. While the detail was amazing, this commercial version of the highly classified technology available to the armed forces allowed only a bird's-eye view, directly from above. State-of-the-art versions allowed digital enhancement to convert such images to ground-level views, making facial recognition possible from two hundred miles in space.

"Zoom in to about thirty feet," Jonathan instructed as he squinted at the screen. "Let me see one of the workers."

"Which one?"

"Your choice."

While it was possible to manipulate the images from the laptop, it was far simpler for Venice to do it with her controls. The image moved to a section of the screen where the thirty-foot elevation would actually give them a view of four workers. In a single frame.

"I'm seeing children," Harvey said. "Are you seeing children?"

"Turning you on?" Boxers jabbed.

"Fuck you."

"Can it," Jonathan snapped. He keyed his mike. "We're seeing a workforce of kids, Mother Hen. Is that what you get from the big screen?"

"Oh, my God, that's terrible," Venice said.

Jonathan took that as a yes.

"Okay, back off to a hundred feet again." The children seemed to fall away into the screen, and they saw the southwestern corner of the factory. Jonathan touched a spot on the screen with the tip of a retracted ballpoint pen. "Let me see this building right here," he said to Venice. "Get me to ten feet."

As the image started to move, Boxers asked, "You want to see the thatched roof?"

"Exactly." The building he was calling up was the only structure in the compound that had been built outside the jungle canopy. It was therefore easy to see construction details.

When the image stopped moving, and the software finished its resolution process, the picture of an open-sided hut was as clear as if it had been snapped by a visitor. As he'd expected, the roof was made of what appeared to be palm fronds. Admittedly, though, he didn't know one plant from another.

"Why is the thatched roof important?" Harvey asked.

"Because they burn really good," Boxers said.

Harvey's jaw dropped a little. "What exactly are we planning to do?"

"Win against ridiculous odds," Jonathan said. Then, to Venice: "Go ahead and pull out again and let me see the compound. Just enough altitude to give me all the buildings."

"Are we looking for something in particular?" Venice asked.

"We're looking for stores of gasoline," he said. He'd keyed his mike for Venice, but the answer was intended as much for Harvey as for her. "Cocaine manufacturing is a bizarre process," he went on. "If people knew how it was made, they'd never in a million years shove it up their nose. After they stomp on the leaves, they soak the shit in sulfuric acid for a while, and then after another step or two, there's a long soak in gasoline. Up here, I figure they've got to have a pretty good supply."

"Gasoline, eh?" Venice said in his ear. "You should have said something earlier. Watch this." The image on the screen blinked as it refreshed, and then it turned from a picture as you'd normally see it to something more akin to a photographic negative. It jumped a couple more times. And then rotated.

Harvey asked, "What the hell is going on?"

"That's Venice being Venice," Boxers said.

Jonathan added, "You learn over time not to ask questions. It's best just to sit still until she's finished. She's good enough with this computer shit that electrons are actually afraid of her." In anticipation of the show that always accompanied one of Venice's digital accomplishments, Jonathan unplugged his earpiece from the radio and ran the audio connection through the laptop's speakers.

"Quit talking about Venice," he said. "She can hear us all now."

"Ha, ha, very funny," she said.

They listened to the clatter of her computer keys as the image on the screen continued to shift and change colors. For the first part of this dizzying display, she trolled around the outline of the main building, zooming in and out of different quadrants. When one quadrant showed a yellow-orange aura, she said, "There it is."

"There what is?" Jonathan asked.

"Just wait," she said.

She zoomed away from the main building and then shifted to the others in the compound. Through the canopy, they appeared more as outlines than real images, but the footprints of the huts were plainly visible. The screen shifted from building to building, pausing for a second or two, and then moving on to the next. She zoomed out and then in, at what seemed to be random intervals, and finally, she paused at one hut, perhaps the smallest of them all. She zoomed in closer, and as she did, a similar yellow aura appeared on the screen.

"There's your gasoline storage," she said.

Boxers blurted out a laugh.

"You'll tell us how you know this?" Jonathan asked. He didn't for a moment question the accuracy—Venice was always right—he just wanted to know how she got there.

"Did you forget what SkysEye was designed to do?" she asked.

Then he saw it. He had in fact forgotten. "Petroleum research," he said.

"Bingo. The program is designed to search for petroleum compounds. Don't ask me how it does it—something about the light signature of vapors—but there you go."

"I'll be damned," Harvey marveled.

"I told you she was good," Jonathan said.

Venice continued, "That first yellow plume we saw was the gasoline in operation. I figured it would be easier to find when it was in use, and I figured that the big building was the actual factory. I just needed to see what it looked like in use, where vapor concentrations are high, so that I could look for it in storage, where vapors are more contained."

"I'll be double-damned," Harvey said. "So, now that we know where it is, what are we going to do with it?"

Jonathan and Boxers exchanged glances, and together said, "Blow it up."

Jonathan expanded, "We're going to need a diversion to get our PC out of there in one piece. If we give the guards a choice of saving one kid or saving the whole compound, maybe we can catch a break."

"Speaking of breaks," Venice said. There was a sudden lightness in her tone. "Wait till you see this." The screen blinked with another refreshed signal, and then they were looking at a clear image of the coca field again.

Not much seemed to have changed. The workers still toiled, and shadows were still sharp. It wasn't until she started to zoom into the workers that Jonathan got that anticipatory quiver in his gut. Was it possible that she'd found Evan in the middle of the crowd?

The answer came when he got his first flash of white-blond hair. He pointed to the screen. "Holy shit, that's him, isn't it?"

The boy stood with a tall black man and another child. It was hard to tell from a still picture, but they appeared to be having a conversation. "Take me in as close as you can."

Even as he said the words, he knew that he'd overstated.

If Venice took the imagery in as close at it was capable of going, they'd be able to count the freckles on his shoulders. As it was, Venice understood his meaning and brought them in to within four or five feet.

"I see a white boy with long blond hair," Boxers said. "Look at the sunburn on his shoulders. That's someone not used to this much exposure. I give it a ninety-nine percent."

Jonathan agreed. "I call that confirmation," he said. "That makes us a go. Mother Hen, can you put a tag on him somehow and keep up with him?"

Silence.

"You still there?" Jonathan asked.

"I'm here," she confirmed. "I just don't know how to answer you. His heat signature is going to be just like everybody else's. I can track him visually, but that gets to diminishing returns really quickly. After dark, he'll be lost."

"Screw it," Boxers said. "We already know he's there. Once we create a little chaos, we just search him out."

"That's a lot of chaos," Jonathan said. "I don't want to have to find a moving target if people start running around."

"Then we'll find him before we blow the gas. Eyeball the kid, then bring hell to life."

"Then we'll be the only things moving in the camp," Harvey said. "I'm not the tactician that you guys are, but that sounds scary."

Boxers laughed. "Scary, huh? You do know about the guns and stuff, right?"

"I've got it," Venice said.

All heads turned to the computer. "Got what?" Jonathan asked for all of them.

"How to track him after dark—at least until he goes under cover. It's not about *acquiring* his heat signature. It's about *eliminating* all the other identical heat signatures."

Jonathan looked to Boxers. "Did you understand that?"

"Absolutely not."

Jonathan smiled. "So it's not just me."

"It's a simple concept," Venice continued. "Normally, we

worry about heat signatures as a way to differentiate one target from others. That doesn't work in a population of targets who all have a signature of ninety-eight point six degrees, give or take a couple of tenths. So what we do instead is teach the computer to ignore all but one of the identical signatures."

"Oh, I get it," Jonathan said. He wasn't sure he actually did, but as he said so, he made a slicing motion to the others, telling them not to pursue it any further. When Venice said it was possible, it was possible. Understanding the hows and whys really wasn't all that important.

"It shouldn't take all that long," Venice said. "First I want to mark the GPS coordinates for every target and download them to your equipment. We don't want you getting lost in the dark."

Jonathan smiled. Technology had changed so much of warfare over the years; and it wasn't just in the weaponry. In fact, the business of the actual fight hadn't changed much at all. You still had to pierce the flesh of other human beings to kill them, albeit with progressively greater accuracy and effectiveness. The real changes came in the noncombat elements. When Venice was done with the download she'd just mentioned, the specific coordinates of every landmark in the enemy compound would be documented to within inches, as would the details of their infiltration and exfiltration routes. On a cloudy, foggy night with zero visibility, they could arrive at their destination and get home again. It was a whole new world of land navigation.

While Venice worked on her cyberspace easel, Jonathan and his team hammered out their assault plan. Given the limits of their intel, it was necessarily straightforward. Get in, create a diversion, and get out. Any enemy with a weapon would be killed without hesitation. Unarmed enemies would be spared as long as they stayed out of the way.

"Tactically, Box, you're the explosives king. Harvey, you're the medic. I'm the lead on whatever entry we need to make. We stay together as a team, we cover each other's asses, but once we have the PC in hand, nothing stands in the way of getting him to the vehicles. And I mean *nothing*, understand? If things go to shit and we get separated, whoever gets to the vehicle with Evan leaves immediately and goes to the exfil site. The reason we have two vehicles is specifically to plan for us getting split up.

"Once the PC is secure and on his way, if we're separated, there's some room for improv." He looked directly at Harvey. "You're the new guy on the team, so you need to know the rules of engagement. We will *not* leave you behind if you're alive, unless it's the only way to exfil the PC. Understand?"

"Us jarheads aren't big on leaving people behind, either," Harvey said.

Jonathan nodded. "Didn't mean to imply otherwise." He checked his watch. "It's five twenty-eight. That gives us fifty-six minutes till sunset, and that's when we step off. Figure three hours to get to the compound, and then the night gets interesting. One way or another we should be clear of this shithole country in thirteen hours, tops."

CHAPTER THIRTY-SEVEN

"Spit that shit out," Charlie said when Victor finally walked away. "It'll mess up your head. These people are all half crazy anyway. Don't need anybody being any crazier."

Evan hooked a finger into his cheek and pulled out the foul-tasting leaves. "How do you keep him from hitting you?"

Charlie's expression said, *Give me a break.* "Remember the scars? That's the part I'm not good at." He walked to one of the few trees that were growing amid the field of bushes and pulled off a few of the green leaves. "Suck on these."

"What are they?"

Charlie shrugged. "Not a clue. Not that other shit, but after you suck on 'em for a while they look the same, and they don't make you feel like crap."

Evan took the leaves gratefully and slid them into the space formerly occupied by the coca leaves. "Why are you here?"

"We better get to work," Charlie said. "There's nothing to this. You just pull the leaves off and stuff them into the bag." He demonstrated. Using his thumb against the first knuckle of his forefinger, he could clear a whole branch in a single swipe.

Evan mimicked the motion, then shook his hand in the air to relieve the hot spot caused by the friction. "That hurts."

"Yeah, you might want to pluck them for a while till your skin gets tough. After a few weeks, you won't even feel it."

Evan gaped. "A few *weeks*? I'm not staying here a few weeks."

Charlie chuckled.

"What's funny?"

"Nothing's funny," Charlie said. "That's just the same thing that everybody says. But nobody ever leaves. Not the way they want to, anyway."

"Why not?"

Charlie gave him a glance, but kept stripping leaves. "You'd better keep plucking. That whip hurts like shit." He craned his neck to see if they were being watched. "They don't leave because there's no place to go. You walked in here, right? You see any places to escape to?"

"I could go to the police."

This time, Charlie laughed in earnest. "Don't bother—they'll be here. They come all the time. And don't bother looking all hopeful like that. Helping you will be the last thing they're about. They come here to get paid by the bosses, sample the product a little, and then do the village girls down the hill. This is like Rain Forest Disneyland. A damn amusement park. You go lookin' for police, they'll just grab you and bring you back. Then you get to have a serious talk with Victor and his toys. Trust me. You're not going anywhere. It's better if you get used to being here."

The knot of fear returned, churning Evan's stomach. "How long have you been here?"

Charlie shrugged. "I have no idea. I was ten when my parents were killed in a robbery in Bogotá. I shuffled around to orphanages and stuff for a while, and then I ended up here. That was a long time ago. I really don't know. It's not like we celebrate holidays. No birthdays, no Christmases.

And the weather never changes. How can you know? How old are you? We're about the same size."

"Thirteen," Evan said.

Charlie stopped and gave him a look. Color had drained from his face. "Thirteen? Really?"

Evan nodded.

"You small for your age?"

"Not really." As soon as he said it, Evan wondered if he should have lied.

Charlie looked away. He didn't do or say anything for a long time. Maybe a minute. When he went back to work, he kept his back turned.

Evan felt like shit. If Charlie had really spent three years of his life out here, doing this, how could he keep going? Could he really not have known how long it'd been? Evan shouldn't have said anything.

"Why is your English so good?" he asked.

"My parents were American," Charlie said. His voice was softer, huskier. "Victor likes me to keep up with English for when people like you come."

The knot tightened in his stomach. "People like me?"

Charlie let it go.

"What do you mean, people like me?"

Charlie shook his head. "Forget I said anything."

"A little late for that."

Charlie stopped working again and looked him in the eye. "They can get a lot of money for American kids who look like you."

Evan didn't get it. Maybe he didn't *want* to get it. "What do I look like?"

"Find a mirror, you don't know."

Evan shoved him, knocking Charlie off balance, but not enough to make him fall. "Tell me, goddammit!"

Retribution came swiftly and out of nowhere. Charlie landed an open-handed slap just in front of Evan's ear, reeling him into the bush he was plucking.

Charlie stepped forward and stared down. His eyes glis-

tened red, and they were wet. He seemed breathless. He
shouted, "You're white, you stupid fuck! You're white, and
you look like a girl. People pay real money for boys who
look like girls. Are you following me?"

Evan stayed on the ground, waiting to see what came
next. For the longest time, Charlie just stood there in a fighting stance, one foot slightly in front of the other, his hands
up and ready to box. But then something drained out of him,
and his shoulders sagged as he dropped his hands. "Remember you asked," he said softly. Then he went back to work.

Evan raised himself to his haunches, and then he stood,
brushing himself off. "I'm sorry I pushed you," he mumbled.

Charlie's hands never stopped their work on the branches.
He turned and said, "And I'm sorry you can't fight worth a
shit." The broad smile sold it as a joke, and a friendship was
born.

A burst of machine-gun fire made Evan jump a foot and
dive to the ground.

Charlie saw it happen and then started laughing enough
to make himself choke. "They're not shooting at *you*," he
said. He adjusted his slung bag of leaves to a better spot on
his shoulder.

"What were they shooting at, then?"

"Nobody," Charlie said. He started walking. "Come on.
It's dinnertime."

Filled, the bag that Charlie pulled along behind him was
huge and heavy. It trailed behind him by a good six feet, and
it dragged enough to make him lean heavily into each step to
keep it going.

"Do you need help?" Evan asked.

"No, thanks. Victor wouldn't like it. You'll get your own
soon enough."

Evan stayed with Charlie as he dragged the bag to the
crest of the hill, and then down to the compound. As they got

closer, the aroma of dinner mixed with the stink of the gasoline and the rotten-egg smell to form a mixture that soured
the thought of eating anything. They took the bag to the edge
of the big building in the center, where a line of workers
formed in front of a rusty scale that looked like one you'd
see in a doctor's office, but much bigger.

One at a time, each of the boys dragged his bag over the
scale. One of the men in the compound slid the counterweight to the balance point, then made a note on a clipboard.
As they waited their turn, Evan saw that every kid in the line
had strips of scar tissue across his back. Some had more than
others, but no one, it seemed, was able to avoid Victor and
his toys forever. There was an uncomfortable silence about it
all. Evan wondered if maybe talking was forbidden, but he
didn't dare ask for fear of finding out that it was.

As they awaited their turn, Evan examined the pads of his
fingers. They were sore and sticky, whether with his own
blister juice or from some kind of sap from the bushes he
didn't know. But he was glad he'd listened to Charlie and
plucked his share instead of stripping them the way the others were doing. If he'd done it that way, he'd probably be seeing bone under his skin.

Finally, they were at the front of the line. Charlie dragged
his sack onto the wide face of the scale. The man on the platform adjusted the counterweight on the bar, then said something in Spanish. Charlie responded in kind, and the man
smiled. After a quick nod and another few words, they were
dismissed with a quick flick of the man's head.

"What did he say?" Evan asked.

"He said I was a hard worker today." Charlie giggled. "I
didn't bother to mention that you were working with me."

Evan felt a glow of pride that he'd done a good job to help
his new friend, and then the glow dimmed when he realized
again what lay ahead for him. Sold for rape.

No, that definitely was not going to happen. He didn't
know exactly how he was going to stop it, but that was not
going to happen to him again. He remembered Mr. Jonathan's

words from one of the ridiculous Stranger Danger talks at RezHouse: *It's better to die on the street than get in the car.*

Yeah, well, just wait to see what happens when someone waves a dick at him. One way or another, there was going to be a lot of blood on the floor.

"Okay, here's how dinner works," Charlie explained as they approached the center of the compound, where someone had produced a bunch of propane-powered grills. "Take whatever they offer and smile when you do it. Victor's got a rod up his ass about showing gratitude. Once we get the food, we'll go to one of the tables and eat. Just eat what you can choke down. If you don't work tomorrow, you're gonna get beat, and they're not going to care that it's because you passed out from hunger, okay? Whenever you get a chance for food, take it, understand?"

Evan nodded. The closer they got, the worse it smelled. "What are they cooking?"

"Never ask," Charlie said. "It'll get you beat for asking, and then worse than that, you'll actually find out. You might think you want to know, but I guarantee you don't."

The rank of grills served as a divider of sorts for the compound, separating the adults who clustered around the main hut from the workers who clustered on the far side of the grills. Charlie showed him the way. He grabbed a plastic tray—a lot like the ones in the dining room back at Rez-House—and handed one to Evan while keeping one for himself. Charlie went to the cook first, silently holding out his tray. The cook put a hunk of meat on the tray, and then ladled some disgusting yellow shit into a cup and set it on the tray next to the meat. Charlie smiled politely, and headed toward the ranks of dilapidated picnic tables that served as the dining area.

Evan followed his moves exactly, focusing all of his energy on not showing revulsion at the animal leg that had been plopped onto his tray. It had toenails. Next came the cup of crap. At closer inspection, it looked like it might have corn in it somewhere. One way or another, he told himself, it was corn. He liked corn. If he convinced himself that he liked this stuff, then maybe he could get it down and keep it down.

Charlie led the way to a table that was otherwise unoccupied. Evan sat across from him.

"You don't want to talk too much to the other workers," Charlie said. "They don't like gringos. Gringos killed a lot of their relatives and raised a lot of hell a while ago. Speaking English is a problem out here. Not speaking Spanish is a *huge* problem out here, so you'd better get that taken care of right away."

"Well, you speak English," Evan said, stating the obvious.

"Do you see a lot of friends hanging around me? These assholes all know that I'm not one of them. They know that I don't suck their weed, and they know that if just one or two things break my way, I'll actually be able to make a life for myself someday. They don't like that." He took a bite of his meat and winced at the flavor. "If I was them, I'd probably hate my guts, too."

Evan didn't know how to respond to that, so he let it go. He picked up the meat and smelled it. Still clueless, he closed his eyes and took a bite.

Oh, Christ, he had to find a way out of here.

Evan was keenly aware that he was being watched and talked about. Boys at the other tables craned their necks to see him and point. Farther away, some boys stood for a better view.

"A little like being in a zoo, isn't it?" Charlie observed.

"On the wrong side of the bars," Evan said. "Everybody's so quiet. This many kids in one place, you'd expect there to be a lot of noise."

"That's the weed," Charlie said. "That's why they want everybody to chew it. Shit does weird stuff to you. Makes you work harder and care less. Can't sleep worth anything, though."

Evan's ears perked. "Sleep? We get to do that?"

"That's all there is after the sun goes down. That's what those huts are for." He pointed to a row of four thatch-roof huts just like all the others, but with walls. They stood taller than the others to accommodate a line of wire-mesh windows that started at maybe five feet off the platform and rose for about three feet over that. "They lock us in just before the light goes away, and they open it up when the sun comes up."

Evan's heart rate picked up. He wasn't exactly claustrophobic, but the thought of being locked into a room with strangers who didn't like him—in the dark, no less—was his vision of a living nightmare. "What happens if you have to piss in the middle of the night?"

Around a mouthful of food, Charlie said, "I try not to. But if you have to, there's a cut-off drum in the corner with a seat on it. One of the punishment jobs around here is to clean it out. Never once saw anybody do it without puking."

Okay, living nightmare didn't touch this. Evan was getting out of here. Maybe he'd die trying, but there was no way this was going to be his life.

A pall fell over the compound, almost as if someone had sucked away the atmosphere. Charlie said, "Uh-oh. Speeches are never good."

Evan pivoted on his bench to see Victor standing up near the grills, his fists on his hips, somehow looking even more menacing from a distance than he did up close. His skin glistened in the fading light. He said nothing until silence had fallen over the compound.

When he spoke, his voice boomed. Even without understanding the words, Evan understood that they were important. Just a few seconds into the speech, he pointed right at Evan and said his name.

Evan looked to Charlie for a translation.

"He says you are a special guest. But he doesn't mean it. He's making fun of you."

As one, the entire crowd pivoted to look at him.

"He says that you can't be trusted." Charlie struggled with the translation, as if trying to interpret the words instead of merely reporting them. After just a few seconds of that, he abandoned the effort and started translating directly.

"Mr. Evan Guinn is not to be harmed. No marks may be put on his face. He does not speak our language, so it would be foolish to try to talk with him. Because he is special, he will not be required to work as hard as the rest of you, but he will still live among you."

"What the hell is he doing?" Evan hissed.

Charlie shushed him. Apparently, it was hard enough to translate one person without having to answer questions from another.

He continued to channel Victor. "Be sure to watch him closely. He is more valuable to me than any of you are. If he is hurt, I will punish you all severely."

Victor emphasized that last point by brandishing the Louisville Slugger.

"If he runs away, or if someone comes to take him away, I will hurt all of you very bad. If he does not return, some of you will die just because I will be angry."

Evan felt his ears turning red as his stomach cramped. Victor was fixing it so that everyone would hate him.

"Our newest resident has friends who will try to take everything away from us. One day soon they may try to kill me and all of you. They may make some kind of excuse, but whatever they say to you will be a lie. These strangers when they come will try to take Evan away, and if they succeed, you might as well die. It will be like the old days all over again when the Americans killed so many of your fathers and mothers."

Victor paused for effect, pacing dramatically down the ranks of tables. He stopped next to Evan, and he glowered. Moving with speed that made Evan jump, Victor clamped his hand on the boy's ear and lifted him from his seat. Evan yelped and grabbed Victor's wrist to keep him from peeling the ear clean off his head.

"And if these people arrive for our friend Evan, what are you going to do?"

For a few seconds, no one said anything. Then one boy stood up. He couldn't have been more than ten. "*Mataremos*," he said.

The other boys cheered.

Victor cupped his ear with his free hand and leaned in toward the crowd. He said something, and then everyone said in unison, "*Mataremos!*"

"Kay?" Victor said, leaning in even more.

"*MATAREMOS!*" The boys all cheered at that. Victor let go of Evan's ear and shoved him down into his seat. Around him, the word he didn't understand became a chant: "Ma-ta-re-mos, ma-ta-re-mos . . ."

For his part, Charlie looked very uncomfortable. To Evan's silent inquiry, he replied, "It means, 'We will kill them.' "

CHAPTER THIRTY-EIGHT

"Scorpion, this is Mother Hen."

Jonathan pressed the mike button on his vest. "Hi, Mom," he said. The three of them walked in single file up a hill that seemed to have no end, Jonathan in the lead and Boxers taking up the rear. In near total darkness, the night glowed green and bright thanks to the enhancement of their night-vision goggles. Their GPS showed that they'd hiked about two miles since leaving the village, and for every step, Jonathan had kept his fist lightly wrapped around the grip of his battle-slung M4, his finger outside the trigger guard, but poised for action with an instant's notice.

"I've got good news from Alaska," Venice said. "Wolverine came through. Our friends are airborne with special transportation arranged through channels. Word is that everyone is safe and they hit a home run."

Jonathan smiled. "I'm sure that will be a story worth hearing."

"I've heard some of it," Venice said, "and you have no idea how right you are."

"Looking forward to it. Got any good news for us jungle jockeys?"

"I do," she said. "I think I have a final location for the precious cargo," Venice said. "He's in Building Golf. It looks like it might be some sort of a dormitory, judging from the number of people who filed in."

Without referencing his map or his computer, Jonathan knew that she was referring to the third hut down the eastern edge of the compound. He stopped and let the others catch up. Boxers and Harvey were both equipped with the same communications gear, but as commander, Jonathan was the lone voice back to Fisherman's Cove. "How sure are you?" he asked.

"I'm one hundred percent certain I saw him enter Building Golf. After that, reliability drops," Venice said. "I'll monitor for people exiting the building, but if that happens, we'll have no way of knowing who it is."

"Roger that," Jonathan said. "I show us two miles out. Do you concur?"

"I do," she said. "But I've got some troubling news. They've got the compound lit up like daytime. I compared that to images from SkysEye last night, and the floodlights appear to be new."

"That means they're expecting us," Boxers whispered. "Fuckin' Josie."

"It means they're expecting *something*," Jonathan corrected. He keyed his mike. "Have you found the generator?"

"I believe so," Venice said. "I've got a heat signature in the five hundred–degree range, consistent with the burning temperature of gasoline, along the western margin of the main building. Problem is, it appears to be in the wash of the light that it's creating. You're not going to be able to get to it."

"Take it out with a sniper shot?" Harvey asked.

Jonathan shook his head. "We're firing five-five-six millimeter, and you're firing nines. They're not reliable for that." He cursed himself for not having spec'd out a 7.62-millimeter rifle to Josie. There was nothing like the proper application of M60 fire to raise havoc with electrical generators.

"We'll just have to plant a second charge," Boxers said.

Jonathan always got a kick out of how easy the Big Guy made complex operations sound. He was right, of course. "That one will be mine," Jonathan said. He turned to Harvey. "That'll put a lot more pressure on you as the sole cover. Are you up to it?"

Harvey cocked his head and smirked. "If I say no, do you have a replacement?"

It was a point well made in response to a stupid question.

"Don't worry about me," Harvey said. "I'm falling back into the habit. Since I haven't shot a gun in a while, I might not have the most accurate aim, but I can pull the trigger enough to make the barrel hot."

The radio crackled, "Hey, are you still there?"

"Sorry, Mom," Jonathan said. "We were just doing a little strategizing."

"Well, strategize this: I show two people leaving the compound and heading your way. They're carrying flashlights, and from their posture, I'd say they're holding rifles, too."

Boxers snorted out a laugh. "Way to be stealthy," he said on the radio.

Jonathan took comfort from the use of artificial light. It put the enemy at a double disadvantage. Not only were they visible before the fight began, but they'd likely be blind afterward because their night vision would be shot. That's what he was hoping, anyway. Not counting on it, for sure, but hoping very hard.

"Are you sure they're heading our way?" Jonathan asked.

"I know that they're heading down the trail that leads to you," Venice said. "Time will tell if you're the ultimate target. I'm guessing no."

"I'm guessing no, too," Jonathan said. "If they know we're coming, the last thing they'll want to do is engage us in anything less than strength."

"I think they're setting traps," Boxers said offline.

Jonathan thought that, too. "Mother Hen, keep an eye on

them. If they stop for any length of time, note the location for us on the GPS."

"I'll try, but remember the four-minute delay."

"I understand. Do your best to keep us informed. Now let's clear the channel for a while."

Venice was unsurpassed in her skills and her commitment to mission, but left to her own devices she could get very damn chatty on the radio. Sometimes you just had to cut her off early, before she could develop an unmanageable head of steam.

"I've got a question," Harvey said after a couple of minutes had passed in silence. "In The Sandbox, we had a problem with Hadjis faking shit for the satellite coverage. They knew we were watching, so they'd put on a show. Any chance that our bad guys are doing that?"

"Impossible," Boxers said with hesitation.

"How can you be so sure?"

Jonathan took that one. "Because Josie never knew about the satellite imagery. We kept that just for us. If he didn't know it, then he couldn't have told anyone."

There'd been an argument between the guards as it came time to herd the boys into their sleeping huts, but Evan had no idea what it was about until Charlie explained it to him after the fact. "Some of the *guardia* think it's a mistake to put you and me in the same hut. They worry that we can make plans that no one else can understand."

Evan shrugged. "Well . . . *yeah*." When he said it, "yeah" had two syllables.

The argument had lasted long enough for them to be the last to enter. Charlie's feet had barely cleared the jamb when the wooden door slammed shut and something heavy slid across the opening. After the bolt or whatever it was slid into place, Evan heard a heavy rattle that sounded like a lock being snapped closed.

The hut held ten army-style cots, arranged in two ranks

down either side of the rectangular interior, but with everybody inside, Evan counted only nine occupants, including himself. The heat and stench of the place were off-the-chart awful. Ten seconds in, he was seriously thinking about vomiting; but then the puking plan was derailed when one of the hut's residents threw a pair of flip-flops at Charlie, beaning him on the forehead with the first one, and missing with the second, which sailed into the corner near the shit can. The rest of the kids cheered at that, and then there was a long string of angry Spanish, punctuated with pointing and derisive laughter.

The kid who threw the shoe jutted out his neck and made a move on Charlie, his shoulders and arms set for battle. As the distance closed, the fight seemed inevitable, so Evan stepped out to help his new friend. He met the attacker with a football-style forearm block to his chest, and the force of the collision knocked the other kid to the ground. His eyes hot and angry, the attacker tried to stand, but Evan knocked him down again. On the far end of the hut, the other boys started to shout, and they surged forward.

Evan didn't care. Every one of them was smaller than he, and he was tired of being pushed around. If they wanted a fight, he'd give them one. He needed to hit someone, to break something. If it had to be noses and teeth, that was fine. God knew it wouldn't be his first time.

The boy he'd knocked down crab-walked backward toward the others, who helped him to his feet. The war was on. Shit was going to fly.

Amid all the shouting, he never heard Charlie yelling at him to stop. He was surprised as hell, then, when arms clamped across his chest from behind and swirled him away from the fight. "Stop it!" Charlie yelled.

Evan was appalled. "Stop? Are you kidding? That kid just threw shoes at you!"

"It doesn't matter," Charlie said.

Behind them, the door to the hut flew open, and three guards stormed in, rifles at the ready.

Charlie darted over to them, his arms outstretched to show restraint. "No, no, no, no," he said. And then there was a long string of Spanish. The guards seemed unmoved at first, but the longer Charlie talked, the more the men seemed to relax. On the far side, the other occupants of the hut had fallen silent, and went through the motions of climbing into their cots.

After thirty seconds, the incident had passed. From body language alone, Evan could tell that Charlie was finishing up some kind of negotiation. Cautiously satisfied, it seemed, the guards nodded and backed out the door. The locks slid shut, and it was over.

Charlie turned and glared at the residents, then walked the few steps to pick up the flip-flops that they'd thrown at him.

"What the hell's going on?" Evan asked.

"Don't ever try to fight my fights for me, okay?" He pointed at the end bunk—the one closest to the shit can. "That one's yours. The newest guy gets the stink."

Evan cocked his head, stunned. "You're welcome," he said.

Charlie turned on him. "I didn't thank you," he snapped. "Don't think you understand this place, Evan. We have rules here, and one of the rules is that the new guy gets the stink. Because I'm your guardian angel, I get *you*, which means that I get the stink, too." He moved to the second-to-last cot, leaving an empty one between himself and the next guy. He sat on the edge, then lifted his filthy feet on the end of the cot closest to the aisle and lay back. "Now try to sleep."

Evan followed, but sat on the edge of his own cot, facing Charlie, his elbows resting on his knees. "He threw shit at you, man. You can't let that happen. I live in a dormitory, too, and I'm telling you, you've got to fight for your reputation."

Charlie rolled his head to make eye contact, his expression one of mild amusement. "Does this really look like a dormitory to you? This is a concentration camp. Siberia without the air-conditioning. Around here, you can fight every day or live every day. The fuck do I care how close to the shit can I sleep? This whole fucking place smells the same. Up there, back here, what difference does it make? Its not worth getting your nose broke or balls beat. It's just not." He shifted his gaze back to the ceiling, then closed his eyes. "Now go to sleep."

Outside, in the distance, an engine fired up, and a moment later, bright light flared through the windows, turning the inside of the hut to day and casting sharp shadows on the walls and ceiling. Almost as one, the boys in the hut all sat up and whispered their concerns to each other.

"Well, that's different," Charlie said, sitting up. "People really coming to get you?" he asked.

Evan screwed up his face and shook his head. "I wish. Anybody wants to, I'm happy to come along."

Charlie chuckled, then lay back down, placing his forearm over his eyes.

Evan followed suit, but was so many miles away from falling to sleep that he was already worried about how long the night was going to be.

After about five minutes, as the kids at the far end began to fill the room with the sounds of sleep, Charlie whispered, "You awake?"

"Oh my God, yes."

"I want you to do me a favor. If some away team does beam down here for you, take me back to the mother ship with you, okay?"

Sometimes, it's the stupidest images that give you the giggles.

Jonathan's earpiece crackled, "They're moving again. Away from you."

Venice had been tracking the movements of the two men who had left the compound with guns, and had been fortunate enough in two four-minute cycles of pictures to catch them in the act of setting a booby trap on the trail they were walking. Because of the jungle cover, she wasn't able to determine what munitions they were using, but the fact that it took them so long told Jonathan that it was something pretty rudimentary. By zooming in closely to the operation and using a stylus on her computer screen back in Fisherman's Cove, she'd been able to mark the location of the trap to within a fraction of one second of latitude and longitude, and she'd already uploaded that location to the GPS devices Jonathan and his team were carrying.

It only made sense that the team would travel to the farthest point to set the first trap and then work backward. Reversing the order would be a terrific way to get snared by your own genius.

"Scorpion, I show you only about a hundred and fifty yards from the location of the trap," Venice said.

Jonathan keyed his mike. "Keep focused on the bad guys, Mom. I've got the coordinates of the trap here. We'll find it. I want to make sure that we find the second one if they set it."

"I'm liking my decision to come along less and less every minute," Harvey grumped. "Booby traps. Jesus."

Jonathan admired Boxers for just letting it go. It was safe to say that the Big Guy didn't like strangers in general—make that *people* in general—and he *hated* having tagalongs on missions. For him to keep his mouth shut on a setup like Harvey just offered took enormous self control.

It took all of five minutes for them to close the distance and arrive at the site of the first trap. When the GPS said that they were ten yards away, Jonathan brought the team to a halt and gathered them around, combining them into an unacceptably compact target, but judging the risk to be low at this point.

Besides, given the darkness of the night, they'd have been invisible to anyone more than just a few feet away.

They spoke in whispers. "Okay," Jonathan said, "the trap they set is about ten yards up the trail. Harvey, go find it."

"*What?*" His tone was one of abject horror.

Jonathan laughed. "I'm kidding," he said.

Harvey brought a hand to his chest. "Holy shit."

Jonathan turned serious again. "From here on out, we're prepared for battle. I want weapons charged and safeties off, which means special attention to trigger discipline. Roger that?"

Harvey made a show of thumbing the safety switch on his MP5 to three-round burst. Jonathan and Boxers had both been in fire mode since they'd slung their weapons. Trigger discipline meant that you kept your finger away from the damn thing until it was time to shoot. The American public would be horrified to know the number of their sons and daughters who had been killed in various wars by some inattentive yahoo who tickled his weapon's trigger at the wrong time.

Jonathan continued, "I'm going to go on white light to find this trap, so keep your eyes averted. Box, I want you for close cover. Harvey, stay back here and turn your back to me. One of us needs continued good night vision. We good?"

"Good as gold," Boxers said.

"Oo-rah," Harvey grunted.

Jonathan smiled. *Oo-rah* was the Marine Corps version of the Army's *hoo-ah* (Marines always had to be different), and it meant that Harvey's Inner Marine was being reborn.

Snapping his NVGs out of the way, Jonathan brought his muzzle-mounted flashlight to life and pointed it at the ground at a spot three feet in front of him. He bent low at the waist to a half-squat and advanced cautiously, scanning the light from one edge of the path to the other to search for any signs of a trip wire or other triggering device. Next to him, his hips pressed to Jonathan's ribs, Boxers advanced in lockstep with him, his rifle trained on the trail up ahead, trusting Jonathan to find any hazards they might step on. The two men had depended on each other so completely and so successfully over so many years and through so many battles that it seemed sometimes as if they knew each other's thoughts.

They advanced with agonizing slowness—the kind of advance that made younger soldiers impatient and frequently cost them their lives. A minute or so into it, Jonathan stopped and consulted his GPS, which said they should be within a foot or two of whatever they were looking for.

Where was it? *What* was it? He took another few tiny steps forward, then stopped and consulted his GPS again. "Okay, Box," he said, "don't move anymore, okay?"

The Big Guy froze. "Am I in danger?" he asked. He never stopped scanning for potential targets.

"I don't know. This is definitely the spot that Venice marked, but I'm not seeing anything. I was expecting a trip wire. A grenade or something. I'm not seeing anything."

"What about a mine?" Boxers asked.

Wow, Jonathan thought. Could these guys be that sophisticated? He pulled the light from its muzzle mount and stooped to his haunches, scanning the dirt of the path for any signs of disturbance. "I don't suppose you have a ground-penetrating radar on you," he quipped.

"I left it in my other pants."

The hairs on Jonathan's arms and the back of his neck felt electrified as he lowered himself to his knees and leaned to within a few inches of the dirt. "They're damn good," he mumbled. He saw nothing. Leaning closer to the ground, he moved the light to the side, hoping that the different angle might give him a different perspective.

He was about to abandon the effort and move on when he saw the brush marks. They were just light track marks in the dirt—an obvious effort to even out the ground—too regular in their appearance to be a natural occurrence. There was only one reason Jonathan could think of for someone to brush over an area like that, and it was to conceal a hole that had been dug for a mine. (If anything else had been concealed, the burier would have just used his foot—something a mine installer would be foolish to try.)

"I found it," Jonathan announced. "Good call, Box."

"I live to serve," Boxers replied. "Now mark it, and let's get on with it."

"No, we need to pull it out."

Big Guy sighed loudly. "I hate it when you say macho shit like that. I hate it even more when you play with toys that can turn us both into humidity."

"If we leave it, we'll have to worry about it during extraction," Jonathan explained. "We'll be moving a lot faster then, I expect. For now, we've got the luxury of time."

He wasn't soliciting votes on this. He unclipped his M4 from its sling and set it on the ground. With the light clamped in his teeth like an old stogie, he drew his KA-BAR from its scabbard on his left shoulder and gently inserted the blade into the disturbed earth. As he'd expected, it went in easily, indicating that the hole had been gently backfilled. Using the tip of the blade, he began the painstaking process of exposing the face of the mine. After three minutes, there it was.

"Well, well, well," he mused aloud, removing the light from his mouth. "The Soviet Union lives on. We've got a PMN-2 here." He returned the KA-BAR to its sheath.

"Of course we do," Boxers growled. "What's the sense of finding a mine if it's not a nasty one?"

The PMN-2 anti-personnel mine first arrived in large numbers in Southeast Asia. Smaller and lighter than its predecessors, the weapon was extremely man-portable, and with an explosive load of one hundred grams of a TNT/RDX mixture, it carried a hell of a wallop, guaranteed to rip off the foot that tripped it, and presenting a high likelihood of doing substantially more damage than that. Troops in Iraq and Afghanistan had seen more than their fair share of these nasty buggers.

On the positive side, because they were so widely carried by so wide a spectrum of soldiers, the trigger mechanism was a forgiving one, thus explaining how so many untrained insurgents survived long enough to get them into the ground.

Jonathan said, "If you want to take a few steps back, I won't think badly of you."

"If you blow me up, I'll beat your ass blue for all eternity," Boxers said. "Just do what you've got to do, and let's get on with the fun part."

Smiling around the flashlight he'd returned to his mouth, Jonathan used the first two fingers of both hands to oh-so-gently excavate the loose dirt from around the mine. Fully exposed, it was about the size of his hand.

"I'm lifting it out now," he said around the flashlight. "Last chance to walk away."

"A daily ass-whuppin' for all eternity, boss. Just think about that. Succeed or fail, I figure I win either way."

Fair enough. Jonathan raised to his haunches and then to a squat, his feet straddling the hole he'd just dug. He reached between his feet, tickled his fingers under the explosive mechanism, and stood. On a different day, if stealth were not a priority, he might have just Frisbee'd the mine into the jungle and let it blow up, but today he didn't have the luxury. He was reasonably sure that he remembered how to defuse a PMN-2, but reasonably wasn't sure enough. He settled on carrying the weapon five feet into the jungle and gently setting it down.

He stood tall again, clapped the dirt from his hands, and reassembled his weapons load.

"I guess some spider monkey is in for the surprise of his life, huh?" Boxers joked.

Jonathan smiled and turned off his flashlight, then snapped his NVGs back over his eyes. He keyed his mike. "The booby trap is secure. Have our friends set any more?"

Venice's voice said, "Negative. I'll keep watching them and let you know if they stop again."

Harvey rejoined them. "What was it?" he asked.

Jonathan caught him up on the removal of the mine and its current location.

"They mined a trail that the locals use to travel to and

from the compound," Harvey recapped, his voice heavy with disdain. "These guys are assholes of a whole new order."

"I don't know," Boxers said. "When your business is using kid labor to produce a product that kills kids all over the world, I think you might have already set the asshole bar as high as it can go."

CHAPTER THIRTY-NINE

Jonathan saw the aura of the compound in the sky twenty minutes before they reached its outer perimeter. The factory glowed like daytime, thanks to slung arrays of incandescent lightbulbs that gave the place the look of a 1960s Route One used-car lot.

Any remaining doubt that the enemy had been alerted to this raid evaporated the instant Scorpion and his team got to see the compound up close. In addition to the lights, teams of soldiers wandered about in random pairs and trios, most with rifles slung, but enough with them at the ready that it was clear they'd been alerted to something.

But for all their nervousness, they'd forgotten the basic tenets of defense. By turning the center of the compound to day, they no doubt took solace that no one could sneak around the interior; but they'd rendered themselves blind to intruders' approach from outside their perimeter. Even worse, the noise from the generator they used to create the light masked the intruders' approach.

Jonathan and his team approached from the southwest corner of the compound, the one nearest the generator. Their location put them on the far side of the compound from the sleeping huts that lined the eastern perimeter. To their left, maybe forty feet away, sat the storage shed for the gasoline, while to their right, only twenty feet away, sat the enormous trailer-mounted electrical generator, which, to Jonathan's surprise, was enclosed in a sticks-and-chicken-wire fence, the gate for which was on the eastern side. The enclosure contained all kinds of tools and equipment that apparently were of great enough value to warrant extra protection. To gain access through the gate would require Jonathan to expose his presence to the entire compound.

"Who the hell builds a fence around a generator?" Boxers whispered.

Jonathan eased quietly out of his rucksack and laid it on the ground to make himself smaller and quieter, then dug into the thigh pocket of his trousers and removed his Leatherman multipurpose tool, one of God's greatest inspirations. Opening the tool, he folded back the handles and revealed the needle-nose pliers and wire snips. Out of another pocket of his ruck, he removed a coil of detonating cord, from which he removed a four-inch length with a slice of his KA-BAR. Then he cut the four-inch strip in half again. Yet another pocket produced two electronic initiators and a roll of black electrician's tape.

"A grenade would be easier," Boxers quipped.

And if they hadn't needed a delay in knocking out the power, he might have done exactly that. As it was, stealth trumped everything. He made sure he had both their attentions when he said, "Keep an eye out, but don't discharge your weapon unless there's no other way."

He got nods from them both, then went on with what he had to do. A distance of about twenty-five feet separated the periphery of the jungle from the nearest side of the fence. Pressing himself on his belly, as close to the ground as his vest and extra ammo would allow, Jonathan belly-crawled like a lizard through the open space, and then aligned himself with the wire wall, hoping that by keeping the lines of his body parallel to the lines of the fence he could remain invisible to all but those who would know what to look for.

He started at the bottom of the fence, peeling the lowest edge out of the ground to expose it. Using the snips on the Leatherman, he cut ten of the one-inch hexagonal links vertically, and then another ten across, forming a kind of sideways doggy-door for himself. He bent the snipped panel out of the way and rolled onto his back so that he could guide himself past the sharp edges of the mangled wire. He offered up a silent prayer of thanks for the thrumming noise of the generator to mask his activities.

Shoulders and head were always the most difficult. Pressing himself into the moist ground, he wrapped his leather-palmed fists over the sharp protrusions with his hands joined thumb-to-thumb above the bridge of his nose to protect his eyes. He flexed his knees, dug his heels into the ground, and pushed. Conditions cooperated, and with relatively little effort, the top half of his body was free and clear, inside the enclosure. From there, all he had to do was sit up and draw his feet in.

Jesus, it was bright in here. With light streaming in from every angle, there weren't even any decent shadows to hide in. He moved quickly. Keeping low, he duck-walked past a collection of stacked buckets, funnels, troughs, stir poles, and piles of accumulated drums of diesel fuel to the generator, which itself was situated near the front gate. It was a monstrous old thing, about the size of a big desk on a trailer platform. His mind conjured images of the team of workers it must have taken to haul this bad boy all the way from the road to here; then he wondered if maybe they didn't get help from a helicopter.

From here out, speed and luck would play a big role. He steadied himself on the unseen side of the generator, taking a deep breath through his nose and letting it go through his mouth. Then it was time to go.

At a deep crouch, he peeked to make sure no one was in

the immediate vicinity, then swung himself around to the front of the machine and pulled open the front panel to reveal the controls. There were two basic parts of the machinery: the generator itself and the diesel engine that drove it. Each part got its own little bomb, the latter with a charge around the fuel line, and the former with a charge around the main outgoing electrical line. Det cord made the life of a demolition expert a piece of cake. All you had to do was insert the detonator and tape it around what you wanted to destroy. He was using radio-activated detonators tonight, but he'd used all kinds of initiators in the past, including OFF—old-fashioned fuse, the kind you see in cowboy movies where they light the bomb and throw it—and det cord had never once let him down.

"Someone's coming your way," Boxers' voice said in his ear.

Jonathan dropped to his haunches and drew his .45. Two seconds later, he'd scooted back around to the far side of the generator and the limited shelter it offered.

With his back pressed to the noisy generator and his weapon at the ready, he pressed his mike button. "Did he see me?" Jonathan whispered.

The answer was slow in coming. "Hard to tell," Boxers whispered. "He doesn't seem spooked, but he's by-God coming right this way. Maybe he needs to refuel the beast or something. He's got an AK slung, but the muzzle's down. I think we're okay. Did you get done what you had to?"

Jonathan gave a thumbs-up, knowing that Boxers had an eyeball on him.

"Then get the fuck outta there and come back to daddy."

Of the choices available to him, that truly was the best one. Normally at night, the smart move was always to remain still when there was an increased likelihood of being seen because the human eye is much more sensitive to movement than to static objects; but when bathed with this much light, such nuances didn't matter.

Still bent at the waist, Jonathan holstered his weapon and

threaded his way back through the accumulated clutter and aimed for the hole he'd cut in the fence. Dropping to a push-up posture, he rolled over onto his back to inchworm back out into the night. His chest had just cleared the opening when Boxers hissed, "Stop, stop, stop. Abort. He's going to be right on top of you. Shit."

Jonathan froze. Without any cover now, he cranked his head to the left and then to the right, trying to eyeball the threat. And there he was: a uniformed soldier quick-walked into view from his right, making a beeline for him. Jonathan thought he was a dead man. He reached for his .45 and realized with a flash of horror that the small opening in the fence blocked his access to his weapon.

Shit indeed.

Only the soldier, it turned out, wasn't heading for him, after all. The beeline he was making had nothing to do with Jonathan. It had everything to do with a need to urinate. Even as he passed within ten feet of Jonathan, the soldier was unzipping his fly and his eyes were trained on the shadows. The urgency in the soldier's body language reminded Jonathan of a man who'd sat at the bar for one beer too many. Two seconds later, Jonathan heard a forceful stream being released into the jungle foliage, and you could almost feel the man's sense of relief.

With the soldier's back turned to him, Jonathan used the moment to drag himself the rest of the way through the hole in the fence. He rolled over and brought himself up to one knee just as the stream died away and the only remaining sound was the steady churn of the diesel engine.

As he'd feared, the soldier sensed the movement and turned to face it.

To call the soldier a man was to overstate it significantly, but like soldiers the world over, this teenager's eyes showed lethal intent even as his face showed utter shock. His hand reached for the grip of his assault rifle.

Jonathan drew his Colt in an instant and leveled it at the kid's forehead. They were close enough to each other that

Jonathan could have counted the pulses in his neck. The kid froze, his shock turning to terror as Jonathan raised his left forefinger to his lips to signal for silence.

The soldier's face was a mask of indecision as duty and obligation battled with survival and pragmatism. Jonathan could almost hear him deciding to be stupid. He shook his head to talk the kid out of it, but youthful resolve is a strong force to deal with.

As the soldier opened his mouth and took a breath to yell, Boxers' enormous silhouette rose from the shadows behind him. Big Guy grabbed a fistful of the soldier's hair and lifted him while at the same time thrusting his KA-BAR knife through the side of the kid's neck. In half of a second, the blade severed both jugulars, both carotids, and the voice box. Amid a fan of blood spray, the soldier dropped without a sound. In less than a minute, he'd be dead.

Jonathan watched for a few seconds as the kid's body struggled against the inevitable, and he offered up a silent apology. If there could have been a way to let him live, they would have; but it was the nature of war that sometimes you just wander into a place where you don't belong. The price for doing so was always unspeakable.

Harvey watched in horror, swallowing the urge to vomit. It wasn't the gore, or even the fact of the killing; it was the efficiency of it. He'd spent five years of his life in the company of professional Marines, three of those in a no-shit killing, shoot-'em-up war, so he was no stranger to the product of battle; but in the past, there had always been an element of hesitation, a humanizing sense of fear. Here, there was none of that. A young man strayed to where he'd no doubt strayed for the identical purpose hundreds of times, and he'd been dispatched with no more hesitation than if the same act had been perpetrated on a troublesome insect.

As the soldier bled out and the fountain of red subsided to a trickle, Boxers wiped his blade on the dead man's trousers before sliding it back into its sheath. Harvey had no idea why he found that one gesture as horrifying as he did. Perhaps it was because he knew to a certainty that he would never be able to do such a thing himself. He understood now why the Big Guy didn't want Harvey to be there: Hesitation was a sin that could cause others to die.

For Harvey, though, that meant that being human was a sin. If a moment of hesitation in taking a life triggered the loss of another life, was that so bad? Wasn't it better than the alternative—to kill indiscriminately on the off chance that a bad guy might win?

Perhaps Boxers was right. Maybe it had been a huge mistake to invite Harvey along on this mission.

They caught a break at the gasoline shed. This structure had a front door and a back door, and Boxers was able to get in and out quickly while Jonathan and Harvey covered him without incident. While they waited, Jonathan used a ten-power monocular to examine the hut where they believed Evan Guinn to be imprisoned. He took in the blocked windows, and the single door that appeared to be secured with a sliding bolt and a garden-variety padlock that should be easy fodder for Boxers' bolt cutters.

Far more troubling than the lock were the two guards who flanked the door holding their rifles at a loose port arms that telegraphed readiness to engage the enemy that they knew was on the way.

"I hope those guards take the bait when we start blowing things up," he whispered to Harvey.

The other man made an odd grunting sound.

Jonathan pivoted his body to face him. "You okay?"

Harvey seemed to have aged a couple of years. "It's just been a while."

Jonathan nodded, showing none of the concern he felt for what he saw. "Just do your job," he said. "You're more about fixing people than breaking things, and that's fine. Any luck at all, you won't have to do anything but a lot of running."

The door to the shed reopened, and Boxers emerged with a big grin. "I used five GPCs," he reported. Jonathan recognized the acronym as general-purpose charges, Unit-speak for half-pound blobs of C4 explosives with a tail of detonating cord. "There's three on the drums of gas and two on the building itself to make sure we get the most fire. I armed them all with initiators, but then I also daisy-chained the charges on the drums. We should get one hell of a show." Daisy-chaining meant running a hefty length of det cord between the GPCs to form a train. The det cord would transmit the explosion from one charge to the other at a speed exceeding five thousand feet per second, with the result being a pressure wave that would significantly exceed the overpressure that the charges could produce individually.

"The bigger the fireworks, the better our chances," Jonathan said. He smiled at his team. "Everybody ready?" He phrased the question for both of them, but the target was Harvey.

The medic nodded.

"Remember the girl they raped," Boxers said. "The people they killed. Nothing we do can beat that."

Jonathan gawped at his friend. That was as close as he'd ever heard the Big Guy get to being sensitive. And he seemed to mean it. How about that?

Jonathan led the way back into the cover of the shadows. Staying inside the dark perimeter, they circled clockwise around the compound, over the northern end on their way to Evan's hut. Animated voices rolled out of the hut at the very northern edge of the perimeter—Building Delta. From what Jonathan picked up, it was the idle chatter of men off duty— a combination of good-natured insults and sexual innuendos.

Boxers placed a hand on his shoulder to get his attention, then poked a thumb at the barracks and mimed an explosion with his hands. Jonathan shook his head and gave him a thumbs-down. As tempting as it was to place a charge on the barracks building just for the hell of it, there was a lot of ground to cover between here and the exfil point, and it made no sense to squander resources.

As always happened with modern planning tools like satellite imagery and computer mapping, Jonathan felt as if he'd already been here. The layout of the compound was exactly as he'd anticipated. Distances were a bit deceiving—in this case, the place was bigger than he'd expected it to be—but once you got accustomed to the scale, the relative position of the buildings and the nature of the terrain came to feel very familiar.

Finally, they'd worked their way around to Evan's hut, the one they'd designated as Building Golf (letter *G* in the military alphabet). From the black side like this, the compound was invisible to them, and they were blind to the positioning of the soldiers. Jonathan placed a gloved hand on the wooden siding of the hut and leaned on it. Pretty stout construction, overall.

Jonathan beckoned Harvey close enough so that his words were more breath than whisper. "Remember, as soon as we cut the power, snap your NVGs in place and don't look at the fire."

When he looked at Boxers, the Big Guy already had his cell phone open and ready to send the signal to his detonators. Jonathan slipped his own out of its narrow pocket on his thigh, thumbed the three-digit code, and hovered his thumb over the send button.

"On three," Jonathan said, and then he bounced his arm with the phone as if they were playing a game of rock-paper-scissors. "One, two . . ."

CHAPTER FORTY

After a while, Charlie stopped translating the whispered threats that were directed toward Evan. They were going to kill him in his sleep or put a snake in his cot. It was all stupid shit that was not entirely unlike the crap that went on in the dorms at RezHouse when no adults were around to hear. Of course, such words were idle noisemaking back in civilization. Out here, they carried the weight of a promise.

Charlie had done his best to make him believe that they were all talking through their butts—that they'd get the crap kicked out of them by Victor if anything happened to him—but the combination of heat and artificially lit darkness made the threats seem very real.

Better to die on the street than get in the car.

Well, one thing was for sure. There wouldn't be many more—

The whole world came apart.

The explosions combined into a single shock wave, ripping the night apart with a devastating burst of sound and pressure. Even on the far side of the hut, the concussion hit Jonathan like a fist in the chest.

In the first milliseconds, total darkness enveloped them just as surely as if they'd blinked their eyes shut. Then, just as the first half-second was expiring, the night seethed yellow-orange. Gasoline drums launched like missiles through the destroyed walls of the storage hut, spewing roiling trails of fire that splashed to the earth like flaming latticework, setting the entire world ablaze.

Almost immediately, automatic weapons fire added to the cacophony. It started as a single burst from somewhere nearby, and then others joined from different parts of the compound. One of the great mistakes made by inexperienced or frightened soldiers was to fire indiscriminately at whatever you think is the source of your fears. If your adversary knows what he's doing, it's always a mistake.

Jonathan counted to three silently, then went to work. With his M4 at the ready, the stock pressed into his shoulder, and his body bent at the waist, he swung the corner to his left, cleared the short side of the building in five quick strides, and then turned the corner again. What he saw impressed him.

Boxers by God knew how to build one hell of an inferno. The explosion of the fuel shed had launched a literal rain of fire over the compound, igniting hundreds of spot fires from tiny to large. Only ten seconds into the assault, the big center structure—the one that Jonathan had identified as the factory—was consuming itself with fire, growing exponentially as the flames found additional stores of processing chemicals and touched off secondary explosions. Behind him in the dormitory shack, the children had begun to scream.

Their screams were nothing compared to the sound that tore the night from the other side of the compound—the sound of people on fire.

The sentries who had been posted to the door were completely absorbed by the diversion of the drums. With their rifles at the ready and their backs turned to the door they were assigned to guard, they uselessly scanned the yard for targets. Jonathan killed them both with single shots to the head.

See guy with gun, kill guy with gun. The Hollywood sense of honor, in which it was cowardly to shoot someone in the back, was pure fiction. The trick in real warfare was to kill the bad guys before they could pose a meaningful threat to the good guys. If he'd let the sentries live, he'd just have to confront them again on the way out.

Harvey appeared on Jonathan's right, looking for all the world like a dedicated warrior. His weapon at the ready, he sank to a knee and took over the work of covering the door. "Don't you have a job to do?" he asked Scorpion.

He did indeed. Per the plan, Boxers had taken bolt cutters to the lock, and the bolt was ready to be slid out of the way. Jonathan joined him on the stoop and locked his gaze just as he'd done so many times in the past. Once the door was crashed, Boxers would go in high and to the right to engage targets, and Jonathan would go low and to the left.

The snapped their night vision back into place and threw open the door.

Evan was terrified. The explosion startled the crap out of him, and the gunfire was downright horrifying, but it was the blast of heat through the windows that completely undid him. He rolled out of his bed onto the floor and curled himself into as tight a ball as he could manufacture. Throughout the barracks, all pretense of toughness or machismo evaporated. They were now a roomful of boys who were terrified of dying.

Next to him, Charlie was on the floor, too, doing his best to slide under his cot. Evan's mind screamed to get out of here—to claw at the wire over the windows or maybe slam his shoulder into the door to bust it open—but his body refused to respond. He was frozen. He'd heard that expression before—frozen in fear—but he had no idea that it was possible in the literal sense.

"What's happening?" Evan screamed to Charlie.

The other boy's eyes were wide and red. He shook his head.

Evan heard two gunshots, really close ones, and then a rattling sound at the front door. It was like every bad dream he'd ever had, where the monster is clawing at your door to get in, and you can't do anything to stop it.

He shot another panicked look to Charlie, then flattened himself on the floor as if to dissolve through the wooden planks.

Please God, he thought. But then he realized he didn't know what to pray for.

That's okay, Father Dom had told him once. *God sees your heart. He doesn't need to hear your words.*

So just *please God* would do.

The door burst open, and the monster entered. Actually, it was two monsters, and they had guns.

"*En el piso!*" one of them yelled. He was huge—from this angle bigger than the door he'd just come through. "*En el piso!*"

Immediately, on the far end of the room, there was a clatter of beds and people as boys dropped to the floor.

"Evan Guinn!" the other one yelled.

Something dissolved inside him, launching him to a new plane of fear. They were coming to kill him. Then all of that changed with the man's next words.

"Evan Guinn, we're here to take you home!"

Inside on the left was for shit—literally, it turned out—so after a quick glance to clear that part of the room, Jonathan shifted his attention to the right.

Boxers yelled, "On the floor!" in Spanish, and then repeated it. To a person, the kids obeyed. Instantly. And kids they were, too. Not a whisker among them.

By Jonathan's estimate, they were already two minutes into the assault, and that meant they were behind schedule. It wouldn't take long for somebody to connect the dots on what they were doing, and then the heat of the fire would pale in comparison to the heat of the battle.

"Evan Guinn!" Jonathan yelled. Details of skin tone and hair color were hard to discern with the NVGs in place. "Evan Guinn, we're here to take you home!"

Two seconds later, there he was. The closest bed to the door on the eastern side of the building. He saw the boy first as movement, and then there was the mop of hair and the white skin. So much for skin tone and hair color being hard to discern. In here the kid was as visible as chalk on a blackboard.

"I've got him," he announced to Boxers.

"Roger that," Boxers said. The Big Guy sidestepped closer to the western wall to give Jonathan space to grab Evan, but he kept his weapon trained on the room.

The boy was still finding his feet when Jonathan grabbed his upper arm to help. When he was in the aisle Jonathan stooped to the boy's level and snapped the NVGs out of the way. "We're the good guys, Evan. From America. We're here to take you back where you belong."

In the dancing, deflected light of the fires, Jonathan saw the kid's eyes go wide. "Mr. Jonathan?" he said.

Jonathan smiled. "The one and only."

"What are you doing here?"

"That's a very long story," Jonathan replied. "For now, I need you to keep quiet, stay close to me, and let's see if we can all get out of here alive."

One of the other children scrambled to his feet and rushed toward them, but Boxers planted a hand in his chest, stopping him in his tracks. "Take me with you," the boy said.

The English startled Jonathan, but he started for the door anyway.

Boxers said, "Go back to bed, kid. We're here for just one."

"No!" the boy shouted. "Evan, you promised!"

Evan squirted out of Jonathan's grasp and buttonhooked

around his hip to beckon Charlie to join them. "Come on," he said.

Jonathan grabbed Evan's arm again, tighter this time. "No, *you* come on."

"But he's my friend."

"You'll make a new one," Boxers growled. "Scorpion, we need to move."

With his rifle trained on the other boys, he started to back out as Jonathan half pushed, half dragged Evan through the door. "Mr. Jonathan, Mr. Jonathan, listen to me. That's Charlie. He was the only one who helped—"

"We can't," Jonathan said. "We just can't."

Evan yelled, "Come on, Charlie! He said you can come!"

Boxers appeared at the door, his jaw dropped. "What the hell?"

Jonathan was stunned. And then the other kid was there. Well, shit. What was he going to do, shoot him?

It would take less time to capitulate than it would to argue. "Fine," he said. Then, to Boxers, "Let—"

A chorus of screams whipped Jonathan's head to the far end of the compound, where the fire had reached the farthest of the barracks—Building India—and was starting to consume the west wall—the one that faced the interior of the compound. Tongues of flame licked up the siding and up to the eaves and the thatched roof. At a glance, he realized that the fire would be rolling into the interior of the building through the high windows. If they didn't do something, the children would burn to death.

Harvey said, "Boss."

Jonathan shot a look to Boxers. "We have to," he said. He let go of Evan's arm and said to the boy, "Stay with me. Step for step, you understand?"

He didn't wait for an answer. He turned on his heel and ran toward the growing conflagration, his rifle at the ready. This was the nightmare scenario—the one that he had driven home a thousand times to Unit wannabes when he was an instructor at the OTC—operator training course. On an 0300 mission, the precious cargo *was* the mission. Everything was secondary to the rescue. And by God, once you have the PC in your grasp, you never do anything to risk their safety. Yeah, well, that was the training course. He'd survived it once and taught it three times, and he knew for a fact that there was no scenario involving the incineration of a dozen children.

The fire grew with startling speed. In the ten or fifteen seconds that it took Jonathan to cover the distance, the far end of the barracks was fully involved. The screams from inside were as terrifying a sound as he'd ever heard. He was certain that they were screaming words, but he didn't try to catch them. The timbre of the voices told him everything he needed to know. As they closed within the last few yards, Harvey sprinted past him to get to the door first. Jonathan didn't think the little guy knew how to move that fast.

A burst of machine-gun fire from close behind made Jonathan slide to a stop and bring his weapon to bear. It was Boxers, and his weapon was up, his eyes focused to the southwest corner of the compound. He followed his sight line and turned in time for a second burst to drop a soldier who'd been readying a shot of his own.

"Make it fast, Dig!" Boxers shouted. "This is spinning out of control. We are officially in trouble."

Jonathan could count on two hands the number of times he'd heard his friend sound this unnerved. Whatever advantage they'd earned through their massive diversion had now been lost. In fact, the diversion itself had become their biggest problem. With the element of surprise squandered, this whole mission would come down to marksmanship.

Harvey pulled on the barracks door, trying to get it open. It was not lost on Jonathan that none of the local soldiers or bosses were doing anything to help the children.

"Move, Harvey," Jonathan barked. He let the M4 fall against its sling, and raised the Mossberg. He jacked the breech open, ejecting one of the buckshot rounds, then reached to his bandolier of shells and thumbed out a slug round. He slipped it into the breech and closed it before sweeping Evan and his friend behind him. He placed the muzzle two inches away from the shackle loop, calculated the ricochet angle, then pulled the trigger.

The Mossberg bucked, and the lock disappeared. He slid the bolt to the side, pulled open the door, and children tumbled out into the night. They coughed and cried, their faces blackened with soot and smoke, but Jonathan didn't see any burns. Next to him, Harvey did his best to examine them as they streamed by. Apparently, they were all healthy, because he didn't stop any of them for further treatment.

A ripple of bullets chewed the wall just to the left of the door, followed an instant later by the sound of the gunfire that launched them. The children yelled and scattered, causing Jonathan to reflexively look for Evan. He was still right where he was supposed to be, his friend close enough for them to share a heartbeat.

As much as he wanted to bolt out of there, he had to look inside to make sure that he hadn't left any living children to burn. He cleared the two steps in a single stride. Keeping close to the floor, where the air was still breathable, he crawled a few feet inside and took a look. Just an empty room on this end. On the far end, a wall of fire had become a living monster, consuming everything. If someone had been left behind, they were dead now.

He scooted back outside.

The children from the burning barracks weren't going anywhere. They clustered around Boxers and Harvey, and now that Jonathan had rejoined the scene, they clustered around him, too. One boy of about twelve who appeared in the firelight to be missing his right eye and ear from an old injury grabbed Jonathan by his web gear and said in Spanish, "What do we do? Where do we go? Please take me with you."

Others were doing the same with Boxers and Harvey. These kids were in a total panic, yet somehow they knew that the strangers with the rifles provided a better future than the locals who paid for their labors.

Jonathan said nothing. What could he say? This mission was coming unzipped in enormous proportions.

"We've got to move!" he shouted to his team.

"Guns to the north!" Boxers yelled.

Jonathan pivoted right and dragged Evan to the ground by cupping the back of his neck with his left hand while shouldering his M4 with his right. A dozen or more men in various stages of uniform undress had left their instinct to fight the fires and were dialing in to the real threat. Word was passing quickly among them, and many were assuming shooting positions. Jonathan dropped two with two three-round bursts.

Bad guys opened up from what felt like every compass point. It was panicked fire, largely unaimed and therefore not particularly dangerous, but the old adages of war still applied: If you throw enough lead out there, something's bound to get hit.

The children scattered. Most of them. In the barracks hut behind them—Building Hotel, the one still locked but not burning—children screamed and pounded on the walls, no doubt terrified by the bullets that missed the intended targets and slammed through the wooden panels as if they were not even there.

Jonathan and Boxers both dropped to their bellies to present smaller profiles, Jonathan's body covering Evan, who was squirming like a grounded fish to get the weight off him. "Get the PC under cover!" Jonathan yelled to Harvey, who seemed momentarily to be frozen in place, neither standing nor crawling, but stuck somewhere in between.

"Harvey!"

That snapped him back to awareness.

Jonathan rolled off of Evan. "Take Evan behind Building Hotel and sit on him. Anybody comes close you don't recognize, shoot him."

For the first time, Harvey seemed to fully understand the stakes, to become fully aware of his surroundings. He stooped low, grabbed Evan under his armpits, and pulled.

Evan needed no additional encouragement. Once he was free of Jonathan's weight, he darted like a loose rocket behind the center hut. Charlie, too. Harvey had to hurry just to keep up.

"We can't stay here!" Boxers shouted. Bullets kicked up dirt in the space between them, and the Big Guy drilled the shooter.

Jonathan knew he was right. There was no way to spirit Evan out through all of this. Two- and three-man battle teams were forming all over the compound now. Their movement and their muzzle flashes marked their locations, but with so many of them and one common target, it was only a matter of time.

"We can't defend this position!" Jonathan yelled, firing at a running target and missing.

"Oh, ya think?" Boxers yelled back. He dropped a magazine and slapped in another one.

"We're gonna move left," Jonathan announced, this time using the radio so Harvey would know, too. "Harvey, stay put. Box, our rally point is the black side of the burning barracks." He dropped a magazine that still had six rounds in it and inserted a fresh mag of thirty. "Okay, Big Guy, you shoot everything north of two-seventy, I'll take everything south. Covering fire!"

Moving with remarkable harmony, they let go with a hail of barely aimed bursts of machine-gun fire as they rose to a deep crouch and made their move for cover. Jonathan dumped his first thirty rounds in seven seconds and two seconds later had a fresh mag that he emptied in six seconds. The goal here was not to kill—although he'd take whatever he could get—but rather to land rounds close enough to the enemy that they hit the dirt. Another basic rule of warfare was that you can't cower and kill at the same time. Calmness under fire was the single deadliest trait that separated professional soldiers from amateurs. Well, that and the ability to hit what you're aiming at.

To Jonathan's right as they moved to cover behind the inferno that used to be Building India, Boxer managed to unload ninety rounds with such speed that Jonathan never heard his pauses to reload.

Jonathan arrived to relative safety in the shadow of the burning building first, followed by Big Guy just a couple of seconds later.

"No return fire," Boxers said. His eyes were wide with anticipation, his face as anxious as a kid awaiting his turn with Santa. "We can take them."

Jonathan nodded. Covering fire, or suppressing fire, was as much a test as a strategy. You learned how thoroughly the enemy cowered under fire. If the roles had just been reversed, and two amateurs had been fleeing a dozen pros while randomly shooting into the night, the amateurs would have been easily dispatched.

"We have to move fast, though," Jonathan said. "We'll roll them up from left to right."

"They're gonna seek shelter in one of the remaining buildings," Boxers predicted.

Jonathan smiled. "With any luck." Hand grenades were invented for eliminating enemies hunkered down inside buildings.

There was no need to review the strategy. They'd both done this drill so many times that it was nearly as instinctive as breathing.

When the radio broke squelch, Mitch Ponder heard the sounds of battle before he heard any voices.

"They're blowing up the whole factory," Victor shouted in Spanish. "Huge explosions! There must be twenty of them! Hurry!"

Without having to be told, the pilot cranked up the engine of their luxurious, leather-upholstered Sikorski S-76 chopper. They'd been standing alert, thirty miles away in the yard of a business associate, awaiting the attack that Ponder had known was on the way. The spin of the turbine woke up the machine gunner in the back.

"Everything's on fire!" Victor hollered. "They're killing everyone. The factory is being destroyed."

Something jumped in his chest. "What do you mean, *destroyed*?"

"Listen!" The mike remained open, and in his mind, Ponder had visions of Victor holding it out a window. The sound of gunshots was unmistakable.

"Well, stop them," Ponder commanded. "You've got a whole fucking army. I know because I paid for their weapons."

"We will try," Victor promised. "But I can no longer guarantee the safety of the white boy."

"Fuck the white boy," Ponder spat. He owed a debt to the American secretary of defense, but nothing was worth the millions he would lose if the factory was destroyed. Most cocaine manufacturers were lucky to manufacture a few kilos a month; his operation made hundreds of kilos a week. There was no bigger operation anywhere in South America. "It's better to keep him alive, but if he has to die, he has to die. We're on our way."

He nodded to his pilot, and the ground dropped away as the rotors bit into the humid night. As they cleared the trees and pivoted north, the glow of the attack was evident on the horizon, a dome of yellow and orange that tore the darkness like a floodlight.

"My God," Ponder muttered. It wasn't supposed to go like this. He'd agreed to shelter the Guinn boy at the factory because it was the only place under his control where he could be constantly watched and where he could earn his keep.

Victor and his soldiers were supposed to have stopped the rescuers from taking the boy. This helicopter was supposed to have been the last-resort insurance policy to be used only if the rescue had succeeded and the attackers disappeared into the night. Equipped with forward-looking infrared technology, and with each of the crew members wearing night-vision goggles, there would have been no hiding for invaders retreating through the jungle.

In a perfect world, they wanted the Guinn boy to stay alive; but if he died, no one would ever have to know. The father would be told that he was fine, and they would manufacture reasons not to show his picture again. If that turned out not to be enough to keep the man from talking, well, that was not Ponder's problem.

The distant dome of light pulsed and grew brighter. Ponder set his jaw, ready to kill.

CHAPTER FORTY-ONE

Because the enemy was likely to expect them to emerge from the far side of the building, Jonathan and Boxers instead emerged from the same spot where they'd entered. They cut left when they were clear of the building, through the searing alleyway between the barracks fire and the factory fire, shooting the same fields as before.

When it felt like they'd passed their enemy's left flank, they buttonhooked to the right and began killing in earnest. Any silhouette with a gun was a legitimate target.

They moved together, their bodies nearly touching, firing and reloading without pause, zigging and zagging at random to frustrate any effort to stop them. This wasn't about covering fire anymore. This was all about accuracy on the move, firing two bullets at a time, each pair finding their target and killing it. Where an enemy shooter presented a frontal profile, Jonathan went for a double-tap, a bullet in the heart followed by a bullet in the head. If it was a sidelong silhouette, he aimed for the ear. If they were running away, the choice target lay between the shoulder blades.

Where they pointed their weapons, people died. Jonathan made no attempt to count, but he knew for a fact that he dispatched five in the first ten or fifteen seconds. The enemy returned fire, but it was all wild and random. As far as Jonathan knew, not a single round came within five feet of him. By comparison, not a single round that left his muzzle missed its intended target.

Twenty seconds into the assault, the enemy was at a dead run, their instinct to survive obliterating their desire to win. All but a few ran in straight lines, among the surest ways to meet one's maker during a firefight.

Jonathan and Boxers never slowed. Where bodies clogged the path, they vaulted over them. Under other circumstances, with an enemy who was better trained or more operationally aware, this kind of full-on assault would have opened the door for a counter-flanking maneuver, where bad guys would hold back and wait for the attackers to pass and then assault from the rear or the side. As they charged forward, Jonathan continued to check his six o'clock, but the maneuver never materialized.

They charged northward along the eastern edge of the compound, and as they passed what was left of the gasoline shed—Building Alpha—Jonathan saw asses and elbows retreating into Building Bravo, which, judging from the construction design was a mirror image of the kids' barracks, but minus the locked doors and wired windows.

Jonathan and Boxers slid to a halt against the near wall of the building, well below the window, but easily vulnerable to anyone who thought to shoot a rifle through the thin siding.

The shooting had stopped, but Jonathan knew that the silence couldn't last.

"I say we blow the building," Boxers whispered.

Jonathan agreed. It was the only—

He glanced out into the center of the compound. "Oh, shit," he breathed.

Evan thought this was like living the scariest movie he'd ever seen—only the explosions were real and the bleeding bodies were real. All of it was real. There wasn't a single moment of the past few days that made any sense to him, but this topped the charts. People were dying, for God's sake. Things were blowing up.

And Mr. Jonathan! Jesus. He'd always seemed like a tough guy and all—friendly, but in a hard kind of way—but never in a million years did he imagine the man killing people to rescue him. He felt like his head had been stuffed with glue. There was too much going on for him to understand any of it.

"Evan, what's happening?" Charlie said way too loudly, unused to the sudden silence. "Who are these people?"

"The guy out there is Mr. Jonathan. He's—"

"Quiet," snapped the man who'd joined them back here. Evan had never seen him before, but he seemed nervous. He had the helmet and the gloves and the gun of a soldier, but he seemed scared. That was the thing about Mr. Jonathan: he didn't seem even a little bit scared. Evan didn't know if he liked that or not.

"Who are you?" Evan asked. He changed his voice to something north of a whisper but south of a shout so that he could still be heard.

"I'm a friend. My name is Harvey, and I need you both to stay quiet." As an afterthought, he held out a gloved hand. "You're Evan Guinn. Nice to meet you."

Evan cocked his head, confused, but he shook the man's hand. "Nice to meet you, too."

"I'm Charlie," the other boy said, thrusting his hand between the two of them.

"He's my new friend," Evan explained. "He's been here a long time. They killed his parents."

Harvey shook Charlie's hand, too, but something changed in his face as he did. He looked sad. "Well, I hope we can find you a nice home," he said.

"What are we doing?" Evan asked.

"We're getting you out of here."

"But *how*?"

Harvey gave him a funny look, as if he didn't know the answer to the most obvious question in the world. "Watch and learn," he said.

"Are we hiding?" Charlie asked.

"Damn straight we're hiding," Harvey answered. "Their job is to eliminate the threat to you. My job is to make sure you stay safe while they do it." As if to punctuate his point, he readjusted the grip on his machine gun. "To get to you, they've got to come through me."

Harvey heard the tough-guy words coming from his mouth, and he nearly cringed. He hadn't felt this terrified since The Sandbox. Nor had he felt this alive. Warfare was the God-awfulest experience life had to offer to anyone; but out here, in the middle of this firefight, he recalled the addiction he'd felt back in the day. Bathed in mortal terror, the world became supernaturally vivid; the colors brighter, the fear sharper, the jubilance greater. It wasn't until after it was over, when the enemy dead and friendly dead all looked human again, that the remorse and doubts sneaked in to steal your soul. It wasn't until it was all over that the thrill transformed to horror.

At this moment, the reality of his life back home—the tent, the perpetual state of fear, and his general sense of uselessness—felt light-years away. They felt as if they belonged to someone else. Here he was in the middle of a by-God war, and he had something worth fighting for. Something worth dying for. He remembered his drill sergeant from a million years ago in Basic Training telling him that the only life worth living is the one worth dying to protect.

He'd understood the words intellectually back then, but now they resonated in his heart. Maybe he needed to lose everything once before he understood the need to protect those things that were important to him. These two kids were his responsibility. If they died out here, it would be his fault, but if they lived to see tomorrow, that would be his fault, too. His victory.

God help anyone who threatened that.

Out in the compound, one of the boys ran in a tight, panicked circle, clearly not knowing what to do. He stopped at the body of a soldier who'd fallen dead just thirty feet away. Jonathan remembered shooting him.

He didn't know where the other children had gone, but this one was very much in harm's way. Jonathan yelled, "*Tú! Niño! A cubierto!*" You! Boy! Take cover.

The boy didn't respond. Instead, he wandered closer to the corpse, where he bent at the waist to look more closely at the face. Then he stomped on it with his heel. Once, twice, then a third time.

Jonathan spat a curse under his breath. "*Parar!*" he yelled. "*No hagas eso!*" Stop! Don't do that! But the kid wouldn't listen. "Shit. Cover me, Box."

"What the hell are you—"

Jonathan was already gone. The kid kept kicking the corpse. No cadre of soldiers would stand by and watch—

Gunfire erupted from Buildings Bravo and Delta, ripping the night and the ground. And the boy. He dropped where he stood.

"Motherfucker!" Jonathan yelled, and he brought his M4 to bear, spraying the windows and walls just inches from Boxers, who in turn unleashed withering fire on Building Delta on the north end.

Return fire ceased as the enemy dove for whatever cover they could find.

After reloading, Jonathan knelt and scooped the boy's limp body into the crook of his left arm while he emptied another mag with his right as he ran for cover.

Back in the shadow of the building, he skidded to a halt and let the boy slide to the ground. Most of his throat was gone, and two holes had been punched through his chest. In the light of the fires, the boy's fixed pupils looked as lifeless as glass.

"He's gone, Dig," Boxers said. "Nothing you can do."

He couldn't have been more than eleven years old. That's a blink. What had the kid been thinking? What would have driven him to stand in the open like that and assault the body?

"Dig, we gotta go. He's dead. Fuckers killed him."

Jonathan felt terrible thoughts encroaching on his consciousness, and he pushed them away. This was warfare, for God's sake, where the entire world consisted of current facts and future objectives. The past becomes irrelevant the instant it passes. You can't worry about the dead at the same time that you're planning to protect the living. But he was so young.

"Focus, Dig," Boxers said.

"Fine," Jonathan said. "None of these assholes gets out alive. Not one."

Boxers nodded. "Works for me."

Jonathan reloaded his carbine, then let it fall against its sling as he lifted a fragmentation grenade from his vest. "Keep their heads down in Building Delta," he said. "I'm gonna frag these fuckers in Bravo and then roll 'em up."

"You're making me hard," Boxers grinned. He slid a fresh magazine into his rifle. "Say the word."

Jonathan settled himself with a deep breath. "The word."

Standing to his full height, but using the corner of the barracks for cover, Boxers aimed at the farthest building and raked the front windows with three round bursts.

Jonathan used the cover to push out in a crouch and moved to the left, down the front of Bravo, keeping his left shoulder pressed against the wall. Behind him, Boxers threw out an amazing volume of fire, while ahead of him, in Building Bravo, nobody seemed to know what to do.

Jonathan nestled the spoon of the grenade in the web between his thumb and forefinger and pulled the pin. He duck-walked three feet out from the wall, barely in sight of anyone with the courage to peek out, and let the spoon fly. At this range, he didn't want to give the enemy time to throw it back, so he let it cook off for two seconds before he threw it through the open window.

"Frag away," he whispered into his radio, cuing Boxers that an explosion was coming. Jonathan dropped to the ground and two seconds later was rewarded with the crisp *bang!* that meant victory. The screams of the wounded followed instantly. He moved down two windows and repeated the procedure. "Frag away."

After the second detonation, it was time to finish the job up close and personal. "I'm going in," he said into his radio.

"Rog."

Jonathan snapped his night vision back into place and reached for the Mossberg again, stretching it against its bungee sling. All of this in one continuous motion as he charged up the three steps to the stoop and kicked open the door.

Outside, Boxers reduced his rate of fire by two-thirds. It made no sense to waste the scores of rounds in suppressing fire when the man he was covering was inside a building and invisible.

The instant he crossed the threshold, Jonathan pivoted right to clear the area behind the door and damn near yelled when he came face-to-face with a soldier. The man just stood there, disoriented and bleeding. The man held an M16 in his hands, but it seemed foreign to him. Such was the disorientation that commonly followed a blast in close quarters.

The temptation to let him live gave way to the reality that once recovered, the dazed soldier would be lethal again. Jonathan killed him with a blast from the Mossberg at point-blank range, shredding his chest with nine .32-caliber pellets.

Then he turned left and took his time strolling down what was left of the center aisle between the ranks of bunks. When he kicked at an arm that was protruding from under a bunk, intending to check if its owner was alive or dead, the arm itself skittered freely across the floor.

Ahead and to the right, a man writhed in agony, his midsection wet and black in the night vision. Jonathan assessed the wound as lethal and had just decided to let him be when the man raised a bloody pistol. Jonathan shot him.

Fifteen seconds after he'd entered the room, Jonathan pressed his mike button. "Bravo's clear. I'm coming out."

"Holy shit, they're running!" Boxers' voice announced in his ear. He started shooting again.

Jonathan darted to the open door and dropped to his knee, switching again to his M4. He watched as a stream of men poured out of Building Delta. They stumbled and bumbled out the door and down the stairs, some of them dropped by Boxers' bullets, but most just tangling their feet in their panic to get out. They streamed into the woods on the far side of the compound.

Jonathan pressed his mike button.

"Heads up, Harvey. They're coming right at you."

Harvey's stomach flipped. "Fuck."

"What?" Evan asked, keenly dialed into the change of emotion.

Harvey hadn't been aware that he'd spoken aloud. He pressed a hand to the boy's shoulder. "Get down," he said. "Lie flat. Bad guys are coming. No matter what happens, you stay put until one of us comes for you."

Both boys showed alarm. "Who?"

"Your old bosses. Now get down." Harvey snapped his NVGs back over his eyes, and right away saw them scattering into the jungle. At a glance, he saw seven or eight of them, but they weren't interested in seeing him. They were interested in getting the hell out of there.

Should he shoot or let them go? It was a tough call. His mission was to get Evan Guinn home alive and healthy. By opening fire, he'd give away his position and invite return fire that would endanger the boy. But by letting them get away, he let them live to attack again.

"*Los banditos están aquí!*" shouted a voice from above and behind. The bandits are here! Harvey whirled on the sound, but when no one was there, he realized that it was one of the kids who were still inside the barracks they hadn't unlocked. Somehow they knew, and then the one voice was joined by others. "*Los banditos están aquí!*"

They started to chant it. And it worked. The fleeing soldiers turned. The closest one raised his weapon to fire.

Harvey's MP5 chattered out a three-round burst and his target dropped; whether dead, wounded, or just scared, he couldn't tell. The important part was that he didn't shoot back.

But a whole bunch of others did. The jungle lit up with muzzle flashes, the staccato pounding of a dozen automatic weapons combining to form the sound of tearing fabric. A fierce and deadly stream of bullets shredded the wall behind them and the foliage surrounding them. Harvey pushed the boys deeper under the barracks hut, while above them the boy who had brought the fire this way screamed in terror and pain as the enemy's poorly aimed fire passed through the plank walls as if they were made of cardboard.

Harvey knew he couldn't stay here. If he returned fire from this spot, the response would bring a deadly fusillade that would as likely kill Evan as him.

After all this—after all the blood and the suffering—the one unforgiveable sin would be for Evan to get hurt.

"Don't move," he hissed to the boy. "No matter what, don't move."

"Where are you—"

Harvey didn't stick around for the rest. Staying pressed low to the wet ground, he crawled the remaining length of the barracks and emerged into the darkness on the north side. Brilliant muzzle flashes marked the location of the attackers. Where Harvey saw a flash, he fired two three-round bursts at it. The flash suppressor on his own weapon kept him invisible to all but those who would have happened to be looking directly at him when he fired. With all the noise of the continuing battle, his were just more shots fired amid the cacophony.

He damn near jumped out of his underwear as a hand landed on his shoulder. When he spun to confront the danger, another hand blocked the swing of his weapon. "We're the good guys," Jonathan said, and then he and Boxers added their firepower to repel the new attack. Within fifteen seconds, it was all over.

As their ears recovered, they could once again hear the subtle sounds of the night. Like the moaning and whimpering of wounded children.

And the sound of an approaching helicopter. Jonathan and Boxers exchanged looks.

"You didn't call for cavalry, did you?" Boxers asked.

Jonathan kicked at the dirt. "Shit. That's just what we need. An aerial assault."

"We need that chopper," Harvey said. "These wounded kids. We can't carry them down to safety." He shot a hard look to Boxers. "And don't even think of saying that they're not our responsibility. We did this."

"If you've got an idea, I'm listening."

Harvey sighed and shook his head as he undid the Velcro fastener on his vest and lifted his helmet off his head. "Oh, I've got an idea," he said as he pulled his vest off. "It sucks to be me, but I've got an idea."

To make it work, though, he had to move quickly.

Even from a mile out, the scale of the destruction was ten times worse than the worst Mitch Ponder could have imagined. Bodies lay strewn everywhere, as if dropped from an aircraft. Everything was on fire—even the ground itself in some places—and what wasn't burning had instead been chewed mercilessly by gunfire. An airstrike could not have produced more thorough destruction.

"My God," he breathed. "My God, my God, my God . . ." He couldn't begin to calculate the millions this was going to cost him. Into the intercom, he said in Spanish, "Look for white-skinned soldiers. Kill any that you see."

Behind him in the cargo bay, the gunner made ready his AK-47.

They came in low and fast, barely above the treetops, sweeping by quickly to make the helicopter a harder target to hit. No one shot at them, however. No one moved. The dead remained still, but the physical devastation stood out in sharper relief.

"Incredible," the pilot said.

And then it was gone, the tableau of destruction giving way to the blackness of the lightless jungle. "Make another pass," Ponder ordered. "More slowly this time."

The chopper slid to a stop in the air and then pivoted on its axis to reverse direction. "If we go too slowly, we're more easily shot down," the pilot warned.

"If they wanted to shoot us down they'd be firing their guns," Ponder said. "And if they don't they're either dead or they've made their escape." He took a deep breath. "It looks to me like everything's dead."

"I see movement in the jungle," the gunner said. "On the right-hand side."

Ponder turned. Thanks to the night vision, he could see them now. A dozen people moving about. They were children.

"Those are the workers," Ponder said. At least they were still left to him. Even as the thought formed in his mind, he realized that with his soldiers and supervisors gone, the children would have to die now, too. He could not afford to let the story of his weakness filter back to the villagers.

"Look there," the pilot said, pointing. "One of the supervisors is still alive."

Sure enough, a dark-skinned man, barefoot and shirtless, staggered out into the clearing, waving his arms and beckoning the chopper down to the ground. The pilot parked the aircraft in a low hover, blasting the man with the rotor wash and making him cover his head.

"Do you recognize him?" the pilot asked.

Ponder shook his head. "I don't know. He looks half-dead." The man stood with a distinct list to his left, and he appeared to be wounded in the leg.

"It could be a trap," the pilot said. "What do you want me to do?"

Harvey hoped he wasn't overselling the limp. Playing decoy had never been a part of his repertoire in the past, and as he staggered out into the open, he couldn't help but fear that his hunched, staggering gait was a little too Quasimodo. As the chopper slowed and drew to a hover, he knew that he had their attention, but as they continued to hover, he could feel the gun sights settling on his chest and head, readying to call his bluff.

He'd removed his protective gear, shirt, and shoes just to look more like the guards he was impersonating; but the lack of clothes meant no place to conceal a weapon. He was entirely dependent upon his acting ability and on Jonathan's and Boxers' marksmanship. Otherwise, he was going to die right here in a place where he'd never in a million years choose to live.

The roar of the rotor wash kicked up dirt and soot and firebrands, enveloping him in a cloud of crap that made it impossible to see anything.

Careful to keep in character, Harvey closed his eyes, covered his head, and hoped that God and great aim would make it all right.

When something changed in the pitch of the helicopter noise, he knew they'd made their decision to land.

Then the shouting started.

* * *

Crouched low, with the corner of the barracks as conceal-
ment, Jonathan settled his sights on the helicopter's cockpit,
while above him, Boxers had taken a kneeling pose to aim at
the cargo bay, where the doors had been removed from this
Cadillac of executive helicopters to provide for a door gunner. The plan was simple: the instant the wheels touched the
ground, Jonathan would take out the pilot first and then the
front-seat passenger, while Boxers killed anyone in the cargo
bay. The whole thing shouldn't take more than a few seconds.

Jonathan found himself feeling an odd paternal pride in
Harvey and his willingness to take this risk. To willfully disarm oneself in the middle of a firefight took a unique brand
of courage. When this was over—

A terrified scream split the night from behind. "Help! Mr.
Jonathan! Mr. Jonathan! Help!"

As Jonathan scrambled to see, something heavy hit the
side of the barracks building hard enough to create the
sound of splintering wood.

Evan worried that he might have pissed himself. It was
hard to tell in the pooled water under the sleeping hut where
the crying and moaning and pleading continued without
break. It probably didn't even matter, except to him. It was
just such a baby thing to do.

Lying here like this, unable to see anything that was
going on around him, but hearing the sounds of so much violence, he had to talk himself into believing that they had
not been abandoned, that Mr. Jonathan was stating a fact
when he assured them that everything would be fine if they
just didn't move.

Next to him in the muck under the hut, Charlie had fallen
completely silent except for his breathing, which sounded a
lot like the old steam trains from the movies, chugging and
huffing at a rate that couldn't be healthy.

"Are we going to die?" Charlie whined.

"I don't think so," Evan said. He tried to sound more certain than his words, even though his mind was screaming the same question. He didn't have the luxury of panicking, though, because Charlie had gotten there first, and one of them had to keep a level head.

"Who are they?" Charlie asked.

"It's a long—"

Before Evan could finish his answer, his head exploded in pain, and he found himself being dragged through the miserable soup of mud and cold water. "Ow!" he yelled, and when he reached for the top of his head, he found a fist wrapped around a handful of his hair. By touching the fist, he seemed to have accelerated the rate at which he was being dragged out from under the hut.

He clawed at the ground with his heels, but there was no stopping his attacker. In just a couple of seconds, he was completely clear and dangling on tiptoes from his hair.

It was Victor, towering huge as ever, and now slicked with what looked in the dim light to be blood. His eyes burned with an anger that Evan could actually feel.

Evan wrapped his hands around the man's forearm for leverage and kicked out for the man's crotch, scoring a hit solid enough to make him lose his grip, but not enough to make him drop.

"Help!" Evan yelled. "Mr. Jonathan! Mr. Jonathan! Help!"

Victor still had his Louisville Slugger. He unleashed a two-handed home-run swing at the boy's head. Evan ducked, barely dodging the blow that splintered the hut's wall, and fell back into the mud. He screamed again.

In the flashing, dancing light of the fire, he saw Victor smile as he brought the bat high over his head. Evan shrieked, first in terror, and then in agony.

Jonathan understood in a single glance what was happening, and he kicked himself for having dropped his guard. You never put all eyes in one direction, and you never leave the precious cargo alone. He had done both, and now a large and very pissed-off local was threatening to ruin everything with a baseball bat.

Jonathan pushed away from the wall. "Stay on the chopper," he commanded to Boxers. With Harvey's ruse on the edge of working and the helicopter flaring to land, Jonathan couldn't afford the noise of a gunshot. He drew his KA-BAR and rushed the man.

Evan was on his left side on the ground, cowering, his knees up and arms protecting his head, screaming like a terrified animal as the attacker raised the bat high over his head, as if it were an axe. Jonathan sprinted toward him, but he was still two strides away when the bat came down with everything he had on Evan's raised shin. He saw the bone break, heard the resonant *crack*.

The agonized shriek churned his stomach.

Jonathan hit the attacker hard, driving his shoulder into the man's side and burying the knife to its hilt into his belly. The man tried his best to yell, but it was a weak effort. Jonathan's blade had found the descending aorta that he'd been aiming for, dropping the man's blood pressure to zero in an instant. By the time he withdrew the KA-BAR from the gaping wound, the man had already gone limp.

Behind him, as Evan wailed, "My leg! Oh, God, my leg!" Boxers opened fire on the chopper.

Ponder sensed that something was wrong the instant after he gave the order to land. The man in the rotor wash—the man who, on closer inspection, truly did not look familiar—became distracted by something off to the helicopter's right-hand side. Ponder looked, but he didn't see anything.

When he returned his gaze to the front windscreen, the man in the rotor wash had changed. His posture seemed to have recovered.

Ponder yelled, "It's a trap!" the instant the wheels touched the ground. "Get us up! Up!"

The pilot jumped, and his hands shifted on the controls, and an instant later, his head burst open, dousing the windscreen and the controls with blood and brains. Behind him, in the cargo bay, the gunner made a sound like a barking dog, and when Ponder heard his weapon clatter to the floor, he knew that the gunner was also dead.

He also sensed that he was next. He reached for the door handle, but in the panic, he fumbled the effort. Something big and invisible kicked him in the chest, driving the air from his lungs. Whatever it was—and he knew it was a bullet—had rendered his arms useless.

As blood spilled down the front of his white shirt, he was surprised how little it hurt to die.

CHAPTER FORTY-TWO

While Harvey tended to the wounded, Jonathan and Boxers secured the scene. That meant walking the entire perimeter of the compound looking for living threats and then dispatching them. The fact that he'd heard no gunshots told Harvey that the first round of destruction had been successful.

As the time stretched to ten and then twenty minutes, children who'd run away began to wander back into the camp and to gather around the rescuers. They wanted to know what they should do. Some of them wanted to come along with Jonathan's team, not even knowing where they would be going.

"We can't take them all," Boxers said.

"So how are you going to choose who gets left behind?" Harvey asked.

"The wounded get first priority," Jonathan said. "We'll decide on the others later." Until Evan was safely at home, everyone understood that the rescue team could not return for the stragglers.

"So what happens to the rest?" Harvey asked.

Jonathan shrugged. "They have to be patient. They can

fend for themselves. For a while. Hopefully, the villagers will take care of them. Maybe someone else. We're not in the refugee business. Not today, anyway."

Harvey listened to the words, and he knew right away what he had to do. "I'll stay with them."

"Oh, no," Boxers objected. "I'm not getting to safety and then have to fly all the way back here to pick you up."

"I don't expect you to," Harvey said. "I mean I'll really stay." He looked to Jonathan. "I've got nothing to go to back there. I'm a predator, remember? No job, no place to live, lots of people pissed off. This'll do for me for a while."

Jonathan stared, unsure what to say.

Boxers objected, "You're talking shit. Boss, say something."

Jonathan gave Harvey a long, hard look. "We're talking a career decision here. Think about it carefully."

Harvey smiled. "Hey, I've got no passport in a country that I invaded outside of any law-abiding entity. What could possibly go wrong?"

When he saw that the humor landed flat, he changed his tone. "Seriously, Boss. Over here I get a new lease. Back home, I'm nothing but an embarrassment to everybody." He spread his arms to include the crowd of kids. "I have my flock." His eyes bored into Boxers. "And I'm not what they say I am."

The Big Guy grew uncomfortable. "Suit yourself," he said. Then, to Jonathan, "I can have the bird ready to fly in five minutes. If we're getting out of here, we need to start loading up." He walked off to attend to it.

Jonathan said, "Harvey, this was never the plan."

Harvey laughed. "It certainly wasn't mine. But sometimes opportunities come wrapped in odd packages."

"How will you make a living?"

"Adapt and improvise. Isn't that your motto?" He shrugged. "Look, back in the world, nothing went right for me. I pissed on some opportunities, and some stuff just spun out of my control, but when it's all said and done, I've got noth-

ing back there. Seriously, these kids we liberated all need to
find their families. They all need an education. Maybe I'll
copy your example and build the Colombian version of Resurrection House. I'll do fine."

Jonathan could not have been prouder. "Help us load,
then?"

It only took a few minutes. The most seriously wounded
got the white leather sofas, while the rest took up space on
the floor with Evan, who seemed to be handling the pain of
his leg pretty well. Because of weight restrictions, they drew
a solid line in the sand that the dead would all be left behind,
as would the uninjured children. As Boxers put it so suc-
cinctly, "We're not a damn school bus."

After some fierce debate, though, an exception was made
for Charlie. A promise was a promise, after all.

With the cargo bay full, and increasing numbers of children pressing to climb aboard, it was time to go. Jonathan
turned to Harvey one last time. "We can make room for you.
Say the word."

Harvey smiled. "I've already said my words. Someone
should stay. I want to stay."

Jonathan found himself speechless—a condition that
rarely afflicted him. He held out his hand. "Thank you," he
said. "We couldn't have done this without you."

Harvey accepted the handshake. "Oh, I bet you would
have found a way. Thanks for thinking I would be crazy
enough to come along."

They held the handshake long enough for it to become
uncomfortable. Jonathan wanted to tell this Marine that he
should be proud of himself, but he knew that speaking the words
would cheapen the moment. Instead, he said, "We gotta go."

"Yep," Harvey said. "Give my best to anyone who gives a
shit."

"I'll do that. You take care."

"I'll take care of me," Harvey said. "You take care of those
kids. I hope you kept current on your combat medic skills."

"It's only about a fifty-minute flight," Jonathan said. This, down from a nearly ten-hour truck ride under the original plan.

"You've got the ambulances arranged?"

"They should be waiting for us. Venice said she'd take care of it, and that's as good as dispatching them ourselves."

Harvey offered his hand again. "Then get the hell out of here."

Before climbing into the cargo bay, Jonathan stripped himself of all weapons and armor, keeping only his Colt on his hip and his .38 in his pants pocket. He'd be moving from one patient to another, and the fewer encumbrances he had, the better off he'd be.

Up front, Boxers turned in his seat to look back at him. He offered a thumbs-up as a question, and Jonathan donned the bulky headset intercom with its long cord. "PC is secure." Even before the final word had cleared his throat, they were airborne.

Evan had never had the experience of flying in a helicopter before, but even though he knew that he should be impressed and grateful, he found himself overwhelmed with a feeling of sadness. May-be even a little shame. Surrounded by all of these wounded boys, he couldn't help but feel responsible for their suffering. No matter how you cut it, he was the reason they'd been shot. When he thought of the ones who'd been killed, he felt his eyes go hot.

And he still didn't know why any of it was happening. He didn't understand why he had been taken in the first place, and he didn't understand why Mr. Jonathan and the others would risk so much to get him back. Yet they did. And they did it for *him*. How are you supposed to live with something like that?

"Does it hurt much?" a voice yelled over the sound of the engine and wind.

Evan hadn't realized that Charlie had repositioned himself at his side. While Evan felt like he'd aged thirty years,

Charlie seemed to have grown younger. He seemed meek. Needy, maybe. As he answered, Evan touched his leg without thinking about it. "The splint helps."

"You know your friend killed him, right? Victor, I mean?"

"He killed a lot of people tonight."

"But he killed Victor with a knife. I saw it. I saw the look in his eyes while he did it. I think he liked it."

Maybe by mere coincidence, a pain shot through Evan's ruined shin, and he grunted against it. "I'd have liked it, too," he said through gritted teeth. "Son of a bitch said he was going to break my legs with that bat if I tried to escape. Guess I'm lucky he only got one."

They fell quiet, but in the silence, Evan sensed that Charlie had sat with him for a reason. He liked the company, so he just waited for it.

"What's gonna happen to me?" Charlie asked after a while.

"What do you mean?"

The boy shrugged. "Just that. Where am I going to go when we get wherever we're going? Is your friend going to take me back to America with you?"

"His name is Mr. Jonathan. And I'd guess so."

"And then what? I don't know anybody in America. I don't have a place to live." Charlie waited for Evan to get it. "I'm going to need a place to live."

Finally, Evan understood. "You want to come and live with me at RezHouse? It's a nice place." He gave a wry chuckle. "And they come and get you if you get kidnapped."

"Would they let me?"

Evan shrugged, and in doing so somehow made his leg hurt again. "I don't see why not. If anybody complains, just let Father Dom know. He'll take care of it for you."

"Who's Father Dom?"

"He's a priest. A nice one. He kinda runs the school. You'll meet him."

"Will he like me?"

"He likes everybody."

Charlie thought about that, nodding his head gently. Then he scowled for a moment before dissolving into deep, racking sobs.

It had been a long time since Jonathan had played medic, but he proved to be pretty adept at it. It helped that Harvey had gotten the kids stabilized on the ground before they took off, but for the duration of the flight, vitals all stayed stable. He worried a lot about the kid with the chest wound. Twice during the flight Jonathan had had to lift the occlusive dressing to allow his lung to reinflate. The good news was that even though the boy remained unconscious, his vitals all stayed good, and his pupils remained equal and reactive to light.

Like any flight in any aircraft, this one had certain rhythms associated with it, such that Jonathan knew without being told that they had begun their approach to the little-used general aviation airport on the distant outskirts of Santa Marta. Using Jonathan's money, Jammin' Josie had arranged for Gulfstream transport back to the States for the tail end of the mission, using a plane that belonged to a former Nicaraguan Contra who'd done very well for himself. As it turned out, flying *out* of Colombia was no problem at all as far as the government was concerned.

"Hey, Boss," Boxers said over the intercom. "I think you want to take a look at this."

Jonathan stepped around one of the wounded kids and over Evan and his friend to rest his hand on the back of the pilot's seat. Boxers pointed to the airport runway up ahead, where a cluster of ambulances stood at the ready, awaiting their arrival. "What can I say?" Jonathan quipped. "Venice's true to her promises."

"I'm not talking about the meat wagons," Boxers grumped. "Look at the line of soldiers."

Several dozen had clustered around one of the jets on the

tarmac, and Jonathan could only guess that it would prove to be the tail number they were looking for. "Well, shit," Jonathan cursed into the microphone.

"What do you want me to do?"

Jonathan ran the options and couldn't come up with any. Clearly, they'd been made. Jonathan had known all along that it was a possibility given Josie's betrayal, but he'd been hoping for a break. If they aborted this landing and headed for another airport, they'd just prolong the inevitable, and they certainly couldn't fly all the way to the States in a helicopter.

"Go ahead and land," Jonathan stated.

"What's Plan B?"

"I don't have one," Jonathan admitted.

"Maybe Panama will take us."

"Look at your gas gauge," Jonathan said, pointing. "Even if they'd take us, we don't have enough fuel to get there."

"Well, we can't fight that many."

"True enough."

"And I ain't rotting in some jungle jail cell."

"One crisis at a time, Box," Jonathan cautioned. "Put us on the ground and I'll give diplomacy a shot."

"I've still got about a hundred rounds of five-five-six diplomacy there on the floor," Boxers quipped, eyeing his cache of weapons on the seat next to his.

"There are more lives than ours in play, Big Guy. Just get us on the ground."

Boxers sighed loudly enough to be heard over the ambient noise. He shook his head in disgust and squared up the aircraft for a landing. "This shit grows old, Digger," he said. "This shit grows very, very old."

Jonathan pulled his .45 from its holster and placed it on top of the other weapons. Depending on the mood of the soldiers, he'd get to say a lot more without a gun on his hip than he would with one.

He turned to his passengers. In Spanish, he instructed them to stay where they were after they landed, to wait for the ambulance people to come and get them. Then he told Evan in English, but with the addition, "You don't leave with anybody but Big Guy or me, okay?"

"You mean die on the street before getting into the car?" Evan asked.

The familiarity of the phrase startled him, and it must have shown in his face.

"You told us that at an assembly," Evan clarified.

That earned him a wink. "I remember that. One way or the other, we're getting you home today."

Jonathan positioned himself in the doorway to the cargo bay as they made their final flare to land, standing there like a human X, his hands and feet braced in the opening. As the wheels touched and Boxers killed the engine, the soldiers moved forward, even as the rotors were still turning.

"I have wounded children in here," he called out in Spanish. "I'm bringing them in for medical care. Please don't harm them any more than they've already been harmed."

A young officer—a lieutenant—peered beyond Jonathan, and his face showed deep alarm. He saw the rivulets of blood on the floor and the clusters of small people who created them. "My God, what happened?"

"Slave drivers up in the mountains shot them. The drug manufacturers. They shot these boys just as they shot their fathers before them. My friend and I rescued them and brought them here for medical assistance."

Confusion invaded the officer's look of horror. "That's not what we were told."

"Well, it's the truth. In any case, can you please let the medicos through so that they can get to doctors?"

The soldier hesitated.

"They're just children, Lieutenant," Jonathan said softly. "Let's give them a chance to be adults."

The lieutenant nodded and gave the appropriate orders. Thirty seconds later, soldiers and ambulance personnel alike were lifting children out of the helicopter and placing them on stretchers.

"Not the one with the blond hair, or the boy next to him," Jonathan said twice. "They're with me. I'll take them to the doctor myself." It was a long shot, but if he presumed that he'd be allowed to go free, maybe it would come to pass.

Boxers remained still and quiet in the pilot's seat. They'd had a tacit understanding for years that Boxers would never allow himself to be taken prisoner, and Jonathan had no reason to suspect that anything had changed. If it came to that, there'd be violence of a very high order.

As the last of the children were being carried away from the helicopter, two soldiers with little to do suddenly looked startled and snapped to attention. Stiff hands shot smartly to their brows as they saluted in unison.

Jonathan followed their gaze and saw an older man approaching. He acknowledged the salutes, but he did not encourage them to stand at ease. Jonathan knew from his gait alone that he was a general officer, and when he stepped more squarely into the light, the three starbursts on his epaulettes confirmed it.

Etiquette and years of indoctrination made Jonathan stand straighter in his presence. Even if you didn't respect the man, you respected the rank. For all Jonathan knew, he might end up respecting both.

"So you are the invading American army I heard about?" the general asked in impeccable English as he approached.

Jonathan scowled. "Excuse me?"

"I recognize this helicopter," the general said. "It belongs to a friend of mine."

"If that's the case, sir, then with all due respect, you need better friends. The owner of this helicopter was a murderer and a kidnapper."

The general's eyes narrowed. "*Was?*" Clearly, he'd heard the use of the past tense.

"Yes, sir. We killed him."

The general looked shocked. "You admit this?"

"I celebrate it," Jonathan clarified. "He was a rapist and a murderer. He tortured people. I presume we're both talking about the same man? Mitchell Ponder?"

The general peered past Jonathan into the bloody interior of the helicopter. As he got closer, Jonathan saw from his name tag that the general was named Ruiz. "This blood," he said, making a sweeping motion with his hand. "This is all from the children?"

Jonathan nodded. "Yes, sir. Ponder's blood is all in the cockpit. Would you like to see it?"

The general gave him an odd smile. "No, thank you. How sure are you that he is dead?"

"Extremely."

"I see." The general reached into the pocket of his tunic and produced a pack of Marlboros. He shook one out, placed it between his lips, and then returned the pack and produced a lighter from the same pocket. He lit up, took a deep drag, then picked something off of the end of his tongue.

"It occurs to me that you have some very interesting skills," the general said. "Is it safe for me to assume that you have visited my country before?"

Jonathan forced his face to reveal nothing. "It's safer to say that if I had been here, it probably would have been under circumstances that I could never discuss."

General Ruiz arched his eyebrows and aimed two fingers at Jonathan to acknowledge that he'd made a good point. "I've never thought much of the drug trade," he said. "But soldiers like me are merely servants of our governments. Mine has a weakness for the revenue that the drug trade creates. Where there's revenue, there's power. And a politician can never have enough power."

A long pause followed, during which Jonathan was unsure what to do. He remained silent and still.

"I, on the other hand, have a weakness for justice and the health of small children. Something tells me that you've helped to make the world a better place by killing Mr. Ponder. You've done my country a favor, even if the leadership won't agree." He considered his next step for a long moment before he punctuated his decision with a nod. "I will consider it a personal favor if you make this your last trip to my country." He dropped his cigarette onto the tarmac and crushed it with his toe. "You are free to go."

CHAPTER FORTY-THREE

Jonathan stood in the background as Alvin Stewart spent a moment with each of the children, flashing his famous smile and offering up candy treats from the paper bag he held on his lap. Mama Alexander piloted the wheelchair for him, and the room vibrated with the kind of happiness that only comes from learning that a dear friend is going to be okay after all. Jonathan knew that it would be a few months before Mr. Stewart fully recovered, but the doctors said that full recovery was assured.

A shadow fell to his left, and Jonathan turned to see Gail sidling in next to him. "Want to walk me home?" she asked.

It was exactly what he wanted to do. They left the mansion's great room quietly and headed down the wide front hall for the front door. Outside, the evening air had cooled from its blistering afternoon peak, but humidity still hung like a wet towel. Gail moved gently and slowly, leaning heavily on the railing as she favored her wounded leg.

"Can I help?" Jonathan asked. He stood ready to catch her if she fell.

"Nope, I've got it," Gail grunted. "Stairs are still hard," she said. She paused and straightened when she stepped onto the walkway. "You're a piece of work, Digger Grave. I spend the better part of my life in law enforcement, crashing doors and arresting people without a scratch. I've got to join the private sector to get shot for the first time."

Jonathan smiled and shrugged. "Technically, you still haven't been shot. You've been fragged."

"I stand corrected," she chuckled.

Halfway down the walkway, JoeDog found them and ran a couple of circles to get attention for the stick she had in her mouth. The bouncy black Lab was as close to a town dog as you could have, but she'd adopted Jonathan as her occasional master. Jonathan didn't accept the invitation for a game of catch, but the beast's hopes never dimmed as they continued to walk.

"How are *you* doing?" Gail asked, giving Jonathan's shoulder a gentle bump with her own.

Jonathan scowled. "Me? I'm great. The good guys won another one. Did you see Secretary Leger's perp walk on the news last night?" Irene Rivers had always had a flair for the dramatic, so she'd made sure that ample media were around when she personally arrested the secretary of defense on charges of murder and conspiracy.

Gail shot him a look. "Did I *see* it? I live on Planet Earth, don't I? He does remorse pretty well, I thought. And your friend Wolverine is second to none at damage control. Nothing at all about our involvement."

"Do I hear bitterness?" They were on Church Street now, heading downhill toward the water, taking in one of Jonathan's favorite vistas. The low-hanging sun behind them bathed the marina in liquid gold.

"You mean about not getting credit?" Gail shook her head. "Not at all. In fact, I think I'm grateful. She was particularly gracious in praising Doug Kramer for saving Jeremy Schuler's life by hiding him. She's quite a lady."

Jonathan gave a wry chuckle. "Maybe Doug will come to agree one day. He's not keen on accepting credit for something he didn't do."

"It's better than taking *blame* for something he didn't do."

Jonathan nodded. "He gets that. He's just pissed that I put him in that position. As he has every right to be."

As they neared the water, JoeDog got a new idea. She ran ahead of them, placed her stick in their path, and then poised herself downrange for the throw, her tail wagging hard enough to unbalance her hindquarters.

"Look at that face," Gail said.

"She can be hard to ignore," Jonathan confessed. He stooped and picked up the stick, then carried it for a while. "This makes her crazy," he said. JoeDog nearly vibrated with anticipation, walking backward and then running forward for the pitch. When they finally reached the bottom of the hill, they turned right. Jonathan checked for cars, just in case, then heaved the sick as far as he could down the sidewalk. The dog became a black streak.

Gail turned her head and watched Jonathan as they walked.

"What?" he said. "Why are you staring at me?"

"I'm waiting for you to answer my question."

"I didn't know there was a question on the table."

"I asked you how you were doing."

"I answered that one. I said I was fine."

Gail scowled. "*Fine* is not an answer. That's a dodge."

"Oh, Lord," he groaned. "Better people than you have tried to climb into my head, Gail. Do yourself a favor and don't even try. Really, I'm fine. And I'm really fine because I'm really shallow."

"So you would have us believe."

Jonathan felt the leading edge of anger. Sometimes *fine* was all you had. Bad things happen; you live through them, and you adapt. Dwelling on them was as useless as trying to change the past.

"I was watching you while you were watching Jeremy Schuler's reunion with his father."

"Gail, don't." JoeDog returned with her stick, but sensed something on the first sniff. Instead of begging for another throw, she just carried it and fell in step on Jonathan's other side.

"It wasn't what you were hoping for it to be, was it?"

Jonathan wanted to show annoyance at the question, but Gail was right. Father Dom and Mama Alexander had been the front-row players for that drama, and Jonathan could feel the same pain radiating from them. On the strength of the evidence gathered with Gail's help, Frank Schuler had been released from death row, and he'd made a beeline to Resurrection House to reunite with his son. All Frank wanted was to give his son a hug, and all Jeremy wanted was to hide. He hung on to Mama Alexander and begged to stay. Where everyone had been hoping for elation, it was a terribly sad reunion.

Jonathan explained his take: "You spend nine of your thirteen years thinking that your father killed your mother, and you're waiting for the state to kill your father because of it. That's a high hurdle to jump. In retrospect, I think we should have expected it. Dom'll stay on top of it."

He cleared his throat. "On a happier note, I hear that Evan Guinn's reunion with his father went really well."

"Witness protection is a hard life," Gail said.

"No harder than the one he's lived so far."

Gail wasn't so convinced. "Under these circumstances, it's going to be a particular challenge. The marshals will make it easier for the first couple of years, but then there's forever to follow."

Jonathan shrugged. "I do worry about the other kid, Evan's friend Charlie. Guinn agreed to let him join their family, but there's a kid who's got to have issues. I wish he could have come to RezHouse instead. Dom would have been good for him."

"And what about all the fatalities?" Gail asked. "How are you with those?" It was the point she'd been aiming for from the beginning, and to Jonathan it felt like a cheap shot.

"Let it go, Gail."

"I know that they wear on you, Dig. They have to."

He glared. He was not going there.

"I'm not trying to tread where I'm not welcome, Dig. I care for you. Deeply. You can't just swallow all of that. I know. Trust me, I know. I killed my share in this thing, too. But I didn't have to deal with dead children."

They'd arrived at the short flight of stairs that led to the walk to Gail's house. "You can make it from here to your front door?" Jonathan asked.

Her shoulders sagged. "Dig, please don't shut me out."

Jonathan gathered her into his arms. She felt strong yet fragile in his embrace. She smelled of soft soap and fragrant shampoo. She was gentle and kind and tough as nails. Sometimes he thought he loved her. He'd come close to telling her so, but had never wanted to screw things up that way. God knew he loved their time together.

"I'm not shutting you out of anyplace where I haven't shut out myself," he whispered. "Those doors are locked on purpose." He released her and kissed her. From inches away, he said, "Care for me enough not to push too hard."

With that, he turned and started back toward the firehouse. "Good night," he said.

As JoeDog walked beside him, a breeze off the river lifted his hair from his forehead and brought the smell of sea salt and fish. It was the aroma of home, the fragrance of a town that had always been a place of contentment. Never his own, of course, but others'. He'd long ago accepted that for some men, contentment would forever be elusive. Some men were born to do the dirty work that allowed society to live with a sense of peace that itself had probably never been more than an illusion.

Such was Jonathan's lot, and he'd always found solace in the fact that he was very good at what he did. Sometimes bad people got in the way of a righteous mission and they had to be killed. That was the way of his world.

But this mission had been different. Was it possible that saving one child's life wasn't worth so high a cost? Could the happy ending be worth so much suffering?

"It doesn't matter," he said aloud, drawing a curious look from the dog. What's done was done. The mission was *successful*, goddammit. If mistakes were made, he'd make an effort not to repeat them in the future, but stewing over them now made no sense at all. It accomplished nothing. At the end of the day, the losses were many for the bad guys and none for the good guys.

That, sports fans, was the only fact that meant anything in the long run. A crime family would soon be broken, and a murderer had been removed from the president's cabinet, all because of Jonathan and his team. Not a bad day's work.

When he arrived at the firehouse, he unlocked the door and let JoeDog rocket past him to assume her seat on the leather sofa in the living room while he wandered to his library, poured a finger of Lagavulin, and settled in to catch up on unread newspapers.

Ten minutes later, he heard the back door open, and Dom's voice shouted, "It's me!" Dom always announced himself when he entered, no doubt as a hedge against being shot as an intruder.

"Library!" Jonathan shouted back. When the priest arrived in the doorway, Jonathan toasted him and pointed to the bottle with his forehead. "Help yourself."

Dom did just that, and then settled into the man-eating sofa along the adjacent wall. "Gail called," he said.

Jonathan growled.

"What's wrong, Dig?"

Jonathan gave an impatient scowl.

"Oh, please," Dom scoffed. "I'm your oldest friend, I'm a psychologist, and I have a direct pipeline to God. I can read you like a book."

Jonathan stared, wondering whether such a friend was a boon or a curse. Something about Dom erased all Jonathan's barriers. He held the keys to every fence, vault, and firewall that Jonathan had built to contain his demons. As a priest, Dom knew it all and absolved every sin. As a psychologist he helped Jonathan cope with the burden. But he did his best work as a friend, just being there.

"I enjoyed the killing this time," Jonathan said, surrendering to the truth. "Worse than that, I enjoyed inflicting the pain."

"You think that's unusual among the population of people who mete justice to child abusers?"

"I can't speak for them. I just know that in my heart I wanted all of them to die, and that that's exactly what happened in the end." He paused and took a huge breath. "A lot of them were teenagers. Not that much older than the children we rescued."

"The age of soldiers everywhere," Dom said. "They made their choices."

"From a damned short list. Slave, overseer, or death."

A moment passed. The two men respected each other enough not to deal in platitudes. "What could you have done differently?" Dom asked, finally.

It was the question Jonathan had asked himself a thousand times, and the answer continued to elude him. "Become an insurance salesman out of college?"

Dom chuckled politely, but didn't respond. He let the question—and all that it represented—hang in the air.

Jonathan drained his scotch and looked up at the ceiling. "I'm not an assassin, Dom. I don't want to become one."

Dom settled more deeply into the sofa and crossed his legs. "Let's talk about that," he said.

The conversation went on for hours.

ACKNOWLEDGMENTS

Every book belongs to my family, in part because they put up with me, but mostly because they love me back. Joy and Chris, you're the best.

I offer special thanks to the real-life Brandy Giddings, who, through her generous contribution to the American Heart Association, lent her name to a figment of my imagination. I assure you that she is a much better person than her fictional counterpart.

Other real-life characters from my past and present lent their names willingly or otherwise to *Hostage Zero*, and I appreciate their good humor in doing so. Jacques Leger and Jerry Sjogren in particular are both terrific people and good friends, about whom you should think only warm thoughts. They are nothing like the characters who bear their names in this book. As for the actual Doug Kramer, well, he's not a cop, but if he were, I bet he'd be a good one.

Hostage Zero paints a picture of Colombia and its people that is intentionally mischaracterized for the sake of dramatic impact. In reality, Colombia is a beautiful, exotic place, populated by hospitable, hard-working people. I ask all of my South American friends to understand that I meant no harm.

Nothing happens in the publishing business without a lot of help and support from a lot of people. Anne Hawkins is at once a fabulous agent and dear friend. Without her, I'd be adrift. Michaela Hamilton is unquestionably the finest editor I've ever worked with. Equal parts advocate and adviser, she makes me a much better writer than I could ever be on my own.

Don't miss John Gilstrap's next exciting thriller
starring Jonathan Grave

Coming from Pinnacle in 2011!